For Sharon,
my '32'

Echoes of Navarre

Paul Richardson

Published by Paul Richardson, 2023.

ECHOES OF NAVARRE

First edition. January 31, 2023.

Copyright © 2023 Paul Richardson.

ISBN: 978-1739796730

Written by Paul Richardson.

In remembrance of Valerie and Richard

ECHOES OF NAVARRE
by Paul Richardson

. . . .

Introduction

. . . .

ALEX SPELLMAN SAT AT his desk on the sixth floor of Thames house in London, lost in thought, staring blankly at his black computer screen. The dull day had turned from morning drizzle to dark scudding clouds looming over the skyline, ominous of bad weather to come. His fingers tapped the desk in irritation. He had spent the morning on the fourth floor suffering through his bi-yearly cognitive assessment, something which he loathed but had to endure if he were to carry on at his current position. His superior, Anil Bharat, insisted on him taking these tests; it was his way of looking after him he supposed, making sure the past didn't rear its ugly head and start causing problems. It wasn't as if he was the only one who had to submit to these tests, everyone who worked at these offices had a history which lent itself to being a bit more complicated than most other jobs in this postcode of London. He wondered if he had made the right decision, working at a desk, shuffling papers, making phone calls. It wasn't what he was used to. Did he want to be back out there again, in the field, with everything that went with that life. The adrenaline rush, the camaraderie, the travel, the excitement? Was he getting too old for it? It certainly had its down sides too. Then again, it wasn't really a decision that was his to make. He had been...? What had Anil called it? Re-positioned? Re-deployed? No - an assignment translocation, that was it. Regardless, he loved the company, he admired everything it stood for, even if he was sitting looking over the grey choppy waters of the Thames every day, he was making a difference, wasn't he? National security had to be protected on all fronts, not just out there in the field, ninety percent of the work was done from a computer, he knew that. He knew he was doing important work. Work that only he had the background and knowledge-base

3

to accomplish. His sense of identity was instilled in him. The same as his stark sense of right and wrong; a point of view that got him into deep water when having to deal with some of the more delicate areas of his work. Inevitably his job brought him into contact with politicians and senior civil servants, a necessary evil that he despised having to deal with. These jumped up impresarios who came and went after making very little difference in the world. He didn't know if maybe this was part of the reason he was sitting at this desk. Punishment? Surely not. Probably just a bit of cautionary damage liability. The business with the former Chancellor of the Exchequer and the call-girl wasn't something he felt comfortable sweeping under the rug, but what choice did he have? The wheels of government need to be seen to be running smoothly. He just wished that if these people were so arrogant to think they could do anything they liked then couldn't they help themselves, and everyone here at Thames House, by not leaving confidential documents in the back of an Uber? At least with a black cab you had the chance of the unwritten rule of decency and discretion; maybe they taught the cab drivers that while they were studying 'The Knowledge', the first line of defence when it comes to national security. He smiled to himself at the thought. Things could be worse, he knew that. It could have all been so different; instead of scars and memories he could be one of the unlucky ones, one of the men who didn't get out, who didn't have the luxury of being able to breathe the air. Fuck! He thought to himself. No matter where or when it always came back to that. To Navarre. To bad planning. To the real reason he was sitting at this desk.

He opened the drawer and took out a small bottle of Codeine tablets and swallowed two dry as there was no water on his desk. He turned on his computer and waited for the machine to boot up and ask for his encrypted password. He would have to check his phone and retrieve the code through an app, a security measure that changed daily. There was no doubt that the MOD was finally dragging itself into the twenty first century, at long last. He rubbed his eyes with the balls of his thumbs and waited, his mind becoming fuzzy. He felt his waking self detach from his physical being, his head beginning to spin slightly. His eyes could not focus on the start screen of his PC and the password box that had appeared there. It was happening again. It was something he should have mentioned this morning at his check-up but he felt ridiculous doing so. It showed weakness on his part and he didn't want to be put through any more tests, anything that would stop him from doing his job. It would pass as it always had. He closed his eyes and he drifted, waiting for the painkillers to take effect.

Deanna Darby poured another white wine spritzer from her father's bar and re-joined her friends beside the pool. She squinted as she left the cool dark interior, letting the Californian heat envelope her as she approached the outside deck. The celebration had been in full swing for most of the afternoon and looked as if it would go on well into the evening, the sun already beginning to sink into the west to eventually extinguish itself in the Pacific Ocean. All of her girlfriends from college were there and of course, friends of her parents as well as some of the neighbours, probably thirty or more in all. It was a day that she had to try and endure, to keep up the pretence of what she had been conspiring to achieve over the last six months, the secrecy of which she found both alien and uncomfortable. Although some of the girls sitting here with her were her oldest and dearest friends, she could feel herself detach from them somehow, recent events causing her to distance herself slightly. Her closest friend, Becca, whom she had known since they were both seven years old, wore a white two piece swimsuit showing off her tanned body as she sat perched on a lounger talking to Chad, a young man who had already made his first million developing a dating app that seemed to work very well with Silicon Valley types. Becca was live streaming directly to her Youtube channel as she sipped her champagne. Deanna felt terrible that she could not confide in her the real reason she would be seeing less of each other over the coming months. At the time she couldn't even confide in her father, as far as he was concerned she was starting a regular governmental job and needed to go on a training and induction course in Northern California. Becca was an 'influencer', whatever that was; apparently people needed to be told what to wear, what restaurant to eat at and what to order when they got there, the idea of which completely amazed Deanna. Apparently people really cannot think for themselves these days. All Becca talked about was the 'gram, as in Insta, and her Youtube channel, it was her world. A world that Deanna barely knew anything about and cared even less. Becca managed to make a decent living out of it though, judging by her lifestyle. It was all extremely frivolous in Deanna's opinion. Her other close friends, Rachel and Charlie were equally as capricious, Rachel living off her father's trust fund, Charlie moving from job to job as nothing she did inspired her to stay at for more than three months at a time. She was really an aspiring artist who couldn't make the rent most months but seemingly couldn't be happier about it, she enjoyed her transitory lifestyle and Deanna was slightly jealous of her hobo chic existence. Deanna wanted more out of life though, she couldn't sit by and watch the world fall further into decay, she had to feel she was doing something positive with herself and with her life, it must be her father's work ethic rubbing off on her. Becca and Charlie had thought Deanna's choice of subjects in college strange; Social Policies, Politics and Criminology were not exactly what they expected of their sorority sister. Deanna already felt as if she had moved on from them in a way, she looked at them with a mixture of love and pity, although she berated herself for doing so and immediately felt guilty. What they did on a day to day basis, in the long term, didn't really matter, it was as if they were all treading water or waiting for something that would never arrive, it seemed to her an empty existence. She was eager to get on with the next stage of her life and leave her childhood behind her and become the adult she always hoped she would be; independent, strong, forthright.

These thoughts naturally brought her round to thinking of her parents who sadly couldn't be here with her to join in the celebrations. Her father had always hoped she would follow in his footsteps and work for the government and it devastated her not be able to share this day with them both. She had always been much closer to her father and had looked up to him ever since she was a small girl. Her fascination with him was all the more intense as he was usually working away for extended periods, and time with him at home in between those trips was precious. Her mother had been loving and caring but as Deanna had grown through her teenage years they had developed the inevitable mother/daughter relationship, equally antagonistic and affectionate. She would make them both proud. It made it so much poignant, that neither of them could be here to help her celebrate, it broke her heart.

Vasili Konstantin Dragunov paced the room trying to control his anger. He seethed with rage, his fists curled tightly into balls leaving nail marks in his palms. A white noise filled his head and a red haze tinted his field of vision so much so that he couldn't think straight. His hawk-like face flushed and his mouth turned down into a rictus grimace. He had been betrayed. That was all he could be sure of. Who it was and why were questions he would need answers to. And surely when he found out there would be blood spilt, of that he was certain. How dare they? Did the Dragunov name mean nothing anymore? Generations of his paternal family had always been in the employ of the Russian hegemony, he could trace his lineage back to the times of Tsar Nicolas I in the early eighteen hundreds. He would not be the scapegoat to end his line of distinction in disgrace. His own struggle to succeed in the face of adversity was something he had come to terms with long ago. Little was known regarding dyslexia when he was a child, he was called lazy and stupid at school by his teachers as well as his fellow pupils. He overcame his disability by becoming erudite in speech rather than on the page. His great uncle, Pavel, would sit with him patiently and explain to him the lessons he could not learn from the books he was given. He became more confident as the years progressed and by the time he was a young adult could win most arguments with a mixture of bravado and knowledge. It all came fairly easy to him especially when he realised that he was dealing with thick headed dolts who would probably end up working guard duty for the local militia. He used his tongue like a rapier, cutting his adversaries to shreds and leaving them confused into submission. Lately he had become more sanguine, happy to leave the agitating to younger, more passionate fire-brands. Age and experience can do that to a man. He had done his time working the halls of the Kremlin, slowly making his way up the greasy ladder of success only to be kicked down when he had finally seen a ledge of safety. He could have retired without having to look over his shoulder for the remainder of his days. He shouldn't be surprised, he had seen it happen to so many others before him. You can never be sure of your place in the echelons of power unless you are at the top. Only the person at the top of the food chain has the ultimate power, as long as you are answerable to someone you are at their mercy. The big question now, was what to do next, what to do about his betrayers? He still had some supporters he was sure he could rely on. He still had money, money could buy him the support he needed regardless of any affiliation, hired thugs needed no other incentive.

His mind began to focus and a plan started to formulate. Vasili had always been a survivor and most problems usually had their own solutions. A tactical approach to the matter at hand would be the way to clear his name as well as wreak revenge on those who had crossed him. If it all worked out he could come out of this whole situation in a more valuable position than he had held previously. He stopped pacing and calmed himself with a shot of vodka before sitting down in the plush armchair and closed his eyes to think.

The assassin known only as Kapusta sat in the darkened room with the Lobaev in front of him in pieces. He had taken apart and re-assembled the rifle four times now. Each time a little quicker than the last. He needed to acquaint himself with his new acquisition, become familiar with it's quirks and learn it's secrets. He had needed to upgrade his arsenal for some time now, something more bespoke was needed for this particular job. And of course like any other line of work, if he did a good job this time there would be plenty more for him in the pipeline. His fingers were becoming numb from the cold and the incessant handling of icy metal but he needed to persevere regardless. Over time he was becoming more comfortable and used to the various aspects of this new instrument of death. He had always had a knack for hitting targets, ever since he was a boy. Playing with his friends on wintry mornings, the snowballs hitting their mark every time without fail. The other lads getting upset and storming off not wanting to be the patsy every time they played this particular game. When on his own he used to practice with his father's small axe, throwing at trees in the wood, getting a ninety-five percent hit rate. Graduating from the older thicker trees to smaller younger ones, the trunks only inches thick. He never really had close friends when he was younger, or even now for that matter. There was something about his manner that people weren't able to warm to. Was it arrogance? An air of superiority? He definitely felt somehow apart from other people. As if they all knew the secret to living life but he was in the dark about the proper way to behave and conduct himself. It made fitting in harder for him. He was strange looking as a young boy. It wasn't until he got to his late teens that he started growing into his looks, becoming quite a handsome young man. But his insecurity about the way he looked as a kid stayed with him. He generally preferred his own company, especially now, since the accident. He was even more self conscious of the way he looked now. He had progressed from throwing axes and snowballs to using more defined instruments such as his home-made slingshots, each one he designed to be more destructive than the last, honing the bands and pouch and perfecting the frame to suit his arm length and upper body strength. He made better weapons than any you could buy in the stores. Finding the perfect projectile to use with it was also critical, it had to be the correct size and weight. Stones did the job in a pinch but did not have the uniformity he desired. Before going on hunting trips into the nearby woods when he was still in short trousers, he would ask his uncle to bring lead balls from the factory where he worked. His uncle, initially, was not too happy for fear of being caught pilfering, but soon relented when he began receiving rabbit and even pigeon to liven up the dinner table, happily risking admonishment by secreting a few balls each day to take home. They would never be missed if he only took a few a day surely?

As Kapusta assembled the rifle for the fifth and last time his thoughts turned to Dominika, his face flush at the thought of her. He remembered their last time together, how it had been an awkward parting. They had met several times in relation to getting the bespoke firearm made, taking measurements, talking about it's uses and the conditions in which it would be best suited. He thought she had shown interest in him, the way she held his gaze and the odd time she laid a hand on his knee when making a point about ballistics or barrels. Her femininity sending him all the right messages. It had been a long time since he had received that type of interest from a woman. It made him feel good. It made him feel manly again, it gave him hope. It made him feel as if the disfigurement wasn't as bad as he had thought. He could barely look at himself in the mirror. How could Dominika look at him with such warmth? It didn't matter how or why. She did.

He regretted the way things had ended. Once this job was out of the way and done he would contact her and make amends. Take her to dinner and treat her like the lady she was. It would have to be somewhere dark of course. Maybe a restaurant with a private corner table. He would feel uncomfortable if people were staring at them while they ate. Yes, that was what he would do. And flowers too. Dominika would love flowers. Didn't all women like flowers?

With his mind made up he packed the Lobaev into it's case and headed from the steel shed back into the relative warmth of his dwellings. He had lit the fire earlier and it would be getting nicely warm now. Once inside he half filled a tumbler of vodka, glanced at the folder on the table and flicked open the front cover. There staring out at him was the face of the man who was his mark. He gulped the fiery liquid and it burned his throat, warming his belly, the alcohol radiating through his chest. His fingers tingling as the warmth spread through his extremities. He would need more preparation but he would be ready, of that he would make sure.

1 - Motel Mystery

Alex opened his eyes with a jolt. The feeling of disorientation was strangely familiar but still quite disconcerting. He felt a sheen of sweat all over his body, his skin prickled and his eyes ached. He took a moment to gather any information he could about where he was. He didn't recognize the room he was in, it was completely alien to him. He could tell it was dusk, the shutters were half way down and the sun was almost lost over the horizon as it peeked through the grime-streaked window. He could make out the shapes of cars in the glow of the harsh yellow street lights outside. He looked down at his body, his torso glistened in the same yellow light, he could tell he was also naked from the waist down beneath the covers. He felt suddenly susceptible. The thought of his vulnerability panicked him. Where were his clothes? He could not see them. As his eyes got used to the increasing gloom he could make out more of the room. There was a door over to his right, a T.V. positioned in one corner, a dressing table with a mirror attached to the back and doors that he assumed were some sort of wardrobe. The wallpaper was tacky in the extreme, the kind that you would only use if you were decorating on a budget, it peeled in the corners and was grimy around the doorways and light switches. He became aware of faint sounds of movement from nearby, from behind the bathroom door. Faint footfalls now and the tinkling of plastic against porcelain, ordinary noises in other circumstances but ones that were now setting Alex's nerves on edge. He heard the sound of running water coming from behind the door. Slowly and as quietly as he could, he raised himself up onto his elbows and strained to hear more, feeling the familiar ache of muscles that had been beaten and battered, pushed to extremes. As he did so his eyes fell on the area surrounding the bed. There, his clothes lay; Burberry slim fits, Ted Baker shirt and his honeyed tan brogues from Savile Row, along with the clothes, he presumed, of the person in the bathroom. The shoes were red high heels. The dress hanging over the back of the chair was black, a cropped leather jacket hung on the side of the same chair, a red bra beneath it.

'Alex?' he heard from the bathroom.

Alex started but kept quiet, not wanting to say the wrong thing for fear of showing his complete ignorance.

When this had happened previously he had always found it best to let these situations play out, they had the habit of resolving themselves, he could normally get a good grasp on what was going on by just observing and gathering information. This was slightly different. It hadn't happened quite like this before.

'Alex!' This time more insistently, she needed him to answer. 'You awake, honey?'

Alex grunted, a noncommittal sound.

'Bring me a towel would you'

She sounded young, younger than him anyway, her voice had a lilting musicality to it. Alex was nearly forty. He ached, but he was never sure if that was due to his age or of being constantly on high alert, his training so ingrained in his psyche that it was difficult to ever let it go. He wondered if the voice should be familiar to him, she sounded as if she was totally comfortable saying his name.

The door of the bathroom opened and there silhouetted by the bathroom light was a vision of femininity. Alex, being a red blooded man, noticed her curves and the way they stirred him, he could tell she had shoulder length dark hair, maybe black, her legs were slender, her waist petite enough to accentuate her hips, her calves athletic and toned as she stood on her toes. She remained there for longer than necessary knowing that he would be drinking in the image, a woman who knew the effect she had on a man. Steam rose slowly off her shoulders and she dripped water on the carpet. He leaned over to the nightstand to turn on the bedside lamp, wanting to get a better look to see if she was as beautiful as he suspected.

'Don't' she said, flicking off the bathroom light 'Leave it off, I'm coming to bed'

She picked up the towel from the back of the chair and dried herself off, then slipped in between the sheets and cuddled up to him. She made contented sounds, almost like a purr. She smelled clean and fresh. Alex thought her fragrance was somehow familiar.

'Alex?' she whispered

Another grunt.

'I love you, you know that don't you? I'm so glad we are in this together. You make me feel safe. I really couldn't do this all on my own'

Then without saying anything more she drifted off to sleep leaving Alex lying there wondering how the hell he had come to be here at all.

. . . .

AS SITUATIONS GO HE could imagine a lot worse than nestling next to a beautiful woman in a motel bedroom. And truthfully he had often found himself some pretty desperate scenarios. That didn't do anything to ease his mind though especially after what she had just said. He relaxed his muscles and let his body loosen slightly. He wracked his mind about *where* he might be. Her voice sounded transatlantic, she could either be American or just well-travelled. He could hear a slight hum in the room. It was probably an air-con unit, if so he could guess this was probably the US. Maybe the west coast. Alex didn't know why but subconsciously, maybe, he could sense the sea, maybe his nose detected a tang of salt in the air. He carried on looking around the room. No obvious clues. A brown leather jacket hanging from a hook on the back of the door, a bottle of tequila on the table, two glasses, the smell of fast food lingering slightly in the air. The sound of distant traffic from outside and an airplane overhead. What he saw next troubled him. A wedge had been placed under the door, not to keep it open but to keep it closed from anyone trying to enter the room from the outside. Unfortunately it was a ploy he had used before which was all too familiar.

The last thing Alex remembered before waking in the motel room was making the descent in an aeroplane from London to Madrid. The airplane hadn't been particularly full, it carried mostly business types off to parts of Europe for various meetings no doubt. He had eaten the terrible food that only airlines can get away with serving; a pasta dish that he would have sent back anywhere else but on an airline. He had needed two whiskey sodas in quick succession to try and get rid of the taste. He had been laughing and chatting with a beautiful young woman who was sitting next to him. He had excused himself to go to the bathroom and when he got back to his seat the plane had started it's descent so he drained his third whiskey soda before touch-down. He didn't recall arriving in Adolfo Suárez. Alex supposed that, inevitably though, he must have done. He did remember he had been going to Madrid to meet someone, to make a payment, for a service of some kind, he couldn't grasp the specifics yet. There were gaps in his memory which he couldn't explain. Maybe they would come back to him, in time. Recently he was having too many gaps in his memories which he found he couldn't fill easily, it was unlike him, usually his memory was faultless. Although he could feel some recall returning to him, he found it frustrating, as if he was trying to grab on to wisps of smoke.

He checked on his bed partner. As the dark was now all pervasive he had trouble making out her features. He could tell though that she was sleeping soundly and deeply, her breathing heavy and even. Alex carefully slipped his arm from underneath her trying not to disturb her. She groaned but rolled over on to her side and carried on sleeping. Alex got out of bed, naked, crossed the room and entered the bathroom. Quietly he opened the door, not turning on the light until he was inside and the door was closed. He looked at himself in the mirror, searching his own eyes for answers but found none. He checked over his body. There were scars new and old, though the new ones were more than a few days as they had begun to heal. His hair was short and professionally cut, a few streaks of grey above the temples, his sideburns short and neat, his beard maybe a bit longer than usual but he decided it didn't look too bad. The detritus surrounding the sink told him they had been here for more than just today, a few days at least. There were a few bottles of the feminine variety, lotions and moisturizers, lipsticks and nail varnish. His shaving apparatus was there too, obviously bought locally as they were of the cheap and throwaway kind he would not normally use. He leant on the basin, brought his face close to the mirror and peered deeply into his eyes. They were bloodshot, whether due to the tequila on the table or the stress of the last few days he couldn't tell. There was bruising around one eye. He traced a finger along the old faded scar which ran from his cheekbone in a crescent shape up around his eye socket, a constant reminder of Navarre. Even though it had faded away to a pale line it still stood out to him as if it had happened only yesterday.

Alex had been having more and more of these 'episodes', waking up and not remembering what had happened. They had started back in London. He would suddenly become aware he had been kneeling in front of the television in his apartment watching any old garbage or walking in a daze around an area he was not accustomed to. At first the blackouts seemed harmless enough as if he had been in a daydream, but they had grown increasingly worse over the last few months. He really began to feel concerned when he found himself in the middle of The South Bank outside The Tate Modern, a swarm of tourists around him all chattering in German. He had been less able to get a satisfactory nights sleep as he felt that when he lost consciousness he also lost control. He was getting increasingly tired and with the fatigue came a creeping sense of paranoia. He was wont to feel he was being watched, he didn't trust those closest to him and he found himself being secretive because of it. His body could deal with a certain amount of hardship but his mind was beginning to crack. A wave of complete exhaustion came over him, he let his forehead rest against the cool glass and closed his eyes. He knew it could be a mistake but he couldn't help himself.

That's when it came to him, Deanna! That was the girl in the bed. Of course. They had met on the plane. They had hit it off, it was all coming back to him. Then his world once again became blank and his mind entered into nothingness.

Aside

He walked down the corridor on the soft pile carpet, his footsteps not making any sound, past the secretaries typing and talking on their telephones. A few nodded to him in acknowledgement but mostly they were too wrapped up in their work to notice him. He carried on past the men's washrooms where the building began to get quieter and found himself walking into the vacant office at the end of the building on the sixth floor. He sat down at the desk, turned on the screen, waited for nearly a minute for the machine to boot up, checked his cellphone and then tapped on the keyboard entering the pass-code. He stared at the screen vacantly, his face a mask belying the fact that he was recording all the information in front of him into his subconscious. For anyone watching him he could have been reading emails or annual reports. He scrolled down the page his eyes flicking over the text reading everything set out before him; names, places, dates, codes and cover stories; all classified and top secret. His body was rigid, the only movement his index finger pressing the down arrow on the keyboard, his eyes flicking up and down. The only time his eyes moved from the screen was when he heard a noise from outside in the corridor, someone using the washroom and letting the door bang behind them. Then, ascertaining there was no immediate threat he returned to scanning the screen. On completion of this task he left the office making sure everything was as he found it, carefully covering his tracks, wiping down the keys and the mouse. Quietly he slipped out of the door and made his way back to his own work station at the other end of the building, not fully realising what was now stored on his organic hard drive. Information that could only be accessed by certain methods, locked away until the right time and circumstances presented themselves

II - Teaming up

The eight men waited in the large meeting room on the sixth floor in Thames House. They were a mixed bag of individuals, some had known each other since they began in the service, others were known only by reputation. They made their introductions, Alex taking the lead as he had already been informed by Lassiter he was to head up the operation. They shook hands and wisecracked with plenty of man hugs and shoulder punches for good measure. All of those familiar with each other pumped up and excited to be working together as a team again. That was all they knew so far, the files laid out on the table no doubt held more information, and only that time would be of the essence, as was usually the case. A call to see the Elite Squad Leader was followed with sketchy details regarding a problem that needed seeing to somewhere around the globe. It was then up to the hand-picked team when faced with the challenge to formulate a strategy and see that it was carried out without any fuss or publicity. Subtlety and discretion were the keywords they lived by, the name of MI5 was always at stake. It was always a successful day if the missions they carried out never made it in to the daily papers. The smaller the circle of knowledge the better.

Alex Spellman sat at one end of the large mahogany table, on his left his colleague for four years, Graham Devereux; a rangy individual with gaunt features but an extrovert disposition, one of Alex's closest comrades and a friend outside of the job. Next to him was Dan Johnson and Jack Cole, both men looking fit for their ages; Dan had a healthy glow to his complexion while sitting in his chair with languidly muscled limbs draped over the arms, he was a handsome man who had the chiselled jawline of a male model but the buzz cut and scar damaged face of a veteran soldier. Jack Cole on the other hand sat pensively, elbows on the table looking tense and ready to spring, also a man in peak physical shape with salt and pepper hair bordering on blond and pale granite coloured eyes which disconcerted many people on first meeting. He did not seem as comfortable with the group as some of the others present but Alex put that down to the fact that he was a relative newbie to these group operations. On the opposite side of the table sat Simon Chapman, compact and wiry with a fidgety disposition, Derek West, an only son born to mixed race parents brought up in Brixton and as tough as nails. John Watts and their youngest member Jimmy Mitchell both sat together, John being a nurturing sort of character, taking it upon himself to give support and guidance to their new addition. Jimmy looked to have a mix of apprehension, nerves and excitement etched into his, comparatively, youthful features and was eager to get to know the men around the table. The room was swathed in a dimness due to the heavy dark drapes that almost covered the tall windows. The sun shone into the room in beams that picked out the dust motes in the air. The table was more than three metres long and made of Kingwood, an ornate, thick heavy construction. All the men there would not have been able to lift it off the floor if asked to. The room and it's contents were old school comfort, a throwback to the older governmental days when civil servants did not have to divulge to the public what their budget was spent on. The men were swapping stories and anecdotes when the door opened and in walked Clive Lassiter, a man who had been in the service all of his adult life in one way or another. He knew the passages and halls of nearly all the government buildings in central London. He had dallied with all the ministers and politicians who passed through these doors and would more than likely forge a lucrative career writing spy novels in his retirement. He was carrying a sheaf of papers under one arm and tea in a paper cup in his hand. Lassiter had the gaunt appearance of someone who didn't see the sun often, many of the men referred to him behind his back as 'Vlad'. His face was pale and pinched, he wore wire rimmed glasses for reading so had to look over them often when addressing somebody further away, as was the case at the long table at which they now sat. The eight men stood up as he entered as a sign of deference although Jack Cole and Jimmy Mitchell were slower to do so than the others and Alex had to prompt them as a mother would her children.

'Sit down gentlemen' said Lassiter, 'without any further ado we will jump right into things if you don't mind. I gather you've all met. If you don't know each other I'm sure that you will rectify that yourselves in due course. You should all know that I have made Spellman team leader for this operation, so you will be reporting to him. If you don't like it keep it to yourself. Alex is, in my opinion, the best man for this particular job. Which brings us onto why we are here'.

The men around the table visibly stiffened as they were eager to find out about the mission.

'We have just received intel' from an asset in northern Spain that there is a problem brewing in the Pyrenees. As you know ETA, Euskadi Ta Askatasuna, and the Spanish government are trying to engineer yet another ceasefire. The thing is that this time it looks as if it's going to stick, both parties are pretty set on ending the bloodshed. ETA are losing support of the public and have finally realised that the senseless killing of innocents, in fact, doesn't help their end-game. However there is a possibility that an individual named 'Dienteputo' is rallying a splinter group in the Navarre region who are not keen on things going so smoothly. Our information is that the size of the group is fairly modest but the members are extremists and will go to great lengths to obstruct the peace agreement. Even so far as to threaten the life of the Prime Minister, Zapatero. The final declaration for cessation of terrorism is due to be signed by heads of state on 17th October. We think this will be Dienteputo's target, so it is necessary to nip this insurgency in the bud, gentlemen. I am relying on you, a team hand-picked by me to ensure that there will be no further escalation in this territory. Peace in the Basque region has been so close for many years now and it is time it came to pass, it is in all our best interests. However.... and this is where it gets a little complicated, your mission is to be carried out without the knowledge or support of the Spanish government'

This statement elicited a collective sound of surprise from the eight men, they all looked to each other for reaction. Alex was the only one who showed no emotion, he had half expected this type of operation to be 'cloak and dagger'.

'You see, our asset in Spain must remain a secret. I have it on good authority that the intel' is sound. We are to be in and out without anybody knowing we were ever there. It is to be a stealth strike. Dropped in by 'chute under cover of darkness. Destroy any and all ordnance on site. Incapacitate all guerrillas in the camp long enough for the treaty to be signed' Lassiter finished, 'All the information you should need is in front of you in the files. Any questions?'

The eight heads around the table shook in unison, these were men who knew what was expected of them and knew their jobs like the back of their hands.

'Excellent', said Lassiter, 'If you need me you know where to find me. I'll leave you to it gentlemen, you have the room for an hour, make your arrangements... and one more thing before I forget. Don't fuck it up. Alright? I picked you lot because I trust you, and my name is at the top of the paperwork, the buck stops here, so I repeat - DO NOT fuck it up. Dismissed'

With that he collected his now lukewarm tea, his files and dossiers and left the room closing the door behind him leaving the eight men to make their preliminary plans. There was a general relaxation of shoulders as Lassiter left, the men now in the company of their friends and peers, the relationship with the team leader, although higher ranking, was of a more affable nature.

'Now, God knows why I've been given you lot as a team', began Alex taking to his feet, 'but I suppose I'll have to make do. It's a good job a team isn't picked on account of it's looks, that's all I can say'

The men around the table all grinned at the banter that they all expected from Alex. It put them at their ease.

'For those of you who don't know our new team member, this is James Mitchell, likes to be called Jimmy. He may look like he just left 6th form but don't let that fool you, he's an asset to the team. Even though he may have been sucking on formula when most of you were already in the service'. The men around the table all looked towards Jimmy and gave him a nod of approval, welcoming him to the team.

'Jimmy, you may know those around the table, if you don't, we've got Graham Devereux', Graham waved a hand without looking up from the file he was now scanning, 'Dan Johnson, Simon Chapman and Derek West whom I have worked with many times previously and can honestly say that they are some of the best men you will find in the service. We also have Jack Cole and John Watts who have come to me on the highest recommendation from across the river. Welcome gentlemen'

'Now that the formalities are over let's get on with this thing shall we?'

The eight men thrashed out the details of the sortie into Navarre. How they were going to deploy into the area without flagging the authorities, their exfiltration package, what type of timers and explosives to use for the most effectiveness, what to do if things didn't go as planned, a meeting point if they became separated, supplies they would need and equipment they would not. The men all made notes, asked questions, made suggestions, argued points and finally agreed on tactics. Alex listened to each individual and took advice from their specialized areas of expertise. He was impressed that on certain points they would not back down. Cole insisted that he be the one to set the explosives in the ammunition shack as he had worked with the same triggers and fuses before in the field. Alex asked for a volunteer to be the second man setting fuses. The details and minutiae of the other roles were buttoned down; there would be two men outside the shack giving cover, the other four men would be dealing with the guerrillas in their sleeping quarters.

After two hours of organizing, the men were becoming tired and going over the same points over and over. It was time to call it a day. There came a knock at the door and a head peered into the room. It was a pimply young intern who was practically unable to utter the words through fright 'Please vacate the room gentlemen, there is another meeting scheduled in ten minutes, thank you' and then he scurried off in retreat. The men looked at each other relieved that the meeting had been forced to a close.

'If anyone is interested, I think we all deserve a bit of refreshment after all that yammering. The Morpeth Arms, across the road in ten minutes, I'm buying the first two rounds. See you there' said Alex. Jimmy wondered if that was an order or a request, either way he was going to stick close to Alex just in case.

3 - Frantic Search

Deanna dressed quickly, she was enraged with herself for being so stupid. How could she have gone to sleep and not kept an eye on Alex? He was obviously still in a confused state. She was almost certain that he recently had one of his blackouts, she wasn't sure if he even remembered her. She had to find him. Quickly. Before those two Polish brutes found him again. She should have checked on him to see how his memories were. Surely he must have remembered the danger he was in?

The few days they had spent together in the motel had been wonderful. She had Alex all to herself, she could feel herself falling for him although she knew she shouldn't. They had spent hours on end talking, in each other's arms mostly, with Alex going out of his way to make her laugh, despite the predicament they were in. It had all started on the flight to Spain, the ease of which they got on, the obvious attraction, the offhand way that he touched her arm that made her skin break into goosebumps. Then on the way back to the US, running from their pursuers to somewhere they could rally and pause for breath, to come up with a plan of action. She wondered to herself if it was all due to the drama and excitement of being on the run. Osterman would be smiling smugly to himself if he knew. Maybe he had an inkling all the time that she would be a pushover for Spellman. Damn him. Why were things so seldom straight forward? She was afraid not only that Osterman would be livid at her for losing him but she wasn't prepared to let Alex go, not now after all they had been through together. She had seen a chance for happiness and she was damned if she was going to lose it. She had lost too much in the last few years, happiness had been denied her for so long, she deserved some contentment, didn't she?

She checked the room for his clothes. They were all gone along with his coat and shoes, but not all his possessions. His toiletries and such were still in the bathroom. She pulled on her trainers and wrapped a coat around her shoulders. Deanna opened the door a crack and peered out just to make sure no-one was immediately outside. The coast was apparently clear. The morning sun had not yet eradicated the cool of the night but it shone harshly through the buildings, casting long shadows on the ground and leaving a haziness in the shade. A few people were out walking to their early shifts at work, a jogger trotted at an unusually slow pace halfway down the block, an elderly lady was out walking her equally aged pug, all normal sights for the average American town. There was even the homeless man, or was it woman, shambolically pushing a trolley across the tarmac in the parking lot opposite. The trolley over-filled with odds and ends collected from dumpsters and skips, all needed to make the life of the owner that much more comfortable.

Where would she start? Where would Alex be going? She wracked her mind. She thought she had been getting to know Alex and then out of the blue she had been left flailing, not knowing the first thing about where he might be headed. She felt helpless. She felt like an amateur. Another mistake like this or the one in Spain and she would be kicked off the case altogether. Her insecurities welled up in her mind; maybe she wasn't cut out for this type of work after all, maybe she should have stayed where it was safe, in the offices in Fairfax or the field office in San Diego, filing reports, making coffee, going to lunch at the same diner every day. No. She was determined to make this work, she had promised herself and her parents that she would make something of herself. She would not, could not, fail.

As she walked the street her mind wandered back to those first days they had spent together in Spain. Deanna had finagled a seat next to Alex on the British Airways flight to Adolfo Suárez. She had travelled from the US and landed at Heathrow the day before Alex was booked in to leave for Madrid. She spent the night in one of those on-site hotels which didn't do anything for her jetlag, the constant noise of the planes landing and taking off every three minutes was almost too much to bear. Once on the plane, with the steward's warning address behind them, Deanna, now with her hair dyed dark brown and cut shorter, instantly struck up a rapport with Alex. She noticed him reading an article in the in-flight magazine about Paul McCartney so to strike up conversation she asked him if he was a Beatles or a Stones fan. Alex quite definitely stated he was into Jagger & Co. They spent the whole flight flirting and joking with each other, there was obviously an instant attraction. Deanna found Alex's slate grey eyes almost turned to blue when the light from the sun caught them in a certain way through the cabin window. He had the ease and confidence of someone who was comfortable in a woman's company and she let herself be seduced by his easy charm.

After she returned from the bathroom mid-flight she was slightly regretful about what had to be done next, although she did consider it was necessary. Her mission was to get close to Alex, strike up a friendship or even a relationship, find out why he was heading to Spain, who he was seeing and what he was going to do there. During her analysis of Alex prior to leaving the US, she had learned that he often dated; usually women who were five to ten years his junior, although apparently not so much in recent years. He was a conspicuously social person, gregarious at times, although he did have an understandable dark side due to the op' in Navarre that failed so horribly. He had never really got over the fact that he lost men in an operation that was under his control. Not a day passed by that Alex must have thought about the people those four boys had left behind. He must have known their wives and children if they had any.

Towards the end of the flight when Alex had gone to the bathroom Deanna slipped a little something in his drink. This had the desired effect of making Alex more pliable, making it look as if he had had too many in-flight drinks, enabling her to get him through customs and into a cab where she could then get them both back to his hotel room. It was there she could keep an eye on him for that evening and see if she could get any idea about who he was in Madrid to meet.

She walked the streets frantically trying to find Alex, looking in bars, down alleyways, internet cafés, shops and restaurants, he was nowhere to be seen. She must have been looking for nearly an hour when she started walking back to the motel in the hope that he might return there. If he wasn't she would have to admit defeat and contact Osterman who would then send a team out to track Spellman. Her career and her reputation would be in tatters before it had even got off the ground, she doubted she would ever recover from it. Her mood was darkening, she had looked everywhere, where else could he have gone? He couldn't have vanished. Two blocks from the motel now and Deanna passed a small, humble chapel. The file had not mentioned Alex being religious but it was worth a try, she had exhausted all other possibilities. She opened the large wooden door and expected to find a dimly lit, gloomy space with wooden pews and stained glass windows. It was a good many years since she had seen the inside of a church and she was surprised instead to find a bright, airy, albeit modest, space with neat rows of light wooden chairs pointing toward an altar. The stained glass depicting modern versions of the traditional illustrations she was expecting to see and the carpet was new and clean. It smelled pleasantly of incense. The room was smaller than she thought it would be so when she entered she assumed almost immediately that Alex was not there. Her heart sank, her head dropped and her chin rested on her chest. She looked down at the floor, took a deep breath and let out a sigh of defeat. She closed her eyes tight and tried to fight back a tear. Then she heard a voice.

'Deanna? Is that you?'

It was Alex, she couldn't have been happier. He had been sitting at the back of the chapel off to the right where he wouldn't automatically be seen.

They walked toward each other and Deanna began to laugh through the tears, Alex embraced her tightly and comforted her.

'I thought I had lost you' she said 'I've been looking everywhere. Why didn't you tell me?'

'I had a blackout... another blackout, one minute I was in the bathroom at the motel looking in the mirror, the next thing I knew I was standing in front of this church wondering how I got there. As I stood there outside on the sidewalk trying to come to terms with my sudden relocation I decided it might be the best place for me to be alone with my thoughts and try to work out some things in my head. And I think it has helped. Here, come and sit down, I've got a lot to tell you' he said, 'When I woke up this morning or rather last night I had no memory of what had been taking place over the last few days. I came here to see if I could make some sense of what has been happening to me. My memories have been returning to me fitfully. It is a lot like seeing something out of the corner of your eye, I have wisps of images in my head but I can't always grab onto them. It turns out this was the perfect place for a bit of peace and quiet and to clear my mind, it helped me to grab at some of those random images and to make bigger pictures from them'

'Are you religious? Is it why you came to this chapel?' she asked him

'That's a difficult question to ask me'

'Why?'

'I have a religion, but it's probably not one you would understand'

'Try me, I can be open minded, I might surprise you'

'I think from a purely scientific point of view there is no question the idea of a God is a manmade construct, as a pragmatist I believe there can be no other option. There is an argument to be made that the world would also be a more peaceful place if there were no religion. Personally I think that humankind has a deep seated need to believe in a higher power, it solves a lot of problems within the human psyche in dealing with the fact that we are self-aware. No other animal on the planet has a God'

Alex paused in thought for a moment choosing the correct words to carry on.

'Ever since humankind has been self-aware there have been Gods to be worshipped, and not just the one God; the Greek Gods, the Roman Gods, the Norse Gods, Vishnu, Shiva, Buddha, Allah, Yahweh and a multitude of others from a variety of cultures; it just goes to show that there is a human need for a God and there always has been. Humans are spiritual by nature. Personally I believe in spirituality and of the human soul. What makes us different from other animals who inhabit the planet is our fundamental ability to care for one another, to have empathy. It doesn't mean that evil doesn't exist, we all know that it does, but religion gives the majority of people a guide on how evil should not be let into their lives'

'And what about the evil committed in the name of religion?'

'Well, there you have the crux of the matter; it's becoming more apparent that religion per se isn't always all about 'love', some fundamentalists see it being about persecution, ethnic cleansing, subjugation and suppression'

'That's a sad point of view'

'But not untrue, most of the wars fought in the last hundred years have been race related conflicts; Bosnia, Cambodia, Rwanda, Armenia, the Holocaust... But it shouldn't stop us from striving to be kinder people, from trying to change the world for the better'

'You haven't told me your religion'

'I have no religion except the religion I hold in my heart, the fact that I know right from wrong, that I can recognize when I have done wrong and never make the same mistake twice. I believe I am a reputable man fundamentally and every day I try to impact positively on those around me'

'Well you've certainly had an impact on me'

'I hope so'

They sat quietly for a few moments and listened to the muffled sound of the traffic coming to life outside the chapel, of people going to work and beginning their day.

Deanna sat with her head resting on his shoulder as he spoke her hand resting in his, 'While sitting here I remembered that we were in Madrid together, that we had to fly back to the United States after fleeing from the three Spaniards, I know that there are people after us but I'm not sure why'

'That's what we are going to find out' she said, 'We need to know if the Spaniard was working alone, if not, who is pulling his strings. Let's get some breakfast, I'm starving, and get back to the motel to see if we can come up with a plan of action'

They left the chapel and walked arm in arm back to the motel planning on collecting their belongings and going to a nearby restaurant to eat breakfast. They were both getting sick of looking at the inside of the motel room eating take-out. It had been three days now and whoever was looking for them had not given them any cause to believe that they were on their tail any longer. However when they got back to the room they could see straight away that they were indeed not out of trouble just yet; the door had been forced open and left swinging on it's hinges. Alex stood to one side of the door and pushed it fully open with his fingertips, there was no one inside but the room had been ransacked; all their belongings had been tossed over the floor, the bed had been upturned, the drawers left on the floor emptied of their contents.

'This doesn't make any sense' said Alex, 'Why would they toss the room when they are after me?'

'We need to go Alex, we don't want to be here if they come back'

Alex suddenly fell to his knees clutching his head, he buried his face into the bed sheets and let out a grunt of pain.

'Alex! What's wrong?' Deanna said, putting her arms around his shoulders, 'What do I do? How can I help?'

Alex just rocked back and forth until the pain abated enough for him to speak coherently 'It's passing now, don't worry, it must be a migraine of some sort, although I've not been a sufferer before now'

'It must be linked to the blackouts and the memory loss, it has to be. Do you need a doctor?'

'No, I'll be fine, it's passing now, it'll be alright, honestly'

Deanna stroked his head soothing him, doing all that she could to try and comfort him. Alex let himself slide into her arms as he waited for the pain to abate finding contentment in the feel of her soft skin and fragrant smell. Deanna became anxious with the sense that their lives were in the balance, their relationship although new and fresh and exciting could very well be cut short, she may never be able to get to really know Alex Spellman the way she would like to. Compared to Gregg, Alex was everything she had been looking for in a partner, of course he had the rugged good looks of a man of his age. He had obviously looked after himself but it was the way that when he talked to her it was as if she was the only person in his world at that time, that nothing else mattered to him. His eyes would look directly into hers and it would feel as if he could see into her soul almost. She sometimes became self-conscious to the point where she would have to say something random to break the spell he had on her. She looked at him now and her heart swelled in her breast, the crescent scar around his eye, his short hair flecked with grey at the temples, his cool grey eyes like pools of water. They sat that way for as long as they could risk it, the men who had been in the room might return once more and they couldn't be around if they did.

IV - The Morpeth Arms

A lex exited the building and walked out into the cold afternoon, there was a frost in the air that would almost certainly turn the grass of London's parks crisp overnight. The sky was a leaden grey and the clouds scudded ever onward in an uninterrupted flow in varying shades of Stygian gloom. He pulled his coat collar up around his chin, put his head down and headed for the warmth of the nearby Morpeth Arms, fully realising the irony of his choice. It was a popular destination for tourists in the summer who liked the espionage theme of the bar, being near Thames House. Graham and Jimmy both kept pace with Alex covering the ground as quickly as possible to get back into the warm.

When they reached the bar it was not as full as in peak tourist season but there were a some local drinkers propping up the bar. There were a few lone stragglers dotted around as well. Alex by way of habit quickly scanned each face and ran it through his internal files, something he had been doing for a long time now, you could never be too careful and you were *never* off duty. Alex led them into the back room bar down the spiral staircase to the cells, a narrow almost claustrophobic corridor with whitewashed walls and a dank feel about it. It was a throwback from the times when prisoners were kept in holding cells for the nearby Millbank Penitentiary. At the end of the corridor they entered an undersized door which opened up into a meagre but cosy bar populated by a few of their colleagues from Thames House. Alex watched Jimmy's face as he looked on in wonder at the private drinking den that was for government employees only. Alex gave him a nod and a wink and they settled at a table big enough for all eight of the team should they join them.

'What is this place?' Jimmy asked

'Members only, Jimmy, you can only get in to this place if you are with a member of the POMs' answered Graham

'And what are the POMs?'

'Shall we tell him? Do you think he is ready?' Graham asked Alex with a grin

Alex nodded for him to carry on.

'Well, when you've been in the service for a certain amount of time, it's not fixed, and when you've proved yourself in the field of battle, in our cases not so much battle but 'in the field' so to say, you get access to one of the most elite and secret watering holes in London' Graham said with satisfaction, relishing the fact that the world of spies and undercover operatives was as real as the movies made them out to be.

'But why POMs?'

'Ah, fine question. And one that I will let Alex here tell you'

'You know what POM stands for don't you?'

'I don't think I do as it happens, it's some sort of shorthand for being British!' said Jimmy

'Well in our case it stands for Perks Of Millbank, I think that is self explanatory. But back in the olden days, as it were, it used to stand for Prisoners of Millbank. All the scum and villainy from London's sewers and back alleys were imprisoned here temporarily while they waited for the transport to take them 'down under' in the convict ships. Not all of them made it onto the floating prisons, some died here in the cells waiting. That's why these holding cells are said to be haunted, with the spectres of long dead murderers and thieves. They say that there is at least one revenant stalking the passages of this building; Archie Capper, a murderer, a rapist and thief to boot. He was known in London as Dapper Capper, started off as a confidence trickster with his partner in crime Effie Whipple. They would rob the unsuspecting in the wee hours of the night, people coming back late from drinking dens and such. Their ploy was to fake an injury or some such, Effie usually being the one to act injured in a back alley somewhere. Some poor do-gooder would come to the aid of an attractive woman in need and all of a sudden Archie would cosh the poor sod and rob him blind. That was their M.O. for many years, God only knows how they survived for so long without getting caught. But, over time they became not only well known but infamous. Their secret was to not work the same area of London too often, they would move about; Elephant & Castle, Brick Lane even as far as Hampstead. At no time did they ever kill anyone though' Alex took a long sip from his drink and set his glass silently back on the table, 'This is where it gets darker; no one knows why but one night Archie lost his mind, that can be the only explanation, right Graham? He became deranged and attacked poor Effie, so the stories go, nobody knew what set him off. He raped and beat his partner of more than five years, then stabbed her multiple times in the stomach leaving her to bleed to death slowly in a deserted back alley not more than 200 metres from this particular public house. The sheer brutality of the crime was his death sentence. He was caught by sheer luck one day when a victim recognized him in the street and told the police, he was picked up swiftly and sentenced to life in exile. His demise came when he was placed in the holding cells here at Millbank. There was a lot of crime at the time, the cells were crowded, mainly with petty thieves and tricksters. Archie didn't stand a chance, they practically tore him to shreds, the other inmates beat him so bad his own mother wouldn't have recognized him, they didn't look fondly on a rapist of women. Nearly every bone in his body got broken that night, it still took him hours to die of his wounds though. His screams and howls are still heard now in the bowels of the cells where we now sit' Alex paused letting the information sink in, 'It seems like the best place in London to be left undisturbed, don't you think? What'll you have?'

Jimmy sat there looking as if he'd been slapped. The look on his face wavered between disbelief and horror.

Alex took their drink orders and approached the narrow bar.

'Is that all true?' asked Jimmy

'Probably. It depends what you want to believe doesn't it' said Graham, 'What is fact is that in true British fashion we are sitting here having a quiet drink directly below all the people in the upstairs bar who haven't got a clue that this place even exists. The horror and the misery that these walls have seen. Most people think that the Spying Room upstairs is the actual room where Mata Hari did her stuff, it's really called that because you can see MI6 across the Thames. It's why this place is the perfect spot, hiding in plain sight sort of thing. I think you'll find that many places in London have a past that not everyone would like you to know, this city is full of dark history that would chill your bones, sometimes it's best not to know'

As they sat there two more of the team, Derek and John, entered the bar and joined Alex in ordering drinks.

'Is this going to be dangerous? The operation in Spain' asked Jimmy looking concerned.

'Not at all. There will be nothing to worry about. I've done dozens like it. Well, when I say that, there is always an element of risk but the team is a strong one, we should be fine' he said, 'But don't get complacent, never get complacent. That is the real enemy'

'How many of these have you done?'

'Too many to count. Not all the same of course. The secret is to keep your head. In this case we are going to be the cause of panic not the victims of it. As long as we all know what we should be doing and stick to our jobs there should be no problem'

'How come Spellman is team leader?' asked Jimmy, 'Why not you? Or any other man on the team?'

'Alex knows his stuff. You know how when you're given a car on your seventeenth birthday and you start taking lessons. Well you either learn to drive the car over the course of maybe ten lessons and then you start to get up to snuff and know what you're doing, you begin to get a bit of confidence, yes?' Graham waited for a nod, 'Or you jump into that car and you know exactly how it works and what to do to get the best out of that engine and those wheels. That's Alex and this team. He knows the strengths of every individual and how far they can be pushed. I've worked with him many times in the past and there is no other man I would rather have by my side in a tight spot'

'Is that so?' said Jimmy raising an eyebrow

'I owe the man my life, I can tell you that'

'How's that? asked Jimmy leaning forward with eagerness, wanting to hear more tales.

'He wouldn't want me to be telling you this story but that's just because he's too damn modest. I'll tell you quickly while he's still at the bar,' he glanced over, 'looks like it will be a while til we get our drinks anyway, he's chatting to the chaps. Two years ago now we were out near the Kazakhstan border, we had been dropped in by 'chute at night to pick up a Russian defector. The plan was to make our way down the Buzan River to Marfino, a modest village where we were to meet him. The Buzan is one of the many spidery tributaries off the Volga in the south. Our Primary had travelled overland from Volgograd and was hiding out in a relative's basement, he had already been there three nights, the poor sod, he must have been going stir crazy. Anyway, there were four of us in the team. We were all dropped along with a 'chute carrying a self-inflating dinghy and our supplies. We were to exfiltrate him to the Caspian Sea where we would be picked up again by a Black Hawk, one of those new ones at the time specially refitted with noise dampening technology; no-one would even know that we had been there. Now, we were dropped into Kazakhstan a few miles south of Safonovka, then we were to make our way down one of the tributaries and join the Buzan, it was about 30 km but we had a undersized, quiet outboard, then once past Baklanye the current would carry us along out to the Caspian sea'

Graham was interrupted then by Alex coming back to the table with the drinks, 'Are Derek and John joining us?' he asked

'Not for the minute, they're staying at the bar trying to get some food. What are you lads talking about?'

'Graham was just telling me about the Black Hawks' Jimmy blurted without thinking, obviously intrigued by the story.

'Well, I suppose you had better carry on then, don't let me stop you. I'll make sure I correct all the bits you get wrong, as usual,' Alex addressed Jimmy, 'he has a terrible habit of exaggerating, don't believe all that he tells you'

'As I was saying,' Graham began more cautiously, thinking hard to find his place in the story, then taking a big gulp from his pint before resuming, 'Ah yes, everything was going fine and to plan, we were dropped in and managed to inflate that damned dinghy so we could stow all our rig and start the river journey, it was bloody freezing, do you remember,' looking at Alex and getting a mute nod, 'all the work that had to be done kept us warm at least. It would have been better to have had a couple of oars, that would have kept the blood pumping. The river journey took longer than we thought, these things very rarely go to schedule, so we didn't get to Marfino until late morning the next day. We couldn't contact our man there until nightfall so we had to lay low and wait. There was ideal cover by a tiny islet about 3 km up river'

'God, I had forgotten all about that day,' interrupted Alex, 'it was a bloody good job 'Bastian brought along some playing cards, otherwise we probably would've killed each other. It was a long wait until nightfall. Sorry, Jeb, you were saying... carry on with the story, I was quite enjoying hearing it again'

'Jeb? Why do you call him Jeb?' asked Jimmy

'You ever read The Grapes of Wrath by Steinbeck?' Jimmy shook his head, 'Well, read it and you'll see why'

'OK, so yeah, we played cards most of the day, and if I remember rightly 'Bastian and Beaner took about fifty quid off each of us that day, come to think of it I still haven't had the chance to try and win it back off them. So, we had to wait until it got dark to make the approach into town to babysit this Russian, Pavel Polyakov, back to the UK. I didn't think he was such a great catch, he said he could give us information regarding the new regime in the upper halls of the Kremlin, the so-called 'nameless' men who ran everything and answered to no-one. It turned out he did give us a few names but nothing to get that excited about. I think he just liked the sound of living in the West, queuing five hours for bread and cheese isn't everyone's cup of tea. Anyhow, I'm getting ahead of myself. We had the location of his position so we knew where we were going, there was a curfew on in the town at the time so there were a few soldiers and police patrolling the streets, but it is a small town, they were easy to sidestep. Finding him turned out to be the easy part, when we set eyes on this fella we couldn't believe it... he was easily 300 pounds, a huge man who could hardly get out of an armchair let alone make it into a helicopter. He was not going to make it to where we had stashed the boat, we would need to bring the boat to him if we were to get him out. We would need to bring the dinghy up the Konnaya as far as possible, without being seen by the patrols, which was about a kilometre, without much cover. As was usual with this type of conundrum we did what any of us would do in the situation, we drew straws. It was a shitty detail but had to be done, this man was not going anywhere on foot, God knows how he got from Volgograd. Must have been in the back of a pickup truck'

Graham paused and took a long draught from his pint almost finishing it in two gulps. As he did so the barman was passing collecting glasses so he ordered another round. Alex and Jimmy both then tried to play catch up.

'Me and Beaner got the short straws anyway. We travelled on foot back to the main part of the river to get the dinghy while Alex and Bastian were going to bring Polyakov to a bridge that spanned the tributary. The banks of this part of the river were remarkably low lying and you could be seen from the shacks on the northern side although there were barges and house-boats that would give us cover. We gave ourselves an hour to make the rendezvous. This is where things started to get a bit hairy. We ran into a patrol, luckily it was the military and not the local police, otherwise they would have made us immediately. Beaner has better Russian than me so I let him do most of the talking. He tried to explain that we had to go out to our boat and check on the moorings as the soft sediment of the riverbed sometimes let the boat drift. I didn't know if any of this was true but Beaner was selling it, these two soldiers were obviously not locals, thank God. We then had a long discussion whether we were breaking curfew or not. We tried to explain that it was now morning and curfew was no longer in place but they were not easily convinced' Graham paused briefly, 'They wanted to take us to the stantsiya to check our papers and credentials. We couldn't let that happen so without any fuss we put an end to the whole debate, if you know what I mean. We ceased conversing with them and let them rest.... in a pile... on the ground. They were so green those two soldiers, they didn't even see it coming. We then had to move them to somewhere they wouldn't be found so we dragged them to a nearby alleyway and left them comfortable, they'd have woken up with pretty sore heads I'm sure. While all this was going on Alex and Bastian were moving the Russian, I think I'll let you tell this bit Alex, seeing as you were there and not me'

'The Russian was difficult to say the least. 'Bastian was a big fella but Polyakov was nearly twice as wide as him, although not as tall. It took us twenty minutes to get him from the basement of the house up to street level. If it was at any other time it would have looked like a comedy sketch but things were tight enough and time wasn't on our side. We didn't have too far to take him after that but we needed to keep moving. He kept wanting to rest his bulk, he was already sweating like an ox even though it was icy out. Unfortunately the Russian had partaken in a few vodkas, he said they were to calm his nerves, but judging by his face he looked like a hardened drinker, he had the rosy cheeks and bulbous nose of an abuser. We had to stop him from bursting into song once or twice. We were halfway down to the bridge when I thought to myself 'Was all this really worth it?' Babysitting was actually the wrong term for what we were doing, it was more like herding cats or juggling snakes. But still, this was the job. I had to look at the bigger picture, the man was an asset, drunk or not. It was our job to get him home, even though he was a pain in the ass. By the time we got him to the bridge I could see Jeb and Beamer making their way up the river in the dinghy. I was thinking to myself that the boat was severely lacking and was doubtful whether it was able to take all five of us, it was pushing it's capabilities to the limit. Anyway, Jeb can carry on now as he was telling the story in the first place' Alex looked toward Graham and took another long drink from his pint.

'We had no trouble after that,' Graham resumed, 'we got to the boat and were heading toward the bridge in it. We could see the three of them approaching the edge of the bank, you couldn't mistake the big Russian. Getting him in the boat was no mean feat, nearly lost him a few times into the Konnaya. Eventually we set off in the direction we had just come and hoped to God that no-one would see us heading back out toward the Buzan. There was a faint light in the sky now as the sun was making an early appearance. We had to get past the outskirts of the town before we could relax a bit. The dinghy was listing badly with the Russian in it, we tried to keep him centred but he would keep sliding over to one side or the other. There was no talking to him now, he was either singing drunkenly or getting panicky about being in the boat and heading out to open water depending on his focus. The Buzan is mostly a calm river, gently flowing out to the Caspian, except for one part we would have to negotiate where it fell a good fifteen to twenty feet in a short distance, I wouldn't call it rapids but it wasn't to be sniffed at either, we would need our wits about us. The closer we got to this point the more nervous the four of us became. Luckily Polyakov was ignorant of what was up ahead, he was in his own merry wonderland as far as any of us could tell, singing songs in a Russian dialect that none of us could recognize. We began to speed up as we approached the fall and as we did soon realised that we were woefully overloaded, with the big Russian aboard making the descent into an extremely dangerous prospect indeed. The last thing I remember was an almighty roar as the water all about us turned from dark blue to white and the soft shell of the dinghy caught on something sharp underneath the surface. The tear in the side of the boat made it deflate nearly instantly, I must have cracked my head on something because when I woke up again I was in the chopper over the Caspian getting bandaged. Alex will fill you in on the details as I was unconscious throughout' he looked now to Alex to finish off the story.

'It was nothing, I assure you. Anyone would have done the same' Alex said shying away from banging his own drum

'You have to tell it now, Al. You can't leave the boy wondering what happened can you?'

'OK, the short version though. Now let me see' he said finding a place to pick up the tale, 'As Jeb here said, the dinghy ripped on the bottom, due to us being overweight, due to Polyakov being a caviar loving, vodka swilling barrel of a man who wouldn't centre himself in the boat. Beaner and 'Bastian both grappled with the Russian in the water, who was by now screaming blue murder in between gulping down river water, while I managed to get Jeb here from sinking to the bottom. It wasn't easy, the river was flowing pretty fast at this stage and visibility wasn't good. I lost him a few times and had to dive down to drag him back up again. The problematic thing about our situation now was that the chopper would have to find us and retrieve us from the open Caspian instead of the boat. It made everything so much trickier. We all got separated by the time we hit open water. I had faith in Beaner and 'Bastian to look after Polyakov even though I knew they would be struggling to keep the situation under control. Jeb was out for more than 90 minutes and as he said he didn't come to until we were in the air. It was touch and go for a while, I wasn't sure if he was going to make it. I remember the water started to get really cold as we waited for what felt like forever for the Black Hawk to come. Though eventually it did, all we had to do was hang on long enough'

'I owe you my life' said Graham in a matter of fact tone.

'Agh, you would have done the same for me. 'Leave no man behind' that's our credo' said Alex to Jimmy 'I was damned if I wasn't going to do all I could to get Jeb back to the UK in one piece. Anyway, he still owed me fifteen quid from the card game'

'No seriously, I wouldn't be here if it wasn't for you' Graham raised his glass to toast Alex, 'Cheers mate, I'll always remember it'

Derek and John returned from the bar with their drinks and joined the table, 'Now lads' said Derek, 'This could be the last chance we get to have a bit of fun, so... we're going to play a little game. Needless to say it might involve drinking, so if you don't think you're up to it you better leave now'

'What about Simon and Jack? Are they joining us?' asked Graham

'Simon had to head home, his missus is going out with the girls so he has to look after the kid' said John, 'I'm not sure where Jack was heading, he just rushed off, said he had a previous appointment about something or other, I didn't quite catch it'

'That's a shame. It looks like it's just the six of us then. How old is his daughter now?' asked Alex

'She must be nearly five, starts school soon I believe'

'And Jack was going where?' he asked

'See a man about a dog, as they say. He mentioned a girl recently. Kiki I think her name was. Maybe he's seeing her. Why?'

'Nothing. I was just hoping to get to know him a bit better before the sortie. I've only met him in passing a couple of times. Best way to get to know somebody is over a couple of drinks, don't you think?'

'You'll see enough of him over the next day or two, in training' said Graham, 'It's not as if he's a stranger, is it?'

'I suppose not. Now gentlemen, let's get down to business. I believe we have to show young Mr. Mitchell here what it's like to be let loose in the middle of London with five chaps who know where to get bar service all through the night. This could be your trial by fire, Jimmy'

All eyes turned to Jimmy who was now looking quite apprehensive at the prospect of spending the evening with these hardened veterans. He gave a nervous laugh.

'It's alright Jimmy, we'll look after you, don't worry' said Graham putting his arm around his shoulder and giving him a friendly squeeze. 'Now, about that game'

A lex felt the wind first, buffeting his body, like a hand pushing hard against his chest. Then the incredible roar of noise. He could feel his middle being squeezed tightly. His eyes focused and his subconscious brain slowly became aware of his surroundings, at first couldn't take in what was in front of him. His hands stretched out in front holding on to handlebars. The tarmac speeding underneath the huge bike at an incredible pace. The speedometer reading close to 100mph. The bike was dead centre of the road. Alex didn't know what side of the road he should be on, there were no indications. The landscape was flat, no road signs, no trees or buildings anywhere to be seen. He panicked briefly and the bike made a kick, he straightened it deftly, his passenger gasped from behind him. He checked his mirrors. There in the distance, almost at the horizon, was a car. He could tell it was almost doing the same speed as the bike. He, rather, they were being chased. He opened up the throttle, took the bike up to 110mph. Slowly, gradually the car began to fade beyond the horizon and out of sight. This wasn't a great bonus though. If Alex and his passenger were being chased they were on a road with nowhere to turn or hide, at least for the foreseeable distance.

Alex checked his mirrors. He checked his speed. Mentally checked his own body. His pulse was racing, his chest tight, his legs like jelly, electric shocks travelling through his forearms to his fingertips, his head pounding with the adrenaline rush. A muffled shout interrupted his train of thought.

'Alex' he barely heard his passenger yell over the buffeting wind.

'Alex, WE NEED TO GET OFF THIS ROAD' the voice sounded familiar.

'NOW, Alex'

That was it, he realised. Regardless of where the road was going, the bike was much more manoeuvrable than the car would be off road. He scanned both horizons, left and right. Nothing. It was a coin toss. He slowed the bike and steered off to the right. It must have been early morning because the dust didn't kick up, it was still damp from the morning dew. The terrain became more uneven causing Alex to slow the bike down to 50mph. He took a glance over his shoulder and caught the car approaching the spot where they left the road. The car slowed down, then halted. Two men got out. One of them whipped out his cell phone and made a call. Judging by their body language they looked pissed. Alex tucked his head down, maintained his speed and drove on. He would stop the first chance he got. Then he wanted some answers. His mind was so full of questions he didn't know where to start. Hopefully his passenger would be the key.

It was getting hot, the sun rising in a cloudless sky and starting to beat down on the barren landscape. Alex was beginning to sweat in his full leathers, the droplets falling into his eyes obscuring his vision, his helmet making him claustrophobic. He needed to stop, and soon. Creeping up over the horizon, through the heat haze came an object. Alex couldn't make it out at first, but as they neared it, it became more apparent. It was a sign. That meant a road. Thank God.

Alex hadn't known which direction he was travelling. All he had for navigation was the sun. The sign turned out to be in English, but it was only a road number. The bike he was on was a Triumph Thunderbird Commander, probably the 1700cc judging by the power, but that meant nothing as to what country he was in. The car that had been following them had been a dark coloured sedan with tinted windows. Other than that he had not seen it closely enough to gauge the country of origin.

Not knowing where he was Alex kept his speed at 65 mph, he didn't want to garner any unwanted attention, especially from local law enforcement. After fifteen or so minutes Alex could see a building coming up on the right of the highway. To his relief it turned out to be a diner of sorts, one of those places which was everything and nothing. It sold gas and groceries, candy and magazines, though none to be of any use; from the look of it the proprietor had obviously given up on actually stocking what he advertised. It had a sign up outside with a picture of a hamburger though when Alex pulled up he could only smell the burnt offerings of a fire from a barrel outside the back of the building burning God knows what. At least he could get a fill for the Triumph, and maybe a cup of coffee, and some much needed answers.

Alex stopped the Triumph next to one of the pumps and waited for his passenger to dismount before he did. He was curious to find out who had been his companion on this chase through the desert. An unshaven Hispanic looking man sauntered out of the building pulling up his sagging trousers, his shirt opened two buttons too many over his paunch, probably in advance of the scorching heat the day was to bring. The man flicked his head in a questioning manner.

'Fill her up' Alex said, then turned to his passenger.

'You OK?' he asked

As he turned expecting an answer, his passenger was taking off her helmet. He was relieved to see it was Deanna.

'I am now, honey' she replied, with a smile that Alex could tell not many others got.

'Let's go inside, we need to talk', Alex walked in as his partner followed, both of them stripping off their hot leathers.

They sat at the only table in the place, opposite each other. Alex placed both hands down flat on the table in front of him and gazed at Deanna opposite. She, however, was rummaging through her purse looking for something. He noticed his hands had bruises on the knuckles. When she finally raised her head to look at him she was applying lipstick and looking at Alex directly into his eyes. Her eyes, Alex noted, were pale compared to her tanned skin and dark, almost black hair, which she now wore in a ponytail. She wore minimal make-up; a touch of eyeliner, a hint of mascara. The lipstick she applied was a rich deep red. For some reason this made Alex blush slightly. She had an easy way about her, obviously comfortable with her natural beauty; although her lipstick was of a vivid shade, Alex would be happy to see her without any on at all, her cheekbones were defined but not sharp unlike the arch of her eyebrows. When she smiled, as she did now, Alex noticed two dimples either side of her mouth which transformed her face into that of a girl instead of a woman. There was no sign now of the silk evening dress he had seen in the motel room, instead she wore jeans which clung to her legs but left her ankles bare; a pair of Converse All Star runners and a plaid shirt open at the neck just enough to show some cleavage. Alex noticed that although the outfit was different something was the same; he could see just the edge of red lace under the shirt.

The gas jockey returned from filling the Triumph. Without taking his eyes away from the woman opposite Alex said 'Two coffees... and what do you have to eat?'

'Only what you see' answered the man

'OK, give me a couple of those pastries' said Alex, 'and then make yourself scarce, we want some privacy, know what I mean?'

'No problem'

Alex could tell now that they were somewhere near the border. Near Tucson maybe. The man's accent gave it away. Probably not over the border yet, although heading south if the sun was anything to go by. Damn, still in the US. He couldn't remember the last time he had been in the UK. He missed the cool atmosphere of London, he had always thought it was the place he belonged. The coffees came along with the Danish. Alex realised he was famished. The coffee did exactly what he needed it to do, sharpen his focus.

'What do we do now, Alex', she asked

'As soon as we finish up here we need to get over the border, whoever was chasing us didn't want us to get this far, we've bought ourselves some time'

They both ate their pastries in silence, although not in any way awkward. He noticed his companion was quite relaxed in his company, considering they were being chased not more than an hour ago. Too relaxed? Alex's mind was trying to piece things together. He was furiously working out what they should do next. They had the advantage of being on two wheels, and of their pursuers not knowing where they were, for now at least.

If they were near Tucson they would need to get on the I-19 to the border at Nogales then carry on south on the 15 to Santa Ana. They should be able to find somewhere to stay and work out their next move. If he remembered correctly that was nearly 150 miles, nearly three hours by road. Maybe a bit quicker on the Triumph. At least he knew someone in Santa Ana. He needed to get in touch with Graham. Graham would give him some answers. Graham Devereux had retired out of the service to live a quiet life in Mexico, it had always been his dream to go somewhere where it was warm all year round. Graham was happy freelancing on security projects for large oil companies and corporations, as long as he could do so with a tequila in one hand and a blunt in the other. Alex hadn't spoken to him for more than two years but the bond that they had forged would last a lifetime. Alex decided he didn't want to start quizzing Deanna, it was apparent that she had put all her trust in him anyway, no point in muddying the waters by letting her know that he had experienced a memory lapse again. She wasn't going to give him the information he needed anyway. Alex needed to maintain control, be cool and stay focused.

They finished their coffees and pastries. Deanna got up and walked to the restroom leaving her keys on the table. Alex reached out and turned the key ring over in his hands. He tried to remember where the motel was that they had stayed. Was it by Lake Havasu? Phoenix? Or further west maybe Mexicali? Was that the day before, or longer, he wasn't sure. Something must have kick-started his recollection because as he sat there suddenly the last few days came rushing back into sharp detail; the meeting in Spain, Deanna in his hotel room at the Hesperia, the run-in with Quiros' two heavies and then fleeing the country, just in case there would be any trouble with local authorities. Then last night at the motel and having to flee once again as their pursuers gained on them again, only escaping by pure fortune, or you could say by Divine intervention.

Deanna came out of the bathroom, collected her belongings and followed Alex out into the harsh, bright, soon to be, midday sun. While Deanna was putting on her helmet the owner came rushing from around the back of the building.

'Hey, hombre, you owe me... for the gas' he shouted

Alex realised he had forgotten all about paying. He fished out his wallet from his back pocket and found a $50 bill, gave it to the man.

'Keep it' he said

While looking through the wallet he saw he had multiples of different currencies adding up to, he reckoned, thousands of pounds. He checked, along with the Dollars he also had Pesos, that was in his favour, as well as some Euros and a bit of Sterling. He also found his passport in his other back pocket, very fortunate if they were crossing the border. Nearly every page had stamps, South Africa, Bolivia, Argentina, New Zealand, Hungary to name only a few. Another gap in his memories. Why could he not trust his mind?

Alex mounted the Triumph, started her up and turned to watch Deanna get on behind him. She wrapped her arms tightly around his waist, her body pressing up against him. Alex revved the bike unnecessarily, let out the clutch and pulled out onto the highway leaving a spray of dust and gravel behind him, making the attendant cough and splutter in his wake.

'Vete a la mierda y no regresar jamás' he shouted at Alex, spitting the dust from his mouth.

Alex smiled to himself as he opened up the throttle and took the bike up to a sedate 65. The Triumph was capable of at least double that. What a waste of a perfectly fine engine, thought Alex. He hoped that Graham still had his ear to the ground and had the same connections from the old days. If he didn't Alex was in trouble.

They had no trouble crossing the border over into Mexico. The guards were particularly busy as it was market day in Santa Ana and there were many cars and trucks looking to pass both in and out of the US. The only people being stopped were traders with their wares being checked for contraband and drugs, the sniffer dogs working overtime.

Six - Deanna's Orders

Deanna Darby sat in the cozy cubicle office waiting for Osterman. She was the only bright thing in the room. Sitting on a grey plastic chair with her back against the white wall, her hands resting symmetrically on her knees. Deanna studied her nails and checked her varnish for chips, even the best manicure didn't last forever. She wore a dark blue suit with a skirt that stopped just above the knee. Underneath her jacket she wore a crisp white blouse. Her shoes matched the suit and were on the lavish side of expensive, it was the one thing she treated herself to; the best shoes you could get, the pair she now wore were French import Christian Louboutin 3.5" heels in matching dark blue suede with red leather soles. She wore no jewellery and minimal makeup; her lips rarely needed enhancing as they had a natural rouge colouring to them. Her auburn hair was tied back in a ponytail and fell between her shoulder blades. She had been working in Defensive Counterintelligence at Langley for eight months now, a department that was set up to root out and put under surveillance any and all threats to the country and to the service. It was a change in routine to meet her boss in a field office, and San Diego of all places. It was nearer where she lived so she was not complaining, it meant not having to get a flight out to Virginia. She had been enjoying the work but was itching to get out into the field - she was not completely comfortable being a number cruncher in an office but knew it was part of the initiation process. If she had wanted to do that full time she would have become an accountant.

Her pale green eyes scanned the office; there was nothing special about it, no personal pictures anywhere, the only decoration she could make out was the A4 calendar hanging on the wall opposite her. The picture on the calendar didn't make sense to her. Was it ironic? It was an industrial landscape consisting of oil drums in the foreground and smoking chimneys behind. There was one date circled in the month and that was today, the other days were conspicuously empty. On the desk was a phone, a blank pad, pens in a tray and a large brown folder. Oddly there was no computer.

The door crashed open, Deanna started slightly as she had been deep in thought trying to work out what the meeting might be about. She stood up and offered her hand to Osterman which he deemed to either not see or to just ignore.

'Sit down, sit down' he said motioning with his hand, 'Glad you could make it, Darby'

Hugh Osterman was a big man; probably past fifty, bearded with a moustache that had curled tips either side, he stood 6'6" in his socks, getting on for 250lbs but not shabby with it; he was fitter than most men. Underneath the tailored suit his biceps strained at the material and he had the ruddy complexion of an outdoorsman. Deanna didn't know too much about him except that he hunted deer whenever he could find the spare time and liked Irish whiskey. As far as she knew he had been married once a long time ago and there was a rumour he had a daughter but no one was sure what age she would be now, probably in her twenties she guessed. In the CIA he was a force to be reckoned with. His position in Langley over the years had become more vague, only those he answered to knew his official position (that was if he answered to anyone at all), he was head of operations to some, to others he was just 'boss'. Osterman collapsed into his chair almost breaking it, put his hands behind his head and leaned back as far as he could without tumbling over.

'Now, how has everything been since you began at 'Treadmill'? he asked

Treadmill was the colloquial name for their department. The term was seen by everyone in the office as ironic as the work they undertook was not drudgery and never the same from one day to the next, although it did consist of mostly paperwork and computer modeling along with crime stats and recidivist data. Deanna often found herself going over wiretap documentation or studying photographs of crime scenes; she had recently been on a stakeout of sorts, piled into the back of a cramped nondescript van looking at monitors and listening to phone conversations, all in the capacity of shadowing the operatives on point and it was a great learning experience for her. The technical aspect of it was beyond her for the moment but it wouldn't take long to pick it up, she was a quick learner and eager to show her superiors that she was capable of any tasks they could throw at her.

'Fine thank you Sir, everyone here has been extremely pleasant to me. I have finished all my preliminary training; weapons and such and read up on all the recent case files regarding black market drugs. Maris has been looking after me and giving me some interesting casework to go over'

'And what have you found out regarding these narcotics?' he asked

'Only that it's a much bigger problem than I had anticipated. I know we're not talking about street drugs, I understand that Coke and Heroin are way beyond our control, but these 'designer drugs', the so called 'made to order' personalised concoctions are becoming a big problem'

'Exactly, Deanna, although the drugs we are talking about for this case are much more specialized. That's not what you're here for anyway, I've got a another job for you. It means going deep, for how long I don't know, how do you feel about that?'

'As you say, it's what I'm here for. What else can you tell me?'

Osterman opened the file in front of him. He sat silently flicking through the pages stroking his beard with one hand. He was thinking, weighing up how much he was going to divulge. Maybe he was considering if Deanna Darby was the best person for the job.

'How is your covert training? Are you up to date? he asked

'I attended the bi-annual seminar as you well know. I saw you there if I remember rightly' she answered 'We were chatting' she added in a sharp staccato tone but with a touch of humour.

'Ah yes, I remember' he said with a grin 'I was talking to about the ethics of undercover work if I recall'

'That's correct sir'

'And has your stance changed in the meantime? Are you still insisting on being a 'hands-off' agent in the field?'

'Of course. As I said before, sir, I do not see why just because I am a woman I should be expected to prostitute myself. We don't have to be morally bankrupt to achieve our goals'

'Yes, yes, yes. We've been over all that. Your ways may be moral but they are also slow and ineffectual, especially when dealing with men. You know as well as I do that most men respond to a beautiful woman. Especially when they are being flattered. That's why you are so perfect for this job. You can do things I cannot. I assume you have heard of Matahari'

'Yes, I have, and I believe she was caught and executed for her trouble. A demise I have no wish of experiencing'

'I'm sure it won't come to that' Osterman grinned, then checked himself and became serious again clearing his throat 'All I am saying, and I have said it to you before, is that although it is not the official line on the subject you could be much more effective if you slackened your morals slightly. Think about it'

'I will take your suggestions under advisement, sir, but you can rest assured that I will not be jumping into bed with my mark just to get closer to him'

'We'll see about that' Osterman said nearly under his breath so Deanna wasn't sure she heard correctly

Osterman knew full well who the mark was and he also knew that Deanna would find him intriguing if not downright irresistible, as in an irresistible enigma to be solved of course. The fact was Alex Spellman was 38 years old but looked 32. He had salt and pepper hair cut short and an annoying habit, so Osterman thought, of not growing a proper full beard but keeping his chin hair half-way between stubble and God knows what. Osterman was prickled because Spellman looked stylish no matter how he wore his chin. Alex was in the special ops branch of MI5 for six years after being recruited, of all places, from the London Stock Exchange floor. Alex had a knack with money, he knew how to accumulate it but unfortunately hadn't learnt how to hang on to it. He could read the markets better than anyone. He was generally disliked by his co-workers who thought he had to be involved in insider trading, they thought that nobody could be that prescient with stocks and trades. Osterman scanned the pages in front of him while Deanna looked over her copy. He knew Alex had all the trappings of an especially comfortable life in The City; he owned his own top floor apartment overlooking the Thames, had a vehicle for nearly every day of the week, kept in underground garages of course, his most treasured being an old Porsche 928 which he had refurbished with a few extras that Ferdinand had overlooked. He had it repainted a rich dark brown, the wheels were spoked and the side windows tinted; inside was all leather and walnut finished off with deep carpet. Osterman knew the luxury of a good car interior. His cars and bikes were used for a variety of different occasions the way a person would wear a suit, depending on mood and suitability. The 2015 Audi TT, the slightly battered blue 1987 Volvo estate; a car which looked

Lego designed or maybe straight out of a kids Minecraft game. His long-wheelbase Land Rover (this one was an old British Telecom works vehicle he picked up at an auction), a Harley Davidson Sportster Iron 883, a 1962 Lambretta Twist (which Alex had yet to break in apparently), a de Tomaso Pantera 1972 with the Ford V8 engine and lastly a 1974 Citroen SM, possibly Alex's most prized possession after the Porsche. All his vehicles had been tweaked so that they suited Alex just so, for instance the engine in the Volvo was not the original but a hefty three litre beast that ran all four wheels, which in turn had spiked treads for extra grip when it was needed. Old habits died hard for Alex. He was a man that had no time for equipment that was inadequate, a lesson he had learnt that the hard way. Osterman could read between the lines when it came to profiling; it was, after all, one of his specialities. And of course he knew Alex's history.

All this and more was in the file Osterman handed to Deanna, as was all the information he had regarding the 'op'. Deanna itched to get back home and pour over what may be her life for the foreseeable future. She was going to immerse herself into another person's lifestyle, she was to change her look, change the way she thought all the while keeping her objectivity and her eye on the goal.

'This man Spellman is, or used to be at least, one of us. That is he is OffCo. Offensive Counterintelligence, MI5. Ever since Navarre, after he took his six month sabbatical, he has been consulting on overseas threats to UK intelligence. He has unqualified high access to assets abroad, ours as well as the British' explained Osterman, 'You see how delicate this could get?'

'Yes, sir, I understand'

'Take it home and study it, Darby' he said, 'It's your baby now, you decide how you're going to run with it, you'll have full backup if needed but we want to keep as low a profile as possible. We won't interfere unless absolutely necessary. We don't want to let your mark know how important this all is. We don't want to spook him and lose him. Not just yet anyway'

Yes, sir'

'And by the way, if you're wondering why the information in the file is quite detailed. Spellman has a man called Graves who works for him. He actually had a debriefing with intelligence in the UK. They approached him on the off chance of getting some tidbits about Spellman but when it came to it Graves gave them the whole kit and caboodle. Spellman had been acting strangely around the office recently so an investigation was started on him, all run of the mill stuff, just to make sure nothing was awry, you know. Graves was worried about the poor lad, probably a paternal thing. Thought he was helping, which he is really. So the file has a fair amount of personal details, some noteworthy, others maybe not so, but you know what they say 'information is power"

'I'll make sure I go through it thoroughly sir' Deanna said, 'Is he reliable, this Graves?'

'Well, he's been with Spellman for 17 years, ever since Alex's father passed away. You see, Alex's father ran a modest semi-prosperous brokerage firm which, at the age of 21 Alex inherited on his father's death. Alex managed to turn it around, making him and the firm relatively successful, and wealthy. Graves worked with his father and therefore it was naturally assumed that Graves would then go on to work for Alex' Osterman explained.

'And how did this strange behaviour manifest itself?' asked Deanna

'Graves said that Alex had periods where he just wasn't himself, he tended to be walking around in a bit of a daze, watching unusual TV channels at odd times of the day, staring blankly into his laptop amongst other things, it's all in the file'

'Have you met Spellman? Is there anything you can tell me on a personal level?'

'I have met him a couple of times, nice guy, he has a bit of a hard edge to him though. There was a luncheon in London about two years back, I was doing a speech about inter agency cooperation, we were basically showing Millbank staffers that we now had an open hand policy with regard to sharing intel. We were hoping to get the same in return from them, the sharing of info had become a bit like tit for tat, there would always have to be a trade of some sort. Spellman approached me afterwards and reminded me that we had met some years before, although I didn't remember precisely when. He wanted to talk to me about defectors, but not defectors into the West but *from* the West. We had a short conversation in the bar of the hotel, basically we chatted about likelihood and statistics, the reasons someone might turn; it was shop talk really. Although I had the feeling that he was asking for a reason, it wasn't just a random enquiry. I gave him all I could on the matter, the fact is quite a low number of Westerners defect to the East and if they do it's because they have some sort of affiliation that may have been overlooked or even hidden. It is rare that we have been caught out and occasionally sleepers have been found deeply entrenched in the fabric of our society, but not often. Although to tell you the truth it is not just the Russians that are the biggest threat to us now, it is the Islamic State, North Korea, Syria, Iran, the list goes on and on. Even our own citizens are quite often the biggest danger to our national stability, disgruntled employees, kids with guns, cyber-attacks, corporate espionage, riots in the projects; there is an awful lot of unrest in a nation with a population of 320 million citizens. So to answer your question, yes, we have met but I don't know the man that well, and when you have read his file you will probably know him as well as me'

7 - Meeting an old friend

Alex rang the bell of the first-floor apartment and waited. He could hear movement behind the door. He put his ear up closer; papers being shuffled, drawers being opened and closed, the scrape of furniture. Alex rang again. After another moment the noise of a lock being turned, the door opened an inch and an eye appeared between the crack and looked Alex up and down.

'What the fuck! Alex. What are you doing here? Are you alone?' he asked

'Yes, just me, Graham, let me in will you?' Alex replied, 'What the hell is going on?'

'You're sure it's just you?' Graham insisted

Alex didn't answer but gave him a raised eyebrow as if to say 'Did you not believe me the first time?' Alex thought it best not to mention Deanna waiting in a Santafé Express in Plaza Zaragoza, Graham sounded spooked enough as it was. He had left the bike in front of the cafe with Deanna keeping an eye on things and had walked to Graham's first floor apartment on Álvaro Obregón.

Slowly and deliberately Graham opened the three locks on the inside of his apartment door with one hand, the other he concealed behind his back holding a compact 9mm Doubletap. He still wouldn't let Alex inside until he had popped his head out and scanned the corridor. When he saw that Alex was really on his own he opened the door just enough for him to step through, then re-locked the door and put the chain back on, placing the pocket pistol back on the ledge by the door.

'That's an awful lot of security, I thought you moved to Santa Ana to put that all behind you?'

'Well if you've had the few days I've had you would be cautious too' said Graham 'I thought that all this shit was behind me but here I am watching my back like I'd never left the job. There is one bastard who keeps appearing, I swear he is keeping an eye on me, I don't know who he is with. I know he doesn't fit in around here though. Sit down. Drink?'

'What have you got?'

'A beer or I've got some shitty margarita mix in the fridge. It's probably OK to drink'

'Beer's first-rate' Alex said, he was parched, it had been a long time since coffee and pastry at the roadside cafe in the desert. 'You look like shit, Graham' Alex noted that Graham was not the man he once knew, the man he had shared pints of lager with in the Morpeth Arms all those years ago. He had lost weight and looked gaunt, his new beard was long and unkempt and it looked as if he had dressed himself in the dark.

He ignored the comment, 'You shouldn't have come here' said Graham

'Where else is there for me? Are you sure you're not being paranoid? You're certain you're being followed?'

'Jeez, how long have you known me?' said Graham 'I think I would know when something odd is going on, I've been in this game too long. I don't know who it is that's tailing me but I have my suspicions. Did you hear about Johnson?'

'No, what about him' asked Alex'

'He was found dead, not two weeks ago. And you won't believe how'

'Tell me' said Alex

'Strangled, or rather garrotted. Cheese cutter round the throat. His head nearly came off his shoulders, the only thing keeping it on was his spine' Graham fidgeted and nervously twitched at imaginary noises from the street.

'Shit, poor Dan' said Alex

'But you already know that there's something going on otherwise why else would you be here. I haven't seen you in nearly two years. Why now? Is someone after you?'

'Yes I've just come from seeing a doctor who specializes in the problems I'm having, he explained a lot to me but there is so much more I need to find out. There is someone on my tail but I don't know who, or rather if I just can't remember who. I don't know what the fuck is going on truthfully' Alex tried to explain 'I keep having these bouts of memory loss'

'I think I know' said Graham' Do you remember the last job? The job in the Pyrenees'

'How could I forget?' said Alex 'You think I would forget losing half of my team?'

'Of course not. But of the four of us who are left, one is dead, you are being chased and I am being watched. What do you make of that?' asked Graham rhetorically, 'I have a theory. I have been wondering what happened to the four of us after we were held by ETA and that damned mad Spanish quack. You know as well as I do that there is a week that we can't account for. What do you think happened to us?'

Alex shrugged his shoulders 'Before now I hadn't given it too much thought. Was it a week? I can't remember. I know we were drugged, there was a lot of... peculiar memories, things I can't account for'

'Exactly' Graham jumped in 'Drugged, yes. And not only drugged, experimented on'

'Shit, that fits with everything the doctor told us, it's all suddenly making a lot more sense now' asked Alex

'What is?'

'Carry on, I'll get you up to speed in a minute'

'Well, Dan called me, about a month ago. Must have been because I was the one of the team with a medical background. Said he was getting blackouts. Said he had memory gaps and so on. He was worried, he was waking up not knowing where he was sometimes. And you know Dan, he doesn't drink, doesn't do drugs any more' Graham explained 'He also mentioned he thought he was being followed, he was in a bad way Alex, you should have heard him'

'That is all sounding worryingly familiar. Then what happened?' asked Alex

'I said for him to come here to see me, get away from whatever was bothering him. I wasn't sure at the time whether he was imagining the tail. Of course he never showed and now I know why'

'What about Jimmy?' asked Alex 'Have you heard anything from him?'

'No, I was just about to ask you the same question' said Graham

'That must be our next step, he may be in danger, if they've already got to him he may even be dead already'

'I've been trying him at his London flat but I haven't been able to reach him yet' said Graham leaning over to the window and peering through the drapes.

'What else can you tell me about what's happening to us?' asked Alex

'My theory is that we are being used without our knowledge to gather information'

'That much I think I have figured out already'

'The only thing I can't figure out is who it might be. The possibilities are vast; it could be any enemy of the west, China, Korea, Russia. You know what sort of secrets we have hidden in our brains, Alex. To the pertinent people they are priceless. The six years you spent with Level 2 access to all UK and US sleepers in the USSR and you're still active in ongoing defection cases, Dan had spent two years implementing and aiding sleepers in Eastern Europe. Jimmy Mitchell worked on defectors from China and Russia over to the West. Think about it Alex, between us we hold a lot of invaluable information' said Graham 'If any of it fell into the wrong hands there would be hell to pay'

'So, they must have already got the information they wanted from Dan otherwise he wouldn't be dead yet' said Alex 'What about you? Have you been getting these blackouts?'

'That's the strange thing, I haven't. I suppose it's a bit like mesmerism, some subjects are more suggestible than others. Or I haven't been exposed to the catalyst, whatever that may be. There must have been something all three of you had in common that I haven't been exposed to' said Graham, 'Your guess is as good as mine whatever that may be. But I'm telling you Alex, I've got stuff here on my laptop that will blow your mind. I can't say I've ever really been a conspiracy theorist but some of the info I've uncovered is undeniable. I've got proof that these black ops go on all the time. I've looked in to at least three False Flag operations carried out on British soil. I think you need to see what I've come up with'

'I will have to take a look at that, but not now, there are other matters more pressing at the moment' Alex paused in thought 'I think I have an idea' he said, 'You have locked yourself away here in Mexico, cut off from the western world virtually, the one thing you don't have in your apartment is TV. In my fugue state I would find myself watching foreign TV stations, I have sound reason to believe the catalyst, as you call it, would probably have been subliminal messaging in the programming on one of these stations'

'That sounds as if it could be likely' said Graham 'If that is the case we are looking at an organization with means and influence on a grand scale...

Russia maybe... or China? We all know that even the United States are more than likely candidates for this type of thing. You know you can never rule them out either'

That reminded Alex 'This is all sounding rather familiar to what the doctor told us'

'What do you mean 'us'?'

'I haven't told you but I am travelling with someone, Deanna. An American. Don't freak out. She's on our side. I teamed up with her last week in Madrid'

'Shit, Alex, seriously. You brought someone else here? To my apartment? What the fuck is wrong with you? And what do you mean you teamed up with her 'last week'? You better be damn sure she's not going to be a problem'

'Calm down, will you. She's one of the good ones. I'm certain of it. I wouldn't be here if it wasn't for her'

'What were you doing in Madrid?'

'Another long story, and one I can only get you up to speed on if Deanna is here to tell it. She's round the corner in the square, looking after our things. I didn't want to bring her here in case things didn't pan out. The doctor we visited is a very reliable source in the field of passive indoctrination, he is also a bit of an expert in the field of MK, studying all three branches of human conditioning but concentrating on the area of MKUltra' said Alex, 'Basically what he told us correlates with your suspicions, we're being milked for information and then more than likely we will end up like poor Dan. We can't let that happen'

'Obviously' said Graham

'So, what's the next step old man?'

'Hey, watch it, less of the old man stuff. Well, we need to pool our information right now, no time to lose' said Graham, 'You go down and bring Deanna up to the apartment, she's not safe down there out in the open. I'll keep trying Jimmy. Be back as soon as you can, Alex, but whatever you do don't pick up a tail, go the long way around to the square and don't return the same way. OK? As far as you're concerned we are on high alert, Defcon One OK?'

'OK, see you soon, don't let anyone in except me, do you hear?' Alex said closing the door behind him.

Eight - Information overload

Deanna microwaved her spaghetti Bolognese, poured a glass from an already open bottle of Chianti and sat herself at the kitchen table, the fat file in front of her. She donned the glasses she used to read and set about devouring all the information she could. The file, once read, could not be taken with her, it had to go back under lock and key as was procedure. She began to read and started from scratch, not wanting to miss anything.

Alex Spellman. 38. Telfords Yard, Wapping, The City, London, UK. Sometime stock trader. Six years at MI5 in the UK (age 25-31), cutting short his 8 year tenure in the field. Now working as a consultant in Offensive Counterintelligence for MI5. Spent four of those years abroad working stealth; Afghanistan, Israel, the Middle East, Tehran. Now working freelance utilizing his strengths eg: field work, data collection, stealth ops, recruitment. Father deceased, heart attack 1998 at the age of 52. Mother, 76, alive, living in Brighton. One sibling, Vanessa, married to Kieran McCormack, living in Hove, parents to one daughter, Rebecca, born 2005.

Alex didn't frequent any particular restaurants specifically, he did a lot of his own cooking at home with ingredients bought from Borough Market, but when he did eat out he preferred either The Captain Kidd on Wapping High Street, which had a panoramic view over the Thames, (nb - word has it that you had to know the owner to get food as it was generally a public house and only served drinks), or Shad on Tooley Street, south of the River which happened to do one of the best vegetarian biryanis in London.

Glancing through the photos provided Deanna noticed the details of the apartment; a home entertainment system second to none, a Pro-ject RPM 9.2 Evolution turntable, Dali Opticon 8 floor standing speakers both running off a Cambridge Audio Azur 851W amplifier. She could also see that Alex collected vinyl; the type often be found at the London markets, either Petticoat Lane or Brick Lane, albums kept in their plastic sleeves, rarities by the look of it. His taste was eclectic, she could see classical, jazz, lots of Billie Holliday, must be a favourite she thought, lounge, PJ Harvey, even 80s pop. She couldn't see any CDs, she assumed that he was more than likely an aficionado and probably considered them as defunct, a relic from another time.

Deanna wondered how and why Osterman had gathered all this information. Was it all relevant? Graves must have really gone to town. The report proved an extremely in-depth study for a man who was supposed to be known for his low profile. Obviously he had been under close scrutiny for a while now and the Home Office kept lavishly detailed files. She eagerly read on.

Alex employed two people. One was an elderly gentleman named Mr Graves, first name Robert. Apparently Mr Graves was employed to look after Alex's cars; making sure they were always filled with gas for when they were needed, this was a task that needed constant vigilance Graves had told the interviewer, as petrol apparently degrades over time and becomes useless, so if one of the cars or bikes hadn't been driven the tank would need to be drained and filled with fresh fuel. This was a necessary evil of having more than one vehicle in the current climate. Mr Graves also looked after Alex to the extent that he would run errands Alex did not have time for, dry cleaning trips etc. But Graves only gave Alex four hours a day five days a week and no more. He was at an age where money didn't have any real use to him and he helped Alex out because, really, he just liked him and enjoyed being a part of his life, while still keeping to his own. In his own way he was watching out for him.

Madeline Ashwood, or Maddie aka 'Madash' was Alex's housekeeper arriving every day before 8am to see that Alex got a healthy breakfast, something that Alex had not asked her to do but did not complain about as she insisted on doing it. She had been with him 12 years and only been employed to keep the flat straight and tidy. Madeline Ashwood was 52, 14 years older than Alex, dressed like a school ma'am from the fifties and would not put up with any of his petulance. Alex had grown very fond of her over the years and would often sit and chat the morning away over coffee instead of letting Maddie get on with her work. The apartment being pretty minimalist didn't need a great deal doing to it anyway.

Looking at more of the photographs supplied Deanna saw that the apartment was, apparently, quite basic until you started looking at the quality of the furnishings. The bedroom had two diminutive side tables either side of a queen size oak bed, the bed was dressed with crisp white Egyptian cotton of a comfortably high thread count. The bed faced the window which looked out over the Thames, she realised that no-one would be able to see into the apartment. There were two doors from the bedroom, one to the main living area and one to a walk-in wardrobe where she imagined he would dress every morning.

Deanna's cell phone vibrated on the table. She flipped it over and saw it was Gregg. She hesitated for a moment putting off having to speak to him. Then she decided it was better to talk now than to leave this conversation for another day.

'Hi, Gregg' she answered

'Hey, gorgeous, I just had to call to hear your sweet voice' said Gregg

Although they had been seeing each other for a couple of months Deanna wasn't at all sure about Gregg. He was a nice enough guy but came on a bit strong for her liking, she was feeling corralled. She was not in the right head-space for a serious relationship, not with her position at Langley putting her to work in the field, and keeping secrets from him was starting to become tiresome and problematic.

'That's nice Gregg. Listen, I'm glad you called...' she started

Gregg interrupted 'Listen honey, waddya say us meetin' up tonight, I could do with some Deanna-time, we could meet in that bar on Madison and get a late beer, I'd like that. Hey, I know, I'll even come and pick you up on the hog. You know how you like the bike, I'll bring you the set of leathers'

It sounded to Deanna as if Gregg had already been to a bar and was a few drinks deep already. That made it easier to decide not to meet up and to break the news to him now.

'I'm not sure that's such a great idea. Listen Gregg', she repeated, 'you're not going to see me for a while, I've got to go away... on work, you understand, you remember, I did mention it' she felt like she was talking to a child, using kid gloves.

'Oh, sure honey' he sounded crestfallen 'Will I get to see you before you go?'

'I don't think that would be a great idea Gregg. This has been nice, the last couple of months. But I'm gonna be pretty busy from now on, and I'm going to be away, abroad most likely'

'But darlin', I gotta see ya before you go, I just *need* to see ya' he almost pleaded

'Gregg, I can't give you what you need. I'm just gonna make you sad, then mad probably. It'll be no good for either of us. Don't you get it? I'm going to send you back your door key, I won't be needing it any more'

'Well, ain't that a bitch' he spat

Deanna could tell he wanted to call her a bitch but was holding back in case there was still a chance for them. This was partly the problem with Gregg; he couldn't say what he meant and a lot of the time didn't mean what he said. He wasn't a good man for her.

'You'll find someone, I know you will' said Deanna

'Yeah, right' he said slurring and then hung up the phone leaving Deanna feeling bad, and that she hadn't handled that as well as she should have.

She picked up the file once again but couldn't concentrate any more. It was getting late now and she decided she would carry on in the morning with a fresh pair of eyes.

The next morning Deanna took her usual morning run along Black's Beach, part of the Scripps Coastal Reserve. She would run south along the beach and past the pier on to La Jolla Underwater Park which was pretty much as far as you could go. The San Diego sunshine, the sea air, the noise of the waves crashing against the shore and the palm trees all did their usual trick of waking her up and invigorating her, ready for a new day. She found that exercise sharpened her mind and cleared out any mental clutter from the previous day. On the days she could not take her run she found herself worrying unnecessarily about matters that had no relevance. Every day when she ran this stretch of beach she was aware that this was the sea that took her father from her, sometimes it was almost too much to bear. She had lived in La Jolla all her life. Her father had left her the house when he passed away. It was luxuriously grand, too much for a single girl of twenty nine to live in alone, but she knew she could not leave it, there were too many memories of her family in the house. Being an only child made it all the more difficult to come to terms with the loss of both parents at such a young age, often she would find the house too spacious, too quiet or too lonely. Deanna's father, Phillip, was presumed drowned off the coast of San Diego last year. It was only fate that Deanna happened to be at a party and not on the boat with him. The party was a last minute arrangement organized by Deanna's friends to celebrate getting her qualifications as a Foreign Service Officer for The

Department of State, of course this was what she had them believe, in actual fact she had passed the CIA program with honours and was about to embark on her new highly secretive job. The FSO posting was a useful cover as it meant Deanna would be away for a great deal of the time and no-one would think it suspicious, her father would not question the monthly governmental pay checks either. Phillip was taking out his newly acquired Tiara Sovran, a 60 foot cruiser he had been looking forward to getting for the last two years, a beautiful yacht capable of 30 knots with all the luxuries you could want. The night he took her out was her maiden voyage and he planned on staying out a few nights as the boat was well stocked and he needed a break from life on the mainland, he loved the sea. The first night he spent on the calmest ocean you could wish for, almost a dead calm, the only sound you could hear on the water was the seagulls squawking from afar. The next day he pushed further out into the vast ocean hoping to spend a few hours diving in some remote spot. He had called her daily with tales of his adventures. The last Deanna heard from him was a message on the house telephone telling her what fun he was having and that he would be seeing her the next day. The yacht was found adrift three days later with Deanna's father nowhere to be seen. The police report came back as missing presumed dead, without a body that was all they could do. They searched the area in increasing circles from the location of the boat but after 48 hours the lifeguard had to stop the hunt as it was deemed too much time had passed and that the body could very well have fallen victim to predatory apex feeders.

Deanna was, understandably, beside herself with grief, she was too young (or too old) to become an orphan. After the service, which was held two weeks after the disappearance, Deanna decided the only thing she could do was concentrate on her budding career in the CIA. She was extremely adept at compartmentalizing her life so would mourn her father only when she was sure she could give him her undivided attention. Often in those first few months she would open a bottle of wine, sit down and watch old home movies. Unfortunately because her father was filming, he was in only a few of them, with her mother only occasionally being given the camera to wield. She would watch and cry and feel wretched, but somehow she needed to have these evenings to have some sort of closure from losing them both. One film in particular she watched over and over; a holiday when she was fifteen in Paris, just the three of them, the camera set up capturing all of them having a picnic in the glorious sunshine on the lawns of the Jardins du Trocadero, looking across the Seine at the wonderful Eiffel Tower. That was one of her happiest memories, one she would always remember even without the video evidence. It had just been her alone with her father since her mother had passed away from cancer. It was a difficult time for both of them. Deanna regretted not spending more time with her. The only solace to them both was that she was taken from them quickly and did not have to suffer long with her illness. Deanna and her father grieved together and they became closer because of it. She didn't want to make the same mistakes with her father that she had made with her mother so vowed to spend as much time with him as possible. Keeping her new career secret made her feel guilty for not being able to confide in him and the fact that it could actually be distancing her from him.

As time progressed these evenings became less often and Deanna consciously decided it was making her too sad and she was becoming maudlin. She rarely thought of her parents nowadays unless she was out on her daily runs. Glancing over the ocean to San Clemente Island brought with it now a sense of resolve that she would make something of her life, make a life her parents would be proud of, make a difference.

She returned to her house overlooking the beach and showered briskly, the return journey had brought with it the rising temperature of the day and she was sweating freely. When she had dried off she settled down once again, with a clear head and a cup of tea, to learn all she could about Mr Alexander Spellman.

The file fell open at a page titled "Delta", Deanna read the seven names below, each name having a dedicated section headed with a picture of the man. She scanned the first name.

Graham Devereux - 36 - Delta - Corporal - 2011 sortie Navarre
Whereabouts unknown

One part of eight man team led by Spellman to infiltrate ETA arms stronghold in Navarre, Basque region. Mission to quash an attempt at preventing signing of peace treaty with Spanish Govt.

The page carried on to list all of Devereux's awards, achievements and accolades.

The next page read:

Jack Cole - 35 - Delta - Corporal/Marksman
2011 sortie Navarre - K.I.A.
One part of eight man team led by Spellman to infiltrate ETA arms
stronghold in Navarre, Basque region. Mission to quash an attempt at
preventing signing of peace treaty with Spanish Govt.

Deanna flicked through the other pages and found they were all pertinent to the Navarre operation. The names listed were Dan Johnson, Jimmy Mitchell, Simon Chapman, John Watts and Derek West, the last three also killed in action. Apparently all of them had worked together, in one way or another, previously; Alex was closest to Graham Devereux and Derek West. Jimmy Mitchell was the youngest of the group at only 24 years old, the others all veterans of at least ten years' service to Queen and country. They all had their own specialities that they brought to the mission; munitions expert, chemicals training, ordnance background etc. She read a synopsis of the debriefing interviews given by the four surviving men and wondered how the explosion could have happened with men of such expertise working on the operation. The statement from Spellman asserted that the switches and triggers being used to destroy the ammunition shed were all checked by him prior to departure and that he has taken full responsibility for what took place thereafter.

Osterman had scribbled a note at the bottom of the page regarding this passage, it read: '*Anil Bharat, Spellman's superior, took no further action against Spellman in regard to disciplinary measures. Spellman took 6 months sabbatical, location during this time is unknown*'

Nine - Fly Time

Deanna waited in line at the check-in desk. She wore her hair down now cut shorter and dyed a dark brown instead of her natural auburn. She had with her only one piece of luggage which she would be stowing in the overhead locker, keeping her large grey leather tote on her person as she would need the personal items it held on the flight. As per her instructions she had left Spellman's file locked in her safe at her beach-side home but had brought with her the recordings of the interview with Robert Graves on her iPhone. She had been going through the files for the last couple of days and felt that she had a comprehensive overall feel for the man she was about to meet. She had wrestled with the moral conundrum of changing her look to the preferred type of Alex Spellman, the words of her conversations with Osterman reverberating through her head. She knew that it would improve her chances of getting 'in' with Spellman but it didn't make the fact any easier to bear. The fact that she was being used as bait in a situation where a man would not be as successful as a female.

Once boarded and settled in her seat for the lengthy journey across the Atlantic she felt confident that she should be able to befriend and inveigle her way into Spellman's confidence. Her first task would be to listen to the three hour interview with his 'butler' and then go over aspects of her strategy for the rendezvous somewhere between London and Spain. If she found that she had time to kill after all that was done she would sneak a read of The Red Dancer by Richard Skinner, a novel that had been on her 'to read list' for some time. It could be seen as being smug or blasé to take her mind from the task at hand but she had an affinity with the book's subject matter and felt that it could be seen as research and could well be regarded as beneficial to her mind-set for the days ahead.

Vasili Dragunov sat brooding in the large leather chair, his gaunt face animated only by the dying flames of the fire, his usual neatly combed grey hair hanging either side of his face framing it like straw curtains, his cold grey eyes boring into the flames that licked the coals. He sat with his bony hands gripping both arms of the chair staring into the smoldering embers, the weak light dancing in his eyes, the only warmth in them. The snow fell heavier than ever outside. He thoughtfully picked up a log with the hearth tongs and fed it into the fire. It fizzed and spat; the logs here were hard to get dry he remembered, they always had been. He looked calm but his mind was an engine going at full speed. His hideout would only be safe for so long, soon they would realise he had headed to his childhood home near Voknavolok, even though it had stood empty for more than twenty-five years. It was off the beaten track, 1500 kilometres north of Moscow and not too far from the Finnish border, not far in Russian terms anyway. It wasn't remote enough, however, to hide from the long arm of the KGB, they would eventually catch up to him. He had to make things up to Sigalov, he couldn't bear the disgrace. What good was all his wealth if he had no position? He could not go back to his house in Moscow. It was one thing to be asked to make assurances that the Russian athletic team came out with a healthy medal average at the 2012 Olympic games, he was glad to do it, after all Russian athletes were far superior than their Western counterparts. All he was doing was applying a little bit of insurance. They all did it, all these athletes were taking performance enhancing substances; Butch Reynolds, Alvin Harrison, Regina Jacobs, Ouyang Kunpeng, the list went on. Why should the mighty Russians not have the same helping hand as the US and the Chinese? The trick was not getting caught. Damn it. For three years the secret had been safe, for three years he had been basking in his and his country's success; 80 medals! 23 of them gold. Andreyev Sigalov had been so pleased with the outcome that he had given Vasili his assurance that once the WADA investigation had been carried out and passed that he could write his own ticket, he could choose his own posting, anywhere. Vasili couldn't wait to move further south where it was warmer, where he could be away from

The Kremlin and be in charge of his own sector. Instead he had been ostracized, cut off, excommunicated. This is why, now, his insurance policy needed to come into play, he needed some bargaining power quickly, his life depended on it. But not for long. Vasili's plan was taking effect even now as he sat there in his grand leather chair. He would make it up to Sigalov. He would win back his favour. When Vasili brought Sigalov the names of all the sleeper agents residing in the USSR he would be a hero, he would be welcomed back with open arms. Sigalov would not be able to deny him.

One thing that Vasili had learned in his years in the KGB was that you always needed some sort of insurance. He had seen too many fellow countrymen disappear to Siberia or found dead in what Vasili knew to be suspicious circumstances. After all, he was one of the men you met with if you had an embarrassment within the KGB. He dealt with problems, he made things run smoothly, he got rid of the embarrassments. Hence, this was why he had been given the London job. "See that we are resplendent in London" Sigalov had told him. Vasili was given the means and the funds to make everything run smoothly, Greasing palms, destroying samples, paying off the chemists etc. It had all been fine until the World Anti-Doping Agency had uncovered his dealings. Now they were a global disgrace and he was the scapegoat, there was even talk of the Russian team not competing in the 2016 Olympics. It turned out that Alex Spellman and his team were the answer to the predicament he now found himself in.

Many years ago Vasili had had dealings with a Spanish doctor by the name of Ignasi Quiros. Quiros was located somewhere in The Pyrenees and involved with a group of Basque separatists. At the time Vasili had friends who were sympathetic with the communist arm of ETA and they suggested he should meet the members of this particular faction who were looking for funding. He met Ignasi Quiros on a visit to Andorra where Vasili was masquerading as a tourist on a skiing holiday. Quiros was an extraordinary man interested in the use of concocted drug mixtures used in conjunction with hypnosis and autosuggestion. He had been experimenting for years but had not had the success he was craving, mainly due to lack of funds and a limited supply of willing guinea pigs. Vasili talked at length with Quiros and agreed to fund him if he would return the favour. Vasili needed his own sleepers, he needed men who could do his bidding, either American or

British Intelligence. Quiros was willing but asked Vasili 'How are we going to get American spies to take part in an experiment such as this?' Vasili knew they would not get willing volunteers and replied 'Patience, my dear Ignasi, patience. You carry on with your research and soon, one day, an opportunity will present itself, do not worry'

That opportunity came one cold winter's day four years ago. Vasili had heard that MI5 were taking an interest in what was going on in the Basque region. A ceasefire and cessation of armed activity was being negotiated between 'Euskadi Ta Askatasuna' and Zapatero, the Spanish Prime Minister. However word had got to MI5 that there was still a limited faction that was not going to agree to the ceasefire. Intel suggested that this faction would go as far to not only sabotage the negotiations but put Zapatero's life at risk in doing so. MI5 decided to run a covert op and send a team of eight men into the region to stop the plot from taking place. Alex Spellman was heading that team. On January 6th 2011 the eight highly trained elite MI5 operatives made their way into northern Navarre in the Basque region to quell the insurgents. Vasili sent his two Slavic heavies. Casimir Sitko and Vanya Prazak were to see to it that all would run smoothly. Vasili had been in touch with Quiros so he knew where the team would be headed, but he had to be clever; it had to look like an accident, there could not be any retaliation from the British. After all it was a covert op and there would be hell to pay if the British were found in a place where they had no jurisdiction.

Sitko and Prazak were in place at the camp north of Arano two days before Alex and his team. They had been given their orders from Dragunov.

Alex's team were dropped in at night by parachute, all landing within a few hundred yards of each other, although they were still at least two hours trek from their destination. They had time if they wanted to get to the camp before sunrise, it was imperative that they make their sortie under cover of night for their own safety. On arrival Alex and his seven compatriots scanned the area with night vision binoculars. The camp was laid out exactly as the satellite imagery had shown; on the outskirts of the clearing was a tin shed which held the explosives and ammunition. On the other side of the clearing were some ramshackle living quarters made up of tents and lean-tos, beside them a barracks of sorts made out of timber with sleeping bunks inside and then beside that a covered timber gazebo with a table and chairs underneath.

Chapman, Watts, Cole and West were to sabotage the ammo dump while Alex, Graham, Dan and Jimmy were to incapacitate the sleeping men in the barracks. This would be achieved with a gas grenade of Carfentanil, the guerrillas wouldn't know what hit them. Details were sketchy about what happened next. After being debriefed over a week later the four survivors were still in a state of shock and confusion. Alex blamed himself as he had been the one to check all the fuses and detonators. It was obvious something had gone drastically wrong. The Carfentanil grenade was to set everything in motion so the men in the barracks would not come running to see about the explosion of the ammo dump. However as soon as Alex heard the explosion he knew something wasn't right, it had all happened too soon. Cole and West were still inside setting the detonators while Chapman and Watts were outside the shed keeping cover. The explosion obliterated the four soldiers by the hut, also knocking Alex, Graham, Dan Johnson and Jimmy Mitchell across the courtyard rendering them unconscious. Alex had no idea the whole thing was being watched by two Slavic mercenaries from the thick woodland to the west.

Vasili had achieved his goal; knocking out the team that had come to destroy his comrades while also acquiring his future insurance in the shape of four espionage operators. Ignasi Quiros had a week to work his magic. Newly developing subconscious indoctrination techniques were used, before sending the four back to the UK via France, leaving them on the outskirts of Saint-Jean-de-Luz where they were picked up by Interpol and returned home.

Vasili had been informed by his man at Thames House that Alex decided very soon after that he could not carry on in the field. He was also told that he visited the wives and girlfriends of the four men who were lost and apparently tried to explain as best he could how he had been responsible for their deaths. No charges were brought against Alex, as working with extremely dangerous equipment was considered a risk of the job. Word had it that this did nothing to abate the guilt he felt.

Vasili Dragunov had four chances to acquire any information locked inside the heads of the remaining soldiers. Dan Johnson's interrogation had proved extremely fruitful although the information he provided was not so much to do with the threat to Russia but more to do with their allies in

Eastern Europe; sleeper agents in Ukraine, Belarus and Armenia. He would have to wait and see what the remaining two could provide. Unfortunately Graham Devereux had proved to be an unfit recipient of Quiros' ministrations, although he could prove useful yet in luring Alex Spellman back onto his predestined path, he could be used as bait. It was imperative he acquire the names of those who could directly endanger the motherland. Once he had all the information from the remaining two operatives he could bring the invaluable intelligence to Sigalov and regain his position and hopefully buy his life back.

11 - Disaster South of the Border

Alex made his way back to the town square, sidling down a few alleyways and doubling back on himself just to make sure he wasn't followed, all the time checking around for anything out of the ordinary. As far as he could tell no-one was behind him. He approached the Santafé from the opposite side of the square and cut directly across it passing under the bandstand that stood at it's centre. He could see the Triumph still parked outside but his subconscious told him something was awry. He could see one of the panniers had been left open on the bike, someone had been looking for something. He broke out into a run and burst into the café where Deanna should be waiting. She was nowhere to be seen. Shit!

'Excuse me, Senora, the girl who was here, where did she go?' asked Alex panicked

The lady behind the counter just shrugged at Alex and resumed reading her magazine.

Alex headed back to the door and was just leaving when he heard 'Senor, senor'

Alex turned around to find a pint-sized boy of maybe eleven or twelve.

'Senor, she left with a man, not 15 minutes ago. They got into a car' the boy said

'What type of car?' Alex asked

'I'm not sure senor, dark coloured, maybe black, tinted windows I think, not from round here' the boy was holding his palm out while imparting the information

'Thanks kid' Alex dropped a handful of pesos into the boy's hand and with that rushed back out to the bike to check the panniers. Inside was a note with a number written on it. It was contact details, no doubt for a trade of some sort. What the hell did he have to trade? Damn! He should never have left her alone. The only thing to do now was head back to Graham and convince him to join forces and find Deanna, he needed a man who knew the area, and he needed to get Deanna back.

Alex made his way back to Graham's place on foot, wary again of being followed, all the while keeping an eye out for anything unusual. He was on high alert, his nerves jangling, now realising the threat was all too real and closer than ever. If they had got rid of Dan when they had acquired the information they needed, that meant that he himself could soon be dispensable.

Alex began to quicken his pace, the longer he took the more concerned he was becoming. What kind of people were they dealing with? Murder? Kidnap? These were obviously very desperate individuals. He broke into a jog, a heavy lump beginning to form in the pit of his stomach. He began to feel sick, not from the running but at the fear taking grip of him, a sticky sweat beginning to form on his brow.

Alex took the stairs two at a time and made it to Graham's apartment but when he turned the corner he could see that he was already too late. The door stood ajar, shards of wood fragments strewn on the floor. Alex carefully and as quietly as he could pushed the door open. He couldn't believe it was the same room he had been in not more than 40 minutes ago. The place had been turned upside down, furniture tipped over, papers scattered all over the floor, broken glass underfoot. He looked around for Graham, his footsteps crunching across the carpet. He saw Graham's body in the kitchen laying across the floor, blood seeping out from underneath him in a widening pool. Alex approached him and gingerly turned him over, Graham was not yet gone but his breathing had become dangerously shallow, Alex could see three bullet holes in his torso, blood everywhere.

'Alex,' Graham managed to whisper 'I was right....' before succumbing to his fatal injuries.

Alex held Graham in his arms and swore to himself, and to Graham and Dan that he would catch whoever did this. Not only would he catch them he would make them regret the day they were born into this world, they had no idea who they were fucking with.

Twelve - Hesperia Hotel - Madrid

Deanna didn't realise at the time what a big mistake she was making, slipping a Benzodiazepine into Alex's drink on the plane. It had enabled her to escort him back to the hotel on the pretext he had had a few too many on the flight. She was able to explain to the desk clerks at the Hesperia that it had been a last minute decision for her, ostensibly Mr Spellman's partner, to come along on the trip. Alex had been difficult to manoeuvre through customs and into a cab but with the help of the concierge assistant she got him into the elevator and once they were safely in the hotel room she relaxed slightly. She loosened Alex's shoes and collar so he would be more comfortable and urged him to lay down on the large double bed.

Deanna looked around the room, found the mini bar and poured herself a much needed gin and tonic to ease her nerves. Alex would need to be a little more *compos mentis* to answer some of the questions she had for him. She walked out onto the balcony and sat in one of the loungers while she considered her approach. Deanna looked out over the city and watched as the sun dipped beyond the horizon and lit the sky up in a dozen shades of red. She had never seen a Spanish sunset before and it took her breath away.

She heard noises coming from the bedroom, Alex must be coming to. When she entered he was sitting on the edge of the bed holding his head in his hands making nearly imperceptible groaning sounds. Deanna pulled up a chair and sat opposite him. This was the best time to get answers, when he was at his most vulnerable.

'Alex?' she said 'Can you hear me?'

Alex raised his head and looked Deanna in the eye and gave a slight nod.

'Good' she said 'I need to ask you a few questions and you will answer them to the best of your ability. OK?'

Another nod.

'Here we go then. Are you ready to talk?' she waited for a nod, 'What are you doing in Madrid?'

Alex rolled his tongue around his mouth a few times to build up enough saliva to talk 'I'm here for a meet'

'Who are you meeting here, and why?' asked Deana

'I'm doing my job' slurred Alex 'Are you doing yours?'

'Of course I am, but what brings you to Madrid?'

'Defector' said Alex

'Who? Alex. Tell me'

'Contact. Belarus. Months'

'Be more specific. Give me more' asked Deanna

Alex closed his eyes, Deanna thought she had lost him to sleep. Then suddenly he began to talk with his eyes still shut. 'Four months ago... contact in Belarus.... wants to come over.... the West.... told him I didn't do..... field work'

'Then what?'

'Insisted on me' said Alex 'Wouldn't deal with any other agent.... said I was the only one he could trust'

'What was his name?' she asked

'Vasili..... Vasili Dragunov'

'Are you sure Alex?'

He nodded and opened his eyes to look at Deanna directly.

'I thought he was dead, our reports say that he had been killed' said Deanna

Alex didn't say anything just gave her a crooked smile like a fisherman who has hooked a monster catch and shook his head.

'So let me get this straight. You were contacted by Dragunov so he could defect to the West. Is that correct?'

Alex nodded

'Are you meeting him here?'

Another nod

This story didn't sound plausible to Deanna at all. Why would Dragunov, if he actually *was* still alive, want to meet in Madrid of all places? Was Alex so desperate for a 'win' that he could be duped in this way? It would be a novice mistake. Deanna couldn't believe what she was hearing.

'Have you spoken to him directly?'

Alex shook his head.

'Who is the go-between?'

'Spanish... man'

'Who? Alex, I need a name'

She got no reply and changed tack.

'What's in it for the West?'

'Secrets' said Alex blankly

'Tell me exactly how the meeting is to take place'

'I am to wait for instructions regarding time.... meeting place is to be Parque Eva Duarte,' then a pause so long Deanna thought he had lost his train of thought, ' ......exact spot to be confirmed, probably by the statue,' he laughed to himself, 'that's usually where defectors like to meet'

'So all we have to do is sit tight and they will contact you. Is that right?'

Alex nodded again and let himself fall back onto the bed. Within minutes he was snoring.

Deanna left quietly knowing that Alex would not have any recollection of her cross-examination after taking the drug. She would let the game play out keeping a close eye on how things develop. She would tail Alex abd keep an eye on developments.

• • • •

ALEC WOKE THE NEXT morning with a terrific headache. He had no idea how he had got from the aeroplane to his hotel room. He sat on the edge of the bed with his head hanging down waiting until the carpet came into focus. He recalled having a drink on the flight but nothing that could have given him the mother of all hangovers. Maybe it was, once again, one of his newly acquired bouts of forgetfulness, with added headache thrown in for good measure. Once his eyes began making out his surroundings he scanned the room for anything unusual. Everything looked as it would normally look in any regular hotel room, but what he did notice out of the corner of his eye was a slip of paper that had been slipped under the door. He arose from the bed feeling as if he had been ten rounds and crossed the room to collect it, noticing as he did so the ache of bruising from various parts of his body.

The note was type-written and gave the remaining instructions for the meeting later that day. It was as Alex had expected; it specified for him to come alone and that if there was anything untoward suspected the meeting would be canceled.

Alex ordered room service and while waiting for his tray made his own coffee which he took out onto the balcony. He looked out over the city of Madrid, which he had always enjoyed, and began to feel his body come round to some sort of normality; the caffeine beginning to have a subduing effect on his adenosine receptors sharpening his wits and honing his thought process. He looked across the six lane Paseo de la Castellana with its lush tree lined pavements toward the National Museum of Natural Sciences and wondered if a walk around its cool corridors would be of any benefit to his state of mind. As he was finishing his coffee a knock at the door declared the arrival of his breakfast; pisto con huevo but with the addition of chorizo and chilli to give it a bit of bite, along with freshly squeezed orange juice made from Valencian oranges, delivered daily to many of the hotels in Madrid.

Alex had a few hours to spare before the meeting so decided instead of the museum he would spend that time in the hotel spa; he booked a massage which he would have after his hour long session in the gym and would then finish off in the terraced rooftop Jacuzzi. After that, hopefully, he would feel like a new man and would be able to face whatever the afternoon had in store for him.

Thirteen - Jimmy losing it

Jimmy stood in the crowded square struggling for breath, his heart beating wildly, his vision blurred. What had triggered the attack he couldn't say, all he knew were that the attacks were as bad as ever. He heard the explosion again in his mind, deafening, blinding, disorienting. He saw his team-mates strewn around him thrown by the blast, laying at improbable angles on the ground like ragdolls. He knew immediately the four men in the vicinity of the shed were dead, they were too close to the explosion to have survived. His ears were filled with a white noise that grew until he could hear nothing else around him. He shut his eyes tightly to try and diminish the growing pain at the front of his head, his hands went up to his forehead to massage between his eyes, trying to relieve the agony. His heart was beating so quickly now that Jimmy felt sure he was going to pass out, his breath still stuck in his throat like being underwater struggling pathetically to draw air. Slowly he began to gain a little air into his lungs, his heartbeat still trying to make its way into his mouth. Bile started to form at the back of his throat making him feel as if he was going to puke, his arms began to shake uncontrollably, all the energy draining out of them until they ached with apathy. He tasted the dry earth in his mouth once again, felt the pain in his side from the shrapnel wound. He heard a woman's voice vaguely in the back of his consciousness, he couldn't make out what she was saying. He felt an arm around his shoulder and soothing words being uttered along with other voices of concern. A crowd had started to gather around him, people were coming to his aid, Samaritans who could recognize a fellow human being in trouble. Jimmy's legs gave way and he dropped to the ground. The people around him were unprepared and he landed heavily. Jimmy was at his lowest ebb, he began to shout at them, telling them to go away 'Leave me alone' he yelled, and when they didn't he muttered under his breath over and over 'go away, go away, go away'. Eventually the security guard who had been called arrived to find Jimmy on the ground in the foetal position, his eyes tightly shut, randomly muttering names as he was slowly coming out of the fit and beginning to calm down. When Jimmy eventually opened his eyes and saw the uniformed guard standing over him he became panicked and tried to get up onto his feet to flee but all he managed was to crawl a few yards across the floor, his eyes showing sheer terror at everyone gathered around him.

It was the third time he had had a panic attack in public like this, he had been lucky enough that most of the time they struck at home, at least there he did not have the embarrassment of trying to explain away his strange behaviour. Doctor Keegan had assured Jimmy that the episodes would diminish over time but after four years they were becoming, if anything, more intense. The nightmares he had become used to, waking up in a cold sweat three or four nights a week, not being able to get back to sleep after they had struck. It was a miserable existence.

14 - Quiros' folly - Madrid

Quiros put the telephone down and felt smugly satisfied that he had done all he could to lure Spellman into his hands. It had started around four months ago. On Vasili Dragunov's orders he had sent out the initiation codes to the four remaining members of Delta, the task force sent into the Pyrenees in 2011. He had added a little extra coding to Alex Spellman's conditioning knowing that he was a man of proud patriotism. Spellman had a special interest in the safety of the crown which he had served for the past years, he was big on Queen and country. Quiros wanted any information he could glean from Spellman and he especially wanted it before his co-conspirator Dragunov got his hands on it and squandered the intel by merely attempting to regain his seat at the table in Moscow. He could use it to his own ends. Dragunov, however, must never know of his intention, it would mean a great deal of problems for Ignasi if he were to become aware of his plan and that should be avoided at all costs. Ever since the QR initiation code had been sent out in the post the four members of Delta had started to hack into any and all top secret documentation they had access to. They were predisposed to watch the Russian news programming where they would receive subliminal messaging concerning where to concentrate their searches.

Spellman was in Madrid at this moment. A message had been sent to arrange a meeting. He was staying at the Hesperia Hotel in the city centre. It had taken the best part of three months to set up the ruse; Spellman was working at MI5 in London behind a desk, after the fiasco in Navarre he had not been able to go back into the field again, although his sense of duty to Queen and country had not abated; he was still as fervent as ever to carry on in the service. So it would have to be something extraordinary to get Alex Spellman negotiating terms with defectors, and the bait would have to be sizeable. Quiros play-acted as the go-between for a Russian citizen who had ties with the KGB who was generally thought to be dead, killed due to his mishandling of the 2012 Olympic drug tests. All it needed was a convincing story of how Dragunov was willing to trade secrets for a safe pass to the West. The story was compelling as there had never been an official statement from The Kremlin regarding Dragunov's death. It was all very plausible that he had been hiding out somewhere remote. As everyone knew Vasili Dragunov had substantial financial resources at his disposal. Slowly but surely Spellman became convinced that he would be the one to bring him in. Quiros was thrilled with the deception. The information from Spellman would be worth a great deal to the appropriate buyer, whether it would be sold to the enemies of the West or even if he were to hand it back for a tidy ransom, he could double up and get paid twice from the US and the UK. Either way he was going to be wealthy beyond measure, he would have enough money to carry on his research into Project Condon, where he would eventually perfect the concept of producing an in-cognizant sleeper agent; a person who would supply sensitive information without even knowing it.

It was time. He had fifteen minutes to get to the rendezvous point to meet Spellman. From there he would take him to a secure location and extract all the information he had gleaned over the last four months. He was looking forward to it. Quiros enjoyed this part of the process for if the subject did not talk freely there were always more persuasive methods.

He got into the back of his BMW X1. In the front were two men he had hand chosen for today's task; Goyo Vásquez and Pino Fuentes, two men who could be trusted and relied upon. Goyo, who was nearing forty five, wore his thinning hair slicked back on his head, a pair of Aspex Target sunglasses covering his eyes, a red v-neck woollen jumper showing his abundant chest hair and a pair of faded blue jeans that were a size too snug, on his feet were a pair of black leather loafers. Pino who was ten years younger was trying to look more classy in his double breasted suit, however if you looked closely you could see the cuffs were worn slightly too much and the shirt he was wearing a little baggy around his chest. They made an unlikely couple. Ignasi, however, had not hired them for their sartorial acumen, but for their ability to get things done under pressure.

They arrived at the Parque Eva Duarte slightly before the arranged time. Spellman was already there waiting. They pulled up to the kerb and opened the door for him to get in.

15 - Spanish farmhouse

Deanna had followed Alex from the hotel the next day. Alex had walked the two and a half kilometres to the park which took him about half an hour and stood at the corner of Calle Florestan Aguilar opposite the Guardian car repair shop. Deanna had hired a car earlier that day and was watching his movements from a safe distance. When she saw Alex get into the BMW she trailed them making sure she was not spotted. She followed the BMW along Alcalá then onto the M-30 heading north, they didn't leave this road but joined the A1 passing Alcobendas where the road became the E-5 and past Fuente del Fresno finally leaving the main road at San Agustín del Guadalix. They did not enter the small town but skirted around it to the south and then headed west ending up at a farmhouse five or six kilometres from the town.

She watched the four men get out of the car and enter the farmhouse. She would have to abandon the car where it was and proceed on foot if she were to get a better idea of what was going on. She checked her arsenal, the Beretta 21 Bobcat was fully loaded with a spare magazine in her inside pocket, that was sixteen rounds if she needed them. She also carried a David Kurt handmade knife.

Deanna kept off the road and on the side of the hedgerow obscured from any passing traffic, taking it slowly so as to not make any mistakes. For all she knew one of the heavies could be doing perimeter passes so she stopped every few metres to crouch down and make sure the coast remained clear. When she was satisfied all the four men were inside the house she steeled herself to get closer still, the heavy weight of trepidation forming in her chest. She recognized the feeling as fear, the type of fear that could all too easily stop you in your tracks, make you curl up and give in. This could not happen, it was her duty to see this through, Alex was depending on her. She was pretty certain that there was something fishy about the whole set-up, it seemed too good to be true, that Vasili Dragunov would be defecting. She had heard of him and from what she could recall he was a hard line KGB man. It was a question of whether the Kremlin had really lost faith in his abilities and cut him loose once and for all. She edged her way to a window that was slightly ajar. Keeping her back to the wall she got as near as possible to try and eavesdrop on the conversation. She heard Alex's voice first.

'....I need to see something more concrete from you otherwise my patience will run out. Show me Dragunov. You said we were meeting him here, so where the hell is he?'

'Patience Mr Spellman. He will be here. I am surprised, myself, that he is not here already. Why don't you sit down and relax, I'm sure he will be along as soon as he can' said the short rotund Spaniard, 'In the meantime I suggest we have a light refreshment to pass the time and I will make a phone call to see where Senór Dragunov has got to'

The Spaniard pulled out his cell phone and walked into the next room to make the call, leaving Alex with the driver and his partner standing awkwardly in the room.

A few moments later the Spaniard returned with two tumblers filled with liquid. He handed one to Alex and kept one for himself, the other two men were not in the equation.

'What did he say?' asked Alex

'That he will be here ...soon' he replied

'Soon? Soon isn't acceptable. I have come a long way to see this man and when I actually get here, wherever here is, he is nowhere to be seen'

Deanna could hear by the tone of Alex's voice that he was becoming vexed with the whole situation. She then heard;

'What the hell! What is in this damned drink? Are you trying to drug me? Alex began to get quite agitated and stood up to leave. 'I don't know what you're up to but I'm not having any of it, what do you take me for?'

'Please Senór Spellman there is no need for this'

Deanna inched her face around so she could see through the window. The short Spaniard nodded at his two men who then seized Alex by both arms, restraining him. A look of panic appeared on Alex's face as he realised he had been duped.

'I was hoping it wouldn't come to this Senor Spellman, if you had just finished your drink it would all have gone a lot more smoothly. The Soma I used in your drink would pass muster for most people but alas it has a faint aroma and you have a fine sense of smell I see. Very clever of you Senór. Now, unfortunately, I have no choice but to garner my information the hard way' said Quiros, 'but to tell you the truth it is of no matter, I will enjoy torturing you. We have met before, do you not remember? Ah no, I can see in your eyes that you have no clue. Well, let me enlighten you. Four years ago, when I was a little bit slimmer maybe, yes?, we spent quite an intense week together. You were probably not aware at the time but we became good buddies you and I, and your three colleagues of course. I was the one who stitched up that cut around your eye, I probably could have made a better job of it but it was a triage situation'

As Quiros was talking one of the men was tying Alex's wrists to the arms of the chair, the other gagging his mouth. Quiros himself began to open up the briefcase he had brought with him and was tinkering with the implements inside.

Deanna kept watching, frantically trying to formulate some sort of plan to get Alex out of this mess. She could not possibly take on the three of them on her own, even with the Beretta, they were bound to be armed. Then, after a few moments her fortune changed, Quiros dismissed the two men saying he needed to be alone with his subject. He told them to take a walk and check the perimeter of the premises. The younger of the two didn't look too impressed, Deanna imagined he was hoping to watch the show. The older man pulled him by the sleeve towards the front part of the house where they had entered.

This was Deanna's one and only chance. She walked under the window awkwardly on bended legs, then carried on to the back of the farmhouse. She had the Beretta out and ready to use in case she met the two thugs. She had not fired the gun anywhere except at the firing range while she was in training. She checked the safety catch more times than was necessary, her thumb pushing it to make sure it was in position. As she rounded the corner she could see that the door was about 8 feet away. She kept her back to the wall and both hands clasped around the gun ready to take aim. When she was two feet from the door she heard the voices of the two men approaching from the other side of the building. She needed to get inside quickly. Her heart was pounding in her ears, if they rounded the corner shots would be fired and Alex's life would be endangered. Still with her back to the wall she reached out her left hand and grasped the handle of the door in an attempt to open it. It didn't move. The footsteps were getting louder, any second they would round the corner. Deanna spun around and faced the door head on, switched gun hands and tried the door again. This time it opened and she slipped inside, closing the door as quietly as she could behind her just as the two men rounded the corner oblivious to her presence.

Deanna stood inside the door letting her heart return to some normality. That was, after all, the easy part. She still had to overcome the Spaniard. She scanned the kitchen from where she stood and it was obvious to her that she had to take him out without making a noise, the Beretta would bring the other two running. She quietly opened drawers to search for the ideal weapon, something heavy and blunt should do the trick. In the large drawer she found exactly that, a granite rolling pin. Just as she picked the pin up and was feeling the weight of it the door opened from the adjacent room, the Spaniard strolled into the kitchen unaware that he would come face to face with a stranger. He stopped in his tracks, mouth open in disbelief, trying to make sense of what was in front of his eyes. Deanna looked at him deciding what to do next. The brief moment felt like an age, time stood still for them both. Then everything happened at once; the Spaniard drew breath to shout for his men, Deanna swung the rolling pin in an arc catching him around the side of his head cutting off any sound before it could escape his lips. He fell heavily to the floor, blocking the door that led to Alex. Deanna tried dragging the Spaniard out of the way but in the end she had to roll him, it took all her strength as he was a portly man and a dead weight. She managed to move him just far enough for her to squeeze through the doorway.

When she saw Alex she put her finger to her lips to keep him from making any noise, took out her knife and cut the ties that bound him. Alex removed the gag himself.

'What are you doing here?' he whispered to her

'Never mind that, tell you later. We need to get out. Back the same way. We need to avoid the other two' she whispered back.

Alex had no weapon of any sort so looked around the room for something he could use. He looked in the leather doctors' bag Quiros had been using and instantly felt queasy, the tools inside were obviously implements to cause maximum pain and discomfort; nothing about them said curative. His eyes wandered over an array of shiny chrome tools with varying degrees of lethality; scalpels, bone chisels, rasps, forceps and a bevy of apparatus he could not name. He selected what he thought would be most useful, a lancet, a scalpel-like double edged knife, not on the large side but it would slice through skin like butter.

They both exited through into the kitchen where Deanna had left Quiros lying on the floor. Alex bent down and checked through his pockets for anything useful. He found his wallet, a cell phone and a note book. He took them all so he could study them at a later time. He checked his head where Deanna had hit him, blood seeped from the wound, it was bad but he would live, he wouldn't be waking up any time soon. They had no time to spare, Goyo and Pino would soon realise that something was out of place, or they would see Quiros lying prone on the kitchen floor so Alex dragged the body over towards the window and laid him against the sink unit where he wouldn't immediately be seen from outside.

Deanna opened the back door and scanned the area for the two henchmen, they were nowhere to be seen, the coast was clear. Just as they both got outside they heard a shout, then the two men conversing in frantic Spanish. Pino, the bloodthirsty young voyeur, had not wanted to miss the torment of the captive and had been trying to gain a view through the window, seeing that the chair was empty and with Quiros nowhere to be seen all hell was going to break loose.

Deanna and Alex realised they had been rumbled and immediately turned on the offensive to catch the two thugs off guard. As one, they ran around the corner of the house, Deanna with her Beretta held up ready to fire and Alex with his ineffectual lancet, which was only useful at close range. As they turned the corner the two Spaniards were already upon them. The older man, Goyo, grabbed Deanna's wrists and forced her arms into the air so rapidly that she fired off her first shot into thin air. Pino was reaching around into his waistband as he was running, not quite able to take purchase of his gun in his panic. Alex took advantage of this and landed a heavy blow with his fist directly across his cheek, which sent Pino stumbling backward in a daze. Deanna was struggling to free her hands from Goyo so she could try and get off another shot. Goyo being that much stronger was winning the battle. Deanna brought her knee up hard into his crotch and his grip around her wrists loosened. She was able to free her hands from his restraint as his hands instinctively lowered, down to cup his aching groin. With his adrenaline pumping Goyo came back at her quickly. Deanna raised the gun to take aim at him again but Goyo slapped her hands out of the way just as she was about to let off another round. The bullet caught Pino high in the chest, Pino fell down onto his knees gasping for air. Alex seized the moment and grabbed Pino by the arm twisting around his back. He then reached down into his waistband and took the gun Pino had been searching for. Goyo was getting the better of Deanna and was about to fall on her when Alex shouted for him to stop. Goyo, again, had Deanna's gun-hand held in his, with his other he was about to start landing punches. Just as Goyo brought his arm up to smash it down into Deanna's face Alex fired off a shot into his back. All the force of the blow left him and his arm fell to his side, useless. Alex shouted another warning. With his functioning hand Goyo twisted the Beretta out of Deanna's grasp, took it in his hand and turned to face Alex raising the gun as he did so. He gave Alex no choice, he rapidly buried three rounds into his chest bringing Goyo to his knees before he could even level the gun at him. Alex turned to see if Pino was still a threat but Pino had quickly realised that he was on the losing side of this fight and was fleeing the scene. He was young and not as tough as he made out. He didn't want to end up like Goyo. Alex let him go as he was not going to be the one to shoot an unarmed boy in the back.

'Are you OK?' he asked Deanna

'I think so' she replied 'It looks like we are even. I came to save your life and you end up saving mine'

'Well, if it wasn't for me getting into this mess in the first place you wouldn't be here. Judging by your sidearm I'm guessing you are CIA. Am I right?'

'Yes, it's a long story. And I will tell you, I promise, but not here. I think we need to get to safety. There was a estación de policía in town, it's not going to be long before they come to see about the shots fired. Let's go. My car is down the road. I think we need to get out of Spain and back to the US. You need to be debriefed. I'm hoping that between us we can sort out what's been going on with you and sort this mess out'

Both out of breath they got to the car and jumped in. Deanna rammed it into first, crunching the gears and sped off not wanting to be around for the doctor waking up. As she clumsily worked up the gears her heartbeat slowed and she was able to give Alex some explanation.

'I was sent to appraise you' she began, 'I'm working out of Langley for Hugh Osterman. It's a joint effort between us and your MI5'

'But why?' asked Alex, 'Why me?'

'I think you know why, deep down. You are being monitored pretty closely, which is natural considering the post you hold. Feedback from your controller, Anil Bharat, and corroborating information from your man Graves suggest that you have been compromised in some way. I'm here to see if I can find out why you are defecting. I was sent here to see if you were really helping Vasili defect or if it was, in actual fact, a ruse for your own defection'

'Defecting! That's ridiculous. I've never heard such rubbish' Alex was taken aback'

'How can you explain your behaviour over the last few months then? Osterman remembers you particularly asking him about West to East defections'

'If I was going to defect do you think I would ask a CIAS operative how to do it?'

'That would be kinda stupid! How do you explain it then?'

'Well.... I'm not sure I can. I've been wondering myself what's been going on with me. To tell you the truth I thought, well, I still think it has all to do with losing my men back in Navarre. I'm pretty sure it's some form of PTSD. It's just manifesting itself with these damn memory lapses' he said

'I think, judging by what just occurred in the farmhouse that it is much more serious than that. That doctor, if he was a doctor, was after you for information, he was going to torture you for God's sake' she said, 'What do you know?'

'Only the usual. I've been at MI5 for twelve years. I know a lot. But I'm not going to go blabbing to just anyone. Especially some Spanish fanatic who duped me into thinking Vasili Dragunov wasn't dead' Alex paused, 'What a fool I've been. I should have known. I was so desperate in wanting it to be true' he chided himself, 'I was acting like a bloody amateur. Nearly got us both killed because of my God-damned pride'

'Let's just think this through for a moment, shall we?' Deanna said, 'I heard some of your conversation from outside. That doctor said he had met you before, yes?' Alex nodded, 'Four years ago, and that he stitched your face up after the explosion in the hills of Navarre. It's no coincidence that you met with him again. There must be more to it. Do you remember anything after the explosion?'

'No. Nothing. All I remember was waking up north of the Pyrenees outside of a small town made up of only a few buildings. We had been dumped at the side of the road. The four of us walked into town and contacted Thames House from a payphone, totally against protocol but we were in such a state that we didn't know what else to do. From there we were picked up by Interpol and brought in under complete secrecy. We were not supposed to have even been there. A public incident had to be avoided, it would have been an national embarrassment. We were debriefed regarding the operation but could not recall anything at all about the period immediately after. We assume it was the splinter group that held us. Why, we will probably never know. Any more than why we were released when we were' he paused, 'The only positive thing that came out of the whole debacle was that the attack on Zapatero didn't come to pass. Whether we stopped it or not, I don't know. The treaty was signed. That was all that mattered'

Alex became reflective so Deanna decided to leave him with his thoughts for the time being. They drove in silence, both ruminating on their predicament. Deanna wondered how much she should tell Alex at this time, whether to come clean and lay her cards on the table or to be more guarded and play them close to her chest.

She decided to make some small talk while she decided on the right course of action, after all, she wasn't sure yet whether or not she could trust Alex Spellman, she may be a rookie in the field but she wasn't that naive.

'How did they recruit you? I saw from your file that you weren't always in the business'

'Well, it's not a very long, or interesting story I'm afraid. If you read my file you'll already know that I inherited and ran my father's company after his death, I still do to a certain extent I suppose but not as hands on as I used to be. Well, we had one particular investor who would ask to deal with me and me alone, I didn't know why at the time but he worked at Thames House and his name was Lassiter. He was a man who recruits. I later found out that was his one and only job, to seek out viable agents through the world of business. Apparently certain careers hold specific requirements for our line of work'

'How?' asked Deanna

'Well, I'm sure you've heard that to become a CEO or a company president you need to have inbuilt sociopathic tendencies. Now, I'm not saying that I'm sociopathic by any means but I did have certain qualities that Clive Lassiter was interested in. I wasn't completely fulfilled by what I was doing, I was making money sure but there was something lacking'

'In what way?'

'Just the fact that, even though I had everything I could possibly need, there was an emptiness. I knew I could make a difference somewhere but at the time I just didn't know where or how. Clive Lassiter made me realise that I could be doing something worthwhile. It didn't happen overnight or anything like that, we became close through our dealings and at the time I didn't know his agenda but gradually it came to light that he was headhunting. And I was flattered and excited and eager, it seemed that he was offering me just what I needed at the time, a chance to become the man I had always wanted to be. Does that sound trite?'

'Not at all, I can understand that completely. I wasn't recruited the same way you were, I always had it in my head that I would be going into this line of work, the only problem was keeping it a secret from everyone around me, that was hard'

'So your family don't know what you do?'

'I have no family, both my parents are passed'

'I'm sorry to hear that'

'That's OK. It still hurts but I'm learning to live with it. What about you? Do you have family?'

'My mother is still around and I have a sister who has a family'

'And do they know what you do?'

Alex laughed, 'Not exactly, my mother has dementia so even if she did know chances are she wouldn't remember and my sister thinks I live this very lavish jet-set lifestyle that allows me to travel a lot' Alex ruminated slightly, 'So it's refreshing to be able to talk to someone so frankly about what I do and not have to worry about saying the wrong thing'

'I know what you mean'

'Tell me, how did you get mixed up in this?'

'I got assigned, just like any other job. I got called into the offices in San Diego and was given you' she looked at Alex as she said it and appraised him properly, seeing how he reacted.

'So, just another run of the mill assignment, eh?'

'How do you mean?'

'Here's one thing I've learned through all my years working in counter-intelligence is that nothing is coincidental. You may not know it yet, but I can guarantee you that you were put on this assignment for a reason'

'And what reason might you think that is?'

'I'm not sure yet. Who is your handler again?'

'I'm sure you won't remember him. Osterman is his name. He said he met you once briefly a few years back'

'Hugh Osterman?'

'Uh-huh'

'Yeah, I know the man, looks like a bear but not as pretty' Alex smiled

'Funny, he said complimentary things about you too. Sounds like you do know him then!'

'Yep, I don't know what he led you to believe but me and Hugh go way back'

'That's strange'

'I told you, you have to be careful, there are serious players to deal with in our line, you should always be thinking about the other person's motives. What did he say you were watching me for?'

'You know I can't tell you that, I would be betraying a confidentiality'

'Well, just be careful, that's all I'm saying to you'

They were nearing the outskirts of the airport now and Alex needed to get rid of the vehicle, he decided they could leave it in short stay parking as it would be a good few days before anyone noticed it there, maybe even a week or more. The journey back to the US would give them both a bit of breathing space and maybe a chance for them to familiarize themselves with their situation.

16 - Balthazar Browne M.D.

The flight from Madrid turned out to be one of deep reflection for Alex and Deanna, both lost in their own thoughts, their conversation limited to perfunctory exchanges. It was as if they were not so sure of each other and were keeping a respectable distance. As far as Deanna was concerned she had to get Alex to the only person who could shed any light on his condition, the only one she knew of anyway. The flight to New York was over eight hours, then another six hours on to San Diego. At least they would have an overnight stop in New York to recharge their batteries and get some well needed rest from the flight and all that had happened previously in Madrid. Deanna's mind was swirling with all sorts of scenarios and outcomes for their arrival in the United States, hoping for the best but fearing the worst. She was in two minds whether she should check in with Osterman, unsure if there would be time for that luxury. She had a feeling of creeping paranoia and a need to press on for fear of their adversaries catching up to them. She had recalled there was a family friend she knew of in Chula Vista, southern San Diego, a quick search on her phone had confirmed he was still living in the area. She knew him more by reputation as she had only once shaken hands with him at a party her father had held many years before. Deanna, still being a teenager at the time, found most of the guests at the party held little or no interest for her. Although this guest had made an impression on her even in that short meeting, not because of what he did for a living especially, but because he had the peculiar name of Balthazar Browne, MD. It had stuck in her head along with the fact that he had a keen interest in the workings of the mind and it's ability to be manipulated, a subject her father had always found fascinating. Her father found this information to be more interesting to impart upon introductions than the fact that Doctor Browne had not one but three Doctorates, the other two being psychiatry and bizarrely, astronomy. According to a Google search he was still living at 1700 Seacoast Drive, the last coastal dwelling before you got to the border with Mexico, roughly two and a half miles away. The house, Deanna also noted, as well as facing the Pacific Ocean, backed onto the Oneonta Slough, part of the Tijuana Slough National Estuarine Park.

Deanna saw that Browne's wife of forty four years had died the previous fall succumbing to cancerous ovaries after a three year battle. According to her search he had not been practising since her passing and had not been mentioned in any online posts in the last six months. Unusual as he had always been, he had always been a well a known socialite and prolific lecturer. It was a gamble going to see him. Deanna didn't know what she was going to find when she confronted him; hopefully the same exuberant, enthusiastic scholar but in all likelihood now a broken man. Losing the love of your life changes a person.

They arrived at San Diego International at two in the afternoon and were greeted by a blast of dry heat as they left the terminal building to jump into a cab to take them to Southern Chula Vista. The drive took them through Little Italy and Logan Heights taking them about forty five minutes as the traffic was pretty heavy in the latter part of the afternoon. The cab dropped them off at the Seacrest Drive address and after trying the doorbell and finding the place empty they waited in the shade of the carport that sat beneath the living quarters of the main building.

'What are we hoping to achieve here, with this man?' Alex asked

'I am sure he will be able to give us some indication of what is happening to you' replied Deanna, 'He's a brilliant man and I know that he will be able to help us, he and my father were very close'

'That's fine and all, but telling me what I already know is one thing, making me better is another. Can he actually do anything for me? I want these episodes to stop. I need them to stop'

'Can we just talk to him and then we will at least know where we stand and if anything can be done. I'm sure that if he is not able to do anything himself he can send us on to someone who maybe can help. Be patient, I know how frustrating it is for you'

'I'm just tired of it all'

'I know' Deanna took Alex's hand in hers and gave it a reassuring squeeze. She could feel herself warming to Alex despite her better judgement. They both heard a vehicle approaching and stood up in tandem to ascertain whether it was in fact Doctor Balthazar Browne. A small silver Chevy Sonic approached them looking as if it were much older than it's two years, it obviously hadn't been washed or taken care of since... well, since ever; it had a multitude of scrapes and bumps all over the bodywork and a layer of dust which graduated in shade from bottom to top.

The car did indeed roll directly up to where they stood and swung without hesitation into the bay where Deanna and Alex had just been sitting, as it did so knocking one of the beach chairs they had only moments ago been seated on. Alex surmised almost immediately on seeing the driver that Doctor Browne had probably been on a liquor run, unfortunately he was all too familiar with the signs of a man in the grip of depression.

Upon emerging from the car, the occupant all but ignored the two people waiting for him. He grabbed the brown paper bag bought from the liquor store and headed straight to the stairs that led up to his apartment.

'Doctor Browne!' Deanna shouted

The doctor looked around at the two figures and furtively carried on ascending the stairs toward the entrance to his building. Deanna swiftly approached him and caught his arm as he was putting the key into the lock of the door.

'Doctor Browne' she repeated, 'Please, I know you won't recognize me but I'm Phillip Darby's daughter, Deanna. Do you remember? We met at my father's house. You must remember' she pleaded

The doctor paused and looked up at her, taking in her face and features, slowly making the connection between this young woman in front of him and old his friend Phillip, another person who had been taken so prematurely from this world. His face somehow showed a mixture of recognition and melancholy as it dawned on him that he could not possibly turn her away. 'Come in, both of you' he gestured with a nod of his head for them to follow him in to the cool dark of the apartment.

Once inside Deanna expected the living space to be a mess. A recently widowed man in his sixties would not necessarily have the housekeeping habits you might expect but she was surprised at how fastidiously neat the apartment was. Alex took the stairs two at a time to catch the pair up. Once inside Doctor Browne deposited his brown paper bag on the counter and opened the curtains facing the ocean, revealing a beautiful vista of the Pacific with the sun beginning its descent over the horizon. As the apartment became illuminated by the warm glow Deanna and Alex could see just how minimalistic the living space actually was with the few pieces of furniture eclectically elegant while the kitchen was a modernist's dream of simplistic design. The Doctor grabbed three glasses from a kitchen cabinet and the bottle out of the liquor store bag then proceeded out onto the balcony where there was a set of wicker beach furniture. He did all this without saying a word until 'Are you going to join me? Or just stand there gawping?' noting the look of confusion on both their faces.

Deanna and Alex stepped out onto the balcony to find the Doctor pouring them all a tumbler each of an Australian Shiraz. 'You have no idea how much of a pleasant surprise it is to see you Danni. I had known your mother and father for many years, what happened to your father was a tragedy, especially after losing your mother to cancer. I want you to know that I am deeply sympathetic'

'Please Doctor Browne, call me Deanna, no-one but my father ever called me Danni. Well, actually Danni Girl, it was his pet name for me. He liked to tell me stories of how his father had been Irish born and brought their young family over to America at the turn of the century, that was how he used to remind himself probably'

'Of course Deanna, I'm so sorry, it's just that was how he introduced me to you all those years ago, forgive me'

'It's fine, honestly' Deanna blushed, 'It brings back painful memories, that's all'

'I remember seeing you at his service, it was a shame there could not have been a formal burial, it must have been quite a hard time for you, I'm sure it still must be. There have been many times I have meant to visit you and see how you were, it's the least I should have done for Phil, but life always finds a way to throw things in your path. No excuse of course, it's not as if you live on the other side of the country. And then of course my poor wife became ill and from then on nothing else really mattered to me. She was my world, and I miss her terribly. Being in love is a wonderful thing but it's a cruel world that makes you witness your partner slowly fading away in front of your eyes... with nothing you can do about it. But you didn't come here to hear my sob story, I'm sure. Now tell me, what can I do for you? You are not here for a social visit, I can tell by your faces, something serious is afoot! And who is this fellow you have brought to see me?'

'Thank you' Deanna said her eyes welling slightly at the sentiment and at the thought of her parents, still so much of a raw subject for her when brought to the surface, 'It means a lot to me, to us, that you are on our side, we need a friend right now. I saw you at the service too but I couldn't speak to anyone on that day, I was in so much of a daze, I didn't know what I was doing. I'm sorry'

'Don't you dare apologize' he said taking a sip of wine, 'I was so caught up in my own shock and grief I couldn't reach out to you, it was severely remiss of me. If I can make it up to you now I would like to try'

'I hope so. This is Alex Spellman, a friend of mine. We're in trouble, Doctor Browne'

'Call me Barty, please. What sort of trouble? And how on earth can I be of any help to you? I'm a doctor, remember, you both look fit and well to me. I don't see how I can help'

'It's not your medical expertise we need, more your insight into, um, what would you call it? Autosuggestion? Hypnosis? It might be better if Alex explains it to you'

'Please carry on', the doctor said, now intrigued, relaxing back into his chair expecting a long tale.

'Well you see, sir, er, Doctor, I mean Barty, to put it bluntly, I think I have been brainwashed' Alex paused to let that statement sink in for a moment, his face reddening slightly at the absurdity of the acclamation, 'In fact I've become certain of it. It's a long and complicated story but to cut it short, as time is a pressing factor, I possess and have access to a great deal of compromising information regarding certain operatives, western men and women, placed in intrinsically delicate positions within our enemies divisions. That sounds like a spy talking, but I can assure you I am nothing of the sort. I am a civil servant working at Thames House in London. I have in the past been privy to classified documents and am currently overseeing sleeper cells in hostile quarters, but only from the position of handler'

'And what does that mean in plain English? And who are these "enemies" Are they my enemies? asked Barty

'I am assuming they are enemies of all that we hold dear; the delicate balance between our two countries, the peace that we maintain and the factions that would like to see the West crumble into disarray. It means secrets. Secrets that could compromise years of undercover placements in Russia, Eastern Europe and the Middle East. I hold the secrets to where our operatives are placed, what their missions are and of their confidential identities. I not only hold them but have access to them through my work'

'And what makes you think you have been compromised?'

'Well, I wasn't sure of anything up until a few days ago. Thank God Deanna showed up to clarify things for me. It's all becoming much more apparent what's going on now'

Alex took a draft of his wine, to relieve his parched mouth from the waning heat of the day, 'There are people after me, and they have been trying to retrieve the information I have in my head. Why and to what end, I don't know, I'm not even really sure what I know, who knows what is locked in the subconscious. We can only assume the worst. I have been having blackouts, blanks where I can't remember what I've been doing or where I have been. We've come to see you, today, to see if there is anything that can be done to stop these episodes I have been having. Maybe even to stop the information being extracted from me, I don't know. I'm clutching at straws'

'Tell me everything you can in regard to this so called *brainwashing*, and I will help in any way I can, but I must have the full picture, understand?'

Alex nodded and related everything he could recall that he thought was pertinent to his predicament; the episodes where he couldn't remember where he had been or what he had been doing, when he had been sitting as if hypnotized in front of the television, of having migraine headaches which he had never suffered from previously, becoming suddenly conscious of his surroundings as if transported from a deep sleep. A lot of the symptoms and manifestations he found difficult to verbalise as they were made up of deep rooted feelings of unease and anxiety for which he could find no cause or reason. He told the doctor how at times he had a strong feeling of paranoia, as if his movements were being monitored somehow.

He also related everything that had happened regarding the staged defection and his run-in with the Spaniard in Madrid and Deanna's help in getting him out of a potentially serious situation. He remembered, or rather, sensed that he had one of his blackouts on the journey to Madrid. This is where Deanna interrupted and owned up to her subterfuge at having drugged him to gain information as to his intentions and then following him to his meeting with the Spanish doctor. Alex would have had every right to have been angry with her but in their present situation and being from the same governmental background he understood why she would have acted as she did.

After he had finished he took another drink from his glass and waited for the doctor to process all that he had been told. Alex watched as the doctor sat with his fingers arched in front of him, staring at the tips of his index fingers apparently deep in thought.

Eventually he began, 'You might find it amusing, that I am named Balthazar Browne, you may also be interested to know that my middle name is Beauregard, a delicious alliteration' he chuckled, 'This is not because I came from a background of opulence or aristocracy, on the contrary; my parents were mid to lower class, my mother worked two jobs and I barely saw my father as he was on the road trucking long distance for the majority of his adult life. They weren't poor but life for them was a struggle, they were the victims of geography, born into the Midwest dust bowl with no talent or opportunity to drag themselves out of the predicament they had been born into. They did not, however, want the same fate for me. They were determined that I would be educated to the full extent of my capabilities and of their finances. They were under the impression that if they named me as they imagined a person of importance would be named I would then rise to the position of my title. Funnily enough this has been proved to be the case just recently, as some scholars in California have published a paper on this very subject stating it to be beneficial to the individual. You don't get many doctors called Cletus now do you?' he said chuckling to himself, 'My parents may have been semi-illiterate but they had a flair for alliteration, and predestination apparently'

Deanna and Alex both glanced at each other not sure where this monologue was taking them.

The doctor noticed their confusion and carried on, 'You're wondering what this has to do with your problem, well, everything and nothing, if you'll forgive me for saying. First of all I think better when I'm talking, secondly I wanted to let you know my credentials by way of a potted history; full disclosure if you like. I am not a man born into wealth, I had to fight for what I have and to get where I have got in life. I am proud of the position I now hold, I am respected within certain circles of society, I have dedicated my life to helping those who needed it most and I feel I have never in my professional life broken my Hippocratic oath. I am proud of the way my parents raised me to be the person I now am. I married a wonderful woman whom I had to say goodbye to much too soon, she was my best friend. And now I may be experiencing some kind of re-evaluation, if you will. The death of a loved one makes you think hard about what is important in life. And thirdly it's gratifying to be able to talk to people again, people apart from the lady in the wine shop. However beautiful the view is across the ocean, and believe me I have spent many hours gazing out at it, it does not replace or compensate for the ear of a sympathetic soul. Human interaction is key, my friends, do not take what you have for granted for someday it may all be taken away from you without notice or ceremony'

There followed a moment of silence as the three of them sat and silently took stock. Deanna glancing at Alex, feeling her face redden into a blush, a warmth spreading from her stomach and rising up to her chest. If she were a teenager again she would swear it was a crush, not since she was fourteen had she felt so giddy about the thought of the embrace of a man. She lowered her eyes for fear that her thoughts would betray her. Alex reassured her with an imperceptible nod of his head and a softening of his expression letting her know that she was in his thoughts also.

Barty continued, 'Forgive me for being maudlin. It was not my intention to dampen your mood, I have apparently lost the ability for polite conversation. That happens when you are out of practice. The re-evaluation I mention is an oath I have made to myself that life is not over because of the passing of a loved one, I have been lonely and alone for too long, Margaret always told me, especially in her last days, that she would not expect me to mourn her for too long, a month she suggested would suffice, she was quite a practical women in that way. Now it is time to move on with my life and helping you two young people may be a way to begin that process, I will help you in any way I can but I fear that I may not be able to do much for you. Brainwashing, conditioning, autosuggestion... whatever you care to call it, the effects are extremely difficult to eradicate or reverse without knowing how the process was carried out upon you in the first place. So considering what I have learned in all my years as an enthusiastic amateur in the field I can tell you, with a certain amount of regret and reluctance that there is not much that can be done regarding your affectation or rather, your affliction. I know this is exactly not what you came to me to hear and I apologize that I cannot be more helpful....'

'So you mean to say that there is absolutely *nothing* I can do to stop these episodes?'

The doctor sat in silence for a few moments before reasoning, 'No, nothing *we* can do, not here, not now. From my experience in these matters the only way to eradicate this problem of yours is to return to or revisit the particular person or persons responsible for putting you into this predicament, and find the antidote if you like; a process which will cease or reverse the effects of the mind control. The only person who has the ability to do this is the man or woman who put you into this state in the first place'

'So basically I'm buggered, as I have no clue how to find this Spaniard now, who is our only link, and I doubt very much if he'll be waiting around for us in the farmhouse we just left a dead body at'

Barty held up a hand to stop Alex from elaborating, 'Please spare me the details, the less I know about some things the better. And don't be too hasty regarding your fate young man. I could spin you platitudes galore; 'more than one way to skin a cat' etcetera etcetera, but I need time. Time to study you and formulate a plan of action, I could perhaps minimise the effects with a short course of hypnotherapy, it would by no means solve your problem entirely but it may give you some respite from the effects. It would be the safest and least invasive method'

'How safe?' asked Deanna

'Nothing would be for certain. I don't have *any* information regarding what was done to you. How invasive the procedures were, what sort of damage could have been done to your neural pathways. Anything I do subsequently could have an element of risk attached, I could inadvertently make matters worse if I were to apply the wrong treatment' Barty noted the deflation caused by his statement and added with a touch of optimism, 'Or you could wait it out and see if the malady wears off, which is highly probable if there is no stimulus to sustain the catalyst. Of course we have no idea how long it would be until you saw an improvement in your situation but I am fairly certain that in these cases the effects would taper off over time'

'The trouble is we don't know how long. You can't imagine what it's like, the feeling as if you are having an 'out of body' experience, subconsciously carrying out actions but having no way to stop yourself, as if in a trance'

'I can't imagine specifically but I have a good enough idea of what you are going through. I haven't divulged this to anyone but back in the day when we were studying the likes of MK Ultra and all the other psychotropic ways you could alter a man's thinking and manipulate his actions, we, that is the group of us, like-minded men and women who also took an interest, doctors and people of learning, would acquire knowledge about these subjects in the only way we knew how; self-experimentation. It was all carried out in the strictest of conditions, you must understand, we were not doing it just to get high or for kicks. That is probably the reason I haven't been outspoken about our findings, for a fear that it would be taken the wrong way and that people would not understand where the basis of our experimentation came from; a desire to understand, and the only way sometimes to do that is to experiment. Just ask Albert Hoffman, a trailblazer in the area of LSD or Stubbins Ffirth or Jonas Salk to name only a few men who risked their lives for the advancement of our understanding of what the human body can endure. Needless to say back in those days we were probably, no definitely, naive to the consequences of our actions but luckily not one of us was seriously affected in the long term by our foolish experimentation. We did find, however, that the effects of certain procedures similar to the one you are experiencing, I would say, did not have a lasting effect'

'And how long are we talking?'

'It's hard to say as every case is different and every individual has his or her own set of physical and mental values, this in course alters the outcome of the effects wearing off. I know that doesn't help your cause but it's the best I can offer you at this juncture. It could be a matter of weeks or...' Barty let the rest of the sentence hang not wanting to verbalize the fact that it could be much longer.

'Or it could be years?' asked Deanna, a defeated tone in her voice.

After a short lull Doctor Browne offered, 'I hope you will both join me for something to eat, you must be famished and you look as if you haven't had a decent meal in days'

'That would be great' replied Deanna

'And of course you are welcome to stay, if you need somewhere. I mean to say, think of my home as your own, stay and gather yourselves, get some rest, plan your next move and consider what I have said to you'

'Maybe we should stay one or two nights, what do you think Alex?'

The morning gave promise to be another beautiful day in southern San Diego. Even though the sun was barely over the horizon the air shimmered with the presage of a balmy heat that only the sea breeze could alleviate. Alex had taken the hammock out on the viewing platform to sleep on and had been woken by the gulls cackling and croaking while swooping in fervent circles catching their breakfast. Deanna had slept on the futon in the living room on the upper floor of Doctor Browne's beachside condo'. The condominium was designed in such a way that it was upside down to the usual idea of a dwelling; the view was so spectacular over the Pacific that the first floor was the living area that led out to the sundeck where the three had enjoyed their wine the previous evening, whereas the bedrooms were downstairs on the ground floor, which still had access to the beach but did not have the elevation for the panoramic view.

Alex checked his watch and saw that it was barely six thirty and tried to sit up in the hammock making himself rock wildly from side to side. He wondered how the Doctor managed with the thing as he was less agile than Alex, maybe there was a knack to it that he needed to learn. He ended up tipping himself onto the deck hands first before letting the rest of his body one limb at a time slide safely onto the decking. He looked into the living room to check that he hadn't woken Deanna with his noisy dismount and found the futon to be empty. Not only empty but neatly packed away to its former state as if no-one had even slept in the bed. With a slight hint of panic and a feeling that maybe she had skipped out on him Alex scanned the room for any type of clue as to where she had gone. He was pleased to find that her personal items were still where she had left them the previous night so that ruled out her absconding. He felt relieved that he could still put his trust in her. It was a predicament that he felt uncomfortable with, to be in the hands of a person he didn't fully know or trust completely; the people he could truly trust could be counted on the fingers of one hand and even in these recent days that number was seriously in question. In his line of work you were taught to put your trust in no-one but yourself and the Lord above and as Alex wasn't a devout Christian he tended to listen to his instinctual inner voice. He had believed in Deanna and was relieved that his decision hadn't been questioned.

He sat down at the table to take in the view and wait for Deanna to join him from the washroom where he assumed she must be but as he gazed out across the ocean he could see the splashing of a lone swimmer in the surf roughly two hundred feet from the shore. After watching for a few minutes he realised it must be Deanna out there swimming and decided he would walk down to meet her, pleased with the fact that she hadn't in fact skipped out on him.

He sat down on the soft white sand and felt the warmth of the sun on his back. It was a soothing feeling that took him back to his younger days. Alex and his father would be out on the lake at the cabin and the unusually hot Welsh summer sun had made them both wish they had brought more water to drink with them out on their fishing trip. A time when life was much simpler than it was now.

Deanna has stopped her backstroke for a moment, peering through the peaks and troughs of the gentle waves and looked towards shore and saw that Alex was sitting on the sand waiting for her. She gave him a big double armed wave and Alex could see even from this distance she had a huge grin on her face. He raised his arm and gave her a similarly large greeting. Five minutes later she was emerging from the surf and donning the cotton top she had left in the sand that barely covered her toned posterior. As she approached Alex he could see quite clearly that although she was wearing panties Deanna was otherwise naked beneath the sheer fabric of the blouse.

Deanna sat down next to Alex on the warm sand. 'You're a brave woman, going skinny dipping where anyone could see you'

'I figured that at this time of the morning I would have the beach to myself. That is of course until I got interrupted by a peeping Tom' she mocked, giving him a broad grin.

'And what makes you so happy this fine morning?'

'Well I *am* a Californian girl, give me a beach and the ocean and you can pretty much have me as I am. It doesn't get much better than this does it?'

'It is beautiful' Alex admitted, 'What on earth sort of time were you up this morning? I didn't hear you sneak past me'

'I didn't have to, you were out for the count. Even the poor seagulls were complaining about the snoring, you should have slept indoors to give them some peace and quiet'

Alex laughed out loud at the slight. It felt nice to laugh, he had been out of practice for some time now. He liked the fact that Deanna could be cheeky with him, he didn't mind one bit, she behaved like a mischievous 'colleen', as his mother would have described her, a twinkle in her eye and overworked dimples in her cheeks. Looking at her now in the early morning light he could see how, despite all that was going on, she was truly happy sitting there looking out at the ocean, was it just that or was it because he was there with her? He hoped so. Alex found her mood to be infectious and soon began breathing the sea air in deeply and letting himself be swept along in her proclivity.

'I find it incredibly difficult to be this close to the ocean and not to be able to go swimming, even from the time we arrived I was itching to go in. I must have woken up at about five thirty this morning. My home is not too far up the coast, you must come and see it'

'I'd like that'

There were a few moments of silence where both of them put off the inevitable conversation regarding their immediate future. Alex eventually broke the lull, 'I've been considering everything that Doctor Barty told us last night, I think it would be a mistake to stay here for too long'

'I agree' said Deanna

'Not just because the treatment would take too long, but because I don't want to put the doctor in any danger. It's bad enough that you are involved, I don't want to drag another person into this mess if I can help it. Enough people have been hurt along the way already'

'I know, Alex, it's OK, I understand'

'So?' he asked

'So' replied Deanna hoping that Alex would put forward a course of action because she wasn't quite sure what to suggest. She also hoped she would be included in his plan.

'Firstly I think we need to keep moving, and secondly I think we need to gather information. And I think I know who can help us'

Relieved that she was part of the equation, Deanna said 'Well if that's the case we will need transport, and I know just the job. I happen to know where there is a motorbike that cannot be traced to us. It'll be fast and it will get us where we need to go'

And Thank God, Deanna thought to herself, that she hadn't posted the door keys back to Gregg already, they were still in with her personal belongings back at Barty's condo.

They both turned their heads in unison when they heard shouts coming from the direction of the condo, initially alarmed they realised it was just Doctor Barty waving from the deck with one hand and holding a pan in the other. Alex and Deanna both looked at each other simultaneously and said 'Breakfast!' both grinning idiotically at each other like children.

With that Deanna got up to go and fetch her shoes which she had left at the water's edge. Alex stayed put while he watched her lithe body retreat from him. He found it fascinating how the female body could move and sway, he admired the shape of her calves as she negotiated the soft sand and realised just how healthy and vibrant she was underneath her stiff workday clothes. It didn't appear to him that she was in the correct profession, she certainly looked more at ease with a life outdoors. He felt sure she had become the person she wanted to be when she had dived in and began swimming this morning. He could not break his gaze from her as she bent down to pick up her shoes and return to him up the beach. Clearly mesmerized he drank in the curves of her body as the breeze buffeted her cotton blouse making it cling to her breasts where the water had not yet dried, her bare feet kicking up sand and her damp hair cascading over her shoulders. She had that heady mixture of athleticism and femininity that showed in her toned limbs when she moved, she was comfortable in her own body and had the naiveté to be unselfconscious about it. What Alex found amazing about Deanna was that she had no idea the effect she had on him, she was attractive *because* she was unaware of being so, he could watch her like this for hours and never tire of her. He realised it had been a long time that he had courted thoughts such as these about a woman, could it be that he was falling for Deanna?

When they reached Doctor Barty breakfast was laid out for them on the table. If they weren't in the pickle they were in it would have been tempting to stay with the doctor for longer considering the hospitality they were getting. The conversation during breakfast consisted of familiar topics, no-one wanting to ruin the atmosphere by referring to the elephant in the room. The three of them happily discussed the weather, the economy, the presidency and even the state of the music scene in California of which they all decided could be a lot better.

The Mexican inflected breakfast was a superb mix of fiery flavours that you could only achieve this close to the source of the ingredients. Barty had perfected his own version of chilaquiles with chorizo and peppers. Alex had rarely tasted anything so flavorsome and devoured the plate of food without considering the speed at which he ate. He realised he had been living off hotel and café fare for too long and apologized for appearing ravenously impolite. This was washed down with freshly juiced apple and ginger that tasted so refreshing that it just had to be beneficial to your health. The breakfast ended with a sweet, hot espresso which left all three of them feeling contented but not overfed. Barty cleared the plates away refusing the offer of help from both Deanna and Alex. He was turning out to be the perfect host.

Deanna returned from the bedroom and gave Alex the key and the address of where the bike would be, telling him about Gregg's routine, the fact that he would be gone for work at 8.30am and wouldn't be back until after 5. After which they would be long gone. She also told him where the leathers were usually kept, a female set were there as well, although Deanna thought that most probably they weren't bought especially for her. Gregg thought that his hog would be irresistible to most women. God, why was she ever with that loser?

When Barty returned from the interior he was clutching an envelope. He handed it to Deanna and said as way of explanation, 'About a month before your father disappeared he visited me with the instruction that if you ever got in touch with me I was to pass this on to you. It's been sitting here all this time and I have often wondered if I should be the one to track you down to give it to you. But your father's direction was clear; I should wait for you to call on me. I don't know what it is or what it says, I have not opened it and never would. It has been sitting safe in my possession for all this time. It is with satisfaction to be able to hand it to you at this juncture'

Deanna took the envelope and turned it over in her hands and studied the writing on the front; her pet name 'Danni girl' was written in her father's hand. She opened the missive and began to read. All of a sudden and with such emotion her eyes began to moisten and sting as tears fell onto her cheeks making her unable to focus on the words in front of her. She handed the pages to Alex and asked, 'Could you read it to me please? I don't think I can do it'

'Of course', Alex began:

To my dearest Danni-girl,

If you are reading this letter it means that I am no longer with you. Something has happened that has taken me away from you. At this point in time it is hard to say what that may have been, but in this letter I may be able to give you some direction as to what my fate has been. This is a difficult letter to write but one that I feel is essential to finally let you know what calibre of man your father was. First of all I want you to know that you and your mother were and are the most important things in my life and I love you both with all my heart and soul, but also that my life is (or was!) actually rather complicated to the extent that I have had to keep things from you to protect you both from the truth. This truth is for you alone as I know you will be able to appreciate what I have been going through all these years, I doubt your mother would have understood and I think the truth would have been too much of a burden to her when she was alive.

Like you, I was an overachieving liberal straight out of university not quite knowing what I should do with my life...

'Are you sure you want me to read this out loud to you, it sounds quite personal' asked Alex

'Yes, please, carry on. There is nothing in these pages that I wouldn't want either of you to know'

'OK' Alex continued

...when I was approached, by what we used to jokingly call the 'men in black', recruiters for government agencies, it was usual back then for certain departments to cherry pick young, promising graduates and get them started within the realms of the administration. I began at a very junior level within Gain Point, an intelligence gathering agency, working locally, they kept an eye on certain individuals and groups who were perceived as threats to US values. As far as your mother ever knew this is what I did and I wouldn't want her to know any different. She was never to know that my job description changed drastically in the coming years. I know that you, however, would understand that there are certain things you cannot tell even to the ones you love. I know that you, like me, pursued a career within the CIA, and I know that because for the last twenty five years I have also been working there, unable to divulge my position to anyone. I am still, up to this point, unable to give you the details of my rank and position within the agency. I didn't let on that I knew but let me say that I am so proud that even without knowing, you chose to follow in my footsteps and fight the noble cause. And I know that is why you joined, because you have a good heart, and it killed me that I couldn't let on that I knew. Just to put your mind at rest, I had nothing at all to do with you being accepted but I was informed of your progress with your application all along the way. I am sure that you will graduate in due course. I have a friend in the agency named Hugh Osterman and in case anything happens to me I have asked him to keep an eye on you for me. He's an honest man and can be trusted. If you need anything, go to him.

Hopefully it will be many years before you have cause to read this letter, maybe I will be telling you all this while lying on my deathbed when I am a hundred and two, I certainly hope that to be the case.

As to the reasons why it made me feel it was important at this time to be putting pen to paper, I am all too aware that in our line of business things can go wrong too easily, it's dangerous. Maybe it's because I'm getting on in years and my outlook is changing, maybe it's because I'm aware that certain cases I am working on are showing me a different side of our government.

The fact that you are reading this letter means that I am no longer around. Just remember that I love you and always wanted the best for you and your mother. I am so very proud of you.

Always yours, Papa.

P.s. Say hello to Barty for me and look after him too, I have a feeling that you two are going to need each other.

By the time Alex had finished reading the letter Deanna had tears streaming down her face and her cheeks were now flushed with anger. Alex knew that the information in the letter could have so many connotations for Deanna and her reality up to this point. Not knowing too much about

Deanna's life previous to their meeting a short while ago he instinctively knew that the material he had just heard would be shocking and life altering for her.

'I'm so sorry' uttered Barty, 'I had no idea that Phil had so many secrets'

'This doesn't make any sense, it can't be right' Deanna murmured, distraught, 'My father knew nothing about me joining the CIA, he couldn't have. I kept it a secret from everyone. When did you receive this letter?'

'Some time after his death, I assumed it was sent through his lawyer as his estate was being handled'

Deanna scrabbled at the letter to see if there was any indication as to when, exactly, it had been written, but found nothing. 'I don't understand, it makes no sense' she muttered

Deanna sat there, gazing out at the ocean, trying to process the information she had just heard. It was unbelievable. She now had new information which indicated that her father's death may not have been accidental, no body was ever found, was he even lost at sea? Everything she thought she knew was now being called into question.

Barty noticed that Deanna had all of a sudden become extremely pale, so got up to fetch her a tonic to keep the shock at bay, for he knew well what a toll the letter would have taken on her. He returned swiftly with a tot of tequila which he urged her to drink down immediately. Deanna coughed at the pungency of the alcohol burning the back of her throat. 'I think I need to lie down' she murmured in a detached voice and with that moved inside the house to lay on the futon.

'Did you have any idea?' Alex asked Barty

'Absolutely no clue, it's as shocking to me as it is to that poor girl'

'What do you suggest we do now?'

'With respect, that is not within my field of expertise. I am a medical doctor remember, not a therapist or a strategist'

'That's what I mean, in your medical opinion, what can we do for Deanna now?'

'Let her rest for a while, then we will see'

'Do you think it will be OK for her to travel?'

'I would give her a few hours at least. And we will be here to keep an eye on her. And what about your plans? Did you make any decisions regarding the procedures I mentioned?'

'Both Deanna and I decided that we need to keep moving. At this stage it would be dangerous for you if we stayed here any longer'

'I understand that but don't worry about me. Deanna's safety is my first worry now. I'm sorry I can't be of more help to you. But, I think we may need to see how Deanna fares, she may not be fit to travel so soon'

'You have done more than we ever could have expected. Maybe we should stay one more night and see how she is after a good nights rest and a chance to process all that information. Would that be OK with you?'

'Of course it would, I would be glad to have the company'

Both men walked in to check on Deanna who was not laying down as they thought but was packing their things up into a makeshift holdall. Upon them entering she said to Doctor Barty, 'Could you drop me to Pacific Beach?'

'Deanna, I really think you should be resting"

'Why Pacific Beach?' repeated Alex when she didn't respond immediately

'You said so yourself, we need to keep moving. And I had an idea that will help us do just that. We need to get that motorbike' she answered matter of factly.

'I have a better idea, we'll stick to the original plan but what if Barty takes me to get the bike now and you stay here and rest where it's safe. I'll be back before you know it and then we'll be on our way. OK? A fresh start first thing in the morning'

Deanna reluctantly knew this was the only sensible thing to do as she felt a wave of exhaustion pass over her. She was still reeling from all the new information in the letter from her father. Some rest and a chance to think things over would be the best thing for her immediate peace of mind.

Barty gave her a couple of tablets to calm her and ten minutes later she was drifting off to sleep wrapped up in Dr. Barty's throw on the lounger in the living room. She heard Alex and the Doctor pull off in his dilapidated car as she drifted and found comfort in the smell of the throw; her brain trying to work out the mix of aromas she could smell from it. Before she could identify the mixture, sleep took her and she entered a world of blissful peace where her mind could subconsciously begin to cope with her new world order. She didn't hear the motorcycle pull up less than an hour later, shortly followed by the doctor's car.

17 - Escape in the night

Deanna was awoken from her sleep by a warm hand covering her mouth, stopping her from calling out or making any kind of sound at all. The room was nearly pitch, she could see nothing apart from the silhouette of the man silencing her, a faint light behind him. She subconsciously gauged the time as 3 or 4am and panic began to rise in her chest. She grabbed at the arm that was holding her down and felt the hard sinews of a muscled forearm. Before she realised she was doing it she was hitting out at her oppressor, writhing as she did so trying to loosen his grip on her. Only after a few short beats did she realise that the person holding her was not aggressive but was in fact trying to soothe her by making a faint shushing sound. He brought his mouth closer to her ear and whispered 'Deanna it's me, Alex. Stop making any noise. They're here'

Alex didn't release his grip on Deanna until he could see that she understood the situation, the faint light that fell across her face and the slight relaxation of her body told him that the information was sinking in. Her eyes questioned Alex and again he leaned in closer to her ear and whispered; 'They are in the building, I heard them kill the engine up the road, they forced entry through the garage'

As he uncovered her mouth she whispered back at him; 'Who?'

'The same people who have been after us all along. We have to get out of here. Now'

Deanna was glad now that she had hastily half-packed a bag for them both. There wouldn't be time to collect anything now.

'What about Barty?' she whispered

'Barty is going to distract them while we make our escape'

'How?'

'No time to explain. Let's go, come on' Alex could not hide the sense of urgency in his tone.

Deanna grabbed whatever she could find in the dim light from the moon as Alex led her by the arm to the doorway. He stopped at the opening and craned his neck slowly scoping the area that would lead them to the motorcycle. Just as he did so he heard an almighty crash followed by shouting. He could tell from the sound that it was Barty initiating his diversionary tactics for them. Alex could not have been more grateful, his timing was impeccable. He grabbed Deanna's arm and pulled her towards the upper deck where there were stairs down to the beach. Travelling as quietly as they could, Alex knew that once he fired up the motorbike the game would be up. Luckily the bike would be easier to handle over the sandy beach than their vehicle would be, reducing the risk of their pursuers following. Before they knew it he and Deanna would be half a mile away heading towards the border, even if it was a few hours before they had planned. The only concern Alex had was leaving the Doctor alone to deal with the two men, he didn't know how much danger Barty would be in, or even if he could handle himself. The guilt of leaving the old man had already begun to gnaw at his conscience. He felt as if he was letting down yet another innocent person, should he have stayed and confronted the two? No. He had Deanna to protect and Barty himself had said to him that she had to come first, he would never forgive himself if anything happened to her, that was the promise he had made to her father.

Alex made sure Deanna was securely seated on the bike and that their few possessions were present before he pressed the ignition, gunned the engine and took off across the sandy beach. He looked back once and saw a figure on Barty's balcony, then three bright flashes in quick succession, all three shots landing wide of their mark, the motorcycle's engine drowning out the noise of the reports, thankfully leaving Deanna none the wiser. He wondered how they were tracking their movements and if they would ever escape their seemingly inexorable chase. He took the bike south until they hit the mouth of the Tijuana River where they had to cross at it's lowest point. From there they went off-road across the Tijuana Slough National Park until they could once again access a roadway. Two kilometres of bumpy scrubland brought them to Sunset Avenue and Alex could finally relax slightly and concentrate on his options rather than straining to keep the bike upright. The best place for them to cross the border was probably Nogales which, if he calculated correctly was roughly 400 miles, maybe 6 hours journey. Then once over the border another 100 or so kilometres to Santa Ana. It would be a gruelling journey but one that had to be made if they wanted answers, maybe they would need to break up the journey with an overnight stay somewhere en route.

18 - Grand Theft Auto

Daisy Buchanan had worked on reception at the sheriff's office for six years, three months and two weeks and she had loved every minute of it. Daisy enjoyed the feeling of responsibility, she enjoyed the fact that when she was off ill, which was seldom, the officers would need to call her at home for information only she could divulge; not that her filing system was particularly designed to confuse but she liked it all to be done a certain way, her way. Daisy had gone to work for the sheriff straight from leaving school when she was eighteen, she had no other aims in life but to earn enough money to satisfy her one passion in life, to collect Elvis memorabilia. This she kept in a room specially designated in her home where she lived with her father; initially it was all kept in the pokey box-room at the top of the stairs but as the collection grew she ended up moving all the statues, vinyl records, bits of clothing, ceramic plates and tacky plastic souvenirs into her bedroom, which was big enough to accommodate everything. She then moved her bed into the more compact room the collection had previously vacated. As far as she was concerned it was a fair trade, she still had her posters that she had moved from the bigger room and now, somehow, she felt even nearer to him as his pictures adorning the walls seemed closer than ever, she could reach out and touch his face without leaving her bed.

The other reason she loved working at the Sheriff's office was that she knew nearly everything that happened in the town. She got a thrill from knowing who had come into the office and with what complaint, it was like living in her own TV reality show, although she would never let on to anyone, especially at work, that she found all the information she gleaned to be like nuggets of gold. She hoarded the information like a squirrel hoarding nuts for winter, it made her feel superior, knowing people's shortcomings, their difficulties and their disputes. Every day brought with it new stories from familiar faces. Daisy would take the statements, listen to the problems and decide who would be the best officer to pass the case onto, all the while secretly storing the information in her head to digest at a later time. Not that Daisy would do anything untoward with all that she knew, she prided herself on her professional work ethic, she just enjoyed the fact that she knew the town secrets.

This particular day had been slow, it was nearly midday and Daisy was scrolling through eBay looking at an Elvis Presley souvenir pack of playing cards she had been keeping an eye on. She couldn't justify paying $150 for them so she was hoping that she would get a better deal at auction. At the moment they were $75 with six hours to go until the end of bidding.

Just as she was thinking that maybe the cards were in the end were worth the whole $150, a man walked in that she didn't immediately recognize. Daisy minimized the window on her computer and straightened her back giving the man her best welcoming smile.

'Good Morning, sir. What can I do for you?' she asked

'I'd like to report a theft' said the man

'Of course. Please take a seat and you can give me all the details. Now firstly, your name and address?'

'Gregg Butanski. 36 Loring Street. Pacific Beach. San Diego.'

'Now, Mr Butanski, what can I help you with today?'

'My motorbike has been stolen. Well when I say stolen what I suppose I mean is that it has been taken without my permission'

'How do you mean?' asked Daisy

'Well, I keep my bike in the garage; it's a beauty, too nice to leave out in the driveway. So I didn't immediately realise it was gone as I don't take it out every day. So when I went to the garage to get it this morning it was gone' explained Gregg, 'but the funny thing is that there was nothing broken in to, no locks had been busted, only a few people even knew the bike would be there'

'And what sort of bike is it?'

'It's a Triumph Thunderbird Commander, 1700cc, matt black'

'And does anyone apart from you have access to your home?'

'The only person apart from me who has a key to the house is my ex-girlfriend. Deanna Darby. She was supposed to be sending me back the key after we broke up. Deanna's a lot of things but I can't believe she would break into my house and steal my ride'

'Have you tried getting in touch with her?'

'Yeah, but she ain't answering'

'OK then Mr. Butanski. I will pass on the details to an officer and it will be dealt with accordingly. Leave it to us, sir. We will do all that we can to track down your motorbike. Just write the vehicle registration and your contact details down on this form for me and we will ask 'traffic' to add it to their list of missing vehicles'

As Gregg was writing his particulars down on the form Daisy heard a ping from the computer, which meant that there had been another bid on the set of playing cards. She furtively glanced over to the screen and maximised the window. She saw that someone had taken the bid up to $95, at this rate the amount would exceed the $150 'buy it now' price. She may not have any choice but to pay the whole amount.

Gregg passed Daisy the filled form and headed for the door. As he was just about to leave he turned and asked, 'So, you'll be in touch if you hear anything, OK?'

'Of course Mr Butanski, as soon as we hear anything we'll let you know' with that Daisy picked up the form and read through the information checking all the fields had been filled correctly. Having done so Gregg departed feeling quite certain that he would never see his pride and joy ever again. Daisy stood up to pass on the form to an officer for processing when the computer made another pinging sound. She put the piece of paper down on the worktop and reached for the mouse again to check the bidding, in doing so she nudged the form with her elbow which then floated down off the desk, onto the floor and came to rest under the filing cabinet. Daisy was annoyed to find the price had now gone up to $105. Just as she was about to collect the form the phone rang, it was her father, he was in the area and thought it would be nice if he took her out for lunch. Daisy was delighted, she said she would meet him at Henry's in ten minutes, she couldn't wait to tell him about the playing cards, although she probably wouldn't tell him how much she was willing to pay. Daddy thought she spent too much on the memorabilia and that she should be out with normal people instead of stuck at home mooning over Elvis. She would, of course, still have to follow the bidding on her cell phone while she was at lunch, luckily her father knew his daughter very well indeed. Daisy forgot all about the form. When she got back from lunch with her father Mrs Athelny came in complaining of being victimised by her neighbour, claiming Mr Ramirez turned on his sprinklers every time she walked by with her shiatsu, getting them both soaking wet. Daisy took down all the details, remembering all the juicy details but somehow forgetting all about Gregg Butanski and his missing motorbike.

Kapusta

T he man they called Kapusta limped into the room and took his seat opposite Andreyev Sigalov, preferring the shadows at the dark end of the room. Andreyev tended not look at him directly as his face was a grotesque mess of scar tissue and badly mended bone. When he did have to address him Andreyev tried to focus on Kapusta's one working eye, the other being melted half shut from the burns he had received. The broken bones in his face gave him a look of a boxer leaving the ring after going all twelve rounds, and losing. No wonder he likes keeping to the shadows, thought Andreyev. Luckily the eye that remained intact was the eye he used to ply his trade, a marksman and sniper of the highest calibre, the most accurate shot with a Lobaev rifle west of the Yenisey.

'We have a problem,' Sigalov began, talking more to his file on the desk than to Kapusta, 'a problem which calls for your particular talents' he flicked open the document, 'this target needs to be taken care of immediately. We cannot have him making problems for us any longer'

'What is the time frame?' asked Kapusta

'You have a fortnight to take care of it, it will be the usual arrangement' he pushed he file across the table toward the assassin.

Kapusta opened up the first page and read the target's name. If his face had more elasticity you would have read surprise on it, this followed by a grin that stretched his scarred skin painfully.

'Da, priyatno' said Kapusta

19 - Too hot in Mexico

Alex looked around Graham's apartment for any sort of clue as to who had done this to him. He found two of the three casings laying on the floor in the living room. On closer inspection he could tell they were from a PSS, a Soviet made 'silent' pistol, in England they called it 'the woolly'. The pistol had been developed for the 'Spetsnaz', Special Purpose Forces branch of the KGB back in the 80's, its sole use for assassinations. Alex wondered what the hell it was doing here in Mexico. Graham's hypothesis was valid, it must be the Soviets. Alex carried on searching. He sat at Graham's desk and fired up the laptop. As it was warming up Alex checked the drawers and flicked through the pile of old post sitting on the desk. One thing caught his eye, a letter that looked familiar, he had seen one just like this before. He turned it over in his hands trying to think of where he had seen it and put it to one side on the feeling that it may be important. The laptop showed it's start screen, but just as Alex thought, it was password protected. There was no way he could hazard a guess at Graham's pass code even though they made it look so easy in the movies. Three guesses and you're locked out of the system for 24 hours. He had a crack at it anyway, there was nothing to lose at this stage. He tried Graham's initials then date of birth - no. Next his official MI5 id - no again. Last try, his favourite film, Point Break - that was it, locked out. Damn it.

Alex took the envelope and turned it over in his hands looking at it more closely. When he took out the sheet of paper inside the envelope he realised that he had received the exact same thing in the post a few months back just before his blackouts had started. It was a sheet of paper with Graham's name and address in the top left hand corner, a short statement about having won a prize and a large complex QR code in the centre of the sheet. What was odd about the page was that there was no other information regarding who had sent the letter or what you could win, and it wasn't in an envelope you would consider to be a piece of junk mail, it was made of high quality, heavy stationary. He would compare it to his own letter at home, if he ever got that far. Also he must try and find out if Dan and Jimmy had received anything similar.

He put the letter in his pocket, took another last look around the apartment and headed for the door. He would call the authorities when he got a safe distance away. He couldn't get caught up in a local investigation, his priority now was to get to Deanna. He noticed that the Doubletap was still tucked up on the shelf, the assassin must have overlooked the gun in his haste to flee the scene, either that or it had been of no use to him.

He cursed himself now for leaving Gregg's Triumph back in the plaza outside the café. He would waste precious time getting back there. However he did not need to be so surreptitious this time, so he ran directly to the plaza mounted the bike and started her up. Then a thought struck him, where was he going? He had no idea where they would have taken Deanna or what he needed to trade to get her back. He fished the scrap of paper out of his pocket along with his cell phone and dialled the number. No-one picked up, it rang for what felt like an eternity before it went to voicemail, then a message was read out in a thick European accent; 'TL99 1284 3pm Friday' Alex knew immediately that that it was map coordinates and from memory he could judge that it was somewhere in Essex in the UK, although he would have to search the web to find the exact site. He quickly typed in the coordinates into his cell phone; Severalls Hospital, Colchester. It was a derelict lunatic asylum built in the early 20th century and closed down in 1997. It meant he had two days to get back to England, try to find Jimmy and solve this riddle and then do everything in his power to get Deanna back. He opened the clutch on the Triumph and headed for the nearest airport. At least he was heading home

20 - Darkness for Deanna

She opened her eyes but could see only blackness. She tried to call out but found her mouth gagged. She tried to move her hands but they were bound behind her back. Panic began to grow in the pit of her stomach, she had trouble catching her breath through the rag which filled her mouth, her heart thumping audibly in her chest. Hysteria spread through her limbs creating a numbness that she fought to gain control over, otherwise she knew she could all too easily lose her capacity for rationality. Her first operation in the field and she had ended up a hostage, her life at risk, her mission in jeopardy. Osterman was going to be pissed off, she thought absurdly, overlooking the fact that she might not see him again. Her mind wandered to Alex. What had happened to him? Was he dead? She started to put things together slowly, making an objective connection of the dots, although there were not too many dots to connect at this stage. Strangely, working things out analytically began to calm her. She was not yet dead. That was a good thing. Her kidnappers obviously had use of her. She was being transported somewhere. Again, positive news. She was of value to someone. Who? The Spaniard? What was his name? Quiros? Somehow she didn't think it would be him.

The vehicle in which she was being transported came to a halt. She heard voices outside and strained to listen for any type of clue as to who the kidnappers might be. Now movement; the trunk she was in was lifted out of the vehicle and thrown roughly onto a hard surface. The impact made her head ache from the noise it made within the trunk, she began to feel nauseous. Now movement again, a short distance, then being lifted once more to another position and shoved along sideways until the trunk banged into something metallic. There she rested until she could hear the jet engines of the plane begin to whine. The plane taxied and within minutes they were airborne. She began to feel the cold ten minutes after take-off, within half an hour she was shivering. All her energy was now directed at keeping warm, the time had now passed for lucid thought, the cold became all-consuming. She closed her eyes in the dark.

21 - Remembering

A s Alex rode the bike along the desolate stretch of desert towards the airport he kept catching glimpses of memories flash before his eyes, nothing much at first; vague glimmers of another plane journey, being in a motel maybe, drinking and laughing, being furtive and surreptitious, being back on American soil; why?, he wasn't sure. All these little snippets did not make any sense to him, he needed more to be able to piece things together. He recalled being happy for the first time in a long while. Could that be down to Deanna? As he guided the bike along a straight stretch of road he let his mind relax to see if he could dredge up any specific details of the last week. He recalled well enough the set-to with the Spanish thugs at the farmhouse. They were lucky to get out of that mess alive. It was after that things got hazy. They were driving, on Spanish roads, there were explanations from both sides; he learned that Deanna had been assigned to him because the CIA knew that Alex was privy to classified information relating to US sleepers tactically positioned in Eastern Europe. He was shocked and offended that Bharat would have signed off on having him tailed, especially by CIA. He could be trusted. He had proved his loyalty over and again. How could they doubt him?

All of a sudden a memory came back to him in a rush; he had let himself into a house owned by a man named Gregg. He knew that there would be transportation there that they could use. That was where the bike had come from, they had stolen it. Deanna had said to him that they were only borrowing it. Who was Gregg? he had asked; an ex-boyfriend she had said, Deanna just happened to have kept a key to his apartment. The bike, he recalled now, was necessary to evade the two men tailing them both. That was why the motel made sense now, they were hiding out, planning their next move. Deanna suggested coming to the US for safety reasons, to bring Alex in, to protect him. They had severely underestimated who they were dealing with if that was the case, these people would stop at nothing to get their hands on him.

Alex made it to Tucson International in 2 hours 25 minutes. He abandoned Gregg's Triumph outside the terminal assuming that he would get the bike back at some point. He dropped the Doubletap into one of the bike's panniers, the expectation that Gregg might have some trouble explaining that to the authorities gave Alex a buzz of sadistic satisfaction, especially after learning how he had treated Deanna. He grabbed Graham's laptop and went directly to the Delta desk. There he booked a red-eye flight to London Heathrow getting him back onto home soil at 7am the next morning.

The booking agent gave Alex a sideways look as there weren't many people who checked in to such a long flight without any luggage. Alex didn't even have a carry-on bag. But after checking Alex's passport and seeing the payment accepted through the credit card he had no reason to delay Alex, especially as he was paying through the nose for a last minute booking. The concourse was busy with people from all walks of life, wandering in every direction, some with purpose and some with the usual airport fatigue you acquire by travelling too often; businessmen, families, couples and the usual hippy contingent of travelers looking out of place in such modern surroundings. Alex was well used to airports and knew the best thing to do now was to grab a coffee, something to eat and try to get some shut-eye whilst waiting for boarding.

As he sat there on the uncomfortable chair in the lounge unable to let his mind turn off, his thoughts kept dancing around the abduction of Deanna and the death of his friend Graham. Could he have done anything differently? How could he have known events would have played out the way they did? The blame lay squarely at his feet, he should have known, he should have protected the people who were relying on him. The only thing to concentrate on now was saving the people who could be saved and he resolved he would do all in his power to do so. First Deanna then Jimmy. He couldn't let them down.

After an uneventful flight which he made the best of by resting while also avoiding the eye of the stewards, he arrived in London to a fine drizzle, as was the norm this time of year. He had nothing on him except the clothes he was standing in, his wallet, his passport and his cell phone. He called Graves upon leaving the customs gate and told him he would be back home in an hour and for him to meet him at the apartment. Then, knowing it would be needed, he took a detour into Burberry and bought a navy blue double breasted Pea Coat with his platinum card. Ripping the labels off, he donned the coat as he strode through the concourse and walked out into the cool fresh air jumping into the first black taxi-cab in the rank. Alex gave his home address, he then sat back considering his next move.

Alex took out his cell phone and looked up Jimmy Mitchell's contact details. He tried calling him but got no answer, instead he left a message for him to get in touch urgently. He tried his landline on the off chance, but again got nothing. He then contacted his boss at MI5, Anil Bharat, who picked up on the first ring. Alex couldn't explain in much detail over the phone as to what was going on but Anil got the message that something was up and that they needed to sit down face to face as soon as possible. Alex said he was looking for Jimmy and could Anil do some digging as to where he might be. They arranged to meet at headquarters after lunch, giving Alex a chance to get home, change his clothes and freshen up a bit.

The traffic in West London was as usual horrendous. Someone in a dirty white van had decided it would be a good idea to drink his morning coffee on the way to work, spilled it on his trousers and ended up veering his van into the barrier on the Hammersmith flyover, blocking a lane and making the journey take twice as long as it should have done. Every car that passed the grimy white van had to slow down and peer at it to check out just how much damage had been done and if anyone had been injured, after all it would be interesting water-cooler chat for first tea break at work later on. They also needed a justifiable excuse for why they were late for work themselves. It never ceased to amaze Alex just how many people travelled in and out of London on a daily basis. Statistically he supposed the accident rate on the roads was probably rather modest, but one inconsequential accident or incident usually caused enough mayhem on a daily basis to bring traffic to a crawl. Even though Alex owned a few vehicles, driving them in London gave him no pleasure, he would revert to the underground to get about more often than not. The Underground system itself was quite a spectacle at rush hour, with over 3.5 million passengers a day using the trains. While watching the constant stream of never ending people pass through the same spot in a station, life begins to take on strange and new meaning. Where do they all come from? Where can they all possibly be going? It gives one pause to wonder. If you consider the evidence of averages you would be looking at all of human nature pass you by; murderers and paedophiles, alcoholics and drug addicts, sadists and fetishists, thieves and criminals, plus every other deviant and freak you could name, all filing past you pretending to be normal, and Alex knew by experience that there was no such thing as normal when it came to mankind.

When Alex reached his home he gave the taxi driver the £75 fare and travelled straight up to the apartment in the lift. At the doorway, just about to leave, was Madeline Ashwood, the lady who kept his living quarters in order.

'Madash! God, am I glad to see you! How on earth are you?' he asked

'I am quite well thank you, young man. And I don't know how many times I have to tell you but I do not like to be called that. I much prefer Madeline, or Ms Ashwood, or Maddy... anything but Madash' she chided him, 'but you know that already, don't you?'

Alex gave her a warm smile and held out his arms, Maddie gave him a warm embrace and said 'Welcome back Alexander, I've been worried sick over you. Are you alright?'

'I'm fine. Really, I am. Well physically anyway. Mentally we'll have to wait and see... and no clever remarks please. You can't be going already?'

'I was just about to leave because there really is nothing to do since you've been away. I just pop by every day out of habit'

'Please stay and have a cup of tea with me. I've had a long journey and I'm so glad to see a friendly face. Will you stay for lunch? Graves will be here shortly and I'll get something delivered in' he asked

'I'll stay for tea but no lunch for me thank you, even though most of the UK is still eating its breakfast but not to worry. I have to watch this figure of mine, and I know you, you will order in pizza more than likely'

'OK. Tea it is. I'll even make it, how's that?'

'Perfect' she said, 'Darjeeling if you have it, darling' knowing full well he would have it.

Madeline sat down at the kitchen island where there were four bar stools. She sat with her back straight and one leg crossed over the other with her hands resting on her knee. She was a fine looking woman. As far as Alex knew she had never married, but not for the want of suitors. In her younger days Alex was sure she would have been a femme fatale, she exuded sexual confidence even now, twenty or thirty years ago she would have been a man-eater. She was always dressed to the nines regardless of what she had to do around the apartment; she had a classic style all of her own that you didn't see much nowadays. Alex was curious why she had taken the job with him, it didn't appear to be in her wheelhouse. He didn't mind though, it turned out they got along very well indeed and if she was willing to stay on he was glad to have her.

'Now' began Alex, 'what has been happening while I've been away?' handing her the tea.

'I'm more interested in your story Alexander. Where have you been? The last time I heard you were on the way to Spain and then... nothing. Why didn't you get in touch?'

'I met a girl' said Alex deflecting the real question.

'Oh, I see' said Maddie rolling her eyes in mock annoyance 'That's typical, off for a romantic break, were you? Tell me more. What is she like?'

'I wish. Nothing quite so simple. Anyway, you know me, Maddie, never straightforward or easy. She's an American for starters. Her name is Deanna, I think, well, I'm pretty sure it is. No, nearly positive'

'You don't know?'

'Let me put it this way. That's what she told me her name was. I told you it wasn't straightforward. We got together in Madrid. She saved my life. She saved a lot more than that as well' he paused, 'I'm in a lot of trouble Maddie. There are people after me. Do you remember Graham?'

'Of course I do, how is he?'

'Dead' he said flatly

'Oh my God! Dead? How? When?'

'Yesterday. I was with him in Santa Ana. I didn't see him murdered but I was... I should have been... it was all my fault, I should have been there for him. First of all the guys at Navarre, now the remaining men of Delta are all being picked off. And I don't know why. Dan as well. Graham told me he had been killed, murdered' Alex held his face in his hands, 'There's only me and Jimmy left. I have to try and get to him and warn him what's going on, before it's too late, if it's not already. I'm going to go over to his place as soon as I've seen Graves. Then into Thames House to see Anil'

'And what about this Deanna person, where is she?'

'That's another problem altogether. She's been taken'

'How do you mean 'taken'?'

'Kidnapped I suppose you would call it. She disappeared in Santa Ana and I was left a message with coordinates here in London. I can only assume that I can get her back in exchange for something, only I don't know what' he said, 'The doctor in Spain said he wanted information'

'What doctor?' Maddie was becoming understandably confused

'Another long, convoluted story, which I will tell you, over a glass of wine, when this is all done. I promise'

'How do you know you can trust this woman? How much do you know about her? Are you sure she didn't leave you the note?'

'Too many questions, Ms Ashwood, I have my gut feeling and the fact that she has been the one who has kept me safe for nearly a week when bad people have been after me'

They both heard keys jangling in the door and Alex stiffened, out of instinct ready to take action but as soon as he saw Graves emerge from the hall he relaxed.

'Mr Graves, good to see you' Alex said

'Welcome back, sir. Now, how can I be of assistance?' he asked

'Straight to the point, as always, eh? Graves. Wouldn't you like a cup of tea with us first?'

'No thank you, sir. I have many things to do, if you would be so kind. I am not in a position to dilly-dally'

Alex knew that Graves could be abrupt to the point of rudeness, he wondered if he was like that with everyone or just him. He had been with him so long now that Alex was more than used to his brusqueness.

'Well, I need a car. Which one is running the best today?'

'That would be the Citroen, sir' he replied 'Will you be taking her out far?'

'No, not far Graves' he said, then pulled the envelope out of his breast pocket 'By the way, I need you to go through all the post that's on file and see if you can find a letter similar to this one. It's very important and cannot wait, OK?'

'Of course, sir, right away' he said, 'Shouldn't take me more than an hour, how far back would I need to go?'

'About four months' said Alex, 'Now I must get cleaned up and get going, time is of the essence, I will see you both soon'

22 - Thames House

Alex pulled the Citroen into a space outside The City Café not far from Thames House, he cut the V6 and listened to the engine of the car ticking as it was cooling down. He picked up Graham's laptop and stepped onto the pavement pausing to turn back and admire the car, even though it had been in production before he was born, the SM was a very special vehicle. It was Citroens finest hour as far as Alex was concerned, there was a reason they called her Sa Majesté. Modern cars all looked the same to him now with only a few exceptions. In the seventies and eighties cars were unique and individual to their manufacturer, you could tell instantly between a Saab and a Volvo, they had personality. He pondered whether he held more stock in his cars than with the women who came and went through his life. He had never been able to find the right woman, one who engaged him on all the levels he needed; emotionally, sexually, but most importantly of all intellectually. He had loved in the past, of course, but there was always something missing, his relationships rarely lasted more than two months and it was usually Alex who ended them. Since the job in the Pyrenees he had denied himself even the thought of trying to make himself happy, he felt he didn't deserve that level of contentment. After his six month 'sabbatical' he had buried himself in his work at Thames House. He wasn't reclusive but he had been more withdrawn, to the point where Anil had mentioned it to him in a brotherly way; 'You need to get out more Alex, get back into the world, all work and no play etc. etc.' Alex took it all on board but would only be able to move on, he knew, when he could make some peace regarding the deaths of his team members.

He locked the car up and took the shortcut through Art Street which brought him out onto Thorney Street. Walking the short distance to the rear entrance of Thames House he nodded to the security guard at the door who he know only by sight and entered the building to undergo the usual security checks. He was to show his credentials and walk through the recently installed, state-of-the-art metal detector where he put the laptop and his wallet and keys onto the belt for x-raying. The two guards scanning the images did not look up at him as he passed through.

Once inside he turned left into the more modest half of the building and took the stairs up to the sixth floor to where his offices were situated overlooking Horseferry Road. You could not see Lambeth Bridge from the offices because the angle of the building obscured it but the view across to Victoria Tower Gardens and over the Thames was quite spectacular.

Alex found Anil sitting in his office, papers spread out in front of him on his desk, phone cradled to his ear and tapping keys on his laptop, he seemed to be doing more listening than talking. When he saw Alex he held up a finger and gestured for him to take a seat on the opposite side of the desk. Alex put the laptop down and sat, looking around the office with new eyes. He had not noticed before now the amount of oak panelling in the room, the chair he sat in was leather, the type that gets softer with age, the carpet expensively luxuriant for a civil servant. Anil sat at a desk that would probably take six men to lift, it was quite a substantial piece being made from African Blackwood, a close relative to ebony. His eyes wandered to the window where he looked out on the London skyline. It gave him a brief moment of satisfaction and contentment to be back in the throng of his metropolis. His mind then returned to the problem at hand and his face darkened; Deanna, he needed to get her back and find the bastards who killed Dan and Graham. Anil finished on the phone.

'Alex, thank God, am I glad to see you. You look like shit, you know that?' he said holding out his hand to shake

Alex nodded and grinned 'Yeah, I know, it's been a tough few days'

Alex then continued, getting Anil up to speed regarding all that he could remember over the last few days. He had blank periods that he could not account for but told Anil all about leaving for Madrid, meeting with Quiros, realising he had been duped and a CIA agent coming to his rescue. Then on to the US with Deanna, seeing the doctor, acquiring the motorbike, hiding out in a motel, being chased by two men in a sedan. Then lastly finding Graham dead, learning of Dan's death and Deanna disappearing with only a map coordinate to go on.

Anil listened in silence for over an hour nodding now and then but keeping all his questions until Alex had finished. Occasionally he looked out of the window while Alex spoke, sometimes he closed his eyes as if in deep thought. Alex knew he would be analyzing every aspect of the story.

'First of all I have to ask you Alex; what the fuck do you think you were doing going to Madrid on your own without my backing? You were damn lucky the CIA had tabs on you otherwise you could be as dead as Dan and Graham are now. I should suspend you for being so reckless'

Alex assumed he was being rhetorical so wisely kept his mouth shut and let Anil vent his anger.

'I can't believe I'm going to have to get in touch with CIA now and tell them we have 'lost' one of their operatives. Do you know what sort of shitstorm you have created? And a man dead in Madrid! FUCK! No end of red tape' He pounded the table in frustration. 'Apart from all that,' he said calming down slightly, 'I can see that there is more to this than we can surmise at the moment. You say it could be the Russians but I am not so sure, our relations of late have been friendly to the point of cooperative. The cold war is over, Alex. It may very possibly be someone else'

'It may officially be over, but as long as we have cells in Eastern Europe you and I both know that's bullshit. There is still a mistrust between East and West. If you don't want to call it the Cold War call it something else, but it's still real, you know that.

'OK. Of course I do. But we're also in the business of looking like we get on with our former enemies. This is the time of happy-clappy World Peace. We need to be seen to be doing the honorable thing, whether we are or not. You know as well as I do we have to play the game. Listen, we will strip the laptop for any information we can glean' Anil continued, 'but if Graham wasn't targeted as you and Dan have been I don't see what we will find' he paused a moment, 'I am going to hold off getting in touch with Langley until you have had your meet tomorrow. Then we will know more'

'I need to go alone, you know that. We can't risk going in heavy and losing her. If you let me go in alone we can have backup on standby' said Alex

'What if you're wrong? What if they kill you both?'

'No. I don't think that's in their plan. They need me. And as long as they need me Deanna will be safe. Let me go and let me end this'

'And you say you haven't been able to get in touch with Jimmy Mitchell?'

'No, I visited his house before coming here. It's empty. Been that way for a few days judging by the post' he said, 'Let me know as soon as you find him. I'm not going to lose another man from Delta. I'll be damned if I will'

Just then Alex's phone beeped saying he had an incoming message. He glanced at it and learned that Graves had found the envelope and could confirm it to be an exact match to the one he had been given earlier.

Twenty Three - Nightmares

He was once again back in Navarre, the explosion ringing in his ears, he could hear nothing else apart from the high pitched whine of ear drum damage, blood dribbling from his ears onto his neck. He was upright looking around at the devastation, his team-mates wounded lying around him, Alex Spellman on the ground with his face a mess of blood, debris strewn all around. Another body, he couldn't tell who, laying prone and not moving, he couldn't tell how bad the injuries were. His head began to swim, his surroundings losing focus, spinning away from him he tried to grab onto a nearby timber but instead fell on his face. The ground beneath him was dry and dusty, his mouth full of the acrid dirt, he coughed until his body entered into a spasm and after retching he threw up bile along with the dust from his throat. He lay this way for long enough for his pain receptors to kick in. The discomfort began as a tingling and grew steadily until it became an all consuming agony. Blood was oozing from his stomach, soaking in to the dry dusty ground. He looked down and probed the wound with his fingers. He began to sob, felt sure he was going to die. He couldn't comprehend what had happened. It was all like a dream, except for the pain, the pain made it real. He must have passed out, a survival mechanism of the body. When he regained consciousness he was in some new kind of hell, the pain had abated, he could still not hear anything from his damaged ears, he could not see a thing, the brightness of the lights blinding him to the point that it hurt to open them, he could hear voices all around him, but could not understand the language, he tried to pick out words or meanings from the chaos. The effort became too much, he let his head drop back onto the hard cold surface and let his mind leave his body, floating away into the ether and began imagining he was now looking down on himself. What he saw was his damaged body laying on a pristine operating table with all of the most eminent surgeons around him industriously making him well, fixing his torn body, stitching his wounds, nursing him back to health. The room itself so clean it almost glowed, shiny metallic surfaces you could see your face in, surgical instruments glinting in the bright light. He imagined he saw pretty nurses attending to the doctors, wiping their brows of sweat when they needed it, offering utensils for the operating procedure. He liked the way the nurses didn't need to wear masks in the theatre, he could see their pretty made-up faces and noticed how the dresses they wore showed off their fine legs. Were nurses allowed to wear heels in the operating theatre? The doctors had their hair done in elaborate styles the way film stars wore their hair in the forties, two of them had moustaches and reminded him of Errol Flynn or Clark Gable

A surge of intense pain brought him crashing back down to reality. He cried out and when he looked again at the doctors and nurses tending to him he became frightened. Their faces were now twisted and ugly, grimacing at him, their eyes bloodshot and staring. He tried to move his limbs to get himself off the table but he was unable. Out of the blue came a crash, an explosion, the nurse to his left slumped over him after being torn apart by the blast, her eyes staring at him vacantly, blood dribbling from her mouth. The white walls of the surgery were now drenched with blood and viscera, he could hear screams in the distance, moans from nearer by, pain and destruction all around. Through the smoke he saw four figures standing motionless; he recognized Cole, Chapman, Watts and West, where their eyes once were now just black pits of nothingness. They raised their arms in front of them searching, reaching, hands grasping for anything to grab on to, like a zombies vacant quest for blood. Cole's mouth opened and a snake's head slithered out of the orifice and began twisting its way around his neck then down onto the floor. Beetles and centipedes then began to crawl out of the nurse's mouth and scuttle towards him up the bedclothes, he closed his mouth tightly and squeezed his eyes shut hoping they would all go away. After a moment the noise abated so he opened his eyes and immediately wished he hadn't; four faces loomed over him, no eyes in their sockets, the stench of death bearing down on him, eight hands covering his face, blocking his vision, cutting off his airway, he felt himself choking, he struggled for breath.....

He awoke covered in sweat, tears in his eyes, hands made into fists grabbing onto the sheets around him. It took more than fifteen minutes for his heart to return to anywhere near normal, the pain in his chest remained for longer, his head and neck ached from the strain of the contortions. It was the second time this week that he had experienced such a vivid nightmare, they were becoming more frequent, regardless that the doctor had said they should be diminishing. The drugs he had been given to keep him calm were not working, he had stopped taking them weeks ago. He couldn't take it any longer, there had to be a way to stop the nightmares, to make some sense of what happened, to arrive at some sort of closure, he was too young to have his life ruined, he would never have a relationship if he woke up screaming most nights. It was Spellman. Spellman was to blame, it was all his fault, he had checked the equipment, he led the team, it was his responsibility. For months now a growing ball of fury had been growing in his stomach. It started off as a need for somebody to blame, to put a face to the destruction, for his growing inability to cope with everyday life, his frustration at not being able to be normal any more. He hated Spellman for taking away his life, for ruining him, for killing his friends and brothers-in-arms. He would pay, one way or another he would pay. He would achieve retribution for his teammates by seeking retribution on the man responsible

Mistakes Paid For

Anatoli Petrakis loomed over the Spaniard sitting gagged and bound to the wooden chair, his eyes pleading with the Russian to his left. Petrakis was muscular to the point of caricature, his white t-shirt straining as his biceps flexed beneath the thinly stretched material, the sinews in his thick neck standing out in sharp relief, his head atop his huge body looking insufficiently trivial by comparison. In one hand he held a pair of gardening secateurs, the other hand pinning down the Spaniard's forearm to the arm of the chair. 'You think because I am far away I will not find out?' said the Russian 'You think after all these years you could double-cross me? I do not expect a confession from you. I simply want you to know that I will not tolerate insolence' he nodded to Petrakis. Petrakis pressed down heavily on the Spaniard's wrist while grasping his pinkie between the blades of the secateurs. Slowly and with some relish Petrakis squeezed the handles together until the skin and bone between the blades split and crunched under the force. The Spaniard screamed out from behind his gagged mouth, the pain all consuming, tears seeping from the corner of his terrified eyes. With one last squeeze the finger dropped onto the floor and blood dripped from the stump. The Russian picked it up and threw it in the trash can. The Spaniard slumped forward as if the effort had been too much for him. Petrakis looked at the Russian with raised eyebrows, again the Russian nodded. He repeated the process again, this time with his ring finger, although this one proved to need more pressure to sever it from the hand. Petrakis, though, had strength in abundance for the task. The Spaniard passed out this time, long before his finger fell to the floor. It was probably for the best, thought the Russian. 'Bandage his wounds and make sure he is comfortable' he told Petrakis, 'we will still be needing the doctor's expertise'

XXIV - The Crux of it

After separating from Alex Spellman and the rest of the unit Jack Cole entered the shack with Derek West to set the charges for blowing the ammo dump. Chapman and Watts were outside keeping watch as planned. Jack hoisted his pack off his back to get at the equipment. He took out the detonators and plastic explosive and began to set the fuses. Derek was doing the same. There was no chatter, only deadly concentration. This was a job that needed total precision. Jack was keeping an eye on West though, every thirty seconds glancing over his shoulder to check his progress. Timing was critical.

Jack Cole saw that West had nearly completed his part of the job. Silently Cole took his SOG Daggert serrated hunting knife out of his pack and took two steps over to West. West, out of curiosity and about to question Cole, turned his head to see what he was up to as there wasn't any time for deviation. That was the moment Cole grabbed the hair on the back of West's head and pulled it back and exposing his neck. Just as West was about to call out Cole opened up his throat with the Sog cutting off any sound before it had the chance to escape. West looked at Cole in confusion as his life force ebbed away. As the vitality disappeared out of West's eyes Cole let his head and body gently down onto the wooden floor where West's vital fluids seeped out in between the boards.

As quietly as he could Cole made his way to the back of the shed where there should have been an escape route left for him, the only job his two watchers needed to do in advance. He searched around not finding an obvious exit. He began to panic. If he were to get stuck in this damn shed he would be blown to smithereens along with everything else. Then he saw it, at the back of the shed in the corner. Part of the corrugated iron had been pulled away from the timber, not much, but enough for him to crawl through. He got down on his belly and pushed open the rough rusty metal, slowly wriggling, all too aware of how long it was taking, gradually inch by inch getting his upper body through the gap all the while painfully aware that it was taking longer than it should have. Once out he could see where he had to go, into the thick of the forest to find the rendezvous point. He wriggled on his stomach until he felt it was safe to get up and make a run for the trees, it was imperative that no-one from the team saw him, if they did it would all be for nought. Cole was off the ground and upright making his way gingerly towards the trees when, rather than hearing the explosion, he felt himself being thrown forward with the force of a bus hitting him from behind. He was thrown off his feet, into the air and into the trunk of a Douglas fir knocking him out, leaving him with broken maxilla and zygomatic bones in his face, a broken rib, a punctured lung, pieces of wooden shrapnel impaled into his shoulder and his upper thigh and severe burns on his head, face and neck.

This was how Casimir Sitko and Vanya Prazak found him once the dust had settled.

25 - The Madhouse

Bartosz Krol and Jurek Wesolek lifted the trunk out of the rear of the pick-up truck. They looked to Anatoli Petrakis, who was standing at the doorway holding a crowbar, to get an idea where it then needed to be taken. The big Greek stood there looking at the two men with unintentional menace, his face when resting fell into a natural scowl. The two Poles were understandably wary of the man, his sheer size and strength made them both uncomfortable. Wesolek thought to himself that the Greek looked absurd with such a diminutive head stuck on an oversized body, although it was not a thought he would share with anyone else, not even Krol. Anatoli gestured with a flick of his bald head to follow him into the building. The two Poles struggled with the trunk as it was a dead weight; they couldn't get a proper grip on it as the handles were too high on the sides. They shuffled slowly toward the doorway Anatoli had disappeared through, banging their shins on the trunk as they walked. By the time they were inside Krol was sweating and swearing in Polish under his breath. Judging by his size, Krol reckoned that Petrakis could have carried the trunk in by himself.

Their eyes took a while to get accustomed to the gloom in the hospital, they couldn't see immediately which way Petrakis had gone. Then they heard a grunt from the corridor to their left so they followed the direction of the noise. The corridor was strewn with derelict gurneys and furniture that had been left to decay. Nature had begun to reclaim parts of the building; tufts of grass poked up through the tiles seeking the sunlight that shone through the windows and plants reached their green tendrils through the broken panes like long fingers probing. The paint on the walls and ceilings was peeling and flaking, plaster hanging off in places showing the red brick beneath. Eighteen years of neglect had turned what was once a beautiful building into a squalid and wretched atrocity.

Severalls had been designed and built in the Echelon style whereby no staff working there would need to exit the interior to gain access to any other part of the building. Seen from above you could say that it took the shape of the head of a flower, the main entrance being the stigma and the wards being the petals, the central part of the hospital could be considered the ovule, an area where the admin offices, laundry, kitchens and of course the operating theatres were situated; this was where the trunk was now being taken. At its peak the doctors of Severalls were pioneers in performing ground-breaking techniques in the treatment of the mentally ill. They would experiment with 'electro-convulsive therapy' and often perform lobotomies to further their research. Work had begun a few years back to refurbish and modernize certain areas of the hospital. This involved carpenters and electricians on site replacing and refitting all that had been left to decay and rot. It was a long term project for the company Latimer & Lacey who had sometimes up to fifteen men working there throughout the year, and because of this the workmen generally left their tools and equipment on site and locked up. The hospital was quiet at the moment as it was holiday for the workers. Whether they liked it or not Latimer & Lacey shut down for two weeks at this time of year - if the workforce wanted to get away for a holiday this was their opportunity.

Krol and Wesolek found Petrakis in a room decorated in red staring at the wall. It wasn't until they were fully inside the room they could see he was looking at a mural that had been painted there. They dropped the trunk and joined Petrakis taking in the scene. The vista was of boats bobbing on the ocean in front of a town with the sun setting behind the hills in the distance. The style was almost childish but it reminded Petrakis of his home; Mandraki on the island of Nisyros in the Dodecanese Islands of Greece. He wished he was back there and not on this damp and dull island of British complainers, working with these two Polish idiots. Even living on an active volcano would be preferable to dealing with these fools, he thought.

A knocking interrupted their reverie. The two Poles looked at each other then both looked at Petrakis. They all stood for a moment listening, wondering where the noise could be coming from. When it dawned on them simultaneously that the noise was coming from inside the trunk they all nodded imperceptibly at each other. It was the woman. The 'bait'. She had obviously become conscious during the journey and was now sensing that she had come to a halt somewhere and was urging to be let out again. This had been happening the whole journey, every now and again muffled cries from inside the trunk, banging and knocking. It was so inconvenient when trying to manoeuvre a body, a living body. Petrakis knew all too well that a dead body in transit was far less trouble. She would need to be let out briefly so she could attend to herself. Even though it had only taken ninety minutes to get from Southend International Airport, it had been a twelve hour flight and she had only been given a bathroom break once while in the air.

Petrakis took out his knife and severed the zip tie holding the lid shut on the trunk. Deanna pushed out with her bound hands and the lid flew open, at once regretting the action as the bright light from the window almost blinded her fragile eyes. She tried to scream at her captors through the gag but her cries were muffled. Instead she soon realised that her shouts were hopeless and seeing that there were three of them decided to remain passive, at least for the time being.

Petrakis leaned into the trunk and grabbed Deanna round the waist with one arm. Putting his face close up to hers he raised a finger to his lips and urged her not to try and make any more sound, then lifted her out and placed her on the cold tiled floor. Deanna was relieved just to be out of that damn trunk at long last, she wasn't sure how long she had been in there but she knew that the department would be getting a chiropractor's bill. If she ever got out of this alive that was. Once her eyes had adjusted she could see the room she was in and it filled her with apprehension. The three men looked at her with a mixture of curiosity and distaste. The man-mountain with the small head came towards her with a gleaming hunting knife in hand, she could see her reflection in its blade and closed her eyes tight at what was to come. He knelt down and cut the zip tie holding her wrists together behind her back then did the same with the one around her ankles, Deanna's legs trembled with relief. The gag however stayed put.

Bartosz Krol helped Deanna to her feet and took her to the bathroom while Petrakis and Wesolek entered the room next door. Here they found all the locked tool chests belonging to the carpenters. With the crowbar he had brought along Petrakis opened them all one after the other, he made it look as easy as opening ring pulls on soda cans. He was looking for one thing in particular. Inside each chest was a variety of power tools; as well as chisels, saws and hammers. He searched until he found the power cable he was after. In the centre of the room was a bench saw, the type that has a rotating blade protruding from the table top to allow sheets of timber to be slid along and cut to size. He plugged the machine in and checked that it was working, the blade instantly spinning at such a speed that would easily cut through four inches of any type of wood. Petrakis thought back to when his uncle Nik had been cutting wood for wardrobes back in Mandraki. He had been feeding a length of timber through the machine when the wood had bucked on a jagged tooth from the blade, the piece of timber jumped and Uncle Nik's hand was jolted into the spinning blade. He was lucky to have only lost his thumb. Petrakis shuddered at the thought.

Meanwhile in the bathroom Krol kept a close eye on Deanna while simultaneously trying to maintain her privacy, although while she was in the stall he could not keep his eyes on her at all. Deanna needed to pee badly. She sat down with exaggerated care on the grimy toilet seat not wanting to touch it at all with her bare skin, she shivered with disgust and gave a little sob of disgust under her breath. While she sat there she scanned the area within the cubicle for anything that could be of any use to her but the bare tiles showed nothing. As far as she could tell it was bare. She would feel a lot better if she had some sort of back-up plan instead of being at the mercy of these three thugs. When she had finished she stood and turned to flush the lavatory, she was surprised when nothing happened. She leaned forward and tried again, still nothing. She heard Krol step up to the cubicle and give two sharp knocks letting her know to hurry up. That was when she noticed something on the floor almost hidden from view near the u-bend of the waste pipe. She bent over and gingerly searched with her fingertips around the floor where she thought it was. She felt something metallic and grasped at it trying not to make any noise on the bathroom tiles. When she saw what she had recovered it made her feel as if she was still in with a chance, at least she would be able to go down fighting. A nail had been discarded due to having a jagged burr at the tip, a dud for a carpenter but something she could use to her advantage. She slipped the four inch nail into the waistband of her trousers just as Krol knocked again, this time more insistently. Deanna opened up and the first thing Krol had been told to do was zip tie her wrists again. She acquiesced meekly and held out her hands in front of her and was then led back to the red room to await proceedings. They sat her down on one of three chairs in the room and tied her with thick sash cord around her shoulders and waist. As Deanna sat her mind turned to Alex and all that they had been through in such a short time. It was only a few days ago that she would have done anything for Alex, she knew she was falling for him, she felt she needed a man like Alex in her life... well, that was then. Now she cursed Alex, and Osterman, for getting her into this mess, she was alone and scared, she only had herself to rely on, in the end it always came down to that fact; she was on her own.

26 - Uninvited

Alex had been in position for the last two hours, waiting patiently. He had spent his time researching Severalls on the internet and had a pretty good handle on how the buildings were laid out. He had also taken the opportunity to have a scout around for any escape routes or blocked passages. He had on him his serrated hunting knife with a 9.5" blade, a Walther P99 semi-automatic handgun which held nine rounds plus a delicate 3" Japanese bespoke dagger secreted in a holster under his sock. He didn't yet know how many men he would be up against or even *who* he would be encountering, the only thing for certain is that they wouldn't be handing Deanna over to him willingly, he was expecting a fight. The room he chose to lay in wait was in the central part of the complex, an area where if he were going to bring captives would be his choice. Many criminals did not have the originality to think outside of the box or to make unexpected decisions. In Alex's experience people up to no good generally made mistakes by being predictable, it was this predictability that he was going to use to his advantage. He was hoping that once he freed Deanna he would also have an ally in his fight, she had shown him already that she was useful in a tight situation.

He heard the pickup truck before he saw it and moved to the window to get a better look at the three men getting out of the cab. Two of them got out the side facing him and both lit cigarettes immediately. Then Alex saw the pickup truck rise at least six inches on its suspension as another man got out on the opposite side which was blocked from his view. The men proceeded to stand around as hired men usually do; not wanting to rush the job for fear they would not be worthy of their pay grade. They smoked and talked, putting off whatever needed to be done. Alex saw the third man round the rear of the truck and immediately the image of a bull sprang to mind, the only thing missing was the horns. The man was huge; he was wearing baggy weightlifters trousers but even these strained against his massively overworked quadriceps and his chiselled calf muscles. His upper body was equally formidable with pectoral muscles and deltoids clearly visible through the t-shirt he was wearing and his bare forearms showing brawn that you

159

rarely saw outside of weightlifting competitions. As Alex took in the whole man he realised that he looked almost comical; the oversized mass of muscle on the body making his head look insufficient by comparison, the bald head sitting on massive trapezius muscles practically making him a caricature. Alex knew by experience that this was not a man who would appreciate being ridiculed, he had created this body as an act of defiance; maybe he was bullied as a child or maybe he had a stutter, either way he should not be underestimated.

He watched them struggle taking the crate into the building not knowing what it contained. Alex was sizing up his adversaries all the time he was watching them, looking for weaknesses. He could already sense that the two Eastern European looking men were not in league with the muscle man, there was an apparent divide, he could tell by the way they stole glances behind his back. There was a definite lack of respect although there was certainly a heavy dose of fear. A fact he could work to his advantage.

They had been inside for a short while when Alex heard another vehicle approaching. He returned to the window and peered out curious to see who was now arriving at the party. Alex was shocked to see the Spaniard from Madrid get out of the car, he walked around to the rear passenger door and opened it to let out a man with a hood covering his head. The hooded man had his hands bound with a zip tie but he was allowed to walk unaided. The stocky Spaniard led his captive to the same entrance as the other men had used not too long ago. Alex couldn't put his finger on it, the hooded man looked familiar to him but he couldn't think why. He also noticed that the Spaniard did not have the same self-confidence now that he had shown in Madrid, something in him had changed, he somehow gave the appearance of a man cowed.

Quickly putting two and two together, Alex realised that the hooded man was, in fact, must be, Jimmy. It was the only possible solution. He was the last and final piece of this puzzle, it was also why he hadn't been able to contact him. The more he thought about the way the man walked the surer he became, even though he hadn't seen him in a long time. Now was his chance to not only get Deanna back but save Jimmy as well. He had always felt responsible for him, Alex had known that Jimmy looked up to him as a big brother figure and he was more than happy to take on the role. It was unfortunate that everything that had happened over the last few years had driven them further and further apart. Alex knew Jimmy had been seeing a psychiatrist and had been on medication for his PTSD. Alex had reached out to him frequently but Jimmy had become more and more withdrawn to the point where he cut ties with all remaining members of Delta team. Alex had only received news of his well-being through Anil who kept tabs on him through his official medical records.

It was now fast approaching 3pm, the time that the kidnapper had stipulated in the voicemail for Alex to be there. He had to think fast and hope to find some sort of breach in their defences so he could try and grab Jimmy. He had no idea where Deanna was in the equation, he would have to capture one of the men and make him lead him to her. It would need to be the Spanish doctor, the other three men were obviously hired thugs and may not be privy to information such as that. He was also eager to find out who was behind this whole operation, he had a feeling it was not just the doctor pulling all the strings, he felt there was much more to it.

Alex left his position of cover and stealthily moved down the corridor towards the room he knew they would have taken Jimmy to. He had his knife in hand, any attack at this stage he would want to keep silent. The Walther was within easy reach in a shoulder holster to be used as a last resort. He heard foreign voices and machinery being turned on and off, it sounded like a saw of some kind; Alex had seen all the tools and equipment left by the carpenters so he had a good idea where they were now situated. The corridor was desolate except for broken glass that had fallen from the windows covering the floor, presumably damaged by bored kids. The glass made it especially difficult to tread quietly, his feet making faint crunching sounds as he proceeded.

Alex decided now would be the time to implement his diversion. He had strategically placed compact grenades around Severalls and was hoping that the sound of the explosions would scatter the men to various parts of the building. He would be able to trigger the devices remotely from his smartphone via an M.O.D. app; it could handle up to ten devices which could then be detonated separately or all at once. He also had a bird's eye view of the blueprint of the building from real time satellite imagery which gave him his own position in the field as well. The really useful thing about the app was that he could track any other people in the vicinity by thermal imaging. The grenades were Dutch made V40s that had been refitted with potassium chloride for a smoke decoy and not for any damage they could cause, being roughly the same size as a golf ball made them very easy to transport and deploy.

27 - Seeking in the Asylum

Deanna sat tied with lengths of sash cord to the red chair, her wrists bound in front of her, the gag on her mouth remained. Her eyes however were taking in everything that went on within her view. She watched the three men come and go from the room she was in to another room where they would chatter in a language she could not understand. She heard machinery being switched on and off, for what reason she did not know, or rather she did not want to know. A million thoughts were going through her head trying to work out how she was going to get out of this predicament. She was no match for the three men who had brought her here, she had no weapon to speak of except for the jagged nail she had hidden in her waistband, she could barely move her tied arms. The only light that shone for her at the moment was the fact that her hands were now tied in front rather than behind her as they had been for the journey. She was sure that this was an oversight on her captors part and she was damn well going to exploit it at the soonest opportunity.

She sat mute as she heard footsteps approaching down the corridor. The other three men heard them too and came in from the equipment room to meet the new arrivals. Deanna was shocked to see it was the doctor from Madrid who now entered the room dragging with him a man who was also bound at the wrists but with a cloth sack covering his head. She noticed that the doctor had a bandage covering most of his left hand and it was apparent from the spotting of blood that he was missing at least two fingers. He glanced at her with contempt and then passed out of her view. The four of them didn't make much conversation. There was a palpable sense of discomfort between the doctor and the muscle man, they apparently communicated mostly through nods and gestures. Deanna guessed that was for her benefit; they wouldn't discuss their plans in earshot of her, she assumed they would have to communicate in a common language, probably English. They returned, all five of them now, to the room adjacent with the tools where again she could only hear vague conversational snippets which she could not piece together coherently.

Deanna saw this as an opportunity and began to wriggle her arms so that she could reach into her waistband for the nail. She had her back to the room the men had occupied so she tried to stay as still as possible while also trying to manoeuvre the piece of metal into her hands. It took her about five minutes as she had to stop frequently to listen for any approach from behind her, but eventually she had the nail in her hand and was able to begin rubbing at the plastic tie around her wrists. The burr on the nail's tip made it a bit easier to cut with, although it was still difficult work. Thank God the carpenter had thought this particular nail was unfit for use. The plastic was tough but slowly, bit by bit, the tie began to show signs of wear. This egged Deanna on seeing that her ministrations were making a difference. Just as the plastic tie was worn down to the point where Deanna could have pulled it apart with the force of her wrists she heard footsteps approaching from behind. She immediately tried to cover any evidence of her struggles and of the tie being cut and sat dead still. The man-mountain had entered the room and went to a bag that he had left in the corner. He bent down awkwardly, his muscles preventing him from making natural movements, and took out a thick pair of leather gloves, heavy like gauntlets. He rose again and shot a glance back to Deanna and once again put his finger up to his lips to communicate silence. Deanna was afraid that she would be caught out but the giant left the room apparently with other things on his mind. She almost felt as if she were secondary to their plans, something she could hopefully take advantage of. She made a final effort to break the tie almost letting the plastic cut into her skin. The plastic tie gave way with a jolt and at last she was free to untie herself from the chair. Before she did any of that she paused to consider the chain of events laid out before her; it was all very well being free but she needed to plan an escape that left no chance of being recaptured.

At that moment Deanna heard an almighty bang from another part of the building and took that as her opportunity to get out. The four men next door became suddenly animated, there were voices raised and orders shouted. The two Poles rushed through her room both reaching for their firearms as they ran. One of them glanced briefly at her but not long enough to realise that there was anything awry. When they had disappeared through the door she worked in earnest to get the rest of her ties free. Once she had achieved her liberty her aim was to flee the facility altogether, get out and not look back. However just as she was about to sneak out of the room she heard approaching footsteps. She picked up a wooden chair leg that was lying on the floor and pressed her back to the wall beside the doorway. Deanna saw a figure enter the room and quickly realised it was the doctor. He looked around in astonishment that the chair was now empty. Just as his eyes were about to land on Deanna she struck out with the length of timber. Learning from previous experience the doctor ducked his head just in time and the timber whipped past the top of his crown and into the door jamb. Deanna felt herself lose her balance and all of a sudden could feel the tables turning on her but she couldn't let herself be caught again. As her body tipped to one side she used the momentum to bring her leg up and launch it full force into the Spaniards stomach. Being the shape he was in this winded him and put him at the disadvantage. Deanna then held the nail in her closed fist with the tip poking out and brought it down across his face, bright red blood springing from his cheekbone where the nail had caught him. Quiros screamed in pain and Deanna made this her opportunity to escape. She fled for the door not looking back and turned into the corridor, running for all she was worth, away from the nightmare.

28 - Chaos reigns

Anatoli Petrakis had been left guarding the prisoner while Krol and Wesolek had gone to investigate the noise from within the building. He was becoming more and more concerned about the way in which this whole operation was being handled. Sloppy work meant that things got missed and if things were overlooked then that put him at risk. Anatoli had already spent eighteen months in Korydallos prison in Greece for a job that went wrong due to the amateurs he was working with. It should have been a purely straightforward tiger-kidnap of a 14 year old girl whose father ran the post office in Parikia on the island of Paros. The plan was to hold the girl hostage until her father had opened the safe which should have held at least €10,000. Unfortunately, all four of the men they were caught even before they had a chance to set their plan in motion. Spiros had been seen stealing the car they would use for the getaway and had been reported to the Hellenic Police. So they were tailed and then all of them picked up immediately after snatching the girl. Spiros had not told the rest of the team but he was wanted for previous crimes and there was a warrant out for his capture. The venture was doomed from its ill-conceived beginnings. Anatoli did not want to spend any more time behind bars but his abilities in this particular field were undeniable, he was suited too well for this type of work.

Quiros had gone into the next room to check on the girl. He had been gone only a few moments when Petrakis heard a scuffle. He made sure the ties on Mitchell were secure before heading into the red room to see what had happened. He found Quiros on the floor, blood oozing from his face and the girl gone. He must have bashed his head in the fall. He immediately stepped over Quiros and rushed after her, walking out into the corridor. He looked both ways but could not detect any clue to what direction she had taken. He pursued her in the direction they had entered the building, although she would not know which way that had been. His body was not made for running and he looked awkward trying to cover ground at speed.

Alex guessed that the modest explosion would have scattered at least one of the men from the tool room. He was not getting clear readings of the heat signatures from his smartphone so could only hope. He advanced slowly but intently towards them now with his Walther held primed. Just as he was nearing the door to the room he detonated another grenade in a distant part of the building, hoping it might flush any remaining men out. When he turned the corner he was surprised to encounter only Jimmy, tied to a chair in the middle of the tool room surrounded by carpenters' paraphernalia. He quickly untied him.

'Thank God I've found you Jimmy' Alex whispered, 'Are you OK?'

'My God, it's you. I'm good. What the hell are you doing here?' replied Jimmy

'Long story. Are you hurt?'

'Not enough to worry about' Jimmy replied, 'Are you here on your own?'

'Yes, if anything gets out of hand I can get backup but for the moment we are on top of things. Did you see anyone else? There should have been a woman here somewhere'

'I had a bloody bag on my head, I saw nothing until they got me into this room'

'How many are there?' asked Alex

'Four; the Spanish guy that brought me here, two Polish fellas and a huge Greek guy, I think'

'Listen we need to get you out of here but we also need to find Deanna, the woman they kidnapped. They are hoping to trade her for me. The thing is I haven't seen her, I assumed she would be here for the trade. Now let's get moving before they come back'

Once free of his restraints Alex gave Jimmy a brief if awkward embrace, then they both entered the room where Deanna was being held only moments ago. They immediately saw the prone body of the Spaniard laying on the floor. Alex checked his pulse for vital signs and found a shallow beat through his jugular. They looked around and could both see the obvious: broken ties on the floor meaning that somebody else had been captive in this room.

'It must have been Deanna', Alex said almost to himself half in hope.

While he was looking around for any sort of clues Jimmy was frisking the body on the floor. He found a wallet full of cash, a notebook filled with Spanish Euro notes and a Smith & Wesson .38 revolver, a stubby pocket pistol with a concealed hammer, in the band of his trousers. Jimmy then transferred the gun to his own pocket without Alex seeing. He then showed Alex the wallet and the credentials inside.

'Ignasi Quiros', Alex read out loud, 'San Agustín del Guadalix, Madrid, España. It says here on his work permit that he manages a farm north of Tres Cantos. That looks to me an unlikely prospect'

'What does he want with us?' asked Jimmy

'Information' Alex replied, 'All this is for some kind of information we have held in our subconscious from what I can gather. This man has already tried to drug and torture me into giving him what I know. I met him in Spain under the illusion that I was aiding a Russian asset to defect'

'How is it that you are here, now, at the same time as me?'

'They must need both of us now. The rest of the team are gone'

'What do you mean gone?' asked Jimmy with a note of panic in his voice.

'Just what I say, Jimmy. Graham was murdered just a few days ago, Dan was killed a few weeks back as far as I can tell. Now it's just the two of us' said Alex, 'I've been trying to reach you for days now, and so was Graham before he got shot. They are targeting the team, the members of Delta team. It seems it all stems back from Navarre'

Jimmy's face darkened at the mention of Navarre, he visibly shrank and became somehow more uncertain of himself. His hand reached for the pistol in his pocket, comforted by the cool hardness of it against his hand. Alex, however, apparently didn't notice, his mind racing through their options.

'What we need to find out is who these idiots are working for' said Alex, 'I am assuming that you also received the letter with the QR code. We have been the victims of some sort of brainwashing or mind control. Graham was on to the idea before he was shot, he also got the same letter we both received but for some reason the conditioning didn't stick with him'

'There might be some clues in the notebook. You read Spanish?'

'Only enough to get me into trouble. But not enough to be of any use to us unfortunately' said Alex

A noise from the corridor made them both straighten and become alert. Quiros was also beginning to stir. They needed to make some quick decisions.

• • • •

DEANNA RAN FOR ALL she was worth, away from the forebodingly dank and dark building, and into the British equivalent of sunshine: a weak globe of light trying to break through the clouds but not quite managing to do so. She did not look back until she was sure she could do so without risking her advantage. She got herself deeper into the woodland surrounding Severalls before daring to glance back. She saw brief movement through the foliage and was then sure that she was being pursued. She crouched to determine who it was and if they had a keen grasp on the direction in which she had fled. She glimpsed the Greek colossus whipping his head round and about looking for a clue as to where she had disappeared to, thankfully, in a state of confusion. He then set off in an alternate direction to hers. Deanna took the brief opportunity to catch her breath before she continued her escape. She could hear traffic noises not too far from where she now crouched. If she could only get to that road she would be able to get to safety.

Slowly she got up and proceeded at a more measured pace trying to remain quiet. After a few minutes she came upon the boundary of the asylum's grounds. It was a wall of about 8 feet in height, a wall she could not scale without the aid of something to raise her up. She followed the wall along hoping to find a gap or a place where it had deteriorated. The ground beneath her feet was rough and uneven, roots of trees and rubble from atop the wall made the going extremely arduous, she had to be careful not to twist an ankle in the process.

Finally she came to a gap in the wall where she could possibly slip through. The red brick had crumbled leaving an opening, but to keep out intruders Severall's security company had patched the gap with makeshift wire netting. Luckily for Deanna the wire mesh had been attached from the inside and had apparently been in place for a many years, with parts already coming away. She had held on to the four inch nail and was now glad that she had, immediately beginning to gouge away at the points that the wire was attached to the brickwork. It was slow going as the mesh was fixed at six inch intervals but she only needed enough space so she could crawl through on her belly to the other side.

She had three of the fixings free when she heard a noise off to her right. She stopped to listen more carefully as to what or who had made it. Deanna was alarmed to realise that it was the Greek slowly making his way in her direction along the wall the same way as she had come. She reckoned that two more fixings and she would be able to slip through, she began scraping at the mortar in earnest, her hands aching from using the ungainly nail so intensely. When she had enough of the mesh free she stood and gripped it with both hands to pull up the sheet, glad to see that the gap was now big enough for her. The noise of the wire mesh being lifted drew attention from the Greek who now honed in to where Deanna was. He began to advance in her direction, it was now or never if Deanna wanted to get out alive. She dropped onto her knees and stuck her head beneath the sheet of mesh, pushing up with her back to try and make the hole larger, it bent only slightly under the force. Deanna then dropped onto her belly and began to wriggle through the hole, her nerves on high alert from the approaching Greek who was now in no doubt that he had found his quarry. Deanna was acutely aware of how vulnerable she was in this position. She could sense his footsteps speeding up towards her position. She was nearly through when she suddenly felt a vice-like grip around her ankle, she pulled with all her might but the fingers would not let go, they began to drag her back the way she had come. Her fingernails tried to grip onto anything within reach but only scraped on the rough ground beneath her. Feeling that she was on the brink of failure Deanna only then realised that she still had the nail in her hand. She reached back and jabbed at his hand with all the force she could muster. She heard him give a bark of pain and immediately withdraw his damaged hand. She pulled her leg to safety and scrambled to her feet on the road side of the wall, relieved at being out of his clutches. As she stood with her back to the wall catching her breath she heard the mesh fence being torn from its moorings against the wall. The Greek had pulled the whole thing away with one fell swoop making an unearthly howl as he did so. She picked herself up and ran as fast as she could away from him. Glancing back over her shoulder she saw that although he had torn the mesh away he still could not get his huge bulk through the gap in the wall. He was left with one arm reaching out toward her and his shiny bald head poking through above it, the veins in his head and neck popping out from the effort.

Deanna turned the corner and practically fell over the car in front of her. She recognized it as being an old Citroen but it took a few moments, while she nursed her leg and her pride, to realise she recognized not only the make of car but who owned it. It was Alex Spellman's Citroen. She remembered seeing pictures of it in the file and she knew the number plate was an unusual one, that was why it had stuck in her head. He *was* here after all. She tried the doors but they were all locked, the boot too. As a matter of course she tried under all the wheel arches to see if there was a spare key hidden anywhere, and was relieved to find that Alex had secreted one in a magnetic box under the rear offside arch. She opened up the car and sat inside, searched the glove-box, not knowing what she was really looking for, but found nothing of any use. On the back seat was a jacket, the pockets of which yielded nothing, but, starting to chill after the adrenaline rush, she wrapped the jacket around her shoulders and breathed in the scent of Alex, being both comforted and worried by it at the same time.

Alex was obviously inside Severalls and looking for her. She had been kept in the dark all along regarding what was to be her fate, only now realising that she was the bait they were luring Alex with. She decided there and then that she had to go back. Go back into the building and give Alex the help he needed, she couldn't leave him in there at the mercy of those thugs. For all she knew they might have captured him by now and started their extraction procedures all over again. She got out of the car and circled round to the boot. If she knew anything about Alex at all, it was that he would have something useful in there, even if it was just a tyre iron. She was in luck, underneath a heavy blanket was a roll of canvas which held a serrated hunting knife. There were gaps where other weapons were usually kept but were now empty. She took the knife and cut off a square from the blanket, to use as a makeshift sheath and she slid the whole thing into her belt. She felt the nail still in her waistband and took it out and looked at it. She decided to hang on to it as it had served her well so far, now considering it a lucky charm. Armed now with a weapon of some effectiveness she made her way again to the main entrance of the institution. None of them would dream that she would be trying to get back in to the hospital, as far as they were concerned she would, more than likely, be long gone by now.

. . . .

ALEX AND JIMMY BOTH dragged Quiros into the chair that Deanna had vacated and tied him up with the rope that was now lying on the floor. Quiros was semi-conscious but coming around rapidly, beginning to make groaning noises and trying to raise his head from his chest. They could hear distant voices echoing down the corridor getting closer, the two Poles were returning to the red room. Alex realised quickly that they were in deep trouble, they were outnumbered and more than likely outgunned. If the big Greek also returned it would be curtains for the both of them. They would need to leave Quiros where he was for the time being, make a retreat and regroup, if they stayed where they were they would get no answers, and they still needed to find Deanna. Alex silently gestured to Jimmy that they were going to make an exit back out towards the periphery of the estate. Once down the corridor they rounded a corner shielding them from the two approaching men, Alex whispered to Jimmy, 'We need to get to the Spaniard, but we must get rid of the other three first, any ideas?' Just as Jimmy was about to answer, they rounded another corner and ran straight into the Greek, literally; Jimmy's face smashing into his rock hard pectorals. Petrakis grabbed Jimmy by the throat and began to choke him, with the other hand he attempted to grab on to Alex before he could go for his weapon. Alex proved to be quick on his feet so Petrakis lashed out with his fist smashing him around the side of the head dazing him briefly. Petrakis had his work cut out trying to subdue both men at the same time but he was certain he would be able to keep the younger of the two under control while dealing with the other. He kept Jimmy firmly in his grasp, as he fought for air and clutched at his tormentors arm to release him from his death grip. Alex feigned dizziness laying on the ground. When Petrakis leaned down to land another blow Alex brought his foot up with such force into his temple that he loosened his grip on Jimmy enough for him to free himself. Jimmy stumbled away gasping for air while Alex righted himself ready to battle the enormous Greek. Petrakis stood his ground, clearly the kick to the head had little effect. Alex, still feeling protective of Jimmy, took the space in between the two men and squared up to Petrakis. Alex, keeping an eye on his assailant, warily began to reach for his Walther, while doing so he motioned for Jimmy to retreat down the corridor and to safety. Jimmy took the opportunity and fled, anything that happened to Alex now was out of his hands, saving his own skin now was his priority. He had no obligation to Alex and he would be damned if he was going to risk his neck again for a man who played fast and loose with people's lives. Every step he took further away from him decreased the weight in his heart, Karma was levelling out the score, Alex was getting what he deserved.

Alex raised his gun and took aim at the big Greek, who was still advancing steadily regardless of the firearm. Jimmy stumbled over some rubble behind him while making his escape causing Alex to briefly whip his head round to check that he was OK. Petrakis took advantage of this opportunity and lunged forward to grab the gun but Alex sensed his approach and all at once took a step back, turned his head and fired off a shot. The report was deafening in the enclosed area, but as soon as he had fired he knew that he was wide of the mark, the bullet only glancing the Greek's shoulder. The shot barely slowed the brute down and he was upon Alex almost immediately swatting the gun out of his hand and landing a fist into his face with the force of a heavyweight. Alex fell down and stayed down, too disoriented to make it back to his feet.

Petrakis grabbed Spellman by an arm and dragged him back the way they had come, looking like some kind of perverse caveman bringing back his kill from the hunt.

When he arrived back at the red room, still dragging the insensible Alex, Krol and Wesolek were back and untying, the now fully conscious, Quiros from the chair. Quiros, although still groggy from the trauma was pleased to see that he now had at least one of the men he was after.

'At last we have what we need, gentlemen. What happened to the other two?' he asked Petrakis

'They both got away' he answered sheepishly with a shrug of his shoulders, 'I will go and find Mitchell, bring him back'

'No, I need you here. You two, go. And this time don't fail me or there will be consequences. The girl will not be returning, but we must now make haste, as she may well be on her way to the authorities. Jurek, you go and find the two of them before they get too far. Do not hesitate to use deadly force with the woman, we don't need her any longer as we have Spellman, but don't come back without Mitchell. Understand? Time is of the essence gentlemen. I have the serum in my bag, if you would be so kind, Anatoli, bring me Spellman and I will begin the process'

Jurek Wesolek looked confused at the instruction but sauntered towards the main entrance, followed by Krol. To attempt to find a woman who would by now be long gone and a man who also did not want to be found. He didn't even know where to start. It wasn't what they had signed up for and way above their pay-grades.

Petrakis manhandled Alex on to the chair and rolled up his sleeve to access a vein. Administering the drug would be the easy part, getting all the information would take a bit of time. Quiros was setting up recording equipment with microphones positioned next to the subject. He was now feeling better and was warming to the task ahead of him, although every now and again the missing fingers on his left hand would make things more difficult for him and he winced with pain. Every time he did so he cursed Dragunov under his breath. He struggled to get the SP-117 into the syringe, a Soviet made medication based on the sodium amytal mixture, which had proven itself to be effective in loosening the tongues of even the most stubborn subjects. It was Quiros' preferred method of interrogation, of the pain free variety anyway.

The table-saw in the middle of the room was to be used as an incentive if things did not go as planned. Many men had crumbled at the sight of parts of their anatomy inching towards the ferocious spinning blade, one that could slice through flesh and bone as if it were butter. Usually it only took the thought of it but occasionally losing a finger or letting the blade stroke the underside of a foot was more than enough convincing to play along. Tradesmen's tools were, in Quiros' mind, some of the best utensils for use on the human body. Hammers for knuckles and fingertips, box cutter blades for faces and ears, roof punches for knees and so on, the varieties were endless for a person with imagination. His background in the field of medicine only honed his expertise in torture techniques and made him all the more practiced in the art. Alas he knew all too well the pain that could be inflicted by a simple tool as he had learnt first-hand only a few days ago.

The evening was drawing in now and the dull day was fast becoming a sombre evening bereft of warmth or grace. The chill was such that you would not venture out without being bundled up, the interminable damp in the air getting through your clothes and somehow into your bones. The darkness continued to draw in and the two men draped tarpaulin over the window to shield what they were up to from any passer-by. They would prefer anonymity at this stage of proceedings. Inside the hospital it remained cold, not something any of the Europeans in the room were used to.

The drug was beginning to work its magic on Alex, Petrakis gave him a few sharp slaps around the face to enliven him.

'Not so hard,' Quiros berated him, 'we don't want to knock him out again. You don't know your own strength Ana'

Petrakis particularly disliked being referred to as Ana, he considered it too 'girly'. He chose to ignore it for the time being as, after all, it was he who chopped off the poor man's fingers and he had every right to be angry and upset with him. Anatoli however was only following orders from Dragunov, the man ultimately calling all the shots, and the one paying his wages. If he carried on with the 'Ana' though there would be a price to pay for sure.

29 - Bright Ideas

Deanna watched the two Poles searching the grounds from where she was hiding. They were systematically scanning the area around the buildings and the wooded scrub that acted as a border between the institution and the perimeter wall. She thought to herself that their search was futile as anyone else in her position was likely to be long gone by now. Of course she wasn't, that was the irony. Were they just looking for her or had they lost Alex as well? And what about the other man? Her hiding place wouldn't be secure for much longer, she would need to make a move soon. She had to assume that they were looking for her only and that Alex and the other guy were still inside. Therefore she had to make an attempt to get inside and free him. As she sat there hidden from view she saw another figure edging his way through the wooded area moving from tree to tree, out of sight from the other two. She didn't recognize this person's face and couldn't figure out where he fitted in to the scheme of what was going on. It must have been the man they had brought in after her. So they must be out looking for him too, and maybe Alex was still inside alone needing her help or rather their help. It was getting progressively darker as time went on which, she hoped, would be to her advantage. It gave her a confidence that was perhaps foolhardy but never-the-less she needed all the help she could get. The two searchers had now disappeared from view and were likely to be going through the woodland making their way toward the front of the buildings. The stranger had made his way to the front of the facility where he would be able to escape the clutches of the gangsters who were pursuing him.

Deanna felt that the time was right to make her way back into the building to see if she could be of any help to Alex. She would need to be stealthy and try and stay one step ahead of those who were running this show, it was now her chance to begin turning the tables on them. She decided to off-foot them by killing the power and plunging them into darkness; she had remembered passing a doorway when she had fled earlier, one that looked as if it could be a utility room of some kind judging by the warning signs on the door. As she made her way back into the corridors of the facility she kept to the edge of the walkway in the shadows, her back practically pressed up against the wall for fear of being seen. Soon enough she came upon the door. Trying the handle she was relieved to find that it opened without the need for any strong-arm measures. Peering in she was surprised and a little concerned that it was not a cupboard at all but a door which gave access to a flight of stairs going down to a basement; a basement that was dark and foreboding, smelling of things she did not and could not recognize. Her primal instinct was not to enter into such a squalid, fetid, unknown pit of darkness but judging from the signs on the door this was definitely somewhere you would find electrical equipment, hopefully fuses and junction boxes and the like. She closed the door behind her and slowly descended into the darkness. Any dim light from above, trying its best to shine through the grate in the door, did not reach down into the depths of the basement. It felt like she were sinking into an inky chasm, her eyes not yet able to adjust to the blackness. She counted the steps as she made her way down, in the back of her mind trying to remember how many steps to a flight, anywhere between ten and fourteen she guessed. Her hands reached out to her sides as she progressed and her fingertips trailed along the wall, feeling the damp and flaky bits of plaster as she felt her way along, hoping not to feel anything worse than that, her imagination beginning to work overtime.

As she reached the bottom stair she felt around for a light switch and found it round the corner on the wall to her left, she flicked it on and waited for the room to illuminate. The strip lights flickered casting brief splashes of light over the murky room. What she saw in the strobing light made her draw breath, it looked just as if the floor was writhing and moving, alive with something. As she concentrated on the image in front of her she realised that the floor of the basement was covered in a layer of water and in this water were black objects moving incessantly from one place to another. Her heart sank. Rats. She hated rats. But she could see where she now needed to go, the power grid controls she was looking for was on the far wall, all she needed to do was cross the floor and shut off the grid for the building.

It took her a few moments to build up the gumption to begin the short crossing, knowing that in reality the rats were likely more afraid of her than she of them but that didn't make it any easier. The thought that they would attack her and begin taking chunks out of her ankles, running up her clothes and nipping her fingertips kept jumping to the front of her mind. She had read James Herbert's rat trilogy too often as a child and now she was regretting it. As she waded over to the power bank in the brief flickers of light, she could see in actual fact that the rats were clearing a path for her and she relaxed slightly at the realisation. She approached the grey metallic boxes lining the wall and realised she didn't know the first thing about what she should be doing. If her fuse box at home was anything to go by all she needed to do was pull all the switches down to turn them all off. With sudden realisation she knew that cutting the power to the building meant cutting the power to the room where she now stood, a thought that filled her with icy dread. No matter, it could not be avoided. She would need to get her bearings and know exactly where to head once the power was cut. She looked back to the stairwell, noticing that the rats were now swimming to and fro across the path she would soon be travelling. She felt nausea rise in her chest at the thought, it was silly she knew, but humans must have an instinctive fear of vermin for good reason.

Deanna began pulling the switches. Each box had an arm in the upright position so she started at one end and pulled each one down as she walked along the bank of cabinets, not knowing which would be the one to plunge her into darkness. She found herself holding her breath every time she pulled an arm, feeling like she was playing a type of roulette. By pure fortune she reached the sixth cabinet and the light still flickered. She now knew this would be the one, so looked around once more to get her bearings and then pulled the arm down. The room was now inky black. It was as if she had been plunged into a barrel of tar. The hairs on the back of her neck tingled and she became acutely aware of every sound and movement in the room. She could hear drops of water she had not noticed before, the rats making a paddling noise as they made their journeys to and fro and the hum of the electrical machinery was now conspicuous by its absence.

Deanna slowly headed in the direction of the stairs, wading through the ankle deep icy water covering the floor, flinching at the objects, real or imagined, that brushed against her lower legs. She held out her arms in front of her like a blind person not wanting to bump into to any hard surface, protecting herself from injury. After about fifteen steps her hands touched a wall. Confused as to where she had actually ended up she side-stepped to her right and felt for the gap that would be the stairwell. Three steps took her to the gap, how could she have gone off course in such a short distance? Now she ascended the steps, glad to be out of the frigid water and away from the repellent rodents. She could see the dim light of the early evening barely making an impression through the grate in the door. She made it to the top and opened the door into the corridor knowing that the easy part was over, now came the part she was really dreading.

30 - Black Out

Quiros had set out his stall, the implements of his trade all neatly in front of him on the table. Alex's eyes had been taking in what was going on since he had regained consciousness some minutes ago, eyes that were beginning to grow wide with dread. His mind had been looking for an escape plan, but judging by his restraints he would be going nowhere any time soon. His forearms were strapped to the arms of the wooden chair and a rope around his chest fixed him to the chair back. The implements he was now looking at were the same ones as in the Spanish farmhouse, an array of tools that were used to cause maximum pain and discomfort while keeping the subject alive and able to talk. The drugs he had been given had dulled his sensibilities but he doubted they had done the same to his pain receptors and Alex was having trouble keeping his thoughts in any kind of linear fashion. He had noticed that the window had been blocked using an old dust sheet. The light in the room now came from a dull bulb hanging from the centre of the ceiling and a halogen lamp plugged in at the wall casting a harsh light across the faces of his kidnappers. Petrakis sat in the corner, arms folded over his huge pectoral muscles, eyes kept firmly on Alex.

'Now, Senor Spellman. I am glad that we get the chance to finish what we started in Madrid' said Quiros, 'You have caused me a fair deal of trouble, do you realise that?' The question was rhetorical, 'Once I have got all the information I can from you I will be carrying out my own private version of retribution. As you can see from my hand I have been in the wars, so to speak. The blame for my missing digits falls at your feet, I'm afraid, my dear friend'

'I'm not your fucking friend, you sick bastard'

'Maybe not, but we will be getting to know each other very well over the next few hours. I will know you better than you know yourself before this is over, your strengths, your weaknesses, what keeps you up at night... You shouldn't have run from me in Madrid, you know that? You caused me a lot of problems having to explain myself to the local policía. You have made it all so much harder than it needed to be. But to tell you the truth I was probably going to torture you there as well, it is, after all what I do best, or rather what I enjoy the most'

'Fuck you. I'm not going to tell you anything'

'Oh, but you will'

'I don't know anything'

'You know more than you realise. This is not some half-baked plan that we made on the back of a napkin. You have no idea what you are involved in. This has been years in the making, nothing you say now is going to change the fact that you will become a traitor to your country whether you like it or not. You will join your other comrade as a traitor, a defector'

'What comrade? Who are you talking about?'

'Ah. You don't know?' Quiros chuckled to himself, 'This is going to be interesting. For someone that works in intelligence you know, in actual fact, little about the important things. These things are going on under your very nose. I suppose it can do no harm to let you in on our little secret, now that you are part of it anyway. It would be nice that you appreciate the lengths we have gone to after all'

Quiros sat himself down opposite Alex, making himself more comfortable to explain himself.

'You remember Navarre of course? How could you forget? I remember it vividly. You see I was the one who nursed your wounds after that awful explosion. No-one knew quite how big that explosion was going to be, it wasn't something we had the chance to rehearse. We could not take the ordnance out of the shed in case it looked suspicious and we didn't know how much you would be using to destroy it all. In the scheme of things it was lucky we didn't lose all of you in the blast' Quiros paused and took a packet of cigarettes out of his breast pocket, ignoring the other two men in the room he lit it from a brass lighter he kept in his shirt. Inhaling deeply he carried on, 'Luckily your wounds were not too severe. Your friends also were not too bad. We stitched you up and tended to your burns, which, thankfully, were only first degree. It is thanks to me that your face bears such a gallant looking scar. We kept you in the infirmary for the duration of your stay, while I worked my magic on you. That part of your stay you have no recollection of. I put you through a highly experimental series of brainwashing techniques that would only come into effect when you were exposed to a catalyst. Some of this you may have figured out already, I'm sure. After all you are not stupid'

'I don't understand. What do you have to gain?'

Quiros held up his hand for silence, 'All in good time, if you would just let me finish, your curiosity should be sated soon enough. I have been developing a program where the subject is unknowingly deployed as a gatherer of information. It is perfect; a spy who doesn't know he is a spy. You see? All this time, since 2011, you have been gathering information for me and my colleagues to glean at a later date. Unfortunately because it is still in its early stages it didn't work on poor Graham Devereux. Dan Johnson, however, proved to be quite useful before he met his end. He gave us as much information as he could, although he is not as big a fish a you are. You must realise that since you all received the catalyst you have been gathering intelligence for us. It has been a productive few months. You ask what I have to gain. Why does anyone do what they do? Money. Glory. A means to an end. A sense of duty. Pick one. I have my own reasons for why I do this but it is also part of a much bigger picture, one that you do not need to know about. Although I'm sure you can fill in some of the blanks. My research has proved satisfyingly effective, I have learnt a great deal with my four guinea pigs. Although it seems that your young friend has made himself elusive for the time being. Never mind, we will catch up to him soon enough. He is a small fish for us to fry at this time, he turned out to be unstable and uncooperative anyway. The fiasco of the operation in Navarre sent him spiraling into a depression giving him bouts of Post-Traumatic Stress Disorder, which I'm sure you are aware of. I would still like to extract any information he can give us though. So you see Alex, you didn't really have a choice, your fate had something of predestination about it, one way or another it was always going to be you and I in a room as we are now. The details, where and when. These are the only things that may have been altered'

Quiros sat back satisfied that he had explained himself to Alex, although Alex would have preferred to know who was pulling the Spaniard's strings. The light outside had now diminished, night-time was nearly upon them. Quiros dropped his cigarette butt onto the floor and ground it under his heel. He then rose from his chair and took an implement off the table. Alex could see that it was something sharp and shiny, the light of the overhead bulb flashing it's reflection in his eyes. He flexed his arms under his ties, straining at them, his muscled biceps becoming sharply defined against the fabric of his shirt as he did so.

Quiros approached Alex slowly bringing the scalpel into view as he neared him. Alex strained his head trying to gain distance between him and the blade, 'How can I tell you what I don't know?' he grimaced. Quiros now remained silent as he placed his bandaged hand upon Alex's shoulder to steady his quarry as well as to soothe him. From behind, two massive hands grabbed Alex around the sides of his head, then he felt one of the hands slip around his throat until he was in a lock he could not manoeuvre from. Although still able to breathe with some effort, his head was now locked in place, the scalpel looming ever nearer to his unprotected eyeball. Alex clamped his eyes shut in an automatic reaction at self-preservation, but the other hand from behind reached over and pulled his lid up from his eyebrow again exposing the now bloodshot white of his exposed sclera.

'You have heard the expression '*an eye for an eye*' I assume? Well my dear Senór Spellman, I blame you for my recent amputation. Ustedes han oído que se dijo: Ojo por ojo y diente por diente. Matthew 5:38. In this case it will be an eye in payment for my two fingers. Only then will we get to work on gathering the information you have for me. I hope you did not think there would be no consequence for deserting me in Madrid. I am a firm believer in the saying 'what goes around comes around'

As Quiros leaned further forward blocking out the light from the naked bulb overhead, Alex could smell the distinctive mixture of spices used in the Basque dish Pipérade on his breath.

Then all of a sudden the light in the room extinguished plunging all three of them into utter darkness.

'Mierda!' shouted Quiros 'Malditos entrometidos'

Alex felt the grip around his throat loosen as he gasped to refill his lungs with much needed oxygen. A white noise filled his ears as the blood came rushing back to his head. He needed to act quickly while the two men were trying to figure out what had happened to the lights. Alex closed his eyes and immediately stood and lurched backwards towards the wall where he used all of his body-weight to crack the wooden chair against the brickwork. Without being able to see anything he could feel that the chair had now splintered into pieces and was in bits around him. His arms were still strapped to the wooden arms of the chair but his instinct was to retain them for both defence and attack in the coming moments. He could hear his captors flailing around him, speaking in their respective languages, neither of which he could understand in the moment. He knew that the few moments of his eyes being shut would give him an advantage when he opened them for the first time as the pupils would dilate and hopefully give him a brief glimpse as to his whereabouts. When he did open his eyes he made out the faint shapes of the other two men in the room and deftly lashed out with his forearms landing cracking blows to each of them in turn. He took pleasure in the crunching sounds the wood was making on their unprotected bones. He was fairly sure that he had got the Spaniard in the nose judging by the crunching sound it had made. The shouts of pain emanating from the darkness convinced him that his assailants would, for the time being, be indisposed and unable to give chase. In the chaos that he had created Alex made his way gingerly toward what he thought was the exit of the room, making sure he would not trip over anything in his haste to escape. He hit a wall and edged his way along to the left, hoping it was the right way to go, and soon found the door aperture of the doorway. With his back to the wall and his arms up in defence he edged around the doorway and out into the corridor where the blackness relented slightly and he could make out the vague details of his surroundings. If he could keep his cool he could take advantage of the hand fate had dealt him. Then out of nowhere seemingly, he could sense rather than see, an iron rod arcing it's way toward his head. He lifted his arm automatically to shield himself from the oncoming blow but even so the bar split the arm of the chair strapped to his forearm and his arm dropped uselessly to his side as he crumpled to his knees. He saw the Spaniard appear from the doorway raising the bar one more time, Alex wasn't in a position to protect himself from another blow, all he could do was wait for the inevitable. The bar came crashing down and his world plunged into darkness.

When he opened his eyes he could see nothing except the faint glow of the waxing moon lighting the outside of the building, bleaching the scene of any colour and casting weak shadows making his surroundings look like a black and white photograph. Alex was disorientated from the blow to the head, the pain still very much apparent. He could feel the cold steel of a blade pressing against his neck, a strong arm twisting his own arm painfully up and around his back and the foul breath against his ear.

'Don' you fuckeeng struggle' the voice said, Alex could hear the thick Spanish accent. A voice he realised he recognized. Could it possibly be Quiros? Alex wouldn't have thought the portly Spaniard had this amount of strength in him.

Alex didn't think he could. He daren't anyway. He could feel the blade drawing blood. The arm that was free was throbbing painfully, probably incapacitated. His eyes began to adjust to the dark. He couldn't exactly remember just how the tables had turned on him, it was like a macabre game of chequers; the upper hand being lost in an instant.

'Just back up slowly with me and you probably won't get hurt'

That was all Alex needed, an enemy with a sense of humour. Alex's mind frantically thought of ways out of his assailants vice like grip, any rapid moves would cause the blade to injure him or worse, sever his carotid artery. The attacker was shorter than Alex and was reaching upwards to keep the blade held at his throat. As Alex's eyes grew accustomed to the dim light he saw they were backing down a corridor. It wasn't a house they were in, more like a hospital but not exactly. The floors were hard and there were rails down either side of the corridor. There were strip lights down the centre of the ceiling, Alex could see the warm, almost imperceptible red glow underneath the plastic covers. He remembered now, the asylum. He was here to save Deanna.

'Anatoli?' the attacker called in a hoarse whisper, 'Anatoli?' a little louder, 'ANATOLI, where de fuck are you? Mierda!'

Whoever Anatoli was he was not answering and Alex's attacker was getting panicky. They both carried on backing toward a door at the end of the corridor. It came to Alex suddenly that Anatoli was of course the man-mountain who had been with Quiros in the red room. He hoped to God that he wouldn't show up otherwise his fish would be well and truly fried.

As they both turned through the door and into the room Alex saw movement out of the corner of his eye. Shit! he thought, it's the Greek. Alex expected more pain to arrive in the form of retribution for what he had dealt out upon trying to escape their clutches earlier, angry with himself now for showing mercy. Ignasi Quiros didn't have a chance to deflect the oncoming blade as it was sunk deep into his throat slicing his carotid artery, all thoughts of his prisoner quickly left him as he dropped his own knife and clutched at his throat to try and staunch the hemorrhaging. Without any delay he dropped to his knees gasping for air and leaned forward bleeding into an ever growing pool of blood.

Alex turned and saw Deanna standing there with a look of surprise on her face as if she didn't think she could get the better of the Spaniard again and the shock of taking a man's life so intimately. She was holding a knife he recognized, the one he kept in the back of his car for emergencies. He felt a wave of pride and appreciation that Deanna had been so resourceful to think of arming herself. He approached her and enveloped her in his arms. She began to sob quietly, killing was never easy, even if it was necessary. All Alex kept whispering to her over and over was 'Thank you'. So much for him saving Deanna, he now owed his life to her.

Deanna kissed him gently now realising that Alex had been quite badly hurt. They were not out of danger yet. Apart from the Greek there were two other henchmen working with Quiros and they didn't want to run into any of them. They also had to find Jimmy and get him out to safety if he hadn't already fled on his own volition.

'We have to split up' Deanna said pulling herself together and taking charge, 'We need to find Jimmy and we will cover more ground if we separate. I don't want to leave you like this but it's for the best. We will all meet out at your car in fifteen minutes, all being well. OK?'

Alex knew Deanna well enough by now to know that it was no use arguing with her. 'OK, we are pretty central to the main part of the building where we are standing now, so if we just head in opposite directions we can work our way to the east side where the car is parked. For God's sake be careful and keep out of sight. If for any reason you need help or get in to any deep water make as much noise as you can and I'll come running, but that's a last resort, avoid trouble at all costs, don't try and do anything brave, OK?'

'After spending the last few days tied up and kept in the dark, the last thing I want is to fall into their hands again, don't worry. One objective, find Jimmy then get out. I know.'

'Good. And... I know it's not the right time but I just wanted to say, sorry. I fucked up. I shouldn't have left you alone in Mexico. It was a rookie move. Or maybe I'm getting too old for this shit. Either way it won't happen again, I promise.' Alex didn't immediately realise the irony of that statement

'Be careful,' whispered Deanna, 'don't make any promises you may not be able to keep' She pulled Alex towards her and gave him a long hard kiss on the lips, steeling them both for the dangers still to come.

They then set off in opposite directions, into the murky corridors of the asylum, broken glass and tiles strewn over the floors hampering their attempts at remaining quiet. Alex took a look back over his shoulder before Deanna passed out of sight around the corner and she instinctively turned her head in response. He gave her a reassuring nod of affirmation, it was all he could do in the circumstances.

Alex hoped he would come across Jimmy and that they would both avoid all three of the goons. He was sure they would find out soon enough that Quiros was lying dead in a pool of his own blood. Then, depending on how devoted they were to their boss, they would either be seeking vengeance or would slink off into the night to avoid any more bloodshed. He hoped it would be the latter. By chance he looked out of the broken window to where the vehicles had been parked. It seemed like an age ago that he had watched the men bring in the chest which he now knew had contained Deanna. He saw two men getting into the car Quiros had been driving. They were leaving, good. Two less to worry about. He watched as they drove out towards the main gate under cover of darkness, not turning on the headlights of the car until they were a safe distance from the building. Obviously just hired hands for dirty work, getting out while they still could. That just left the Greek oak. Alex hoped it would be him rather than Deanna who would run in to him, if it had to be anyone.

He turned a corner and, wishing that he hadn't tempted fate, practically came face to face with Petrakis, catching them both by surprise. Immediately Alex went on the offensive and did the only thing that would buy him any time, kicking Petrakis as hard as he could between the legs, knowing that it would incapacitate him. Petrakis let out a cry of pain and went down on his knees, swearing in Greek as he did so. Alex took his chance and ran, knowing that the other two men were gone and that he could now only meet Deanna or Jimmy. Just as these thoughts were forming in his mind he could hear the footsteps of the Greek behind him. It couldn't be, he thought to himself. It was impossible, not after that kick, he must have balls of steel. He knew he would be no match for the man if he let him catch up with him, better to outwit him or outrun him.

Alex had a decent head start but could hear the footsteps gaining on him with deadly reliability. He flicked his head from side to side looking for possible escape routes but found nothing. He began trying handles but this slowed his progress dangerously, none of them turning out to be unlocked doors.

Thankfully before his pursuer could see his luck change he found an unlocked door leading to what looked like a kitchen. Alex limped into the room closing the door as quietly as he could behind him. He heard the running footsteps slow as they approached, his nemesis doing the same thing with the doors as if reading his mind. Alex scanned the kitchen for weapons. Nothing was within reach. He couldn't leave the door as it was, there was no lock. He stood with his heel against the wood holding it shut. Hopefully his pursuer would be fooled into thinking it was locked like the others. Alex reached out to his right with his hand, groped on the worktop to try and find something useful but found nothing. As quietly as he could he opened the drawer closest to him, gently feeling around for something, anything. His hand touched a variety of metallic objects, all steely cold but not weapons. He felt a long pin-like utensil, picked it up and saw it was a bbq skewer, industrial strength with a wooden handle. Not a bad weapon, he could inflict a great deal of pain with it if need be. He heard the footsteps arrive at the kitchen door and stop. A slight turn of the doorknob. Alex put more weight against the wood. The door didn't move. Then Alex heard the squeak of leather and rustle of clothing. He was crouching. He must have a damned sixth sense, or he could hear him breathing or something. Alex felt sure he was looking through the keyhole. This may be his one and only chance. If his attacker got him alone again Alex would be finished, he was no match physically. Alex only had an instant to make the decision. As deftly as he could he moved the skewer around so the point was facing the keyhole, then with the palm of his other hand, through luck and a bit of judgement jammed the skewer through the hole. Alex would always remember the scream, even for a grown man of 6'2" and 220 pounds, he sounded like a child. Alex tried not to think about his eyeball being pierced and bursting, let alone the pain that would have followed.

Alex opened the door and found his attacker lying on the floor with both hands covering his eye socket, blood oozing out from underneath his palms. He was now whimpering and not able to get himself into an upright position. Alex knew by looking at him that he would give no trouble for the near future. He was a broken man. Alex stepped over him, reached down and pulled the injured man's id from his inside jacket pocket, briefly checked his name and credentials then walked towards the exit. Alex decided that as soon as he was within a safe distance he would call it in and have him picked up, having his full name and details would make it very difficult for him to flee the country now.

He made it back to the car without coming across Jimmy and considered going back in to make another search, but before he could, he saw two figures approaching, nearly jogging towards him and he recognized almost immediately the silhouette of Deanna, thankfully alongside her was Jimmy.

31 – Back to London

They drove in silence, all three of them trying to process the events of the last few hours, and in Deanna's case, days. It was an hour and a half drive from the asylum back to London. Deanna understandably fell asleep in the back seat using Alex's coat as a pillow to rest her head on. It wasn't until they were passing Canary Wharf that Jimmy realised they were not heading towards his home.

'Where are we going now?' he asked unable to hide the irritation in his voice

'I'm taking you somewhere safe, at least for a few days until we can figure out that the threat to us all is over, I'm not taking any more chances' explained Alex, 'We are going to the Morpeth Arms, there is a safe-house there that you can stay at. The firm owns the top floor and uses the apartments for various reasons. Anil has had it on standby for this specific scenario, you'll be safe there, the circle is very tight, just the four of us know about it.'

It was past midnight by the time they had reached their destination and the public bar was now shut so the only thing for it was to head down to the private bar deep in the cellar of the building. Alex would have to sign Deanna in as a guest as she was not part of the firm. This was not something that was usually accepted but due to Alex's long standing within the establishment it wasn't a problem, as long as he could vouch for her.

They made their way through the large front bar and into the smaller back room bar. To the left was a small door, which could all too easily be missed, it led to a narrow spiral staircase that took them down to the cellars. Dampness was all around them, Deanna could tell from the brickwork that the cellar dated back a very long time. On their right, as they walked down the short corridor, were three arches reaching back far enough to swallow any light there was on offer, used in the past to store barrels of beer and such. It gave Deanna a chill, reminding her of the basement in the asylum, and imagining the furry bodies of rats moving around in the darkness.

Upon opening the door into the private bar a swathe of warm light beckoned them in and suddenly the whole tableau changed from cold and clammy to cosy and inviting. The smell of alcohol and flavoursome food filled their nostrils and all three of them simultaneously realised just how hungry they were.

They ordered food and drinks and sat down in a corner booth where they would have a bit of privacy. Even though the bar was nearly empty, there were a couple of faces Alex knew but none that he wanted to engage with.

'What is this place?' asked Deanna

'It's a place that you can't tell anyone about, ever' Alex said half jokingly, 'It's our secret'

Alex glanced at Jimmy to share the joke but saw that his mind was elsewhere. 'What's up, Jimmy?'

'Well, where the fuck do I start Alex?' he answered with vehemence

Alex was taken aback by the aggression in his voice, 'I don't understand'

'You know what I'm talking about. If it wasn't for you we wouldn't be in this fucking mess!'

Alex had been so involved with himself over the last few days that he hadn't thought about the effect it had all had on Jimmy. All of a sudden the guilt of Navarre came flooding back to him. He knew that it had changed Jimmy but he also didn't realise quite how much Jimmy blamed him.

'Listen, Jimmy, I'm sorry. I know this is shit for all of us. But I'm trying to get us out of this trouble'

'The trouble started when you were team leader in Navarre and you know it. Do you know what it's been like for me? The nightmares, the crippling anxiety. I haven't been able to have a relationship since then. My whole world is a fucking mess. And all because of you'

'Hey, now listen, I know you're pissed but you can't put it all on me, you signed up for it, you knew the risks involved. And it's not as if we all weren't affected by what happened'

'Yeah, you're not the one taking anti-psychotics, not being able to leave the house. Don't talk to me, you just don't get it do you?'

'Jimmy, I get it that you blame me. But you don't know what it's been like for me either, I'm not looking for sympathy, but seriously... most of our team are dead. Graham, gone. Dan, gone. We are the only two left, we should be looking out for each other, don't you think?'

'You look out for yourself, Alex. Like you always do. When this is all over and I can go back to my own flat I won't want to see you again'

'I'm sorry you feel that way, Jimmy'

With that Jimmy stood up and downed the rest of his whiskey and headed up to the apartment three flights up.

'I'm sorry you had to see all that, it has obviously been brewing for some time. He's been suffering from PTSD ever since he came back from Spain all those years ago. I don't know, honestly, what I could have done differently'

'I'm sure you did everything you could' Deanna reassured him, 'and I'm sure he doesn't hate you'

'You saw him, he seems pretty pissed to me'

'But who else does he have to blame? You are the obvious candidate for directing all that rage and frustration'

'It doesn't make it any easier though does it?'

'Alex, you mustn't beat yourself up too much about it, it could have happened to anyone, remember I have read the files extensively. You can't go on living with the weight of this forever'

'Easier said than done' sighed Alex, 'all I do is go over again and again what I should have done differently... I honestly don't know where I went wrong. I remember checking everything and all the equipment being sound. I even got Cole to have a look at the triggers and the mechanisms. That poor bastard didn't stand a chance'

After a pause, Deanna not knowing quite what to say changed the subject, 'What now? Where are we staying tonight? I'm getting tired'

Alex gave her a crooked grin, 'Getting tired? You must be on your last legs. Tired is an understatement. There is a place around the corner, The Worcester on St Georges Square' Alex pronounced it as 'Wooster', 'A very private residence where we won't be disturbed' As he was talking he was tapping at keys on his cell and then looked up, 'Excellent they have my corner suite, overlooking the river *and* the square, I've just confirmed it. Let's go'

The walk should have taken around five minutes except that Deanna all of a sudden realised that she was in the heart of one of the most beautiful cities she had ever seen and wanted to stop every few yards to take in the views. Her excitement brought out her inner child as she was now eager to see as much of London as she could while she was here. Alex promised her that he would give her the full five star tour after they had dealt with the matter at hand.

32 - Closing In

Vasili Dragunov heard the car before he could see it. He stood in front of the door to his childhood home and checked that all the locks were secure. There was no denying there was somebody home, after all there was smoke rising from the chimney. He was relieved when the car that rounded the corner was one that he recognized as belonging his nephew from the other side of the valley, one of only a handful of people who knew of his whereabouts. Usually his nephew, Evgeny, would call prior to visiting, so alarm bells were now ringing as normal protocol was not being followed.

Vasili waited until the car had stopped and his nephew had got out, alone, before he started unlocking the front door. By the time he had the four dead-bolts undone Evgeny was at the threshold. He let him in then closed and bolted the door behind him keeping an eye out for anything unusual all the while.

They greeted each other with a manly bear hug, 'Nephew, so nice to see you. How is it you are here but I had no clue you were coming?' asked Vasili.

'I'm sorry, Uncle, there was no time. I have news from Moscow, let us talk in the warm'

'Of course, come through, the fire has been lit since this morning, it is warm'

They both walked through to the room in which Vasili had been sitting at his desk moments ago. The fire blazed and it was in complete contrast to the bitter cold outside the house. Evgeny walked straight to the fire and stood warming his hands and the backs of his legs while Vasili took to his worn leather armchair and settled in to hear what he had to say. Evgeny was a handsome looking boy not yet twenty five years of age. He was dark haired with an unmistakable Russian air about him. He had a strong bond with his uncle and would do almost anything for him. When Evgeny was just a boy of twelve Vasili taught him the game of chess, they would play any chance they could and soon enough, by the time he was fourteen, Evgeny was a player of equal standards to Vasili, who had been playing all his adult life. A precocious player for sure, one who took unnecessary chances but had the audacious flair of a lateral thinker, perfect for the game. From then on they would play on a regular basis and whilst playing discuss the ways of the world, Evgeny had lived a sheltered life being from the country and Vasili was all too keen to teach him in the ways of life as he knew it, his dealings in Moscow had taught him much and Evgeny should also benefit from his experience. They discussed and argued over a range of diverse topics; communism, socialism, western politics, eastern values, the price of oil, the Middle East's grip on the west, religion; no issue was off limits. Vasili admired the boy for having a strong view on such worldly matters, he found himself loving the boy as a father would love a son. Dimitri, his own father and Vasili's brother, had remained in the country to work on the land and for that reason had drifted apart from his brother. They kept in touch through Evgeny but relations had not been the same since they had fallen out over a woman when they were in their twenties. Dimitri had gone on to marry Ulyana and after she had given birth to a baby boy had begun treating her with an increasing disdain that Vasili found unacceptable so that any pretence at a brotherly bond had dwindled to nothing. It was Ulyana who thought that Evgeny had the right to know his uncle and who made the effort to visit Vasili when he was old enough, taking advantage of Dimitri's failing health and diminishing faculties.

'Tell me nephew, what is so urgent to break protocol? I hope you did not risk my whereabouts on a whim?'

'No Uncle, it is no whim. I have grave news. The search for you is expanding. The KGB are heading this way, it was only a matter of time but that time has now come. They have systematically searched all your premises. The houses you own are now guarded and the offices are being scrutinised for clues as to your whereabouts. You must leave, quickly. I have had word from my source within the Kremlin that officials will be here before the week is out. It was pure luck that we were able to have more than a day's notice'

'I see', said Vasili, 'this is indeed much sooner than I had anticipated but is not unexpected. What do you suggest, nephew?'

'You must leave obviously. They are coming here to kill you, or perhaps worse...' he left the sentence hanging.

Dragunov knew all too well that being captured by the KGB could in fact be a lot worse than a bullet to the back of the head. He would be made an example of, it was possible he would be sent off to a labour camp in the far reaches of the motherland, never to be seen or heard of again. The thought of spending the rest of his days breaking rocks in Siberia was not something he would like to consider.

'And where shall I go?' he asked, knowing well what his plan would be in this event, but he wanting to see if Evgeny had the insight to judge what would be his next move.

'If I were you Uncle I would of course head to the West. I know it is not your home but at least you will be safe from capture' said Evgeny, 'You should again travel over the Finnish border and make your way to the UK. They would take you in, surely? If you gave yourself to them, they would treat you fairly'

Vasili had only recently done this trip to deal with his errant employee, Quiros, for trying to steal what was his; the information of a valuable asset. Quiros had paid dearly for that mistake. Just because a man is in hiding does not mean he has no teeth to bite. Quiros had had two of his fingers bitten off to remind him of his betrayal.

'You are of course correct, Evgeny. My business takes me to the UK anyway, it was only a matter of time until I had to leave. I shall make arrangements immediately. Do you need anything before I go?'

'No, Uncle, I will be fine, I am going back to Moscow in a few days, it will look strange if I also disappear, and from there I can keep a better eye on the progress they make with their pursuit of you. I will of course let you know if they are getting too near'

'Of course, but I do not wish you to risk yourself for me. You have your whole life ahead of you, young boy. Do not throw it away on my account. Take no unnecessary risks. Understand?'

'Yes, sir' answered Evgeny with a slight bow of his head.

'And tell me, how is my brother?'

'Father is not well I'm afraid. His condition grows worse. Every morning he awakes and panics saying he cannot see, that he has been blinded. Each time it takes longer to calm him down. He remembers eventually, he has not been able to use his eyes for, I think, over four years now, but it is quite traumatic for him, very difficult. He doesn't always recognize me... he...' Evgeny trailed off choking back his emotions at the thought of his ailing father.

Vasili placed both hands on his shoulders and comforted Evgeny, softened by the years and acutely aware of the sadness of losing a parent to dementia, although he was suspicious that Dimitry's recent problems were divine retribution for the way he had treated people, and said, 'Tell him his brother sends his love and hug your mother, for no reason, just hug her. She loves you more than you know. Now, leave before it gets too dark for driving. And thank you, I am in your debt, you are a good boy, I will not forget what you have done for me, and not just today' said Vasili, 'We will gain a check mate soon, yes? The pieces are all falling in to their correct positions, I have my next moves all planned out, have no fear'

With that Evgeny left the cottage to return to the other side of the valley, a ninety minute drive if conditions were favourable. There was no time to lose for Vasili, once again he was to leave his childhood home, perhaps never to set eyes on it again if things did not go well for him. He packed a meagre travel bag for his journey into the West. This would be his redemption. Before he knew it Andreyev Sigalov would welcome him back with open arms and he would no longer need to hide in the shadows or he would be confined to living in the West with no chance of seeing his nephew again. All the fortune he had amassed in his years in Moscow would either be lost or retained, if so one day to be bequeathed to Evgeny when he eventually passed, an act of kindness as much for Ulyana as for Evgeny, knowing that there was nothing of value his own brother could leave to his only son. The only thing he may pass on to him was the possibility of a hereditary condition. It was for this reason that his plan should succeed, he couldn't leave his Ulyana and her son with nothing.

He was now to drive himself to the border of Finland where he would meet his Swedish driver who would take him the rest of the journey, a roundabout route, by road and sea, low risk and low profile. He was going to meet his destiny one way or another, the culmination of many years of hard work and planning. He would leave at first light, the four day journey would give him plenty of time to get his affairs in order and to focus his mind on the job in hand.

Thirty Three - Cross Country

Six months previously Vasili Dragunov had been sitting opposite Sati Chatterjee in a cramped stuffy office just off a main thoroughfare in the Chor Bazaar in Mumbai for a particular set of reasons. Firstly to acquire three fake passports in different names and of different European nationalities, secondly to acquire various visas to gain entry into certain European countries especially the UK, and thirdly to tidy up some unfinished business that had been hanging over his head for too long now.

It was so easy, when you came from Moscow, for India and the Indian masses to have little impact on your day to day thoughts. From the few individuals you may have met on your travels they came across generally as a warm and generous race of people who were happy to spread their culture, be it food, music or Bollywood movie sensibilities beyond their own continent upon the western world of Europe and the Americas. What you realised after visiting a bustling conurbation like Mumbai is that there is an awful lot more to India than you could ever dream of. Like any other large metropolis, Mumbai has its grimy underworld where for a price you could buy anything your heart desired and where unlike any other metropolis you could sink without a trace either willingly or possibly unwillingly. Much of Mumbai had changed over the last thirty years since Vasili had first visited, many areas had been modernized and cleaned up. The dismantling of the slums being first and foremost to go as they discouraged tourism. The sprawling mass that sat at the foot of the World Trade Centre that had housed the many labourers who worked on the project had been eradicated. Colaba was now a respectable tourist destination that could not put up with the open sewage systems and the wild packs of dogs that roamed the streets after sunset, the dark and dangerous underbelly that came with slum living. Many of these builders and tradesmen had moved on after the completion of the towers, along with their few possessions, their families and very little else, often to the next building job which could be another five year or ten year project. Mumbai had not dragged itself entirely out of the previous century, Chor Bazaar sat proudly in the centre of the city, resisting change while still drawing tourism; it was a market where you could buy almost anything you could imagine, spices from Marathra, snake oil from Bangladesh, local breads, flour, ornate carvings, the latest fashions, exotic fruit, freshly cooked rotis, pudachi wadi, batata vada or zunka bhakri; all exquisite local dishes, the list was wondrous and endless. It was a place where Vasili could lose himself in the culture of another world, a million miles away from Moscow and all that it entailed. When in Mumbai it were as if nothing else existed, so consuming was the city. What drew him to the bazaar now were the expert skills of Sati Chatterjee, the infamous forger extraordinaire, who could, for a price, depending on what you desired, create a dual identity that could only be detected by the most thorough scrutiny. Chatterjee was proud to be able to tell his clients that his passports had been used in all major destination airports without being flagged. The few clients who had been caught while holding a forged 'book' were the ones who had not had the strength of character to carry off the deception and had blown the deceit themselves.

Vasili sat opposite Sati and looked over the three forged passports and nodded in admiration, Mumbai really was the epitome of excellence when it came to forgeries, 'I am thankful to you for having these ready for me in time for my trip home, I wasn't sure whether three months had been long enough to craft them'

'It is not the crafting that took the most time' answered Sati in his thick accent, 'We keep a store of foreign passports in reserve as well as the ones which we will supply to order. We had plenty time to fulfil your wishes'

Sati Chatterjee, a man of diminutive stature, some would say peculiarly diminutive but not to his face, peered over his wire rim spectacles, sat calmly knowing that his work could not be faulted, 'It is only a matter now of the payment. You advanced me fifty percent of the cost when you made the order so it is the remainder you will be paying me now'

'Of course. I had already anticipated the work being first class so I took the liberty of wiring you the funds earlier today, they should be in your account now'

'That is very fine, I thank you. I will have my assistant check the account directly and we can finish up our business together'

'And while that is being done there is the other matter I had discussed with you. Did you have any success?'

'Of course Vasili. As I told you before 'If the man is in Mumbai we will find him for you' And with that he slipped a piece of paper across the table top. Vasili opened it up and read an address.

'Unfortunately it was slightly more difficult this man to find. I think he may not have wanted to be found. The price for you is three thousand dollars, it is very fair price'

Vasili didn't blink an eye, 'That is more than reasonable', drawing a wad of notes from his jacket pocket and counting out the denomination, 'And of course this matter will stay between you and I'

'It is our matter alone and no-one else's'

Sati nodded that the money had indeed been successfully transferred and closed his laptop.

'Wonderful, then it just leaves me to say thank you and I hope that God is with you. I will see myself out'

Dragunov exited the offices into the busy market place where upon leaving the cool, quiet interior of the building there was an immediate rush to the senses. The early afternoon heat was becoming overbearing, his cool tailored suit doing nothing to inure him to the beating sun, the noise and smell of the market bombarding his senses. He looked again at the scrap of paper with the address written on it and upon committing the words to memory screwed it up and threw it in a nearby cook's brazier to where it immediately burst into a blue flame and disappeared.

Tonight he would visit that address and finish his last piece of business in Mumbai.

Dragunov was brought back to reality with the realisation that the vehicle he was travelling in would soon be descending below sea level. An action that made him unreasonably nervous even though hundreds of cars make the same journey every single day. He closed his eyes and calmed his mind, ridding his thoughts of the undeniable, irrational urge to panic. Some deep-seated survivalist instinct bubbling just below his conscious mind was warning him of the danger. He breathed deeply to calm his heart-rate, reassuring himself that it was all perfectly normal. The car was crossing the Øresund Strait on the bridge of the same name, some locals called it the 'salt and pepper' crossing after the Saltholm and Peberholm Islets, one natural and one man-made. Two thirds of the way across the strait the four lane highway gradually dips into the Drodgen Tunnel and the remaining part of the journey to Copenhagen from Malmo is taken underneath the water.

The soft evening sunlight suddenly gave way to the harsh fluorescent strip lighting of the tunnel and within a few minutes the car was swallowed up by the concrete surroundings of the underpass. Vasili considered the engineering that had been involved in the construction of the twelve kilometre crossing from Sweden to Denmark. Built with a four lane motorway as well as a rail link it also boasted having the highest concentration of internet data flowing through its cables running parallel with the road, connecting Sweden and Finland to the rest of mainland Europe. The man made Islet of Peberholm was also a marvel of human endeavour, it was a structure so huge that it was hard to imagine that at one time it had never existed. Recently it had been made mandatory to show your credentials upon entering the crossing from either country, something that up until last year had not been considered necessary, another civil liberty thwarted in the name of the War on Terror. Once immersed the tunnel runs along the seabed in a groove nearly forty metres wide and at a depth of ten metres, a fact that Vasili knew all too well and which was reason enough to give him cause for concern, his primitive subconscious rising up to challenge his natural pragmatism.

As his driver, Yusef, began the ascent from the depths of the ocean floor the car emerged again into the dying light of the evening, the setting sun casting it's warm glow on the airport buildings to the south, a passenger jet roaring overhead making its final descent into Københavns Lufthavn rattling the vehicle with the down force from its huge wings. It was a convoluted journey they were taking to reach their destination in the U.K. but it was necessary to avoid needless risks at airport customs. They had travelled through Finland around the northern edge of the Gulf of Bothnia, then south taking the route of roads less travelled to avoid the capital, Stockholm, and crossing the Storebæltsbroen, a 16 kilometre suspension bridge spanning the 'Great Belt', the strait separating Denmark from mainland Europe. Leaving Denmark they would drive on through Hamburg and Bremen in Germany, which was unfortunately unavoidable, eventually ending up in Amsterdam in The Netherlands where they would seek a sea crossing over the channel into Britain. It was a long and arduous trip that had given Vasili plenty of time to consider his past as well as his future. His mind again drifted back to Mumbai where he had that appointment with a man at the address he had committed to memory.

It was the very same evening after having collected the documentation from Sati Chatterjee that Vasili had been sitting in the undersized dilapidated one-room dwelling above a spice vendor's market stall not too far from the Chor Bazaar. He waited no more than forty five minutes before the bane of his current predicament came shuffling home in a semi drunken stupor, muttering some Russian shanty under his breath. As soon as he saw Vasili's gun trained on him from the murky shadows of the room he abruptly stopped in his tracks, the colour drained from his face and the effects of the vodka he had consumed reduced considerably as it dawned on him the amount of danger he was in. Vasili watched him intently as each expression on his face clearly showed what he was thinking. Initially the automatic reaction to bolt, followed by the reasoning that a shot to the back would soon stop his retreat, next the scan of the immediate vicinity with nervous flicks of the eyes for weapons that may be of use in this situation, then the realisation that he was in fact helpless and at the mercy of the man sitting in the pale linen suit.

Vasili flicked the barrel of the gun gesturing for Gregor 'Ryba' Tarasovich to take a seat in the wooden chair in the centre of the pokey room. He had earned the nickname Ryba meaning The Fish because of his wide mouth and thick lips as well as his cold demeanour when it came to running jobs for the lower echelons of middle management at The Kremlin. He was lying low in Mumbai trying to avoid exactly this scenario, his life being cut short for screwing over the wrong person. Vasili knew from his nephew that Ryba had been instrumental in tarnishing his copybook with Sigalov back in Moscow and it was time that he should repay that debt. Once seated Vasili took from his jacket pocket a handful of thick black zip ties. Handing one to Ryba he instructed him to attach his left wrist to the arm of the chair. Once secured he tied the right wrist to the other arm of the chair and repeated the action on both ankles to the wooden legs of the chair. When finished Ryba and the chair were as one and were not able to move separately. Vasili ignored the pleading that began to emanate from the ugly thick mouth of the traitor, someone who for his own gain without a shred of integrity or honour, had taken a part in his downfall and put him in the position of exile he was now in. To stop the pathetic whimpering Vasili stuffed a rag into his mouth to quieten what was next to be done, he was not here to kill Ryba, only to send a message; a message that would echo from here to Moscow with resounding reverberations. When Ryba realised he was not to be killed he began to panic all the more, his eyes widening, the only form of communication he had left, knowing that what beheld him was more likely to be a fate worse than death.

Vasili stood behind Ryba in the darkened room and donned a pair of leather gloves, unusual apparel for this time of year in Mumbai, but he had brought them along with him for a reason. With the tips of his left hand he gripped the upper incisors and pulled Ryba's head back until he was staring wide eyed at the ceiling. With his right hand he rested the ball of his thumb against his lower row of teeth and began to gradually increase the pressure. Slowly but with an inevitability Ryba's jaw stretched and in doing so the pain he felt increased exponentially, the rag in his throat stopped anything but a stifled scream from escaping his throat, again his eyes told the story of his agony, pleading for his tormentor to stop. Vasili was surprised at how far a human jaw could be prised before the ultimate disjunct between the mandible and the maxilla, the jolt and crack that followed had two outcomes; the lower part of Ryba's face took on the eternal terrifying form of a silent scream, conversely his eyes had at last closed due to the fact that he had passed out from the agonies that had been inflicted on him. This suited Dragunov as the next part of the job would be so much easier now that he was unconscious, he took out a compact oblong box from his breast pocket and removed from it a surgeon's scalpel. If a man couldn't keep his tongue from wagging he would have to learn that lesson the hard way.

The car rolled along incessantly, south bound along the E45 soon to be leaving Denmark behind and entering Germany for a brief period. This being the border with the most probability of being heavily scrutinized, they would counteract the risk by deviating via Krusa just before reaching the checkpoint and crossing over where the security was not so heavily maintained. They would be stopping in Neumunster for something to eat and a chance to stretch their legs and refresh themselves. The hardest part of the journey was nearly behind them.

Thirty Four - Going Sour

Kapusta got out of the black Volga Siber and walked stiffly with a slight limp towards the enclosure's entrance and rang the buzzer. He was dressed all in black, a thick long woollen coat covering the length of his body, snow-worthy boots, thick leather gloves and a typical ushanka on his head with the flaps let down over his ears. His scarf covered the lower part of his face so only his eyes were visible, his undamaged eye kept half closed in the face of the biting wind blowing across the reservoir, the other eye persistently weeping. It was -10 degrees but the wind made it feel colder, the sky above was made up of many shades of grey but held no snow in it, although remnants remained with more than a foot covering the ground. The tree's branches in the nearby wood sagged with the weight of the recent snowfall and made a stark contrast to the scudding sky behind. Visitors to Ribinski Reservoir may have described it as beautiful in the more clement months of the year but Kapusta knew it to be a barren and inhospitable place when the cold took hold of the landscape. He had driven the 300 kilometres from Moscow arriving at the facility for the designated time of 7pm, stopping briefly in Kamenniki for a bite to eat as the evening may very well turn out to be a long one. It was his fourth trip up to the facility to see Dominika Zotov, the woman who was personally assembling the Lobaev rifle for him.

Dominika had taken over the bespoke arms service from her father, Dima Zotov, fifteen years ago after learning everything there was to know about Russian firearms. As he had become more aged her father's health had begun failing and he had moved to Moscow to stay with his younger sister who could take him on his frequent visits to the hospital. Sadly he had died six years ago after a long and painful battle with cancer. His funeral in Moscow's Vagankovsky cemetery in the Presnensky District was only attended by a handful of people, Dominika noted that there was only one man whom she didn't know by sight who she assumed was from a governmental department judging by his attire. Probably sent there to check and make sure her father really was deceased, no doubt to return to Moscow HQ and tick a box on a form proving so, the Russians liked their bureaucracy. She lived and worked in The Facility, as she liked to call it, which was about 10km north of Kamenniki on a spit of land overlooking the vast expanse of water. Visitors were by appointment only and had to go through her own vetting procedure before initially being let through the fortified gates. She liked the fact that it was a cold and forbidding land in the middle of nowhere, it deterred any unwanted visitors wandering around. Many people were not suited to the solitude or to the barren landscape but she found beauty in the bleak skies and the slate-grey water of the reservoir, she found comfort in the snow flurries blocking out the sky in the winter, she found no need for the gayness of flowers in a vase as some women might, she found their gaudiness distasteful and out of place.

Dima Zotov had made bespoke firearms ever since he found he had a knack for doing so at the age of fifteen. In the beginning he made them for himself, as a hobby, taking existing parts from similar weapons and retooling them to make more superior models. His talents became well known in Rybinsk and Yaroslav and soon enough he was being asked by the upper echelons at The Kremlin and in the military to build specific guns for particular individuals, certain specially trained soldiers, expressly snipers. He set up Fabrika, The Factory, when he was twenty-one, on the site that Dominika now carried on his tradition. It was specifically built to house everything he would need to fabricate and assemble his works of art, as he saw them. Behind the austere grey concrete exterior were rooms specifically designed for crafting the barrels, carving the stocks and fashioning the actions of the rifles. Of course times change and so do techniques; Dominika's work was now quite different to how her father had made weapons for all those years. She understood what he did and appreciated the beauty in his creations but the modern sniper wanted an amalgamation of state-of-the-art weaponry designed with accuracy and efficiency in mind. She specialized in Lobaev rifles, although they may not have the beauty of her father's designs they were said to be the most accurate sniper rifle over the longest distance and they were the rifle of choice for many marksmen.

Kapusta waited in the cold for the gates to be unlocked from the main building. When he heard the sharp buzz from the keypad the lock sprang free and the gate proceeded to glide open on silent hinges to admit him onto the property. He knew not to bring the car up the drive, he had been told quite emphatically that any vehicles were to be left outside the compound. As he walked towards the entrance he noted how the grey building practically disappeared into the background of the slate sky almost as if it were camouflaged. Kapusta cursed Zotov for being so eccentric, she had so many odd rules that you had to adhere to, if you chose not to obey them she could quite simply cut you off. Admittedly she could afford to be awkward as she might be the only person within a thousand kilometres who could assemble the weapon just the way he wanted. He trudged with his head pulled down into his woollen coat, up on through the layer of snow on the ground and made his way to the entrance where Dominika was waiting for him. She stood in the doorway with the bright light from inside framing her. She was wearing her working apparel, loose jeans, a buttoned work blouse and a thick leather apron tied around her waist and neck, her short dark hair held up with a bandana to stop it flopping over her forehead. She stood there ostensibly not feeling, or maybe not minding, the cold as if it had no effect on her whatsoever. Kapusta pushed past her into the atrium of the building and stamped his feet.

'Welcome back Kapusta' she said over politely but with a warm smile.

Kapusta said nothing as he peeled off bits of outer clothing one by one, grumbling to himself as he did so.

'I knew you couldn't stay away' said Dominika with a mischievous grin, knowing full well that today was the day Kapusta was collecting his beloved rifle, after being given the full breakdown of its workings of course. She enjoyed teasing him as he didn't intimate having the verbal dexterity to counteract her wordplay. 'I have been thinking about you since our last meeting. Have you been thinking of me? My dear Kapusta' she teased

'This meeting has been on my mind every day since the last time we met' he said matter-of-factly, 'but not for the reasons you may be suggesting' He didn't know how to read Dominika, he was almost certain that she was just playing with him, trying to trick him into playing his hand and admitting that he found her attractive, which he did. She made him flustered. She had a boyishness to her that aroused him; slight perky breasts, narrow hips, shorter hair than was usual for most women that he knew. She was confident in her natural beauty and as a result did not feel the need to use make-up. Her high cheekbones and perfectly arched eyebrows didn't need any enhancing although Kapusta would have preferred seeing a splash of colour on her lips to deny her androgyny. By definition the trade in assembling firearms was a manly trade and a thing you rarely encountered women doing, it stirred up feelings of confusion in Kapusta. He didn't know what she could see in him, his face and body deformed almost beyond recognition. He knew he wasn't an easy man to look at, many people looked on him with disgust or pity. Dominika, however, either didn't notice his scarring or didn't care about it, she didn't take any heed of it at all. She spoke to him as if he were just any other person, which was what made him suspicious, he didn't like to be made a fool of.

'I am here for the gun and nothing else' he stated

'You are not even a little pleased to see me?' she asked 'It can be so solitary here in the Factory for weeks on end, I am pleased to see you. I enjoy your company. You are not an apple-polisher, as they say in Vologda'

'I polish no man's apples' Kapusta retorted with a wry grin

'That's what I like about you. Now, come. Follow me and I will show you your weapon. I think you will be very pleased with me and the work I have done for you. I can tell you are a man who demands perfection, yes?'

Kapusta nodded agreement and followed Dominika into the heart of the building through the workshops. He had not seen this part of her operation before as his previous visits had been held in the more relaxed meeting rooms at the fore of the structure. He took everything in around him with a curiosity that he would have liked to have satiated, but Dominika strode on with a purpose that did not encourage questions. He was impressed by the sheer magnitude of the machinery and the apparent meticulous attention to detail and precision. The concrete finish to the floors and walls gave this area a sense of being the factory floor where all the work would be done. Many different varieties of gun in many states of assemblage were stacked neatly on racks in cases on the far wall. He could tell that mostly they were Lobaev rifles with a few other Russian models there being used for their parts. Kapusta craned his neck as they left the area and entered a well-lit corridor, then returned his gaze to Dominika's rear swaying gently as she walked ahead of him. Conversation was not forthcoming as her purpose now was only to reach their destination. He was now being led, impossibly it seemed, in the direction of where the lake should be situated. His sense of direction and orientation became more confused the further they walked, they turned corners and walked along curved passageways. He followed her down dimly lit corridors passing doors with compact windows inlaid into their upper halves, the interiors showing nothing as no light entered these rooms from any exterior windows. He may have been imagining it but he sensed they were descending slowly as they progressed, could it be possible that they were now under the lake? It was difficult to tell at this point and he was sure that disorientation was part of the factory's structure.

Eventually they came to a large steel door which opened up into a room lit by a dim entrance light, Dominika flicked a switch upon entering which began a sequenced activation of lights throughout the length of the room. Kapusta looked on astounded as each light that turned on revealed an impossibly endless room going off into the distance. The illumination of the room took perhaps thirty seconds and when finished he could only just make out the far end where there were a selection of targets and cut-outs. The ceiling had an illusory effect of bearing down upon his head as he looked down the shooting range, an optical illusion to be sure. It wasn't possible that this room could exist considering where the building was in relation to the body of water.

'Seven hundred and fifty metres' she said apropos of nothing

'Where are we?' he asked

'Isn't it obvious?' Dominika replied, 'We are in the shooting gallery'

'I realise that, but where in the compound?'

'The compound is large. All you need to know is that you are in capable hands my dear friend. Now, would you like to see your rifle?'

'Of course'

'Then I shall fetch it. Wait here one moment'

Dominika opened the door to a small anteroom where she had the gun kept safely until it was needed. When she returned she was carrying a large, black hard-cover rifle case reminiscent of an elongated suitcase with a handle and two clasps, the letters SVLK-14S branded on the leather. Kapusta noted there was also an option of locking the case with a code, this small detail pleased him. She laid the case on its side on the table and waited for Kapusta to open it up. She enjoyed the moment when a client first laid eyes on the finished product. She noted how his eyes fell on the rifle and took in all the aspects of its beauty before reaching in and taking it from its bespoke, black velvet resting place. She reached into the desk drawer and took out a box of ammunition and placed it on the table beside the gun.

'After you' she said to Kapusta, giving him permission to pick up the weapon. He felt Dominika's gaze on him as he turned the weapon over in his hands feeling the distribution of weight and the quality of build. In the back of his mind he was considering what the weapon was going to be used for and in what scenario the rifle would be best put to use. He tried to ignore Dominika's eyes on him as he checked the rifle's barrel and firing mechanism but he became more self-conscious than ever while doing so. She was getting under his skin and he didn't like it.

'You will need these' she said and held out her palm which held two lumps of putty. Knowing he would need to put down the weapon to insert the ear defenders she saved him from doing so; taking a piece of putty in each hand, rolling them between her thumb and forefinger she stepped toward him, the putty would warm from contact with her skin and mould to the shape of the inner ear. He could feel her light breath on his face and detected a pleasant aroma of mint intermingled with her scent that was unmistakably jasmine. Dominika gently pressed the two pieces of putty into Kapusta's ears letting her soft hands lay against his damaged skin for a beat before slowly removing them by letting her fingertips trail down his chin towards his lips. 'Now I think you are all set' she said before inserting her own defenders. Kapusta's blush did not show but something deep inside of him stirred, a thirst that would need to be quenched.

He drew his attention back to the gun. The 'Twilight' certainly was a thing of beauty, this particular model as requested was finished in matt black and had a length of nearly a metre and a half, about two-thirds of that being the barrel. Making kill shots at 3 kilometres was not unheard of, although being a relatively new gun on the market he would have to find out the qualities of the weapon for himself, something he would start now with a few shots at target in the range. Even if the range was a fraction of the rifle's capabilities. He would need to test the rifle in real world settings to determine its true strengths and weaknesses.

He took one of the .408 Cheytac rounds out of the box pulled back the bolt and inserted it into the chamber before getting down onto his belly to personate his prospective position in the field. He pulled out the spiked bipod feet and rested the weapon on the ground before making himself more comfortable. He was impressed by Dominika's attention to detail as the floor below him was apparently padded so as to not cause any discomfort while lying prone. He offered his eye to the scope and looked through to the various targets at the end of the tunnel. He was quietly impressed that the miniscule bullseye targets loomed large in the viewfinder and were clear and bright beyond reason.

'You will notice, Kapusta, that the optics I have used in the scope are of the highest quality. It will prove useful even in the lowest of lights, enhancing the subject by using Swarovski optics and an optional zoom. But just in case you have to use the rifle in the dead of night it can be fitted with a night vision scope, which, unfortunately, because of the nature of the beast, does not have the same distance capabilities'

Kapusta did not answer Dominika but instead was waiting for his breathing and heart rate to settle and for his body to become at one with the weapon. He held it lightly in his two hands, one on the barrel and the other gently on the grip. He would not move his finger on to the trigger until he was sure he would be taking a shot, that was the first rule; engage the weapon only when you are certain. He heard Dominika behind him humming gently under her breath and tried to ignore the distraction. In the field there would be much more in the way of disturbance but it exasperated him that she could not keep quiet. He began pranayama, a breathing exercise he had been developing himself, it had been a way to cope since the accident that had caused all his bodily wounds. It was a version of Sama Vritti, a yogic relaxation tool that dealt with calming the mind and body. It had been part of his recovery and a way to come to terms with what had happened to him. Soon he found himself focusing in on the targets only and blocking out all extraneous noise and diversions.

Kapusta eased his finger onto the trigger and squeezed gently. The shot rang out and he could see immediately that the sight was in need of a slight adjustment. He had hit the target but the damage was high and wide by a few inches. He rectified this by turning the fine tune dials on the scope just so slightly. Not moving from his spot he pulled back the bolt and inserted another round of ammo. This time the round hit the mark without any deviation. He reloaded and fired one more to ensure the second shot was not a fluke. Happy with his progress Kapusta put the gun through its paces, trying out different types of ammunition and switching scopes to get to know how the gun would feel and perform. This included blackout conditions, Dominika killing the lights for him and donning her own night vision goggles while he made the shots. He was methodical in his evaluation of the weapon, Dominika lending a hand whenever was needed. He spent the best part of two hours lying down in that same position, so much so that when he eventually decided it was time to put an end to the testing Dominika thought he would need a hand to get into an upright position again. She offered him a helping hand but he refused and sprang out of his prone position with a vitality that surprised her.

'What do you say, Kapusta? Judging by your exhaustive trials I think you are happy with your purchase, yes?'

'I am happy. She will do nicely' he said, 'Your fee has been wired into your account prior to my arrival. I had no doubt that you would not satisfy my expectations, your work is as always of the highest calibre. I would not have come to you unless I knew I was getting the best service'

'Then I think we need a drink to finish off our deal, I will not take no for an answer, follow me into the living quarters and I will show you the hospitality of a Dubna. That was where our family home was before I moved out here permanently' she talked as she helped Kapusta pack away the gun back into the case, 'We lived in a modest house on the south of The Volga, not the most beautiful of towns but it was home to me and my three brothers'

'Where are your brothers now?' he asked, 'and why did they not follow in your father's footsteps, why was it you who took on his work?'

'I had a passion for it. Unfortunately my brothers did not have the temperament for the work. Dimitri and Anatoly both joined the army, being both older than me and both similar in age they had always wanted to serve, even from such an early age they had no other dreams. They always wanted to be fighting whether it was with each other or with the boys from the north side of the Volga, it broke my mother's heart. They would ride their bikes over the bridge where the hydro station was and take on gangs in the parks, they enjoyed it very much. The army was the best place for them to vent all their aggression, and they also needed a firm hand which they got in the military, they were not suited to civilian life, that's to be sure. Viktor, who is younger than me, preferred a less manly role in life, I am more of a man than him. He has worked in a shop in Moscow for the last six years selling clothes, it suits his less masculine side. If I tell you he has never had a female companion you will get the idea what sort of man he is'

'Do you keep in touch?'

'Only with Dimitri and Anatoly, they visit me when they are on leave every four months or so, depending on where they are stationed at the time. I have no time for Viktor, he has cut ties with our family and I am OK with that'

With the gun now packed away they started off back the way they had come, Kapusta carrying the weighty case this time, again walking behind Dominika as he was still not sure he had the route back clear in his mind with all its twists and turns. He happily fell in behind his host where he could take in her elegant gait as she led the way back to the softly furnished living area. Talk again was sparse as they walked but he did not mind as his thoughts were full of the contradictions he was trying to work out and separate. It had been too long since he had 'known' a woman, and it suggested to him, impossibly, that Dominika was attracted to him. Or was it that she was playing with him? He did not know. He found women difficult to work out. On the previous visits here he had found it curious how Dominika had never mentioned his burns and scars, her eyes always fell on him with compassion and not pity. If he did nothing about it now he wouldn't know how she really felt about him, it may be the last time their paths would cross.

They entered the sumptuously comfortable but sparse room that Dominika referred to as her salon, although Kapusta didn't think the name was suitable. It looked cosy enough but lacked the furniture or decor that would make it suitable for relaxation. He noticed a Lempicka painting on the wall along with some other locally sourced art and he was pleasantly surprised by Dominika's taste. She walked to a cabinet and opened it up to reveal a bar that would put most taprooms in Moscow to shame. There were bottles lined up that covered most of the European countries as well as oddities from around the globe; whiskies from Scotland and Ireland, Gins from the UK, Absinthe and Pernod from France, Arrack from Sri Lanka, Bolivian Singani, Romanian Tuica and of course a selection of the finest vodkas from The Motherland. Kapusta noted there was an extremely rare and aged bottle of Hrenovuna that he had not had the pleasure of appraising, the horseradish root lay in the bottom of the bottle continuing to flavour and enhance the pungency of the alcohol. He was pleased to see that the bottle's contents were as clear as water, not like the mixture he tried to make in the shed at home when he was a teenager. He enjoyed the bitter taste and strong bite that the garlic infused concoction gave off, he liked the way that it made your eyes water and burned the back of your throat, it was somehow comforting and reminded him of his younger days.

After telling Dominika of his preference she poured them both shot glasses of the clear liquid.

'Pey do dna' Dominika said with a broad grin, pleased that their business was complete and that her client was gratified with her work. Kapusta looked at her quizzically as this was not the usual toast for a Russian to make from this part of the country, or any part of the country for that matter. They both drained their glasses in one and slammed the shot glass down onto the counter ready for a refill. Dominika's cheeks immediately flushed as she was apparently not used to such strong spirits.

'I am more used to Australian Shiraz' she said as way of explanation and then laughed giddily enjoying the prospect of letting loose.

'If you would prefer to drink wine, I will not think any less of you. If you are not used to this particular vodka it could have a powerful effect. Be warned'

'Maybe just the one more then, as it is already poured'

Kapusta took the next drink, knowing that the initial toast was the only drink you tossed back, and moved to the leather sofa to savour the next one, Dominika followed his lead and sat not exactly next to him but in his vicinity on the same sofa. He noticed she had somehow changed in his eyes since he first saw her earlier on in the evening, she had gone to the trouble of applying an imperceptibly subtle amount of make-up; a little blusher, some eyeliner and a hint of lipstick. She had lost the leather apron and the blouse she wore was unbuttoned showing the perfect line of her clavicles. The effect was immediate and dramatic, his cheeks warmed and he could feel himself stiffen, he only hoped that she did not notice.

'You must meet people from all over the country, in your line of work' he stated

'Not only Russians. We, or rather, I have been supplying to most of Europe for the last four years and have been making headway expanding the operation worldwide in the last two. This is why, you may have noticed, there are so many different tipples in the cabinet. I find it always helps matters when you can toast a successful transaction when it is in the national drink of the client'

'Surely you can't cater for all tastes. Have you ever been caught out?'

'Only once, it happened to be a lady from Scotland of all places, I can't tell you too much about her and her business for obvious reasons. We had gone through more or less the same process as we have done. We got to the point where she was picking up the merchandise and we were as we are now, toasting to the completion of the trade. Being Scottish I had assumed she would be a whisky drinker, which she was, but she wanted to mix the single malt, '89 Pulteney with something called Irn Bru. Have you ever heard of it?'

'No'

'She wouldn't drink the whisky without it, she said it wouldn't taste the same... I could tell from the start this woman was going to be a problem. I had vetted her like any other client and she came up clean, maybe a bit too clean if you ask me. I couldn't put my finger on it up until this point but things were turning sour fairly quickly'

'What happened?'

'She insisted on going to her car for a can of the stuff, can you believe it? So I let her go. The weather was not as wintry as it is today. I stood at the door and watched her walk to her car, which was parked a bit further away than yours is now. The outer gate had closed behind her, she would need to be allowed access to the building again to collect her gun. Unfortunately for her I was not inclined to let her mix a 27 year old vintage single malt with some vile orange concoction that teenagers drink in the streets of Glasgow. She returned to the gate and I saw her ring the buzzer then I turned heel and closed the door behind me'

'Are you serious? You blew the whole deal over a mixer?'

'What would you say if I mixed my Hrenovuna with some Coca-Cola?'

'I would say you were mad'

'Why?'

'Because it is a pure drink not to be diluted with anything, let alone Coke, it would ruin it'

'Exactly so. This was a woman I was not willing or capable of doing business with. If only I had found out earlier it would have saved us both a lot of time and money'

'Kapusta laughed, 'And what happened after? Were there any repercussions?'

'It was quite funny actually. I watched her scream at me from the upstairs window for a while until I got bored. She became extremely vexed indeed. Next time I looked out at her she was sitting in her car with her head in her hands. Who knows what she was up to? I gave her another half an hour before calling the local politsiya from Kamenniki who arrived within ten minutes and advised her to move on. Officer Mikhailov is a close and dear friend of mine, he looks after my interests as a single woman living all alone out here'

'And nothing after that?'

'No. Not a word'

'I am really glad I didn't ask for cranberry in my vodka. I wouldn't have known who to go to for a gun such as the one you have made for me'

'You are a very resourceful man, I am sure you would have coped'

They had both finished their second glass and Dominika got up to go to the bar for another refill. As she did so she stumbled only slightly and with the back of her hand she brushed her forehead, feeling slightly flushed with the alcohol.

'I told you it was strong'

'Maybe I will only have a small one this time. I assume you will have another'

'Of course, it will brace me for my long journey back to Moscow'

Dominika leaned over to him with his drink 'I can think of better ways to brace oneself, Kapusta', he caught a glimpse down her blouse at her perfect bosom cupped in lace as she leaned in closer and caught the faint aroma of mint once more and his reticence left him. With one hand he gripped her wrist spilling the vodka on the sofa as the other grabbed her waist and pulled her to him, their faces lingered a beat before Dominika hungrily kissed him on his scarred lips. Kapusta could feel himself stiffening once again, this time with an ache that would need to be satisfied at any cost. His hands were not as gentle as they once were as he pulled at her blouse to place his hands on her bare skin. He wrenched at the material until the buttons burst and scattered over the floor. He pulled her towards him firmly as they kissed, his hands savouring the heat of her skin in the small of her back, her hand placed on the back of his neck, fingers running through his uneven hair. All of a sudden it became too much for him, he had to have her, now; he broke off from the kiss and twisted Dominika's arm until it was behind her back, she protested but Kapusta pulled her other free arm round behind her also and held both wrists within one large powerful hand. He moved himself off the sofa and pushed Dominika down so she was kneeling on the floor her cheek pressed down onto the leather seat of the sofa. Holding her there forcefully he used his free hand to pull her jeans down over her pale buttocks revealing a pair of white panties, these he also pulled down exposing her silken quim. With his fingers he explored the area between her legs and found that she was misty from her own arousal. He could wait no longer, not letting her wriggle from his grip he awkwardly freed his stiff member from his fly and urgently inserted it into the warm folds of her womanhood. There he let himself experience the warmth enveloping his rod before he started thrusting, slowly at first, savouring the feeling of his cock sliding in and out of her, then gradually, without the ability to desist, speeding up until the pounding from his hips made the sofa scrape on the floor, an ache forming in his loins from crashing repeatedly into Dominika's buttocks. He was aware of nothing else apart from the need to achieve his own climax, he hadn't known a woman in this way for so long, since before the accident, the only pleasure he had in that time he had given to himself. His thrusting was all and everything, eyes closed and head held back his hips rammed her with a cruelty that Dominika had not expected. She whimpered and protested to no effect, his strong arms holding her in place as his thrusting became frenzied. He let go of her arms now and moved his hands to her slim hips and held them tight as his orgasm built, the weight of his upper body bared down on her, all the blood drained from his face as he let out a guttural groan that rasped in his throat, his ejaculation becoming all encompassing, a beautiful agony going on and on, pulsing and jerking, the muscles and tendons in his upper body rigid with the electricity pulsing through his body.

Eventually the spasms relented and Kapusta slid out of Dominika, falling away from her to sit on the floor with his back against the sofa, out of breath, eyes closed, his now flaccid member still protruding from his fly laying against his black trousers leaving a mark of spilled seed. Dominika slowly gathered herself, pulling up her panties and jeans, then crawling up onto the sofa and lying in a foetal position wrapping her torn blouse around her to cover her modesty, saying nothing, too shocked at the speed and ferocity of it all to form any comment, her eyes moist and her mouth dry.

Eventually she uttered, 'I think you should go now', her eyes red from the tears he had elicited.

Kapusta picked himself up off the floor and straightened out his attire, his face now red from his exertions. He knew better than to say anything, to try and justify what he had done, he had been unable to stop himself. He stood with his back to her and leant down to pick up Dominika's glass from the table, knocking it back in one go and wiping his mouth with the back of his hand, any pretence of decency leaving him as if he had given up trying, he then let the glass clatter back onto the glass table before picking up the rifle case and walking into the atrium to gather his outdoor clothes. He solemnly donned his scarf, coat and hat before walking out into the cold, dark night to drive the 300 km back to Moscow with only his demons to keep him company. He walked with his head down, ashamed and downcast, a black cloud forming behind his eyes. He tried to divert his enmity towards a more deserving figure; the man he had to kill, the man he had been hired to shoot with the gun now in the boot of the car; his ticket to a permanent life in The Motherland, not having to look over his shoulder any longer. He would put Dominika out of his mind, he was a fool to have let his guard down with her; it was not a mistake he would make a second time.

35 - The Plot Thickens

Anil let the phone ring for almost two minutes before Alex finally picked up. 'Alex, thank God, are you OK?'

'I'm OK Anil, just a few bumps and bruises, although I'm going to have to come in for a debrief asap, things have escalated and I need to see you. We are dealing with something far bigger than Deanna and I, on our own, have the means to control'

'Before you come to Thames I've found something I thought you ought to know immediately, I don't know if it has any bearing on what you're up against but...'

'What is it?'

'You remember the laptop, Graham's laptop from the apartment? Well, we finally got into the hard drive. The techs had to access the hard drive directly, always much easier than trying to crack a password. Even so the files were all encrypted so it did take a bit of time, but nothing the team couldn't deal with. Graham had been extremely busy down there in Mexico. It looks like he had been researching False Flag operations subsequent and prior to the Navarre mission'

'What does that have to do with what's going on now?' asked Alex with a tone of exasperation and weariness in his voice.

'Bear with me Alex, we don't know if it does yet. But there are things you should know'

'For instance?'

'There is a huge amount of information regarding CHRISYS Logistics, I'm sure you're familiar with them?'

'I wouldn't say familiar but of course I've heard of them, teams of mercenaries for hire, founded by the Norwegian Rasmus Christianson, ex-military, not exactly legit from what I can gather but all I've heard are rumours mostly. I was actually approached by a head-hunter a few years back but I told him in no uncertain terms to 'sling his hook', although I don't think I was so polite, didn't think too much of it at the time'

'Well, Christianson set up CHRISYS in '95 after the downsizing of the Norwegian army. The fall of the Berlin Wall in '89, the Warsaw Pact and the end of the Cold War meant the government couldn't justify such a large military contingent so a lot of the troops were either let go or forced out. Of course Parliament not wanting to be accused for military cutbacks called it a 'restructuring'. Basically they didn't need a large army to mobilize any longer, they made it sleeker, more professional. It left a lot of bitter feelings for the men who had thought they would spend their working lives in the armed forces, you know, career men. I think that Christianson took it pretty badly. He spent a year or so floundering, or so we thought at the time, it now turns out that more likely he was laying the groundwork for CHRISYS; recruiting ex-military, amassing arms and weaponry, making connections within the corporations that run the Scandinavian governments. Looks like he invested his pay-off rather well'

'Then what?'

'We don't know for sure, as you said it is mainly rumours and conjecture. He has a fierce loyalty from any of the people who worked within the organization. We couldn't find one person that had anything to say regarding their work within CHRISYS. However, even in those early days CHRISYS had been linked to a certain amount of 'housekeeping' for the BND, the German Federal Intelligence Agency; clearing up loose ends, getting rid of embarrassing individuals etcetera'

'But what has all that got to do with False Flag Ops?'

'According to Graham's research, CHRISYS are responsible for at least four false flags in Great Britain in the five years prior to your team heading out to Navarre. The only reason I am mentioning it is that Jack Cole's name kept coming up and is prominent in three out of four of these Ops. The most notable one being the West London 'Bomb on the Bus' in 2004. Supposedly a 'terrorist cell' of two young Muslim extremists from West London who left a rucksack full of explosives on a Number 33 bus from Hounslow. As has become apparent from Graham's findings and is common to these terror alert scenarios the passengers were all government patsies. Now what is peculiar about this particular event is that it was either quite poorly planned from the terrorist's point of view, or that is was very well carried out from a governmental point of view. The damage was fairly minimal considering the reported payload of the bomb. There was little or no question whether the brothers, Mohammed and Khaleed Hossein, were the extremists intent on killing a bus load of innocent people. I expect you remember seeing the photos of the wreckage in the newspapers' Anil continued not awaiting an answer, 'there were between fifteen and twenty people being treated in and around the area after the explosion, civilians were on hand to lend first aid and support but were unable to because of the rapid response by the teams of metropolitan police and what many assumed at the time to be another arm of law enforcement. What Graham had unearthed was the video footage and still images from members of the public in the vicinity soon after the blast that show this team to be employees of CHRISYS. This is where it gets into bizarre territory, would you believe they were wearing jackets with the CHRISYS logos on them? As if that wouldn't be noticed'

'What is their logo? Can you describe it?'

'It's a simple outline of the sun as far as I can tell'

'Are you sure?'

'Yes, a small circle with eight triangles around the edges' Anil heard Alex laughing sardonically at the explanation, 'What is it?'

'I'm not sure that it is a sun, it could be alternatively the symbol for chaos, don't you think? It makes a lot more sense considering their line of work'

'My God, you're dead right Alex, why couldn't I see that?'

'But what made Graham think it was a false flag? As I remember reading there were training operations going on that day. The Met were running a series of rapid response scenarios for an airliner coming down in an urban setting, what with Hounslow being directly underneath the Heathrow flight path. I'm actually surprised there hasn't been something like that happen before now. It was perfectly plausible for those teams to be in the area. And if I remember rightly there were people badly injured on that bus'

'That's what you think you know, and think you saw. But believe me you didn't. It was an extremely clever, very effective, but totally manufactured, smoke screen. It made the public believe there was and still is an immediate threat, either from individuals who could be any one of your neighbours, or any one of your fellow travellers. You know what the government has to do to keep the public on high alert, they can't just be told there is a threat, they have to be shown. It looks as if the role of government is to keep the masses scared out of their wits. The way everything is reported on TV and in the media gives you a distorted view on the world. Believe me this is the safest period to be alive on this planet but you wouldn't think it to watch the 9 o'clock scaremongers. Anyway, I've been looking at the footage and in all the photos and videos there is something not quite fitting about the victims. There is a distinct lack of blood, although there is a lot of ripped clothing, yes, but without the injuries to justify them. The bus windows are mostly intact considering a bomb had just gone off and there were no outright fatalities. Luck or design? Additionally, of all the victims taken to West Middlesex Hospital none were seen by triage nurses, they were all taken into an area in the hospital cordoned off for the training exercise and treated by military personnel. I know I sound like a conspiracy theorist but remember it's not me talking, this is Graham's findings and he had been looking into this for the last three years. What made him start and why? I don't know. Sadly we might never know what set him on this path. The crux of all this information is that Jack Cole had become an embarrassment to CHRISYS and the British government. There were certain individuals, members of the public or enemies of our country, who had started to poke around and were threatening to expose Cole *and* the false flag events he had been involved in'

'How come this is the first I am hearing about this? And why was he was put on my team to go into Navarre if he was such an embarrassment? Didn't Vlad have any of this information?'

'That I don't know. He shouldn't have been on your team. I'm sorry, Alex. I knew that he did some outside work but I didn't know it was for CHRISYS. Although, someone up the chain of command must have known, someone whose pay grade justified the information, who possibly had links to Christianson. I'm doing some digging to see if I can come up with the culprit, although I do have a good idea who it might be but as yet no hard proof. This is the first I am hearing about all this as well, remember. I think Christianson was going to cut Cole loose, it must have been a relief to him that he was a fatality in Navarre. Unless of course... now we could be straying off the conspiracy path and into the deep dark woods here, unless Christianson and the CHRISYS team had something to do with what had gone wrong on that operation'

'You can't be serious?' exclaimed Alex

'From what I've been reading Alex, and what I know from working for the British government for twenty five years is that almost nothing is beyond the realms of possibility. Truth is often stranger than fiction. I've worked with you long enough to know that you're a straight shooter and I hope you know that I am, but there are people whose sole aim is to get into a position of power not for the greater good or the good of the people they should be serving, but for their own gain, their own financial reward, their own ascent up the greasy pole of power for powers sake'

'Tell me what else you know. I need to know whether this bastard Christianson is responsible for the lives of my team-mates. If he has the slightest hand in what happened on that day I'll have his fucking guts for garters'

'Calm down, Alex, we don't know anything for sure yet. Christianson might be a mercenary piece of shit but that doesn't necessarily mean he blew up that shed in Spain to get rid of Cole. As I have just said it may be in the realms of possibility but we can't go off half-cocked without any evidence to support the claim. Let me briefly outline what CHRISYS has been up to over the last fifteen years and we might be able to connect some dots'

'OK, but just concentrate on the operations that Cole was involved with for a start'

'Well, we know for sure that Jack Cole was involved in at least three False Flag operations, one of them being the Hounslow bus bomb, the job which brought him under scrutiny. The other two were apparently more accomplished and carried out with greater dexterity from the CHRISYS team as Graham was probably the only person who has shed any light on the two operations. The first one being a pathogen attack on Birmingham's shopping district at Christmas 2001; again it was supposedly an attack by extremists intent on causing as much disruption as they could rather than any actual body count. With hindsight this makes it all the more likely that it would have been a False Flag, two square miles of inner city area had to be evacuated on the last Saturday before Christmas day. It would have been on the news at the time but because it was Birmingham and not London maybe it didn't get all the attention it deserved. The story was fairly short lived, no-one was caught for placing the duffel bag in the shopping centre but it was intimated that it was yet another Muslim attack on our Western way of life. It caused a lot of ill feeling within the immigrant communities in the inner city. It didn't matter what religious background you were from if you had skin of colour, you were looked upon with suspicion. A few scuffles followed between the more extreme groups but thankfully the Christmas spirit prevailed and things quickly returned to normal. But, as you know, with any of these attacks, be they real or imagined, they drive a wedge between the communities that have been coexisting for many years. It's sad but it looks as if there will always be an element in British culture that won't accept multiculturalism'

'I know, I know, the powers that be aren't happy unless we are scared of foreigners and suspicious of our neighbours. It enables them to keep us in line, and we are supposed to be thankful they are looking after us so well' commented Alex sarcastically.

'Now you're sounding more like Graham'

'No-one was caught for the Birmingham attack, although there was CCTV footage of a man placing the bag. Unfortunately the footage is not clear enough to make a definitive identification. A man between the ages of 18 and 45, dark clothing, maybe jeans, dark hoodie pulled up, under a dark jacket, difficult to tell skin his colour and no discernible gait to his walk. In other words a ghost, nothing. It could be any one of a million people. And I know what you're thinking... no, no sign of any type of logo on the jacket. The official line, however, is that it was an amateur extremist, name of Karamat Bashir, a 17 year old, born and raised in Solihull, South Birmingham. I don't know where this information came from or where this individual is supposed to be now, or why he hasn't been brought to book. It looks as if he has just disappeared into thin air, part of an ongoing investigation no doubt. But what if this person never even existed?'

'What links this to Cole?'

'Well it just so happens that as part of the sweep operation after the suspect package was found, Cole was one of the team sent in to scrutinise the shopping mall where the threat was perceived to be greatest. What was really strange about the footage from the CCTV was that many of the sweeper team were apparently too laid back considering what they were potentially dealing with. There was a definite lack of urgency or trepidation in their demeanour'

'Yeah, that sounds highly suspicious to me. And it was definitely Cole in the video?'

'No doubt about it'

'Who was he supposedly working for at this time?'

'Probably CHRISYS, as well as guns for hire they also helped out from time to time with other operations within certain parameters. It's just too much of a coincidence if you ask me'

'And what about the next one?'

'Well the next one is really interesting. Do you remember the supposedly peaceful demonstrations in Hackney regarding Muslim rights in Britain about five years ago? There was talk in Parliament about curtailing entry to the UK from certain Muslim countries. From what I can gather from Graham's findings, and I've found a lot of online chat-room banter to back this up, the demo had been infiltrated by agent provocateurs specifically there to incite violence. The march was supposed to end up at Downing Street to deliver a petition to the Prime Minister but it didn't get that far. Somewhere between Fleet Street and the Thames embankment the number of protesters swelled to unmanageable proportions. Maybe some of these were bona fide and were just late to the party but nevertheless a violent element joined the crowds and racist chanting began, objects were thrown, windows smashed, property vandalised, you can imagine the rest. The whole rally ended up as a battle against the police in attendance; six policemen injured, twenty one protesters hospitalised, fourteen arrests and of course columns and columns of press coverage that the Muslim protesters attended the rally with the intention of causing trouble. So you see where we're going with this?'

'I imagine that Graham has found proof that members of CHRISYS were the ones at the rally, and that one of those members was Cole'

'Exactly. Which leads us back to the fact that Cole was a common denominator in at least three False Flag Ops, that he had been exposed, that he was an embarrassment to either Christianson, the British Government department linked to CHRISYS or both'

'We need to find out everything we can about Cole as soon as possible'

'I've started on that already'

'Is there any proof at all that the explosion in Navarre was anything but an accident?'

'It's very difficult to find that out this late after the fact. We can't exactly send anyone out there to survey the scene, any more than we could have done at the time. Remember it was a covert op, we weren't even supposed to be there. And what would we find now anyway?'

'I suppose' lamented Alex, 'What's the next step then? If there is any chance that there are others responsible for those men's deaths...' he left the sentence hanging. A spark of hope had begun to ignite deep down in his gut, a chance maybe that after all he may not be solely to blame for the deaths of his four men in the Spanish mountains.

'Leave it with me Alex, I'll do what I can. I just thought you needed to know'

'Thanks Anil, I appreciate it'

'I have emailed you the pertinent files in encrypted format so you can have a detailed look at what I've been talking about. I think you'll be surprised at the weight of evidence that Graham had amassed. I'll let you know when I find out anything. Now, take care of yourself and get in to me as soon as you can'

'I'm not sure when that's going to be, I have to deal with a few things first. Can you text me the contact for the techies who worked on getting Graham's laptop unlocked? I need to speak to them. And thanks Anil, I'm glad someone has got my back, I'll be in touch'

Alex hung up the phone and sat silently trying to process all the information Anil had just landed on him. So many questions were spinning through his mind, he didn't know where to start.

He flipped open his laptop and opened the email attachments that Anil had sent him. He would have to access them using MOD decryption software which could take anywhere between five minutes and half an hour depending on the size of the zip files. While this was set in motion he called Jimmy and left a message to meet him in the Ravenous Rook later that evening, a cosy London pub dating back to the late seventeenth century. He needed to let him in on the information he had just been given.

36 - The Ravenous Rook

When Alex entered the cramped tavern with Deanna he could see that Jimmy was already seated at the bar and had been taking advantage of the range of whiskies available to him. A pint of bitter stood half empty next to two glass tumblers, one empty and one nearly diminished of its contents. Alex could see immediately that Jimmy had that glassy eyed demeanour of being at least one sheet to the wind as he was trying once more to gain the barman's attention. Alex had the feeling that there might be trouble brewing.

Alex greeted him with a friendly grip on the shoulder and was met with a start. Jimmy shot him a baleful glance while not being able to hide a sneer of disdain. Alex took this to be the effects of the alcohol and assumed Jimmy might turn out to be a belligerent drinker. He ordered three coffees from the barman to be delivered to the snug.

Alex sat opposite Jimmy with Deanna at his side.

'Jimmy, you need to sharpen up, I can't have you falling apart on me like this. We're in some deep shit here and you can't be going off the deep end, do you hear me?' Alex was trying to summon the authoritarian air of his rank

Deanna put her hand on Alex's arm to urge him to not be so hard on the young lad. 'Jimmy, I think what Alex is trying to say is that, we know that what you have been through hasn't been easy, in fact what has happened to us all in the last few days has scared the living daylights out of me, there were times I didn't think I was going to get out of the asylum alive. But then you and Alex came to my rescue. I have you to thank that all three of us sitting here in one piece'

Alex stiffened slightly at the direction Deanna was taking in dealing with Jimmy. He would have preferred the more austere military approach of 'pull your socks up and get on with it', but he kept quiet and let the gambit play out.

The coffees came and Deanna let Jimmy take a few sips before she carried on.

'Alex and I have been coming up with a plan to end this once and for all. I don't know about you but I am sick of running and hiding. I can't go on like this any longer'

Jimmy's eyes became more alert and sparked with interest, 'What do you have in mind?'

'Listen, Jimmy, I know that it's been hard for you...' started Alex

'Yeah, you've got no fucking idea, really, how hard it has been. Do you?'

Alex was taken aback by the venom that remained in Jimmy's voice, 'What do you mean?'

'I mean, leading us all into a trap that got all of our team killed, because even if I didn't die on that mountain back in Navarre I'm sure as hell looking down the barrel of a gun now!'

'Let's not go back over trodden ground again, Jimmy. Anyway, that's not true. We're not going to let anything happen to you. The three of us, together we are strong. And we are safe. We will look after each other'

'I thought I was safe with you in Spain and look what happened. You do realise I can't sleep nights, I lie in bed awake with the horrors of that day in front of my eyes and I can't get rid of them. And when I do sleep I have nightmares, twisted and dark and....' he trailed off

'I'm sorry, Jimmy, I didn't realise how much it had affected you'

'Yeah, well... So what's this damned plan you have cooked up, then?'

'Well, I pulled the wallet and phone from that man-mountain back at Severalls after he got an eyeful. I couriered them both to Bharat who sent them to tech to see if we could gather anything useful from the chip in the phone. The wallet didn't look to me to have anything useful but it got sent in anyway. It turns out that there are only two active numbers in his burner phone, one of them is the Spaniard Quiros who we know well enough but the other is an unknown. But traceable, apparently. The Quiros communications are plentiful and recent but this other number is used less frequently, which got me thinking that it must be to a person higher up in the food chain. As you both know you tend to speak to superiors more infrequently than those you work with on a day to day basis'

Alex paused for a sip of the bitter coffee and to let the information sink in.

'So Freddie in tech has back traced the number using triangulation and has pinpointed its location over the last ten days, which I have to admit is quite remarkable. And this is where it starts to get really interesting. Ten days ago the individual who this cell belongs to was in an area west of the White Sea in Northern Russia. Then only a few days ago the signal began to move. Its journey made a rather convoluted route through northern Europe which, lo and behold, ended up in Broad Oak in East Sussex'

'What's in East Sussex?' asked Deanna

'There is a hotel on the north bank of the Darwell reservoir. Very exclusive and quite expensive. The sort of place you stay when you might not want to be found. They have a reputation for being discreet, to say the least. It is owned by the oligarch Vladimir Semenov although that is not common knowledge among the locality, especially as the hotel is called 'La Maison du Lac'. It consists of the main hotel with thirty five en-suite rooms which from what I can gather are more like apartments, but also has chalets nestled in the woodland and on the northern banks of the lake, all extremely private and inconspicuous. That's where I think our man is in hiding. Who he is exactly and what he is doing there has yet to be defined. Freddie is doing some more checking as to who owns the dwelling in Russia where we first picked up the cell phone signal' Alex waited for this all to sink in with his two companions before finishing his pitch.

'We need to go on the offensive and find out who is behind this. As Deanna has said; we have done all the running we are going to do. It's been a defensive game up until this point, now it's time to bring the fight to them, whoever they are'

'OK. So what is it exactly you are planning on doing? Just walk in and confront this lowlife?' said Jimmy with contempt in his tone.

'Yes, exactly that'

'You're mad. That's a sure way to get us all killed. We have no idea what we'll be walking in to. It could even be a trap'

'I highly doubt it. I can't ask you to help if you feel that way. It's up to you whether you come or not. I won't blame you. It's my mess and I should be the one to sort it out and finish it. I don't even like the fact that you are coming' he said looking to Deanna

'You forget who I work for. I am more than able to lend you back-up support'

'I know you are, but that doesn't make it any easier that you won't take my advice'

'We've been over this already. I'm coming with you and that's final. I want to see this to the end and I'm not letting you go alone. I couldn't forgive myself if anything happened to you'

Alex turned to Jimmy, 'What do you say, Jimmy? Are you in?'

Jimmy sat stock still staring into his cup of steaming coffee, not moving a muscle, so still that Alex thought that he mustn't have heard him.

'Jimmy?'

He slowly raised his eyes to look at Alex and Alex could read a myriad of emotions in that one look. He was all at once angry, scared, doubtful and, just as the old Jimmy would have been, anxious to put the world to rights. Either that or Alex was projecting his own emotions on to him and reading him like a mirror. In that moment, Alex knew that he could ask no more from Jimmy, he had been through enough and it wouldn't be fair to the boy. To subject him to any more danger, to risk making his mental health worse and to possibly put his life in danger would not be acceptable.

'I need you to do something for me Jimmy' Alex said quietly, 'I need you to keep yourself safe and I need you to get yourself better. I know it's been hard for you, and I know that you blame me for it all. But all I can say to you is this. I could swear that all the equipment was good to go, the safety of my team was always my first and only concern and I feel like shit every time I have to face the fact that I may have missed something. I know that you are a long way from forgiving me but I hope that one day that time will come'

Alex stood up to leave and turned one more time to face Jimmy. The tone of his voice now changed to something more paternalistic he said, 'Jimmy, try not to drink any more. I know I'm not your father or your commander any more but that doesn't mean I don't have your best interests at heart, you know? Look after yourself and I'll see you soon, OK?'

With that Alex and Deanna left the pub to head back to The Worcester and work out the details of their next steps. Alex glanced back at Jimmy and saw in his face that he looked relieved, the tension had fallen from his face

37 - Blindsided

Jimmy left The Ravenous Rook feeling slightly the worse for wear. He had never been a very heavy drinker and what with that and the medication he was taking, his faculties were definitely compromised. Anyone seeing him walking down the road trying to flag a taxi would say he had been on a heavy bender. He had tried to order an Uber on his cell but after trying multiple times to navigate the app the battery had died on him making the phone useless.

Eventually after walking much further than necessary he made it back to The Morpeth Arms and his safe house. He was tired and cold and the alcohol in his system was wearing off. As he entered the building by its more discreet doorway on Ponsonby Place. Jimmy was in two minds whether to check in with his security detail and go to bed or to head down to the private bar for a hot toddy to warm up his cold bones.

He stood in the narrow corridor for a few moments weighing up the options and decided a hot toddy it would be, there wouldn't be any need to disturb Sergeant Lowry at this time of night. Lowry's only job was to protect him while he was in the residence anyway.

Jimmy let himself in to the rear bar area and across to the doorway which led to the spiral staircase. It was a narrow cast iron structure that must be quite challenging to heave kegs of ale and crates of bottles up and down. He couldn't imagine anybody of extended girth manoeuvring in the cramped well. It had been a long time since he was here and in those years he himself had filled out slightly. The place was silent, he wasn't even sure if the POM bar was open, it didn't sound as if it was. He supposed that if you could hear it from outside it wouldn't be much of a secret bar would it? The fact that it was deathly silent set his nerves on edge. It was unnaturally quiet, especially in SW1 of all places. London to him had always been about noise and chatter and never being able to find a quiet spot.

He arrived at cellar level and began making his way down the cluttered walkway strewn with crates and kegs, with the arches to his right swallowing up all the light into their depths. He had no idea how far back they went, and didn't plan to find out, on a deeply primitive level the utter pitch blackness freaked him the hell out. Even when he was a younger man it gave him the jitters walking down to the bar on his own. He could almost imagine what it would have been like for the poor souls locked up down in these cells, cut off from daylight awaiting a future containing God knows what? He could almost hear the cries and shrieks of the inmates as they pleaded for their lives. Could he hear them? He could hear something, but couldn't put his finger on where the noise was coming from. The echoes from the tunnels and arches were deceiving, but he was sure there was something. Yes! There it was again. Not moaning as such but breathing, heavy breathing. Jimmy found himself entranced by the sound trying to figure out its precise location wondering what it could be. Was it his imagination? Or was it one of his trauma episodes?

He stepped towards the darkness slightly straining his ears to clarify between reality and imagination, not daring to go any further into the blackness. His eyes trying their best to gather any light information for what lay in front of him, pupils dilated to their maximum but still seeing nothing but pitch. All of a sudden a figure burst from the blackness filling up his whole view. Subliminally Jimmy saw the huge bulk of a body with a disproportionately small head, the head which sported a bloodied bandage over one eye. This was the last thing he saw before the baseball bat swung at him striking him square on the forehead knocking him clean out

38 - Checking in

Dragunov's driver pulled up in front of the hotel, got out and opened the door for him. A hotel doorman stepped forward from the alcove of the entrance and stood silently but expectantly awaiting instruction. Dragunov shooed him away and nodded to his driver to fetch the few pieces of luggage from the boot of the Mercedes.

After checking in he was shown to his private lakeside apartment where he relieved Yusef of his duties and told him to stay within reasonable distance for when he was next needed. Vasili roamed the apartment taking stock of his surroundings, thankful to have the interminable journey behind him. He wandered into the plush bathroom, the tiles underfoot hewn from warm brown Italian marble and the wash basins made from a single solid piece of Sea Pearl granite. He took stock of his face in the mirror and studied the worn features of a man who was too old to be on the back foot and on the run. He washed his face in the water from the golden faucet and let the cold liquid sting his face and sharpen his senses after the long journey. Everything he laid eyes on was in stark contrast to the house he had left in Voknavolok; a modest single story converted farmhouse that had been his family home for more than three generations. His immediate surroundings were almost gaudy by comparison and it took some moments of acclimatisation to adjust to the ostentation. It was an adjustment he would easily slip into as it was the life he was accustomed to before he was ostracized by Sigalov and his cronies; his wealth was something that had not yet been stripped from him. Yet.

He walked through the sitting room toward the rear of the building where he opened the heavy drapes to reveal the breath-taking vista that was known locally as the West Arm. The sun sparkled on the water, swans floated lazily on the surface. He knew that further down the mile long body of water would be fly-fisherman casting for brown trout. Across the 200 metres to the opposite bank was heavy woodland where songbirds chirruped incessantly and to the right the reed beds were thick with warblers. Vasili walked out onto the veranda knowing that he enjoyed total privacy from the other residents of La Maison du Lac. He sat down at the table, pulled out his cell phone and began contacting his colleagues for the final phase of proceedings.

Petrakis heard the door of the bar begin to open as sound leaked out towards him. He dragged the limp, lifeless body into the dark recess to avoid detection, hoping to God above that he had done no lasting damage to the man. Any chance he had of making good at this stage hinged on him not damaging the merchandise. What with Quiros gone he now had to try and make amends by getting into the good books with Dragunov directly. He hoped that something could be saved from the disaster at the hospital. Although he wasn't quite sure who was going to extract the information from the subjects now that Quiros was gone. Still, not his problem. He was sure that Dragunov had others who could do the work, after all he was KGB, a rich man in a prestigious post in the Kremlin, his resources would be far ranging.

He would stick to the arrangements they had made previously; to meet Dragunov at the Maison Du Lac.

I t was still dark when Alex opened his eyes from a deep and disturbing sleep. It took him a few moments to identify where he was and remember who he was with. He gauged that the heavy drapes were keeping out nearly all of the crisp morning sun from streaming into the room, a soft glow trying to break its way through shimmering on the motes of dust dancing in the air. He could tell from the extravagant surroundings that he was in his room at The Worcester and he could sense that Deanna was awake beside him. He turned and looked at her. He couldn't believe that she could look so beautiful without any effort; her hair tousled and creased from the night's sleep only adding to her allure, the swell of her breast beneath the covers and the smooth shape of her hip as the sheet strained at it creating warm sensations down in his loins.

'Where were you?' Deanna whispered gently stroking the hair from his forehead, soothing him, worried that the dream that woke him had been a bad one.

'I was in the back of a Humvee, with you, travelling across the desert' he answered trying to recapture his disappearing dream, 'There was you, Jimmy, my dad and Jack Cole of all people. It was so, so hot...'

'I didn't mean in your dream, darling. I meant where were you when you disappeared, after Navarre? I know you don't like to talk about it, but I just wondered...'

'It's not that it's any sort of secret. It's just that it's not the sort of story you go around telling just anyone. You've got to understand, I was depressed, in a very dark place. I had to deal with my demons'

Alex remained silent for a long time, considering how he would even begin to tell the story of his time in Wales.

'You don't have to tell me if you're not ready' Deanna gently squeezed his hand in reassurance.

'No, I think I want to tell you. I'm ready. The question is; are you? It was a part of my life I am not proud of. It will make you see me in a completely different light. Are you ready for that? Even if it may make you hate me?'

'There is nothing you could tell me that could change the way I feel about you. The person you are now is what's important. Not something that happened years ago'

'Well, we arrived back from France two weeks after the operation,' Alex paused trying to piece together a coherent story to tell Deanna. He reached over to the table and took a long draught of wine from his glass, immediately regretting it, wincing at the bitter tang of alcohol 'we were disoriented, we hadn't realised that we had been missing for fourteen days. We were taken back to the UK almost without any detours, we were in the back of a vehicle, blacked out windows, couldn't see in or out. There was no chatter if I remember correctly, we were all still in a state of shock. I remember just how quiet that journey was, it was the lull before the storm in a way. As soon as we were back on British soil all hell broke loose, we were debriefed aggressively and thoroughly. We were kept in Bagshot for two days, barely able to see sunlight, locked in our rooms when we were not being interrogated. I didn't know who was going to be doing the interviews from one hour to the next, most likely they were deliberately putting us on the wrong foot to keep us from relaxing. Someone, I don't know who, had got it into their heads that we were now some sort of threat, I have no idea why. As far as I was concerned we were the victims. We had *lost* men, didn't they realise that?' Alex was becoming agitated at the memories being stirred up.

'Shh, it's over now' said Deanna trying to calm him

'That's the trouble, it's not over. It's far from being over, can't you see that? We are still pawns in someone else's game. It makes me so angry to think that we have no control over our own destiny. Thinking back now, this has all been inevitable. It was stupid of me to think I could have done anything to prevent what is happening to us'

'At least it brought us together. We wouldn't have ever met otherwise'

'That's true' he admitted, 'They must have got all they wanted from us from the interviews in Bagshot. I told them all I knew, all I could remember anyway, which wasn't much. It was all a blur. I could recall preparing for the operation, all the run up, the jokes and the camaraderie, they were a great bunch of fellas. I still miss them. I remember travelling to the drop and 'chuting in. We grouped up as was the plan, it was dark but we knew exactly what we were doing, it had all been laid out in such detail prior to us going. Then it all went to hell...'

'You don't have to relive it for me' said Deanna softly, 'I'm sure it wasn't your fault'

'But that's where you're wrong, it was all my fault. I was in charge, I had checked the explosives, I had picked the team, it was my operation, I was in charge. The buck stopped with me. When you lead a team of men into battle you have to be able to take the losses as well as the triumphs. When I was in Bagshot I hadn't quite realised what exactly had happened in Navarre. I only became fully aware of the extent of the casualties during the questioning. I think that is what convinced the officers that we were innocent of any wrongdoing. As I became conscious of the fact that we had taken casualties it dawned on me that the four of us that returned that day in the van from France were the only survivors; me, Graham, Jimmy and Dan. I soon realised it would be my task to visit the relatives of those other men and explain to them what had happened to them. That was the part I found the hardest of all. I visited all of their relatives one by one and told them the bad news, Derek had been married but was now divorced so it was his parents I had to go and see, they were devastated, understandably. John had a girlfriend of three years, she didn't take it well, for all intents and purposes they were married they just hadn't got around to making it official yet. I couldn't find Kiki, that was Jack Cole's current partner supposedly, it was a strange thing, he had mentioned her often but when it came to tracking her down I couldn't. Maybe Kiki was her nickname or something but that was all I had to go on. Apart from that Jack had no other relatives alive in the UK. He had an uncle he talked about, worked overseas somewhere, but I was never able to find anyone related to him. Out of all of the men Simon Chapman's family was the hardest, he had a wife and daughter, married for eight years, the daughter was six years old. I had known them since they had got married, I was even at the wedding. I had seen Melissa grow up into a feisty young girl, full of fun and mischief. She wasn't in the room when I was telling Hannah but she could hear her mother crying from the other room and there was no coming back from that. I had destroyed their lives. It broke me. I know that now. I couldn't bear the stark reality that these two women's lives would never be the same again. I did what I had to do and told them, I took responsibility and said all the proper words of condolence, but I knew deep down that in a way it was over for them. They had each other but they had lost such an important part of both their lives. My guilt was all encompassing, I felt nauseous and as I left their house I could feel my throat constrict and I thought I would not be able to breath, I threw up before I could get to the car. Looking back now I would say it was some sort of panic attack, maybe brought on by the guilt or maybe an accumulation of all that had happened over the last three weeks. It all became too much, I had to do something. The company had given us the option of taking time to recover from the ordeal so I took advantage of that and immediately disappeared, it would be the best thing for me, or so I thought. I wasn't really thinking straight to tell you the truth. I didn't even tell Graves or Madash where I was going. They must have been worried sick'

Alex paused. Although the telling of this part of his story may be cathartic it was in no way easy for him to dredge up these old memories. Deanna sensed that he would need some encouragement so let the silence sit not wanting to jinx the moment. After a while Alex carried on.

'I took the Volvo and headed to Wales, it was the only place I could think of that would be quiet enough for me. My father has a modest cottage by the twin lakes just outside Capel Curig, I hadn't been there since I was a little boy, maybe eleven or twelve. I don't know why it came to my mind then of all times. It was somewhere my father used to go on fishing trips, to get away from city life I suppose. The cottage was just a glorified shack really. It didn't have running water or heating. The first thing I had to do when I got there was to chop some wood for the furnace and get the place warmed up a bit. He took me there fishing a few times when I became old enough. The place hadn't changed at all in the years that had passed, maybe it looked a little bit more decrepit, but you only really visited there for the views across the lakes. The cottage stood at the edge of the wood and looked across the water towards Mount Snowdon, I remember sitting in the little fishing boat with my father thinking that there couldn't be a more beautiful spot in the world. The snow capping the top of the mountain while we were bathed in the warmth of the sun down on the lake. Taking sandwiches from the basket and drinking cans of pop from the nearby shop, dangling our rods in the water and sitting in comfortable silence. I knew when to keep quiet in my father's company, but I didn't mind. When he was away from the City he was a man of few words and would often discourage conversation by just grunting. We would take whatever we caught and eat it that evening, frying it in the skillet on the range. Sometimes it would be a perch or maybe a pike. Many people will tell you that these fish are inedible but that's not true, I tasted some of the most succulent fish taken from that lake with my father. He would prepare them, take the heads off, scale them and gut them. I had a go a couple of times but cut myself on the filleting knife,' Alex showed Deanna the scar on the ball of his thumb, 'after that he would do it by himself, I would just help with the cooking; squeezing lemon into the pan or coating the fillets in flour, that sort of thing. I had my first taste of beer in that cottage,' Alex said wistfully, 'can't say I liked it that much at the time but funny how if you stick with something you gain a taste for it'

'What was he like, your father?'

'I didn't really appreciate him until it was too late. We had a pretty amicable relationship but I wouldn't say we were close. I was closer to my mother in that respect. As I said he was a man of few words so it was all too often difficult to gauge his mood. I imagine he was always busy at work during the day so when he got home he no doubt had spent up all of his conversation and needed his solace. My mother understood that entirely but for me as a youngster growing up I found him rather prickly at times. I admired him tremendously, looked up to him, I even wanted to be him. But as I got older I realised we were quite different. It's funny, how I ended up in the same business as him, we must have had that in common at least. That and a love for my mother, there was no doubt he loved her, more than he did me, but she was the bond that held us all together'

'Do you still see her?'

Oh yes, of course, every week. Or as often as I can anyway'

'Tell me what happened to you in Wales' Deanna prompted gently

'The time I spent there after Navarre was nothing like the time I spent with my Dad, they were practically pole opposites. From what I can remember, most of it is still a kind of a blur, I spent a lot of the time holed up in the cabin with a bottle of something or other, any bottle of spirits, whatever Pinnacles had in stock that day. I hit the bottle hard those first few weeks. Clogwyns café was at the end of the road but I can only remember going there a spare few times, only when my body began to crave food so badly it started rejecting the alcohol. The inside of that cabin became both my saviour and my captor, it's hard to explain. I know now that I had to go through some sort of catharsis. Somehow I had to come to terms with what had happened to us all but I didn't know how to do it. After a while I didn't have the energy or the will to even light the stove to keep warm, I think I was punishing myself. The only drive I truly had was to seek oblivion at the bottom of a bottle. Even this became a poor crutch for me, I needed to lose myself completely, so I ended up driving the ten kilometres to Betws-y-Coed in the middle of the night mostly, with a bottle of Jack Daniels between my legs to find the town dealer. The town wasn't big by any standards but I knew from experience that any town has the entrepreneur who was more than willing to cater to the local drug users. These inconsequential towns in the middle of nowhere were supplied enthusiastically, the teenagers who found rural living unbearable had to have some sort of escape. I found Derwyn down at the cemetery hanging out with a bunch of goth type friends, people you wouldn't usually have anything to do with, they wouldn't even show up on your radar on an average day, but these grungy-looking wannabe vampires happened to be the types I was after. Nobody had told them that this look was over, fashions are always last to hit the boondocks. I knew immediately Derwyn was the man to be dealing with. The others although all looking the same, didn't have the sense of business about them, they looked like users rather than peddlers. I didn't need to approach him, he came to me. Anyone hanging around that part of town wouldn't be there for any other reason. He didn't have anything stronger than 'K' on him that first night but it was enough to get me started, or to finish me, I wasn't quite sure. That night was the first time in a long time that I could forget about the look on Melissa's face, when she had realised that she would never see her father again. I sniffed that powder until I reached a perfect oblivion, I was no longer in that dark and cold cabin, I was floating above the lake looking down on all my problems as if they were boats bobbing on the choppy water. I remember throwing stones and rocks at them to try and sink them. Each one I hit would sink to the bottom only to resurface the next day in the cold light of morning. That was when the Jack Daniels would be needed to hold me over until I could see Derwyn again that night. Derwyn, ever the entrepreneur, knew he was onto an earner with me, he knew I had the money to carry on the abuse, and began to bring in alternatives to 'K'. For an increased price he would give me 'Hillbilly H', some 'Drank' or Little Smokes, all of which had the desired effect on me; nirvana. God knows how I never get pulled over on those journeys to and from town, somebody must have been looking out for me, it was a miracle I never hit anything. The roads were often a blur, the Volvo floating down the lanes rather than being driven by me. I vaguely remember one time I had been on Peyote Buttons and decided it would be a excellent idea to climb Glyder Fawr, I began the ascent in the late afternoon in my pyjamas, shoeless with only a bottle of tequila for company, it was obviously the Mexican faze of my rehabilitation' Alex smiled ruefully at his attempt at humour

'It sounds awful. How did you survive?' Deanna asked, 'What made you turn yourself around?'

'I think that *was* a turning point for me. I nearly froze to death up that mountain. My instinct for survival kicked in. I realised deep down inside that if I didn't change my ways pretty soon I could be dead within months. I had lost nearly ten kilos in four months, I honestly couldn't tell you how I had spent most of that time. I was having hallucinations on a regular basis, vomiting was a daily ritual, food was something my body had to ingest just so I could do more drugs. I hadn't looked in the mirror for more than two months but when I did I could barely recognize myself. I climbed to the top of Glyder Fawr. I found out later that it was 1,000m to the summit. I was exhausted, mentally and physically, I was looking death in the face. I decided there and then I was going to pull myself together and get back in the game. I would have to live with the guilt, I could live with the shame. I would live for my mother's sake. I searched and found reasons. I had brought myself to the edge of my own destruction, looked into the abyss and found that the will to live is stronger than anything else'

'Oh darling, I can't imagine what you must have been going through. Why has all this been such a secret these years?'

'It hasn't been a secret. I just haven't found a sympathetic person to listen to my story, it's not something you go around bragging about'

'But what about counselling? Doesn't the department offer you that at least?'

'They would have done I suppose but I think I needed to go through some sort of penance for what I had put those families through'

'But you still haven't forgiven yourself?' said Deanna

'No'

'Do you think you will ever be able to?'

'Not a day goes by when I don't think about what happened to those lads. I don't deserve forgiveness. I am living the life I deserve'

'There's no one saying that you shouldn't be happy, only you,' she said, 'Aren't you happy here with me?'

'Of course I am, you're the only thing that matters to me at the moment. Keeping you safe. Why do you do what you do?'

'You mean work for the CIA?'

'Yes'

'That's a long story. One for another time I think. We all have our demons making us do what we do'

'Yes but some are darker than others'

'How did you pull yourself back from the brink?' she asked

'I had to call in the help of a friend'

'Who?'

'Dan Johnson'

'The man who was killed?'

'Yes, he was the sort of guy you could call on for help. He knew what I was going through. He had an idea anyway. He was there at the cottage the very next day. Came laden with supplies,' Alex smiled to himself at the memory, 'He helped me go cold turkey, it was tough and I must admit it tested our friendship at times, but he persevered with me. He wouldn't leave my side. He made sure I was back to eating properly, my weight started to gain. He even visited the village to see Derwyn, paid what was owed to him and told him the money train had come to a halt; to expect no more business from the city boy. He could be completely convincing, could Dan. Not the sort of guy you would mess with. We even took the boat out towards the end of our stay, can you believe that? He made it a reward for doing so well'

'It sounds as if you were close'

'As close as any of us get when we are on a team together'

'It must have been tough, finding out that he had been killed'

'It was. But it makes me glad that I am here to find his killer. He deserves some retribution. He was a damned exceptional man'

'I hope you do' said Deanna, 'Or rather I hope *we* do. We're a team now, whether you like it or not'

Forty One - Target Practice

He waited in the undergrowth. Unaware of the time or how long he had been there, ignoring the ache in his muscles and the impending cramps that were always threatening. No matter how well he prepared he found that as he got older his body was less able to cope with the demands he placed upon it. He knew that after it was over he would pay the price for lying prone for so long, his concentration taking precedence over the needs of his muscles and tendons, over his need to squash the three inch long millipede that now crawled over his hand, pausing to enquire whether it was worth its while to make its way up his sleeve to a warm spot in the crook of his elbow. He had to overcome his primal instinct to swat it away and kept his body as still as he could while waiting for his quarry to appear. He was vaguely aware of the weather changing above his head, the clouds scudding past, growing darker and threatening rain, the moisture in the air becoming palpable. An insect buzzed around his head and alighted on his eyelid, he could feel as it's legs tickled their way around his temple and then it moving toward his ear. There the insect paused and although not moving he could still feel it and imagined it pondering where to go, what to do next.

He scanned the area far below him moving only his eyes, keeping his head still. He could feel the blood coursing through his temples, his pulse throbbing in his fingers. He allowed himself to slowly stretch his thumb and forefinger on his right hand, knowing that if these two digits let him down at the crucial moment it would all be for nought. The insect noticing that there was movement nearby decided it would vacate the area. He heard it's wings create their buzzing trill as they took the creature out of earshot. He knew the small clearing was a popular spot for wild boar to come foraging for truffles, it being on the edge of the forest where the boar felt relatively safe from larger animals. He knew that he could possibly spend the whole of the day in this position and the boar may not show itself. He also knew that if it were to come, it was more likely to be at dusk, when the light was dwindling and the skittish creature felt safer. Even though the sky was darker than ever he became acutely aware of his skin prickling under his heavily camouflaged rigout. He wore the green, black and tan army issue jacket and trousers. He also wore tan boots that he had altered to become invisible on the forest floor and on his head a woollen hat of the same ilk to hide his blond hair. Every part of his exposed skin was painted to match his outfit so you could not distinguish him at all unless he broke cover. He would sometimes even don brown contact lenses if necessary to hide his blue eyes. But that was only in particular circumstances and would not be a benefit for shooting his boar on this day.

He sensed rather than saw movement over to the right hand side of the clearing. It may have been a bird or a squirrel but he kept his eyes glued to the spot until he could rule one way or the other. Slowly and with supreme caution a large female boar entered the clearing sniffing the air as it did so. After a few moments sensing that it was safe she made a grunting sound that was a calling to her offspring to follow her lead and join her. He watched them both for a few moments noticing how the younger boar looked to its mother for her instruction, it was obviously at an age where it was learning the secrets of the forest that were being passed down from generation to generation. Kapusta watched them, admiring the wonder of nature and the bond between mother and child; something he had experienced all too briefly which made him wonder whether a different childhood would have set him on a altered path in life. It made what he had to do all the more specific, he was not dealing with just one animal but two. Two animals linked by blood, bonded by instinct. The first shot would have to count if he was to make the best of this opportunity.

Slowly and with imperceptible subtlety he shifted the aim of the Lobaev to where the two boars now foraged. Moving his eye behind the scope the whole scene became magnified and crystal clear. He knew where the first shot should be placed for maximum incapacity; his finger curled around the trigger as he readied himself for the shot. He controlled his breath. His heartbeat slowed. He squeezed.

Any sound the rifle made was dampened by the forest around him, the silencer doing most of the work, the only evidence of the shot being made was the large female boar squealing in pain as the bullet ripped through her haunches, leaving her unable to run from the immediate danger she was now in. The baby boar on hearing his mother cry out in pain ran around in circles not knowing what the danger was or where it was coming from but too young to leave her side. As far as Kapusta was concerned it was the perfect shot, the female was alive but immobilized and the offspring was not independent enough to leave her. He would make the best of this target practice. He shifted the nozzle of the rifle once again so that the young boar was in it's sights and waited for it's panic to subside. Realising that it's mother was in pain the youngster returned to her side out of curiosity, not knowing what else to do. It sniffed at the wound and tried to make porcine sense of what had happened. The adult was still standing upright but any movement was now restricted due to the blood seeping from her hind quarters, she limped pathetically. Kapusta squeezed the trigger once more and this time caught the young boar directly in the temple, the bullet passing through its skull, spraying the mother with blood and viscera. Any noise the young boar was making immediately extinguished as it fell to the forest floor. He was pleased that the young boar would not have to experience the pain of the adult. It was all he could do to spare the youngster any suffering, a quick death was a blessing that not all received, or deserved. The mother on seeing her offspring fall to the ground began squealing once again but this time not in physical pain but mental agony as she realised her flesh and blood was no more. Kapusta once again pulled the trigger and caught her in the hind, this shot sapping her of any will that remained.

Seeing the adult boar writhe in pain brought him back to a time five years previously when he was, himself, on the verge of giving up on everything. The idea of letting his injuries, which at the time he thought must be fatal, to take him quickly to death, and to free him from his pain. The burns he had sustained covered most of his face. Lamentably he had turned his head at the point of detonation, the blast throwing him into a tree, wreaking havoc with his body. The initial hours and days after the exfiltration were a blurred miasma of pain and confusion. Many times he wished himself dead so he would not have to deal with the skin on his face and neck tightening and tearing, the doctors strategically slicing the skin in relief to minimize the damage. These injuries put all others to the back of his mind but he could also sense that the damage he had suffered to the rest of his body was of some severity. For the first week at least, he dared not move any part of his extremities, for in the first days when he had tried, shockwaves of pain shot up his limbs taking root in the base of his skull as if a knife were being twisted

behind his ears. It were as if he were a waking corpse, lying there not able
to see through one eye, the other hardly at all, hearing murmured voices in
languages he could not recognize. His life lay in the hands of strangers, he
had no idea if they were friend or foe, whether he had been picked up by his
contacts or whether they had fled and left him to be taken by hostiles. Even
as these thoughts entered his mind he could not make the effort to care one
way or the other, there was always another agony to contend with which took
all of his resolution to battle through.

What followed was months of misery and torment, confined to his bed,
his body slowly, incrementally knitting itself back into some sort of working
entity. He realised soon enough that he had, after all, made it into the hands
of his compatriots. They had been waiting for him in the nearby woods to
take him to safety and to his freedom. Sitko and Prazac had been invaluable
in getting him to relative safety. He learned later that they had waited for
the first opportunity to break cover and drag him from the edge of the
clearing into the deeper woodland and to the refuge of the denser wooded
canopy. From there their exfiltration plan had to be revised drastically to
compensate for his injuries. He was unable to walk without the aid of both
men, not solely due to the shard of wood embedded in his leg but also from
the concussion he had sustained upon colliding with the trunk of the fir, he
was practically out cold. The original plan was to yomp their way through
the north-western part of the Irati Forest to the parked off-roader vehicle
two miles away that had been left camouflaged on a remote dirt track. This
would have taken them about half an hour through the dense woodland,
but instead with the injured man, it took nearly three hours. By the time
they arrived at the vehicle Sitko and Prazac were quite near to exhaustion
themselves, having had to shoulder the burly soldier taking turns with a
fireman's lift, they came awfully close to failing their mission. Spurred on by
the fact that Sigalov would not be best pleased with them if they came back
empty handed, even if the man didn't survive the journey they couldn't be
accused of failure. They had meagre medical supplies at the jeep and did what
they could for their patient and although neither of them had any extensive
training in triage they did the best with what they had. They bandaged his
face and neck with moisturised dressing although they could both see that
it would be ineffectual against the burns he had received. They took steps

to help staunch the blood loss from the wound in his leg. They had already ascertained at the site that he had not severed an artery, the shoulder wound they could not do much with so dressed it as well as they were able. From that time on it was their objective to get him to a safe house in Andorra, the principality between Spain and France nestled in the Pyrenean Mountains. There was a ski chalet on the outskirts of El Pas de la Casa, a pretty but empty town that shared it's border with France. Here they could get their comrade the medical attention he needed and hopefully get him fit enough for the next leg of his long journey back to the homeland and thereby relieve themselves of any more responsibility. Sigalov was contacted immediately and arranged for specialist doctors to attend to his valued asset, all with the utmost discretion. They determined quickly that although his injuries were indeed serious they were however non life-threatening, and even though there was a hospital less than ten miles away they recommended he should not be moved again and could be treated well enough at the chalet. What followed was nearly eight weeks of convalescence and rejuvenation where Kapusta came close to losing his mind; initially battling through the pain which then transmuted into a war against the tedium. He was visited by various doctors and healthcare workers, all speaking languages he recognized but did not understand. They examined him and gave him drugs, they made him exercise when he had no strength or stamina to do so. Sitko and Prazac came and went, dropping in to check on him and no doubt report back to Sigalov with updates. Physiotherapists visited him daily to make sure he did not become sedentary. He hated every minute of it, he felt trapped or worse, imprisoned. What had gone wrong in Navarre that he had sustained such crippling injuries? Had he got the timing on the detonator wrong or was it just that it took so long to wriggle out of the tiny hole at the back of the ammunition shed? Or just bloody bad luck? It was something that nagged at him day and night, that all this torment could have been avoided if things had gone differently.

Eventually things began to improve for him. His ability to walk, although stilted and a little painful was regained within some weeks and he could leave the chalet and wander into the town. This challenge took the wind out of him at first and he could only manage short distances. However, as his strength increased he found himself limping up the steep mountain pass to take in the spectacular views across the valley through his still heavily bandaged face. He had not seen the extent of the scarring left by the burns although he knew they were bad. He could feel the tightness of his skin and the lack of pain you have when your nerve endings are seared. He didn't know whether he would still be able to carry out his duties with any sort of capability. Sigalov had wanted him for a reason. He was being looked after so well on the understanding that he would still be an asset. If he were to find out that he was now useless as a sniper he would be worth next to nothing, Sigalov would no doubt cut his losses and cut him loose or have him liquidated.

He remained stock still looking at the boar and felt that all the worry he had gone through was in the end unnecessary; he had reached Russia four and a half months after the accident. He would never be back to his former self physically but thankfully his aim and his shot were not affected. He drove himself harder now, more than at any time before proving as much to himself as to anyone else that he would not be a burden or a liability. The shock of first seeing his damaged face had been hard to come to terms with. He had never really thought of himself as particularly handsome but he had seldom had any trouble with the opposite sex either. He realised that would all change now that he looked like half of his face had melted into itself. He could barely bring himself to look in the mirror; one eye was nearly covered with scarred skin making it nearly impossible to use, luckily it was not his dominant eye so did not affect his aim. The only thing that made him feel any better at all was when he thought of himself as the villainous Harvey Dent, a.k.a. Two-Face from the DC comics that he used to read as a kid. Although he was not as good looking he enjoyed the fact he was much, much deadlier.

He had second thoughts regarding the boar. Deciding to put an end to her pain, he aimed once more and took a final shot hitting her square between the eyes. She collapsed to the floor with a thud and twitched a few times before assuming an eerie stillness. The light drizzle had begun to get heavier and his leg now ached severely from being inert for so long. It was time to pack up and return to Glavnaya. He was fastidious when packing up all the tools of his trade, scanning the area in which he had lain prone, making sure he left absolutely no traces. An old habit he would not give up, carelessness causes mistakes and mistakes get you killed. He had been through enough in that chalet in Andorra to know he was not ready for death yet.

42 - Catching the Spider

A lex was forced to show his credentials at the front desk of La Maison du Lac and to ensure that the staff should in no way try and warn the guest in question of their presence. He knew very well that hotels such as this one were founded on the principle that the client's privacy and protection were of the utmost importance and should be coveted at all costs, after all, that was what they paid for. Alex knew that by the time he got to the target's door he could well have been tipped off by any one of the staff, so speed was of the essence and stealth was the order of the day.

Deanna and Alex slipped out of the reception and back into the car lot where they dodged in between the guest's vehicles, a ridiculous variety of top end luxury cars, from Bentleys and Jaguars to Maseratis and Bugattis. Alex's mind was racing, he was fired up at the thought that this could be the man who had instigated all this horror on them and that he could finally be bringing this whole nightmare to a close. He needed answers as well and this fact was more important than the justice he would have liked to bring to the perpetrators. He kept checking his hip for his firearm and was comforted by the feel of it's weight against his skin, a tendency that kicked in when the stakes were getting higher and the adrenaline rising.

He looked to Deanna, 'You don't have to come in with me you know. In fact I would prefer if you stayed safely outside'

'You know I can't do that Alex. It's not just you who has to find out what's been going on, I am as much involved as you are now. Anyway, you're going to need me and you know why. We're not going to get past that security detail easily unless we work together' she said nodding towards the burly guard standing outside the door.

'Granted. I just don't want you to get hurt'

'Let me worry about myself for the moment and you worry about getting in without getting killed'

'Ok, but let me do the talking and cover my back, we don't know how dangerous this person is yet. Don't let these surroundings fool you, some of the deadliest snakes have the brightest colours'

'I know, let's just get it done, before I lose my nerve'

The driver stood guard outside the entrance to the hotel apartment where Dragunov had ensconced himself, standing with his back to the door he was motionless apart from his eyes, which Alex suspected were scanning the area constantly from behind the dark sunglasses he wore.

It was an age old trick but one that worked nearly one hundred percent of the time. Whether the ruse would on the middle-eastern minder she would soon see. Deanna pretended she was on a telephone call while walking through the car park, completely swept up in her conversation, all the while trying to fish something from inside of her purse. Alex watched from nearby, out of the driver's line of sight. He could see his interest had been piqued by the attractive woman walking past him as his head followed her progression across the tarmac. Whether it was in the interest of security, Alex doubted it. While the driver's eyes followed Deanna, Alex used the cars and landscaped divides to make his way to one side of the building where he could take advantage over the besuited minder.

As if on cue Deanna made her play, fumbling her purse and dropping the contents over the asphalt. She played the part perfectly. Flustered, she abruptly finished her phone call and knelt down to begin picking up the mixture of coins and detritus that had scattered widely around on the ground. After a slight hesitation the driver decided he could not stand by and let her scramble around on her knees retrieving all the coinage. He approached and without saying a word gestured with his hands that he could help and when Deanna smiled as an acceptance he proceeded to do so. He began by picking up the coins from the outside of the radius and worked his way inwards, gradually becoming closer to Deanna as he did so. Deanna all the time thanking him and remaining flustered and suitably embarrassed by the commotion she had created. He remained mostly silent, Deanna assumed he may not have had good enough English to instigate conversation, but he nodded and smiled as Deanna thanked him.

After gathering all the coins he could see, Yusef, the driver, held them out in his hands to give to Deanna. Deanna with all the concentration she could muster kept her eyes on him and not on Alex approaching stealthily from behind with a rock in his hand raised ready to strike. Deanna's eyes flickered imperceptibly, a micro muscle movement that instantly gave Yusef cause for concern and planted doubt in his mind as to what was really happening. The smile dropped from his face as he sensed another person in the vicinity. Yusef turned a moment too late to see Alex bring the rock down onto his forehead, the element of surprise had been lost. Alex connected well and the driver went down in pain dropping to his knees and clutching his head. Alex took the opportunity to try and retain the upper hand and got the man in a choke hold clamping his arm around his neck by holding his fist tight with his other hand. If Alex could cut off his oxygen supply for long enough he would pass out. He had no reason to kill this man and he had no desire to do so, there had been too much killing recently for his liking.

Yusef rallied at the realisation that he was in mortal danger. Underneath his Saville Row suit was a body that trained in the gym two hours a day, seven days a week. He rose up from his knees with Alex hanging off him like a pillion passenger, and began prizing the arm from around his throat. Deanna could see that Alex would soon be on the defensive and did the only thing she could think of in the moment, she brought her foot, full force into the groin of the driver. The effect was instant. He went down again, this time clutching his nether regions, a man broken. Alex squeezed tighter. After what seemed like an age the driver began to lose his sensibilities and became insensate. The muscles in Alex's arms began to produce lactic acid and it was now becoming a race of who could beat the biological countdown of their rictus embrace. As Alex could feel the energy draining from his arms, the bodyguard began to lose consciousness and went limp. Alex checked his pulse to make sure he was still alive. It could be a close thing between suppression and termination and Alex could ascertain he had judged it correctly, a faint pulse remained.

It took both of them to drag his limp body between two cars where he wouldn't immediately be seen or found. Alex stripped him of his jacket in the hope he could pass off as the bodyguard at his post outside the door. It would only need to be believable for a moment, enough time for the door to be breached.

As they approached the apartment entrance it was Deanna who took the lead and rang the bell to enter. She looked as if she could be hotel management and would try to gain entry by feigning some sort of housekeeping errand.

Deanna composed herself as she stood in front of the door, brushing down her skirt and mentally preparing herself for the lie to come. Alex stood with his back to the door in the same stance that Yusef took. A few deep breaths and she rang the bell. Footsteps could be heard through the door as he approached. The footsteps then stopped and a thick Russian voice crackled through the intercom. Dragunov would have assumed that Yusef had vetted the person now standing at the door as he could still see him in the corner of the cctv screen standing guard. Deanna knew then that she was being scrutinised for any kind of clue as to who she was, 'Hello?'

As brightly as she could Deanna smiled and sang in her best French accent, 'Bonjour Monsieur, housekeeping', she decided to keep it simple.

'Khorosho, zakhodi' she heard as the door clicked open and swung inwards.

As soon as Alex was sure that there was no chain attached to the frame he spun around and stormed the door, crashing it open against the wall making a dent in the plaster as it hit. To his surprise, the old man in front of him stood there with a look of resignation on his face, as if he almost half expected someone to come bursting into the room. Alex pulled his gun from his hip and raised it to point at him, he then flicked the nozzle to intimate that he needed to move from the hall into the interior of the apartment, 'Move'. Deanna closed the door behind them. The captive said nothing but complied with the request and slowly sauntered into the main living area. Alex shed the drivers jacket and took in the living quarters as he entered; overly opulent decor consisting of plush carpet, flocked walls and French period furniture. What really stood out for him though, was the view over the lake and how dazzling the water was as the sun glinted off the surface. It made him squint as he took in the view. As his eyes began to adjust he could make out the swans on the surface of the lake and the reed beds on the far side of the expanse, a breathtaking view by any standard.

43 - Confrontation

Alex looked the old man up and down trying to ascertain where he knew him from. Then it dawned on him. Vasili Dragunov. He looked different in the flesh. The Russian defector used as a lure to get him to Spain. The man who never showed up, who was never meant to show up. The man also linked to Quiros and the Greek. Alex's anger deepened realising that he had been played this whole time.

'Do you know who I am?' Alex asked

'I haven't a clue my dear boy, why don't you enlighten me'

'Don't give me that bullshit, you know me' Alex's blood was up, 'Alex Spellman, Delta squad, Navarre 2011'

Vasili's lips curled in a smile of acceptance. 'So, you finally caught up with me, eh?'

'You can be a difficult man to find, it seems'

'Well that might have something to do with the fact that I am trying to keep a low profile these days. You're not the only one that's out for my blood. How did you find me by the way?'

'The same way we find anyone these days; technology trail, you can't go anywhere without leaving a trace. You should tell your employees to be more careful with their burner phones'

'I see' said Vasili, 'all down to the simplest of factors, I suppose I shouldn't be surprised'

'Why didn't you run when you had the chance?' Alex asked him

'Run. Where would I run to? Dear boy, I am old. Too old to be embarrassing myself by trying in vain to flee. I know when the game is up. I have tried my best. What would happen if I ran? I wouldn't get far, it would just be postponing the inevitable'

'I need some answers from you, I need to know why. Why me and why now?

'Unfortunately for you Alex, you were in the right place at the wrong time or the wrong place at the right time, depending on your viewpoint. You served a purpose for me. Alas in the end it bore no fruit, otherwise I would not be in the position I am in now. You were my puppet, my mole and my salvation. At least you should have been'

'What are you saying? Make some sense'

'I don't feel I need to explain myself to you. I did what I had to do for my own reasons, you need not worry yourself about them'

'That's where you're wrong, Dragunov. I'm taking you in with me. Like it or not you have been cornered and captured and now you will feel the full force of the British government concerning everything you have been up to. The crimes you have committed, of which I am sure there are many, will be your downfall'

'There is nothing you can prove. You must know that. My hands are clean. Even so I could just as easily make a deal. I could trade information for my freedom'

'Regardless, it is my duty to bring you to task, I wouldn't be doing my job otherwise'

'I am impressed, Alex. I was sure that after all that had happened you would not be able to let me live. After all it was me that had Dan Johnson killed and of course Graham Devereux, they were not really as useful to me as I had hoped. The information Dan had for me, although interesting, did not carry enough weight for my redemption. Quiros tortured him solidly for nearly twenty four hours, he had got all the information in the first five hours. Of course you have met my friend Ignasi and you know how much he loves his gadgets. I think he was just enjoying himself. It was a shame about the three deaths in Navarre, I was hoping to sacrifice just the one man, the man in the shed. It was unfortunate that the two other soldiers were so close to the munitions shed, they could have been great sources of information for me also'

'What do you mean? Four of my men were killed in Navarre' Alex spurted out in anger

'You don't know, do you?' Dragunov chuckled to himself realising that Alex had no clue about the defector. 'Can it be that you still have no idea what really happened on that day?

'What are you talking about?'

'I am talking about Jack Cole. Alex' Dragunov said with relish, 'The mission in Navarre benefited the motherland twofold. Jack Cole used it as a cover to escape from the West and bring back with him his skills as an assassin. It wasn't just that he was defecting, more like returning to the fold. He had found his redemption after many years and was then ready to return to Mother Russia. Even after all it had done to him in the past. It also provided me with the guinea pigs I needed to help my doctor friend, as well as provide some insurance for me. In my line of work it is always a smart idea to have some sort of backup in case your employers decide you are dispensable. In my case it wasn't the fact that I was dispensable, it was the fact that I was to be hung out to dry and made to look an embarrassment amongst my peers. I had given my life for Russia and how do they repay me? They asked the impossible. Which I gave them'

'Make some sense old man' shouted Alex becoming annoying at Dragunov's ramblings.

'It was not my fault' Dragunov said almost to himself

Alex turned to Deanna and shrugged as if giving up on his questioning. It was unbelievable that Jack Cole could have defected. He didn't know the man as well as the rest of his team... but still, he was a member of an elite squad, he had been working for Her Majesty's military force for most of his adult life. Then again, maybe the dealings he had with CHRISYS should have raised warning flags, maybe he was not a man you could trust after all. It then began to dawn on Alex that everything he had felt responsible for and all the guilt he had been carrying with him for the last six years could have been someone else's doing. He started to feel as if the cold grip on his heart, one that he had learned to live with for so long now, had suddenly been released. He could breathe again without the constant ache in his chest. It was as if without knowing he had been carrying around the weight of his fallen comrades in his chest and now that was being replaced rapidly with anger, an anger that was directed at the man standing in front of him, Vasili Dragunov. The man who single handedly brought all this pain and suffering to him and his friends, who had put Alex on a journey of doubt and confusion, all due to his own damned self-interest. Alex reached behind his jacket and put his hand on the cold metal of the gun butt. He paused a moment before pulling the gun out and pointing the barrel directly at Dragunov's face. Alex's face became flushed as the realisation of this man's actions continued to take hold in his head. The hell he had been put through, all the lives that had been lost, Alex began seeing red.

'Alex' Deanna said gently. 'Alex, what are you doing?'

Alex didn't reply as he stood firmly rooted with every intention of ending this man's life. His finger gently squeezed on the trigger of the gun.

Again Deanna tried to distract Alex. She touched him on the arm to try and bring him out of his determined trance. Dragunov was not surprised by the actions of his subject, he was fully prepared for his demise to be at the hands of Alex Spellman. He had expected nothing less. 'Alex, please' she said. Alex turned his head to Deanna and upon seeing her soft features, her pleading face, realised that what he was doing was impetuous and exactly what Dragunov would want him to do. He also realised his actions would jeopardize any future he might have with the beautiful woman who stood by him, literally and figuratively. Dragunov had practically goaded him into pulling his gun, but he decided he would not be suckered into making bad choices. Alex realised he had his own free will and was going to choose the appropriate action. He would take Dragunov into the proper authorities to face his punishment. He had admitted to both of them what he was responsible for, the word of two governmental operatives would be more than enough to bring this malefactor to justice. To make his point unequivocal Alex tipped the nozzle of the automatic upwards and jettisoned the magazine onto the floor rendering the weapon safe.

'I'm not going to play into your hands, Dragunov. The machinations you set in motion all those years ago have kept me prisoner for too long, I have been captive to grief and guilt, and I am no longer willing to play your treacherous game. However much I despise you and your cohorts for putting me in this position I am not going to let you off easy by killing you'

'I think you will find that was a mistake Mr Spellman', said Dragunov as he stealthily pulled an object from his pocket, 'You leave me no choice, I will not be taken without a fight. If you do not have the *yaytsa* to finish me off yourself I will have to be the man in the room and finish this myself'

Alex could see as Dragunov raised his arm that he was holding a compact firearm, small enough to fit in the palm of your hand. Alex guessed it was a Pieper .25 Auto, a rare enough pistol, a collector's item for many these days but still dangerous enough to do some serious damage. Alex realised he had just lost the upper hand in the situation and cursed himself for ejecting the magazine. He was now at Dragunov's mercy.

'What do you want?' asked Alex

'What do any of us want? To live our lives, free of tyranny, in comfort. You were unfortunate in that you were drawn into my sphere, by luck or misfortune, whatever it may have been. There was nothing you could have done about it. No action could have altered the outcome of us standing here in this room with me pointing this gun at you. Do you believe in fate?'

'Fuck fate. We are here because you are a conniving, malevolent bastard who will go to any lengths to get his own way regardless of the lives you ruin along the way'

Dragunov chuckled at the damning depiction of himself, 'You would do the same thing if you were in my position'

'That's where you're wrong. You see, I know the difference between good and bad, right and wrong. I would never have made the decisions you have made'

'And what about the men you were going to kill in Navarre? Did they have a choice?'

'There was no intention to kill anyone that day'

Dragunov shrugged, 'It is of no consequence. Your hands are by no means clean Alex. You have been responsible for many wrongdoings over the course of your career, you are in no position to criticise me for my own self-preservation. And not least as you have the audacity to drag this innocent girl into your realm for her to suffer the same fate as yourself. What did she do to deserve this, eh?'

'You leave her out of this, this is between us, you can let her go' Alex pleaded.

'You know I cannot and will not be letting either of you go. I have survived for this long because I am willing to take action when other men back down, case in point,' Dragunov nodded at the magazine lying on the floor, 'would you mind kicking that over to me, we don't want to have any accidents now do we? Thank you' the gun clattered across the floor to his feet, 'You are weak and you know it, you ask for compassion when you know it doesn't exist... and nor should it, compassion is for faint hearted liberals. I care nothing for you or your kind, you make me sick with your kowtowing to the capitalist American pigs, you are as bad as each other, I have no pity for you'

Alex had to find a way to tilt the odds back into his favour, it was naive of him to think that Dragunov would go quietly and let himself be tried in the West for his crimes, 'I can cut you a bargain' he offered.

'You are in no position to bargain, do you not see who here has got the upper hand?'

Alex bluffed, 'We are not alone Dragunov, there will be men here before you know it. If you kill us here, now, you will only be making things a hundred times worse for yourself, you can still turn yourself in and cut a deal, you could turn this around'

'There are no men coming', Dragunov patronised Alex by taking his eyes off them and glancing out of the window. 'And I will not be cutting any...' Cutting him short, Alex took it as his chance to rush at him, it may be his last and only hope. Although the gun was still pointed in their direction Alex knew his aim would be off momentarily. Alex made his move. At that same exact moment the room filled with the spray of shattered glass. Deanna screamed. A rifle's report rang out soon after and Deanna realised that blood had sprayed her shoes. In panic she threw herself to the floor to avoid being hurt herself and saw both men on the floor a few yards away from her, Alex laying on top of Dragunov, neither man obviously moving, broken glass and blood spatter covering the floor around where they lay.

44 - Man Down

The gunman slowly raised the barrel of the Lobaev rifle and aimed, capturing the scene playing out in front of him within his sight. He had been in position for more than an hour and had watched as the couple arrived on foot attempting to be stealthy, one of them approaching the cabin from an oblique angle so as not to be spotted by its inhabitant. Not the way he would have chosen to have done so but it seems that they gained access nevertheless.

This particular sniper rifle, the Twilight SVLK-14S, had been custom fitted for the gunman's precise requirements, it had a single shot bolt action as the gunman rarely needed to use more than one shot to take down his quarry, such was the unerring accuracy of his eye. The designer Vladislav Lobaev boasts it to be the most accurate sniper rifle in the world. The gunman silently watched the three people in the room half a kilometre away. One man had his back to him, he could see the other man's face whilst he did the talking, the woman was standing nearby with a look of consternation on her face. He recognized all of the faces in the room. One he knew very well, the other he knew by reputation. He would have enjoyed hearing what was being said in the room. He found it amusing that very shortly all of their problems would have to be reassessed, they would have a whole set of new troubles to worry about, although sadly from this distance all he could do was watch. He studied the scene intently, noting each man's movements and gestures. Both men were becoming agitated, he saw they were arguing. There was a power play going on and he knew very well what it was over. The woman was the only one remaining quiet. He saw the younger of the two men drop the magazine from his gun to the floor as the other had his arm raised as if holding his own weapon, although from this distance it was difficult to make out that sort of detail. He was a professional, nothing would be left to chance. He didn't know exactly what was being said in that room nor did he care. He was there to do his job. He was there to eradicate a problem. He watched as the older man inexplicably took his eyes from the couple in the room. He looked out of the window directly in his direction. The magnification of the sight gave his actions an unreality of being within his field of vision. Almost instinctively the gunman squeezed the trigger and let fly the inevitable, a bullet to end his life. In the split second he let the missile free the younger man had made a leap in his captor's direction, no doubt to try and unarm him. Both men fell to the floor and were now out of his range of vision. There was no doubt in his mind however that the target had been hit and that his quarry was now laying dead. 'Dlya Rossii-matushki' he uttered with satisfaction

Deanna gingerly crawled over to the two men lying prone on the ground. Even from a few yards away it was obvious immediately that the Russian was dead, his eyes stared vacantly at an abstract angle and blood oozed freely from the dime sized hole in his temple. His face absurdly looking as if he was searching for something up in the sky, mouth agape revealing a crimson interior making his face look starkly pale in contrast. It didn't make sense, she couldn't understand how if Dragunov had the gun he was the one who ended up dead on the floor, the sudden rush of adrenaline had dampened her calculating skills. She crawled closer, careful not to cut herself on the glass strewn across the floor, afraid of what she might find when she got to Alex. She couldn't see him moving either, she felt sick to the stomach fearing that somehow he had also been injured. She called out in a hoarse whisper, 'Alex', surprised at the discordant sound of her own voice, and got no reply.

She reached Alex and saw that he was covered in blood, whether his or Dragunov's she couldn't tell. She used both her hands and pushed his shoulder pivoting his body so he fell from on top of the older man. The action of repositioning stirred Alex and he let out a guttural gasp as he drew in a breath. Deanna could now see that he had been injured and that there was blood all over his face. She hoped that it might not have all been his own. Dragunov's weapon must have gone off in the meleé, at least Alex was alive and breathing. She checked him for injury and found that he had, in fact, taken a bullet high up in his chest below his clavicle.

Kapusta finished dismantling the Lobaev before packing the rifle into its case. The hours of blindfolded practice meant that he could do it in the dark if necessary. He made sure that he retrieved the spent shell, leaving no trace that he had been there at all. He was pleased that the job had been a success and that he had made the shot without any need for a follow up. He rolled up the groundsheet that he had laid underneath him and folded it away into his backpack along with all the other accoutrements that were needed for his stake-out. He was far enough away from the target that he had no fear about being seen, the remaining individuals in the cabin certainly wouldn't be interested in pursuing him. After all they would probably have reached the same settlement in the end, he was just sent as an insurance policy in case things began to head in the wrong direction. He packed his kit away in complete silence as was his habit, taking care to put everything back in the place it belonged; a fastidious person was someone who survived, he had learned that over the years. He had a long trek to make it back to his vehicle but he was fit, the moon was bright and the ground was dry enough for a speedy journey. He threw the backpack over his shoulder, made sure it was strapped down to his chest as he would be yomping most of the way, picked up the rifle case in his right hand and paused before setting off. He scanned the area once more to check that he had not left anything behind to incriminate himself. Satisfied that he had not he turned to set off. As he did so he practically ran in to a figure that had appeared out of nowhere, dressed all in black, as he was, but with a ski mask over his face. In any other situation it might have been comical but Kapusta suddenly knew that he was in deep shit. He knew that this person in front of him was highly trained as he had not heard his approach or even had an inkling that he was in the vicinity. Sadly he was not shocked at his appearance, in his line of work you learned to expect the unexpected. They stood looking at each other for a moment sizing one another up, neither moving a muscle. Kapusta looked the man up and down evaluating the immediate danger he was in and what he was going to do about it. His face belied the panic behind his eyes. His rifle was packed away, although it would be of no use at all at close range. He had a knife but it was in his backpack along with anything else that could be used as a weapon. He was at a distinct disadvantage.

'Who are you?' Kapusta said breaking the deadlock

'That is not important' the Russian voice replied, 'What is important is that you realise why I am here and why you should be saying your prayers at this moment. These are the last minutes you will be spending on this earth'

'Tell me, what have I done?' he replied calmly

'I think you have done many things in your life, and I could be here to seek retribution for any one of them' he said, 'but it just so happens that you bought your gun from the wrong lady... Dominika sends her regards'

Just as Kapusta opened his mouth to say something an arm reached around from behind him and jerked his head back. At the same time a knife was drawn across his throat severing his carotid artery, blood spraying from his wound. Kapusta's arms flailed, trying to loosen his attackers grip on him but all too quickly lost the ability to be effective. The man in the ski mask took two steps back to avoid the arterial spray getting on his clothes but his eyes remained locked on Kapusta until the life began to ebb from him, his shocked expression changing to one of realisation and then resignation. The man behind Kapusta held him with strong, bear-like arms until he could feel his life force had drained away. He then let him fall to the ground, the blood from his wound slowing to a trickle and seeping into the dirt in which he now lay.

The Russian in the mask pulled it off to reveal his face. He spat with disgust on the body lying on the ground and muttered, 'I don't know what my sister ever saw in you, you ugly piece of shit'

'What shall we do with the body, Dimitri?' asked Anatoly

'Nothing. Take a picture of it on your phone so we can show our sister. I will text her now to say the deed is done. Then we must re-join our regiment, our leave is only for 48 hours remember'

'Of course'

'We should take the rifle with us. There is always the possibility that some busybody could go to the trouble of tracing its origin. There must be no connection between the Zotovs and this murdering bastard'

'Of course we take the rifle, are you dim? Dominika would expect us to deal with it. But first and most importantly we must take out the tracker, so the rifle, if found cannot be directly linked to Dominika, OK?'

'OK. What do we know about him? Anything?'

'Only what Dominika uncovered when she was putting him through her vetting procedure'

'What did she find out?'

'He defected from the UK. Used to be with the military as far as I know'

'So his name is not Kapusta?'

'No. Although he did have some Russian connections. His name was Cole, Jack Cole'

'Not his real name?'

'No, nobody knows his real name. Who cares anyway, he is a motherfucker, better off dead. Now come, we must go, we will need to get to Dover before the boat leaves. And we still have errands to run'

The brothers took the gun and relieved Kapusta of everything in his pockets that could identify him. The keys to his vehicle would also come in handy for reasons of haste. Not having to make the return journey all the way on foot was a bonus. The rifle would need to be got rid of first, better off in the sea than in the lake nearby. Lakes are far too easy to dredge, in the sea it would be lost forever, if it was disposed of properly.

The brothers faced each other and raised their right hands in a salute and said 'Bozhe, blagoslovi Rossiyu' in tandem, a ritual they had practised every time they had made a successful kill together.

They both double-checked the area before heading off. The moonlight thankfully still bright enough to let them travel without torchlight, they disappeared into the dense woodland toward the road where the vehicle was parked. Nobody would be any the wiser that they had ever even been there.

46 - Free at last

Deanna rolled Alex completely off of the lifeless body of the Russian and was relieved to see him open his eyes and say, 'What the hell happened?' Even under the grim circumstances her face broke into a broad grin as she realised that he couldn't be too badly hurt. She leaned down to hug him but Alex grunted with pain so she withdrew, she did not want to cause him any additional discomfort. Instead she gave him a soft kiss on his cheek, 'Sorry. How bad is it?'

'It hurts like a bastard, but seeing as I am able to function I think I was lucky I didn't get hit anywhere vital'

'Can you get up?'

'I think so. Is it safe?'

'He's dead, if that's what you mean'

'I mean from the sniper. The gunman who shot Dragunov'

Deanna hadn't been able to process what had actually happened in the last few frantic, confusing moments. Her one and only thought was about the safety of the man that she loved. It dawned on her that, of course, there had to be an assassin, 'Dragunov was the target, not you?' she said as both a statement and a question

'Exactly, and if it was either one of us they may still want to finish the job. Stay low, below the window line. We'll have to find a way out before he's able to take another pot shot. We need to get to the car. The shot came from the south, so we can leave the way we came in and retreat using the cover of the woodland to the east'

'OK, can you walk? Tell me what you need me to do'

'Yes, just give me a hand up. I think the bullet that Dragunov fired is still in my shoulder, judging by the pain'

Alex and Deanna both crawled their way over to the exit of the cabin, staying low all the time and avoiding the line of sight from the broken window. Alex's shoulder wept blood and made his left arm almost unusable. Every time he put pressure on it brought not only burning pain but a halo of soft focus stars around his vision.

Once outside they made their way slowly, not knowing if the marksman still had them in their sights, across to the tree line where Alex propped himself up briefly against the nearest tree to catch his breath. The short distance they had covered taking more energy than it would have done normally. Again they used the cars in the parking lot to shield themselves, not from Dragunov this time but from their unknown assailant, whoever it may be. They weaved their way haltingly, crouching between the Jaguars and Bentleys, taking their time and being careful not to leave themselves open to any area that could hide an attacker. Finally Alex could see his car and realised they would have to risk the last thirty feet of open ground to make a dash for it. Little did he realise when they had first arrived that they would find themselves in their present situation.

'OK, let me go first and we'll soon find out whether there is anybody else out there'

'I can't let you go alone, you're in no fit state'

'Listen, Deanna, this is non-negotiable, I go, you stay. You follow when we know it's safe, when I have reached the car'

'Alright, but please be careful'

'I will' and with that he pulled her towards him and gave her a reassuring kiss full on the lips, girding himself for the next few moments.

Alex felt his adrenaline surge as he tensed his legs muscles for the imminent sprint. He unlocked the car door with his key fob and made the dash, zig-zagging as he went, across the tarmac and after what seemed like an age, to the car. When there, he made his way to the passenger side and climbed in, catching his shoulder on the way in causing him to recoil in agony. Thankfully, to his relief, his sortie elicited no response from any gunman. He leant over, ignoring the pain and opened the driver's door for Deanna and beckoned for her to follow. She took off her heels and held them in one hand before making the dash herself, following Alex's lead, avoiding running in a straight line just in case. Again, all was quiet as she clambered into the driver's seat. Alex had the keys in the ignition ready to go. Deanna gunned the accelerator and let out the clutch and with a squeal the tyres gripped tarmac, the car lurched forward gaining momentum rapidly. Deanna moved up the gears as best shew could and soon they were racing out of the car park and the vicinity of any danger.

Not until they were out of the hotel grounds and on the main road could they relax and breathe a sigh of relief. Deanna knew the first stop needed to be an emergency unit to get Alex's shoulder seen to. 'Where to?' she asked. 'North, up the A21' Alex replied through gritted teeth. Deanna told the SatNav the destination and followed the instructions spoken to her. Tunbridge Wells hospital was only twenty miles away and as any damage from a bullet wound needed to be minimised as soon as possible, this was their main aim. Spire Sussex might have been closer but Alex would rather be heading towards London than away, he needed to know he was close to home if they decided to keep him overnight.

Alex relaxed back into the leather seat cupping his elbow in his hand protecting his injury from the bumps and potholes along the A21.

Deanna drove from the hospital in Tunbridge Wells back to Alex's apartment in London, his injuries making it difficult to work the gear stick on the old car, apart from the fact he was on strong painkillers. She wasn't used to driving stick, her car back in the US being an automatic as most were, but she managed with only a few crunches of the gears this time. Luckily Alex, being on strong drugs, either didn't seem to notice or to mind. He was drowsy and a little bit high, giving the impression that he was slightly drunk, so the conversation veered from topic to topic, drifting happily between childhood memories and giving Deanna a detailed description of his favourite topic; London lore, a subject on which he was very knowledgeable.

Pulling up outside the apartment building where Alex lived, there stood Madash and Graves looking on expectantly, two people who in times of trouble never failed to be there for him. The hospital had rung ahead and contacted Anil Bharat who in turn had called Madeline Ashwood. Madeline of course had called Robert Graves immediately as she would have no idea how or where to park Alex's car in the private garage.

It was as if two completely mismatched parents were welcoming back their son from war. Madash smothered Alex in kisses as Graves gave him a manly hug and swiftly grabbed the car keys to deposit the car into the depths of the underground parking lot.

'Oh, we were so worried about you, my dear boy' cried Madeline as she and Deanna both took an arm and helped Alex up the steps and towards the elevator.

'It's good to see you too, Madash'

'Now Alex, you know what I think of you calling me that name, but as you are incapacitated I will let you off this one time' she said with a smile, secretly enjoying the fact that she had a special nickname from her favourite boy.

'I am Madeline Ashwood, you must be Deanna, you may call me Maddie, but definitely not Madash' she said with a smile, 'I can't say that I've heard a lot about you but you must be somebody quite special to get full access like this'

'Oh, it's a long story. I am very happy to meet you though. Alex has mentioned you more than once. Sometimes in his sleep' she whispered conspiratorially

'So, first things first. Is it kettle for tea or ice for whiskies?' asked Madeline putting on the kettle regardless. In her experience all major life events called for one of the two beverages.

As she made the drinks Robert Graves entered the room and sat down opposite Alex and looked him right in the eye, 'We're glad you're back with us son, we were worried about you'

Alex knew that he was a man of few words and usually none of them heartfelt so it was a big deal to catch Graves at his softest.

'Thanks, Graves, that means a lot. It's good to be home, you have no idea. And it's great to see both of you'

Out of the corner of his eye Alex could see that the landline answering machine had a flashing message so out of habit touched the button to play it. He heard a familiar voice coming from the speaker. A voice, he now realised, that he wasn't sure he would ever hear again.

Just thought I would let you know kids, that I am OK. Apart from a few bumps and scrapes I managed to convince those two imbeciles that you had, in fact, held me against my will and that they were actually my saviours for chasing you two off. Heh-heh. I couldn't quite believe it myself, they bought it hook line and sinker. In any case they were too concerned with catching up to you than dealing with me so I told them that I had heard you talking about heading north to Los Angeles. I don't know if they believed it or not but at least it made me look to be impartial...'

Alex glanced at Deanna with a look of relief in his face that soon turned to a broad grin, another guilty burden had been lifted. She smiled back at him as the remainder of the message played out.

'...I hope you two are OK and that you are home safe and sound. Let me know as soon as you can, the spirit of your resting father will surely come back to haunt me if anything I did led you to any harm. I feel somewhat responsible for you now, both of you. So make sure you contact me. And I wanted to say thanks also, thanks for making me realise that I can still be of some use and that even

though I am now on my own there are still people out there who matter to me. Don't be a stranger Deanna, and that goes for you too Alex. Best of luck, bye now'

Deanna had a tear in her eye as the message came to an end and Alex went to her to comfort her, placing an arm across her shoulder, giving her the support she needed. 'We couldn't have done it without him' said Alex and then took a long draft from his tumbler of whiskey. 'Cheers everyone, it's good to be home'

'I can't tell you how worried we have been about you, I thought that you had put all this behind you when you started to work at Thames House? We were both worried sick!' Madeline now entering full maternal mode, 'And not even a phone call or text to let us know you were alright'

'I am really sorry for that, but as Deanna will testify there wasn't a lot of time. We were under a bit of pressure to sat the least' It was becoming apparent that the alcohol didn't mix very well with the medication and forming his words was becoming a challenge for Alex.

'It has been a demanding few days' Deanna agreed with a weary smile

'Now if you will excuse me I think that I need to go and lie down before I fall down, I have to see Anil tomorrow and debrief him on the last couple of days, no doubt get a bollocking for my trouble as well'

'Is there anything we can do?' asked Graves

'You've done more than enough, just being here for me has made all the difference, you've no idea. As far as I'm concerned it's back to business as usual and as soon as possible'

'Sounds good to me. And will you be needing a particular car for tomorrow?'

'Thanks Graves, but I think I'll jump in a cab'

'And will you be staying with us?' Madeline asked Deanna

Deanna wasn't sure what to answer and looked to Alex for some sort of intimation, hoping it was going to be positive.

'Yes Madash, Deanna will be staying here as long as she would like to'

'Oh' Madeline replied slightly crestfallen

Deanna found it difficult to contain her happiness at the statement and grinned broadly.

'But that doesn't mean that I won't still be needing your services. I would be glad to see you on your usual days if that's OK with you'

'Of course it is' she smiled, also buoyed by the affirmation.

'Now if you don't mind, please let yourselves out, I will see you all when I have had some well needed rest' and he led Deanna by the hand towards the bedroom. He crashed headlong onto the Egyptian sheets and listened to the sounds of Madeline washing up the glasses outside in the kitchen. Deanna lay on the bed next to him and draped herself across his torso, stroking his resting muscles trying to ease some of the pain he must be feeling from his injury. They both dozed off in this position and did not wake until the next day.

48 - Explanations

Alex sat in Anil's office utterly worn down by the events of the last few days. His arm and shoulder, although still very sore, were well on their way to healing. Once again his body felt as if it had been put through the wringer, bruises and wounds all over. He knew he had to hear everything that Anil had to tell him but he didn't know whether he had the capacity to take it all in, let alone process it into something that made any sense. Unpacking all the information had been a complicated business but the techies at Thames House were very thorough when they got their teeth into something.

'Well, what have you got for me?' Alex asked wearily

Anil looked at the sheaf of paper sitting on his desk as if he wasn't quite sure where to start. He then began the long explanation into the background of the enigma that was Kapusta.

'After doing a lot of deep background checks on our man Jack Cole a.k.a. Kapusta a.k.a. Pavel Petrov, it turns out that he was a much more complex creature than we ever could have imagined. Born in a dispiriting Russian town called Desnogorsk on the south bank of the Desna river near the Belarusian border; home to the personnel who worked at the Smolensk Nuclear Power plant. Son to Boris and Natasha, his family were one of the first to have moved there to work at the power plant back in the early seventies. Many people came from the outskirts of Moscow, 300 km away, as well as Smolensk 100 km away, to start a new life with long term career prospects. I imagine Russia was a tough place in the late sixties, early seventies; unemployment was widespread and jobs were thin on the ground. The power plant spelled a new beginning for a lot of families who were willing to work hard and do long hours. These were people who were sick of barely getting by on scraps and who were happy to leave their old life behind them and start anew'

'Pavel spent his first years in that family home, up to the age of about ten from what we can gather. He was an only child and his mother, by all accounts, treated him with all the love she could give when she wasn't working night shifts at the plant; his father however was a belligerent drunk who spent all that he earned on vodka, leaving the family with only the mother's earnings to live off, which she had to protect with a shrewd resourcefulness. What started off as a chance at a new life became, over that decade, a daily roulette game with an aggressive father. Beatings were common apparently. The boy Pavel was victim to his father's tirades on a weekly basis and would often turn up at school with injuries, when they were too conspicuous he would stay at home and lie in bed with his mother who would console him as best she could. But this was nothing to what Natasha had to endure at her husband's hands. If it wasn't the verbal abuse he gave her it was the drunken rages he would launch into and with those rages came the physical assaults. Often it was about money, the fact that he could not get his hands on her wage. Or it was about being sold the Western dream of a new life in the 'nuclear age' where everyone would be happy and want for nothing, a scenario that was not bearing fruit for him. Mainly because of the incessant drinking and the fact that he was stuck in Desnogorsk with no hope of escape. It was a vicious cycle'

'Brezhnev's mishandling of the country's economy during the seventies was such that Russia stagnated financially and fell into a period of hopelessness and despair for the working population. These same people looked to the West with a mixture of veiled envy and animosity, a sure way for despondency to turn into anger. This rubbed off from the father to the son, maybe subliminally, maybe more directly, we don't know for sure, we can only surmise at this point as there are no longer any living first-hand witnesses'

'According to the files from my contact at the embassy, the pivotal moment in all their lives was one wintry evening as Boris had once again taken too many vodkas on his one day off from his work at the plant. Cole's mother was about to go to work on the night shift but for one reason or another a disagreement prevented her from leaving the house, Boris was angry with her and took it out on her by beating her in front of the boy, not caring that he was standing in the corner afraid for his own life. Little did Boris know that Pavel had grown into a strong, sinewy ten year old whose placid face belied an anger broiling deep inside of him. He knew that because of his father's current fit of rage he would not have the strength to stop the beating his mother was receiving. But Pavel could bide his time'

'Inevitably Boris grew weary with the effort of throwing punches and left his wife curled up in the foetal position on the floor moaning softly. Pavel sat with his mother, cradling her in his arms trying to soothe her suffering. It was in the small hours of the morning that she gave up the will to live, she had gradually lost her fight from the internal injuries she had sustained from the beating'

'The young boy left his mother after covering her with a blanket from her armchair and quietly climbed the stairs to the bedroom where his father laid, fully clothed on the bed, snoring loudly, recovering from his drunken stupor. Pavel took his mother's pillow and covered his father's face with it pinning it down with his knees either side of his head, he held his father's arms down with his own and waited until the thrashing of his legs subsided to stillness'

'Additional information was proffered from his adoptive parents, Martin and Natalie Cole of Great Houghton, Northampton. We got in touch with them through Cole's records on file. Pavel was sent to them after the Russian authorities tracked them down as being his closest living relatives. Natalie was a cousin of Natasha's apparently, or rather Natalya. Martin Cole was in the army and met Natalya on National Service deployment in the early sixties. We are finding out the details of where he was stationed but I don't see it as a priority at this time. Jack underwent extensive sessions with a child psychologist where a lot of this supplementary information was held on file. Up until now it has been protected under patient confidentiality. It was released to the M.O.D. after his death. He was initially treated for trauma because of the loss of both parents, a shock that would affect any normal child of ten. His doctor was the only person privy to the fact that he in fact suffocated his father in response to the fatal beatings his mother received at his hands. A crime of passion to be sure. But information reached certain individuals within the Kremlin that this boy had particular tendencies that could be nurtured and developed. Nothing remains a secret for long in Russia. The doctor no doubt knew Sigalov, or one of his close compatriots'

'It was also revealed during these sessions that Jack had inherited his father's animosity towards Western culture but being the resourceful boy he was, managed to keep this covered up from everyone but his confessor, who, unfortunately, was not so discreet. We assume it was why he began working for CHRISYS, he saw it as a chance to undermine the fabric of society by spreading doubt and fear throughout the West and supplying public awareness with credible threat'

'It's quite clever, really, when you consider it; we have the real terrorists creating havoc within cities with random acts of violence against innocent citizens. They create panic and widen the rift between ethnic groups living together. And then we have groups like CHRISYS making us look in the direction that the military-industrial complex wants us to, channelling our perceptions. We are being manipulated constantly, whether it is by the way news is reported with a bias, to the way we are shown doctored images from war zones'

'Regardless, we have ascertained that Jack Cole made contact with Andreyev Sigalov in The Kremlin when he was a young adult, probably in his early twenties. He was welcomed back with the proviso that he should carry out a series of acts on behalf of Mother Russia, the extent of which we don't know at this time. Although now that we know he should have been a person of interest we will be digging up everything we can about his years spent in the U.K., going over his every move with a fine tooth comb if you will'

'We are nearly certain that the failure of the mission in Navarre was in some way due to his attempt at returning to Russia. I don't know what you would call it as defecting gives an erroneous impression as he was after all Russian born. We know he received injuries in the escape, he was identified by his dental records as there were no other clues on his person. What we can't figure out is who killed him and why. By the time his body was found any evidence that may have been left at the scene may well have been destroyed by weather and such. I don't think we'll ever know for sure, although we suspect the assassin known as 'Kapusta' would have had no shortage of enemies. He has been known to us as an operator for a few years but we didn't know his true identity until now. He is responsible for some high profile assassinations within Russia and on the European mainland. It was highly unusual for Kapusta to leave mainland Europe. If it wasn't for your intel regarding the sniper who took out Dragunov he may never have been found in that remote part of forest. It was certainly off the beaten track. What was strange was the fact that whoever killed him took the weapon away with them, there was no rifle found at the scene.

'There was a vehicle left abandoned on Castle Hill Road in Dover. We are looking into the possibility that it could be connected to Cole. It's feasible that his killer made off with his keys and therefore his vehicle and made his escape from Dover on to France, and then... who knows. He could be anywhere by now.'

'And what do we know about Dragunov?' asked Alex

'Not enough, I'm afraid. Obviously we've been able to link him to Quiros and Petrakis, who, by the way, is safely in custody as we speak'

'The man-mountain? How the hell did he end up getting caught?'

'We have Sergeant Lowry to thank for that'

'How so?'

'Well, according to Lowry, he has been trying to stop smoking, unsuccessfully for about six months now. He knew that Jimmy wasn't in residence and he figured that if he went downstairs for a quick smoke he would see Jimmy if he approached. Rightly so, I would say. So he exited the building onto Ponsonby and saw what he thought were a couple of drunks making their way home after a heavy night, a big fellow carrying his smaller, drunker friend. Checking his pockets he realised he didn't have his matches and approached the couple looking for a light. I can't imagine the shock when he realised it was Jimmy being carried off, unconscious, by some thug with a bandaged eye. Luckily Lowry always carries a selection of, shall we say, deterrents on him at all times. Our friend Petrakis got a dose of fifty thousand volts from a Taser, put him on the ground long enough for Sergeant Lowry to cuff him' Anil paused to let the information sink in with Alex, knowing what the next question was likely to be, 'Jimmy is recovering in St. Thomas' and he is doing fine, still in a bit of pain from the knock on the head but he is going to make a full recovery'

'Thank God. And Petrakis?'

'Not talking yet, but he will, don't worry'

'What about the others involved?

'Probably guns for hire, they don't have much in the way of serious convictions. I am checking with Interpol to see what they have on them. From our records it looks to be mainly drugs and arms they have been mixed up in until now. They have definitely stepped up their game, started playing with the big boys, so to speak. They have gone to ground for the time being, but we will persevere and they will be picked up. After all, they are crooks and if only out of habit they will be up to their old tricks soon enough'

'Dammit!' Alex exclaimed, out of frustration as much as anything more specific.

'By the way, Jimmy left a message that he wanted to see you. Seemed important to him that you swing by'

'Yeah, I'll do that'

Alex and Deanna stood at the foot of Jimmy's bed waiting for him to stir, Deanna holding a bag of grapes and Alex a bundle of magazines for him to read. The nurse had told them that he had recently been administered some pain relief and could be asleep for some time. She said that an Indian gentleman had stayed for nearly an hour talking to Jimmy and that he might well be too tired for any more visitors. His head was bandaged and they could see bruising around his eyes, he looked as if he had taken a hefty blow. Alex knew the strength of Petrakis so understood the damage that he could've inflicted.

Jimmy awoke slowly and opened his eyes, wincing slightly at the effort. Noticing that he had visitors he tried to pitch himself up onto his elbows, Deanna touched his arm to reassure him he didn't need to make the effort. He sank back into the starched NHS pillows looking older than he should have done.

'How are you feeling?'

'Oh, you know, I feel like I've had ten too many Glenlivets'

'I'm hoping it looks worse than it is'

'Could be worse. Lowry might not have been there to intervene'

There was a pause as everyone let that fact sink in.

'Jimmy. I'm sorry you got dragged into this, I should have kept you safe'

'I know' whispered Jimmy

'You were my respon...'

Jimmy cut him off, 'I mean, I know Alex. I understand now'

'What do you mean?' asked Deanna

'Anil told me everything. And *I'm* sorry'

'You don't have to be sorry for anything, Jimmy'

'I do. And I owe you an apology. I blamed you all these years. I thought you were the one who fucked it all up for the team. I thought it was you who didn't check the equipment properly. I hated you for so long'

'Shh, now, Jimmy, it's OK' said Deanna

'No, it's not OK. I didn't realise it was Cole all the time, or whatever the fuck his real name was'

'If it makes you feel any better, I didn't know either. I've been punishing myself for all these years thinking that it was my fault. I couldn't see any other explanation either. His name was Pavel Petrov by the way, he also went by the nom de guerre of Kapusta. Apparently he was one of the best snipers Russia had seen'

'Does anyone know what happened to him?'

'No-one has made claim to the killing. We are assuming at the moment that it is a professional job. Apart from actually catching him off guard, which was a feat in itself, there were no clues left at the scene as to who finished him off'

'So probably not the Americans then' Jimmy said with a smile in his eyes

'No, not the Americans' said Alex smiling, then realising that Deanna was sitting next to them, a frown on her face, both erupted into embarrassed laughter.

Deanna scornfully looked at them both but couldn't help but join in as well when she began to see the funny side too.

'And what about Dragunov?' Alex asked, 'Did Anil mention anything about him?'

'He didn't tell me too much, I'm not really sure how much he even knows yet. Information is still coming in about him from our sources within the Russian network'

'What are they saying?'

'By all accounts he was high level within the Kremlin, nobody is exactly sure of his position, but he fell foul of a man called Sigalov, Andreyev Sigalov. You heard the name?'

Alex nodded his head, 'Yeah, I know him, a nasty piece of work by all accounts. Single minded, ruthless, practically untouchable'

'Well, Dragunov, for whatever reason, fell out of favour with Sigalov. It looks as if all this business with you and the team was some kind of way for him to seek his redemption. Judging by the outcome it looks as if it was too little too late'

'I can't see what he was trying to gain'

'It was all about information. From what Anil told me he was trying to buy his way back into favour by supplying information gleaned from you, and me, and the rest of the team. The Spanish guy...'

'Quiros' Deanna prompted

'That's him. He happened to be near Navarre when we were sent in. One of these bands of outlaws hiding out in the mountains. There must have been a connection somehow, somewhere' Jimmy winced as a bolt of pain shot through his head, 'I'm OK, it'll pass'

'Or not, I don't know', he continued, 'Whatever the details, Dragunov knew that we had been conditioned by Quiros after the Navarre attack and he used us to systematically glean information from our files regarding sleepers in the field, specifically in the Communist bloc and eastern Europe'

'Godamn it' said Alex venting his frustration, 'All of this for some bureaucrat to get his job back'

'Looks that way' said Jimmy as he closed his eyes trying to will away another wave of pain.

'Listen, Jimmy, we are going to leave you to rest now, but I'll be back in to see you tomorrow, we'll talk more then OK?'

'Yeah, OK' he said, smiling, 'I'd like that'

'And listen, if I get any more info in the meantime I'll let you know'

They had both felt a great change come over them in that short conversation, all the tension and animosity had vanished and they were once again comrades, bonded by a common enemy, the only two left from the mission. Finally they both knew the truth of what had been haunting them all this time.

Deanna leant down and gave Jimmy a kiss on the cheek that made his face redden, making him forget his pain momentarily. Alex shook his hand and locked eyes with his once protégé, conveying in that look that all was well between them and they could at last move on and maybe once again forge some sort of friendship. Alex felt as if he had a weight lifted from him as he left the ward, he turned and gave Jimmy a wave salute before vanishing from view.

50 - A Warm Embrace

As Alex quietly entered the apartment he saw Deanna as she went about her business around the kitchen. He watched her silently, without her knowing, for a brief moment. She was barefoot and only wearing one of his silk pyjama shirts, he glimpsed a hint of her firm buttocks as the shirt-tails rose when she reached up to the cupboard for the coffee jar. He imagined that she would be wearing nothing apart from lace panties underneath the silk and even in his jaded state he could feel the passion in his loins stir.

In fact Deanna *had* heard him open the door and enter the apartment. She had performed the action with full knowledge she was being watched and of the effect it would have on him. After he threw his keys down on the counter she whirled round in feigned surprise and went to him. They fell in to each other's arms and pressed their lips against one another. Alex happily ignoring the pain it caused him in his shoulder. He could feel himself stiffen as she pressed her body against his, the floral, clean smell of her hair filled his nostrils, his hand in the small of her back clamping her body to his. She smelled refreshing and intoxicating at the same time, a heady mixture that fired his senses. The meeting with Anil and all that he had recently learned fell away from his thoughts and he became at one with Deanna, in the moment. He felt an urgency overwhelm him; he had to make love to her, now. He broke off the kiss and looked into her eyes to see the same pressing need mirrored in her eyes. He took her hand in his and led her to the bedroom where he kicked off his shoes and began to undress. Deanna lay down on the bed and watched him. She stretched her arms above her head, an involuntary act of expectation, and in doing so raising the shirt to show off the black lace panties she was in fact wearing underneath. She rolled onto her side to get a better look at Alex undressing, suggestively lifting one knee upwards in anticipation, subliminally showing Alex what awaited him, offering her body to him in a small act of submission. His body, although distressed by recent events, still had the buff athleticism of a man who took care of himself, his muscles flexed and rippled as he took off his shirt and unbuttoned his trousers, letting them fall to the floor.

He lay on the bed next to Deanna and kissed her again with more passion and urgency, undoing the buttons of her shirt one by one. Her breasts were warm to his touch and her nipples stiffened as he brushed his palm over them. Automatically Deanna reached down and slipped her hand inside the band of Alex's boxers feeling his shaft thicken and throb in her palm as she grasped it in her hand. They broke off the kiss to extricate themselves from their remaining clothes and got under the covers naked. Alex began to manoeuvre himself on top of Deanna but found that he couldn't support himself with his injured shoulder and fell back again onto the sheets in pain and frustrated.

'Don't worry, darling, just lay back and let me take care of everything' said Deanna

Alex did what he was instructed, laying himself down and drinking in the sight of Deanna proceeding to straddle him. He was now as hard as rock and Deanna grasped his shaft to steady it as she guided it towards her moist ingress, gasping with satisfaction as she let it slide in to her, filling her up. Alex made a sound at the back of his throat that encouraged Deanna to carry on, his hands on her hips encouraging her. She moved her hips back and forward feeling his shaft move inside her, steadying herself with her palms outstretched on his firm chest, all the time grinding her g-spot on to his pelvic bone, raising her level of arousal; if she carried on like this she would soon reach her own moment of bliss. But she did not want to reach orgasm before Alex so she slowed down and instead of grinding, lifted herself up from Alex so his tip was nearly out of her quim, then let herself slide down again fully impaling herself, gasping with pure pleasure as she did so. She repeated this action rhythmically picking up speed as she went, biting her lip trying to keep from crying out. Alex had somehow grown even harder as she continued to ride his member up and down and she could sense his orgasm getting nearer as he closed his eyes to try and stave it off. Deanna returned to grinding her pubis against Alex whilst moving up and down his shaft and within a few short thrusts she saw Alex's stomach muscles contract and his abdominals accentuate in relief. As if their bodies were in tune with one another, she felt herself beginning to climax; a warm feeling in her stomach soon becoming an intense quivering sensation that emanated from her core and spread to her legs making her unable to keep any sort of rhythm going.

By now, for both of them, they had passed the point of no return and Deanna fell down on top of Alex wracked with heady paroxysms as Alec exploded inside of her, locked together in the thrall of mutual climax, Deanna's breasts pressed against his chest heaving with the intensity of the orgasm.

They stayed like that for some time, savouring the warmth of each other's bodies, until eventually Deanna rolled off of Alex and cuddled in beside him under the sheets, the phantom of his phallus still present inside her, warming her, echoes of her orgasm still being felt. 'I love you', she muttered almost imperceptibly.

'I love you too' he replied, meaning it, eliciting a feline flex of affection from her.

They slept like that for some time, in each other's arms, locked together. Deanna's head nestled on Alex's chest subconsciously calmed by the steady rhythm of his heartbeat and the rise and fall of his breathing, she had never felt this content before in her life. Even with all his demons Alex was still a man she could trust with her life, and with her happiness.

Alex awoke first and watched Deanna as she also began to stir. He was transfixed by her beauty, without make-up somehow even more alluring than with. Her eyelashes were short but dark, her cheeks still so very slightly flushed from the exertions of sex, her full lips parted as she breathed imperceptibly in and out, he wouldn't change one thing about her. Just as this thought formed in his head Deanna's breath seemed to falter and then caught itself up by making a huge snorting sound instantly waking her up. Alex burst into fits of laughter surprised by the suddenness of her waking, Deanna looked around perplexed as to what had woken her.

'What happened?' she asked groggily

'Oh, nothing darling' said Alex, 'you may have been snoring slightly'

'Don't be silly, I don't snore. You, on the other hand...'

They both began to giggle and could feel the tension of the last days fall further away, becoming more like a distant dream that was becoming hard to grasp.

It was liberating to be safe in the knowledge that the worst was all behind them and that they could finally get on with their own lives together. It felt for Alex as if it was a new start and that he had finally been released from some sort of living perdition, he could breathe again without feeling the weight of guilt with each exhalation.

EPILOGUE

Deanna had just got off the phone from Hugh Osterman. Alex was in the open-plan kitchen finishing breakfast for them both, eggs steamed on the skillet and a toasted brioche each. While he did so he glanced through the morning papers trying to get back up to speed with current events while also casting a quick eye over the stocks and shares that he had stakes in. The smell of strong, fresh coffee wafted through the air, carried through the apartment by the breeze from the Thames. The morning air was cool but the sun had not been up long enough to burn off the dew from the previous night. By mid-morning the heat of the sun would stake it's claim on the day and make London a boiling pot of angry commuters and irritated office workers. Alex was glad he had nowhere to go and was happy he could spend the day with Deanna doing whatever they liked for a change. The fallout from Dragunov and Kapusta now far behind them.

'What did he say?' asked Alex

'He was very considerate actually. He said for me to take some time before making any decisions. I was a little bit disappointed to tell you the truth'

'Why?'

'I was hoping he would say he couldn't do without me, or something along those lines'

Alex brought the two plates of food to the kitchen island wincing slightly at the niggling pain in his shoulder from the small calibre bullet he took.

They both perched on stools at the island to eat breakfast.

'If there is one thing I can guarantee you is that Hugh Osterman is not a man to beg. Has he given you any positive feedback regarding Dragunov?'

'I think I got a 'well done' and a 'glad you're not hurt' from him' she smiled, 'I suppose that's something'

'I think you were lucky to get that much. Osterman doesn't gush. That was probably the best you will get'

'It's just nice to be wanted, that's all'

'I want you' said Alex with a grin, 'I would go as far as to say can't do without you'

Deanna smiled at the sentiment 'And what happens when things go back to normal?'

'What do you mean?' Alex becoming worried that Deana wasn't happy with him in London

'I'm not saying I don't want to be with you. It's just that... I have my home in La Jolla, and I have work. I have no job here. And you'll be going back to work soon, after taking this time off'

'I can support us both. I make enough from the stock exchange to keep us covered. All that practically looks after itself.'

'It's not that though. I can't be a trophy wife' she blushed slightly at the mention of the word wife and moved on quickly, 'I have to be doing something, be productive, be useful. That's the reason I got into this line of work. To make the world a better place. To make my parents proud of me. It sounds silly saying it out loud like that'

'I am sure they would both be very proud of you. You've been amazing' he reached his hand across the granite top to hers and gave it a reassuring squeeze. 'That's why we both do what we do. It doesn't sound silly.'

'Thanks Alex'

'As Osterman says, take a little while and figure out what you want to do'

'That's just the thing Alex, I know what I want to do. I was doing it. It had been my aim for so many years to be working out of Langley. I worked really hard to get where I was. And I feel I can make a real difference. I don't want to give that up.'

'So where does that leave us?' Alex asked half knowing the answer. He realised that things very rarely worked out in the real world. It didn't make it any easier to accept that harsh reality could get in the way of happiness. His mood dipped slightly but he knew deep down that just because you want something badly doesn't mean you should automatically get it. He had been in the world long enough to accept the hard realities of life. If he really loved Deanna it would be wrong to hold her back.

'I don't know' answered Deanna

Alex collected up the detritus from the breakfast and began loading it in to the dishwasher. Deanna got up and walked over to the picture window overlooking the Thames. There were two tourist barges travelling in opposite directions causing the murky water to makes waves from the wakes. She had a lot to think about and no easy way to resolve her conflicted feelings. Her head and her heart at odds with each-other. She thought of the boats on the Thames mirroring her predicament, one coming home to dock the other heading out into open water. She smiled inwardly at the silly analogy. She felt happy with Alex, happier than she had been in a long time. But she knew deep down in her heart that she needed purpose in her life. As much as she loved him, was it enough?

'Deanna' Alex called, 'You won't believe this' he was glancing again at the newspaper while rinsing the few bits of cutlery, 'CHRISYS is being investigated. There's an article here in The Times'

Deanna roused from her introspection, became animated 'Do you think it's anything to do with what we uncovered?'

'I would say it definitely shone a light on some of the shady things going on. Christianson should be brought to book. I'm glad we showed him for what he is'

'A trouble maker is what he is. What do you call them?'

'A firebrand?'

'That's it. Firebrand. What gets me so angry about outfits like CHRISYS, is that they have no affiliation or loyalty, Christianson just works for the highest bidder'

'That's capitalism for you' Alex scanned the article, 'He certainly looks pissed, the paparazzi caught him off guard leaving Taillevent in Paris'

Deanna wandered over from the window to look at the article and to get an idea of what Christianson looked like out of pure curiosity, having never seen him before. Her eyes scanned the picture, the usual black-and-white press shot of a personality trying to dodge the photographer's lenses pointed their way. As her eyes took in the scene something peculiar struck her but she couldn't immediately pinpoint the oddity. Then it struck her, one of the men in the background looked familiar to her, it looked just like her father, but of course she knew it couldn't be.

To put her mind at rest she asked, 'Alex, tell me, do you see what I see'

'What do you mean?'

'That man there, at the back. It's out of focus and a bit fuzzy but I could swear that looks just like my father' The more she looked the more convincing the resemblance became. She held the grainy picture up close to her face then further away to try and gain the best view.

'But how could it be?' asked Alex, 'You're father is dead. And I can't say I know exactly what he looks like'

'I know it sounds crazy. But his body was never found' Deanna said clutching at straws, becoming more focused.

'So you think...?' Alex didn't quite know what to make of the revelation.

'I don't know what I think. But the more I look the more it seems like him. Look. I'll show you'. She got out her cell-phone and opened up the photos folder, flicking through until she found some pictures of her with her parents. She showed them to Alex and they both compared what they were seeing in the newspaper to what was on Deanna's phone.

Alex examined the similarities between the two faces in the pictures and he felt as if there was no doubt, in fact, that they were the same person.

'I think you're right Deanna. I think it is your dad. If it isn't it's his twin. But how can that be?'

'I don't know. Do you really think so? I never even thought...' Deanna had no words to express what she felt about the fact that her father could be alive and well. 'If it is him, what is he doing with Christianson of all people? And is he mixed up with CHRISYS? Is he working for them?' Deanna began to question everything she thought she knew, her world once again being thrown into turmoil upon confronting the unknown.

'I don't know but these are all things we're going to have to find out' Alex thought back to the letter that had been left to Dr. Barty to Deanna from her father, 'I thought at the time that there was more to that letter from your father than met the eye'

'What do you mean?' asked Deanna

'Well, it would be the type of letter I would write if I was going Black-Ops. When I was reading it out to you I thought it could be construed a few different ways'

'But my father was never in that part of the service. He was just an office worker'

'That might have been what he told you. Maybe it was all he could tell you' Alex thought, 'Did you tell him what part of the service you were going into?'

'No, I couldn't. My department is top-secret, no-one should know'

'Even your father?'

'Yes, even my father'

'Do you see where I'm going with this?' Alex waited for the realisation to dawn on Deanna, that her and her father were in fact more similar than she knew.

'I can't believe it' she muttered, 'So all these years, all those times he was away at conferences he was doing what I do? He was undercover?'

'I think you're going to have to come to terms with the fact that you followed your father, unknowingly, into the exact same field. The thirst for adventure obviously runs in the family' Alex pronounced with a slight grin at the irony, 'Obviously you have the same talents'.

'If that's the case it means we need to find him and help him. He's been gone for too long. That is not ordinary procedure for any type of covert work. Do you think he was taken against his will? Or is he deep under cover? Do you think he might be in danger?'

'That is what we'll have to find out'

'Oh Alex, I don't think I can cope with losing him twice. I can't bear to start hoping only for him to be taken from me again'

'We won't lose him. For a start we know exactly who he is with and where he was yesterday, so that is something to go on at least'

Deanna looked distressed at the thought of her father being in any sort of danger. She could barely dare to give herself the hope that she would see him again.

Alex sensing that Deanna was on the verge of mentally crumbling told her what she needed to hear 'Listen, whatever happens Deanna, I'll be with you every step of the way. Whatever you need. We can do this together. We'll find him'

'Do you mean that, Alex?'

'Of course. You and me, we're a team. After what we've just been through together, we can overcome anything'

'I love you Alex Spellman' Deanna whispered putting her arms around him

'I love you too' said Alex

THE END

With Special Thanks To

I would like to give special thanks to Yvonne Tupman for giving the manuscript an early editorial shake-up and for advising me with some constructive criticism. I would also like to thank Mark Curran and Sharon Richardson for being guinea pig readers and giving me the encouragement and support to carry on with the project.

Also With Thanks To

Ben Diamond
Marie-Claire Kane
Sally-Ann O'Gara
Emily Richardson
Sharon Richardson
Lisabeth Lawton
Patrick & Valerie Murphy
Cathy Dennehy
David Donovan
Patricia Evans
Raluca Tuluianu
Emil Brannen
Elena Huxley
Michael Duignan
Henry Washington
Deborah Ashman
Joanna Barker
Nigel & Yvonne Tupman
Dierdre Faughnan
Robert Bannon
Connor Huxley
David Stevens
Simon Barnes
S.W. Watts
Samantha Barrie
Fozia Hamid
Tharshika Senthuran

The True Story of Effie Whipple

E ffie lay in the alleyway off Redmaid Lane in the East End of London. She had been there for maybe half an hour, waiting for a passer-by to come to her aid. The thick fog that had been rolling in off the Thames dampened the sound of the boats upon it. The vessels taking passengers up and down stream made the raucous laughter coming from the nearby inns seem further away than they actually were. The day that had passed was one of exception as the sky had been visible for most of the afternoon due to a brisk wind blowing from the west. This had caused people to pause and look upwards to the skies reminding themselves how blue it could be and how the sun could dazzle your eyes. However, the wind had dropped toward the evening and the city had once again been draped in a thick mixture of smoke from the chimneys and fog from the river, reducing visibility to fifty yards or less. It was not the time of evening to be out on your own and vulnerable. The poor and desperate roamed the streets looking for opportunities when it was dark, no-one was safe. London was a dangerous place to be at night in 1832. Effie could hear the odd carriage pass by, maybe ferrying a couple back from the theatre or a late dinner in central London. A drunk staggering back singing at the top of his lungs eliciting shouts from the residents of nearby dwellings, none of the sort of people she could rely on to offer her help. She needed a good Samaritan. She knew almost by instinct that one would be along sooner or later, all she needed was a little patience.

She heard the footsteps approaching long before she could see the person making them. She began to call out, asking for help, pleading for assistance. As the man approached she could see immediately that he was of a well-to-do nature, slightly squiffy but eager to offer his hand to help out a lady in a predicament. If he had been in a more sober state he may have realised that all was not as it seemed. However, he approached Effie and inquired as to to how he could be of assistance. Effie rattled off the well-worn story of how she had had fight with her fiancé and that he had slapped her about and left her here without a means to get home. She was desperate and willing to do anything to get help from a nice gentleman such as himself. All this flattery gave the Samaritan no reason not to help Effie. He moved closer to assist her up from the wet ground not quite registering why she couldn't have done so herself. He could not see any visible wounds or injuries. As he bent down to take her hand he felt rather than heard movement behind him as a shape appeared out of the shadows. With striking precision and deadly swiftness Archie clouted the gentleman on the back of his head with his leather blackjack filled with lead weights. He tottered briefly before falling face first onto the cobbled alley surface rendered insensate. Quietly and efficiently Archie and Effie rooted through the poor unfortunates pockets and stripped him of all that was of value about his person. They took all of his jewellery, a significant amount of money and a handsomely expensive fob watch that could be pawned in Spitalfields. He would wake up the next day with an outstandingly sore head and a lesson well learned; London was a dangerous place at night.

Effie and Archie were always on the lookout for the relatively new Metropolitan Police force that had been in effect for the last three years. They had made their work that much more difficult. Before 1829 they could work quite freely enjoying the opportunity lawlessness provided. There were nearly nine hundred 'Blue Devils', so called police officers patrolling London's streets looking for thieves and brigands. The public in general railed against Robert Peel's 'constables'. They had been put in place to maintain public order. The public maintained they were curtailing their civil liberties. Many of these officers of the law became targets of public disdain and were set upon and beaten; one peeler, Joseph Grantham, was killed carrying out his duty in 1830, but the coroner described his death as justifiable homicide indicating that perhaps he was not wholly on the side of justice. Maybe it was just a matter of time before Archie and Effie came face to face with one of the 'peelers' in the course of their after-hours enterprises. It eventually happened one of the evenings when they were picking pockets in the bustling area of Charing Cross. They knew full well that it was an area with dedicated patrolling, but the rewards outweighed the risks and after all they both had to eat. Inevitably they were spotted one day and poor Effie was the one that got caught, not being able to flee as fleetly as Archie. She knew that she would more than likely end up at Hoxton House if caught, a private asylum that took in cases who lacked any finances. Lamentably she fell into the pauper category, although this was a preferable outcome to being sent down and spending time in a jail cell.

Archie had partnered with Effie for the last four and a half years, they made a solid team, both enjoying the excitement of the game that they played. Both being willing to learn off each other and both almost telepathically knowing what the others intention was; a useful tool in their circumstances. Archie was without doubt a rogue of the first order, looking every bit the con merchant he was. He was in his mid-thirties, standing about 5'10" and not an ounce of fat on him. His gaunt features that made him look like a cadaver in certain lights. Although he may have looked like a crook he had an easy charm about him and a habit of winning people over with his warm wit and deep soothing voice. He could dress for nearly any occasion if needed but mostly took the appearance of an every-man working-class gent from the East End. Effie on the other hand exuded a mixture of joy and mischievousness, clearly enjoying all that life could throw at her. She reveled in the challenges set before her every day, with a twinkle in her eye that captivated most men, it would take something tragic to set her into a dark mood. Effie and Archie were not partners in a romantic sense. They had a mutually beneficial business arrangement. Archie took the occasional girl for a stroll down along the Thames of an evening, Effie however choosing not to entertain gentlemen for her own reasons. She kept mostly to herself.

Effie was committed to Hoxton House in the spring of 1832 accused of leading an 'immoral life' and having 'vicious vices'. This was more than enough to earn her a stay at Hoxton. She would be locked up, studied and rehabilitated for at least 6 months and only released again after she had shown that she could change her ways and re-enter society as a useful and trustworthy citizen. During these months of incarceration Archie would visit whenever he could in the guise of her fiancé and they would spend a snatched hour here and there talking of plans for the future when she was released. Archie being buoyed by her enthusiasm and she being grateful for some diversion.

One of these days Archie arrived at Hoxton to see Effie. He was told by the guard he wouldn't be able to visit her for the near future and gave Archie no further explanation. He left feeling downcast and vowed to keep returning in the hope of seeing her to lift her spirits. Months passed without any change, his visits grew more infrequent. One day out walking he happened upon Effie in Highbury Fields in Islington. His heart leapt at the thought that she was free from the shackles of the institution where she had been kept for the last nine months. He approached her eagerly but as he neared her he realised that something was not quite right with Effie. She had lost any spark she had once had. She walked slowly with her head bowed down, eyes unseeing gazing at the ground below her feet. She was wandering aimlessly across the park. He caught up to her and touched her shoulder. She did not look up but merely stopped her ambling shuffle. Archie spoke her name aloud and when no response came forth turned her shoulder to look her square in the face. She raised her eyes to his but there was no recognition in them. He could see immediately that this was not the Effie that he once knew. Her face was a mask that hid nothing behind it, any personality that was once present had been eradicated. But how? he asked himself. What had happened to his Effie? On closer inspection he found the answer he was looking for. The reason for the walking shell he was looking at; the scars on Effie's forehead. Evidence that while she was in Hoxton House they had tried to cure Effie of her errant ways by trepanning. Boring holes into her skull to eradicate undesirable behavioral traits. On realising that his friend of more than five years was gone, never to return, he took Effie in his arms and enveloped her in an embrace that he found hard to relinquish. Tears formed in his eyes as he stood there in the fading light of the day holding his dear friend and wondering what to do.

He couldn't leave her as she was, so remained by her side taking her hand in his and walked slowly through the park, keeping her company. They looked like two sweethearts taking a stroll on a cool September evening. As they walked Archie decided that he could not leave Effie in this way, it was cruel to expect her to be able to survive on the streets of London in this diminished state. He knew what would become of her. He had been living in the underbelly of the East End long enough to know that the weak would only too quickly become prey for the more unscrupulous characters who roamed the alleyways. He shuddered to think of what would be her fate. He found them both a bench where they sat until the night became chilly and the park had emptied, he put his arm around Effie's shoulders to keep her from the cold and when the time was right he would do what was necessary.

Archie Capper was found by the 'Peelers' early in the morning before the mists of night had even begun to lift. The chill in the air sending plumes of vapour from their mouths as they patrolled the park. Archie was sat on the bench with his arms around Effie in an effort to keep her warm. For anyone watching looking like a pair of sweethearts making the most of their time together. Only when the officers came to move them both on for loitering did they realise that not all was what it seemed with the picture presented to them. Archie raised his head and looked at them both with an expression of bewilderment. As he did so the officers could see immediately that the lady was bereft of life as her head lolled to one side in the fashion of a ragdoll. What happened next was to be expected. Archie departed quietly with the two policemen. He uttered not a single word, no admission, no denial, only the circumstantial fact that he was found with a female dead from strangulation. The red welts around her neck where force was applied to cut off her air supply in direct opposition to the benign look on her face, almost beatific in it's serenity.

Archie was swiftly sentenced for murder. In the following proceedings it became apparent that Archie was none other than the Archie Capper aka 'Dapper Capper', the notoriously slippery pickpocket and confidence trickster. It also came to light that his victim was his partner of longstanding, Effie Whipple. What puzzled the constabulary at the time was the motive for the killing. If they had fallen out for some reason why was Capper cradling his victim in such a way? Why did he not flee the crime scene? And why when questioned did he say nothing to admonish himself of any guilt? No-one thought to look into Effie's recent visit to Hoxton House and what type of treatment had been administered to her there. If so it may have answered a great deal of questions. It was assumed that he had murdered her while drunk for reasons unknown. Perhaps reasons never to be known. It was as if he passed out at the scene, hence his disorientation when found.

Archie was sentenced to spend the rest of his days in 'penal servitude' at Norfolk Island penitentiary, 850 miles off the Gold Coast of Eastern Australia and nearly 500 miles north of New Zealand. An island renowned for its harsh living conditions and of the draconian servitude the inmates were forced to endure. An island so far from anywhere else that there was no hope of escape. Archie knew that many of the inmates didn't survive the four month journey to Australia, many of the voyages being prone to either violent storms, outbreaks of sickness on board or fires regularly breaking out below decks.

Archie was sent to the holding cells at Millbank where he was to await his passage. He knew all too well that the relatively new building was also a dangerous place to reside for any length of time with many of the inmates falling ill to cholera, malaria and dysentery. These maladies due to the marsh-miasmata and human effluvia from the River Thames and the marshland the gaol was built upon. Conditions there were diabolical, in the sixteen years since it had been in operation word had spread throughout London regarding the squalid countenance human beings were forced to endure there. Only five minutes exercise were permitted each day for the inmates and the rations of bread and water were severely deficient. Many were given the choice of seeing out their sentence at Millbank instead of being sent to the penal colonies, although both choices were often regarded as a death sentence. It was ironic that seen from above the building took the shape of a flower head whereas its interior was described by some as an eccentric maze. It comprised of long, dark and narrow corridors with twisting passages and narrow stone staircases with devious steps, and of having poor ventilation and living conditions generally being unsanitary to say the least. Inmates were expected to remain silent at all times or else they face solitary confinement. Violent inmates were shackled or whipped in the 'Chain Room'. Many took their chances on the long sea voyage to a land where you would at least see the sun shine. Any which way you viewed it Archie's fate was that of a man with limited options.

· · · ·

ARCHIE HAD SPENT NEARLY six weeks in the squalid cell in the depths of Millbank Penitentiary. Of the six levels he was being kept in the lowest, what the guards called 'down under'. This one marked for the inmates destined to travel to various penal colonies in Australia, under the light, under the air and practically under the ground. Any meat that had been on Archie's gaunt frame to begin with had been stripped away and all that was left was a shell of a man barely able to chew the stale bread that was given to him as sustenance. His teeth had begun to fall out due to scurvy, any fight for life he once had was now extinguishing rapidly. His grief regarding Effie's death haunted him day and night. He was no killer. He knew somewhere in his heart that he was saving Effie from a fate worse than death on London's dark streets. But that fact didn't assuage the guilt he felt inside, eating away at him, consuming his every waking moment. From the time he was arrested Archie had not let one word pass his lips, for all intents and purposes he may as well have been a mute. This didn't stop him from receiving the beatings from guards and fellow prisoners alike who had found out why he was in Millbank. And because Archie would not protest, the rumours had begun to spread that he had done dark and deranged things to the poor girl that he eventually murdered. Whether these rumours were spread with full knowledge they were falsehoods didn't really have any bearing. As far as the attackers were concerned Archie raped and mutilated the woman, left her bleeding to death in an alley for the dogs to pick over. Archie believed he deserved the beatings and almost welcomed them. He took them silently as a form of penance, a rightful punishment for the crime he had committed. Then, six weeks to the day, after entering Millbank Archie Capper could take it no longer, he had so little energy left, could barely walk. He could not see out of his swollen, beaten eyes but had come to the conclusion that if he was going to die it would be by his own hand and not in some random act of violence, be it here in the cells down under or on the high seas at the mercy of God's wrath. Archie had found a jagged piece of metal days ago in the far reaches of his cell, at one time it must have been a nail of some kind, now left to rust. He knew what he had to do to end his suffering. Not just from the physical pain but the anguish at having to live with the fact he killed his best friend and partner in crime. He would never be at peace until he ceased to be linked to this mortal coil, breathing this fetid air, the voices inside his head screaming to be silenced. When darkness came Archie opened the veins in both of his wrists with the nail, it took all the energy he had left in him, he watched as his blood pooled around him on the floor. Not pulsing as he had imagined but seeping away as if his body could not muster the effort to exsanguinate the blood from within. Slowly, inevitably he became unconscious. Thoughts of Effie still swirling around his head, following him into the abyss into which he now descended.

www.ingramcontent.com/pod-product-compliance
Lightning Source LLC
Chambersburg PA
CBHW060525180626
46817CB00002B/485